PRAISE FOR THE NOVELS OF SULEENA BIBRA

"Bibra debuts with a sparkling, hilarious rom-com about rival art auctioneers. …laugh-out-loud banter and sensitive heart-to-hearts that will make readers swoon. This enemies-to-lovers tale hits all the right notes."
Publishers Weekly (starred review)

"Fans of Sonya Lalli will love Bibra's impressive and hilarious debut. The witty banter of this feel-good romance will delight readers and have them looking for more from this author in the future."
Library Journal (starred review)

"Bibra's assured debut is an immensely fun enemies-to-lovers story of two auctioneers at rival New York auction houses, Loot and Carlyle's. A fabulous recommendation for fans of *The Hating Game* (2016) by Sally Thorne."
Booklist

ALSO BY SULEENA BIBRA

Love At Auction Series

Two Houses
Two Christmases

Road to Romance Series

The Road to Gretna

For additional books by Suleena Bibra, visit her website,
suleenabibra.com.

THE ROAD TO GRETNA

ROAD TO ROMANCE
BOOK ONE

SULEENA BIBRA

ISBN 978-1-967839-01-8 (paperback)

ISBN 978-1-967839-00-1 (ebook)

The Road to Gretna

Copyright © 2025 by Suleena Bibra

All rights reserved. No part of this book may be used or reproduced in any manner whatsoever without written permission except in the case of brief quotations embodied in critical articles and reviews.

Any use of this book to train generative artificial intelligence (AI) technologies is expressly prohibited.

This is a work of fiction. Names, characters, places and incidents are either the product of the author's imagination or are used fictitiously. Any resemblance to actual persons, living or dead, businesses, companies, events or locales is entirely coincidental.

Cover Illustration: Venika Bibra

Editing: Mackenzie Walton

To me.

If people are reading this, you actually did it. You worked past fear, doubt, anxiety and laziness, and you self-published a book. Now stop procrastinating on social media and go do it again; we're trying to make a life-long career here.

The Route to Gretna
Gretna Green
Whitehaven
Burnley
Bakewell
Nuneaton
Buckingham
London

CHAPTER 1

NAOMI

"I need five Red, White, and Blue Margaritas, please!" I loudly request over the music, in the dimly lit basement restaurant that has become our spot.

Bubba's serves what English people think American food is, mostly burgers and hot dogs with small American flags stuck in them, like we conquered processed meats. The walls are covered in American license plates and pictures of American treasures like the Lincoln Memorial and Dolly Parton, and on special occasions, like today's Fourth of July celebration, they get a real American band. Or four English guys with a banjo.

It's become a second home for us.

I hadn't expected this weekly meeting of Americans to turn into a regular thing. All because of a chance meeting at the American food aisle, where Zara and I almost came to blows over the last Lucky Charms, to her introducing me to her friends at a "real American diner" in the heart of Kensington (which was decidedly *unreal*), I clicked with these people. In two years since, they've become family.

"Can I have an order of the chili dogs, but can I have that with a side of sadness that you lost us in 1776?" asks Zara, a Southern Californian who works on reality shows.

James looks at her pityingly. "Oh, love. We watch the news. We're good with that particular loss."

"Well, you also lost our ancestral homeland of India," I say. Well, not Lucy's. And I guess it's only half mine.

"I'll get you those chili dogs." James, our favorite server, is used to us by now and only engages with us half the time.

"Chili dogs for all, James," orders Jaya, an Indian-American castle publicist (publicist for cultural heritage sites) who always looks glamorous. I met her through my PR agency when we worked together on an assignment, and when I found out she was from San Jose and homesick too, I invited her to our group.

"Did we miss anything?" Lucy, a white mystery writer from Los Angeles, approaches our table and then sits down across from me.

"She means did you order us drinks? And I need drinks after dealing with *Madame*." Dev exaggerates a posh English accent when talking about his (least) favorite person, his boss's daughter. Dev's an Indian-American curator at a big, extravagant, historic house in the countryside and is originally from Southern California. He drops down next to Lucy. They both knew Zara from before I ran into her on the day that is now known as Marshmallow-gate, since they all grew up in Artesia. Zara and Dev were dragged to the same temple against their will one Saturday night a month when they were teenagers, and Zara and Lucy went to high school together. They reconnected when they found out they all lived in London, through social media.

"We have food and drinks coming and we will acknowledge signing a declaration to be independent later. But right now I want to hear Zara's news." I turn to Zara, refusing to engage with anyone until I hear what caused all those cryptic, maybe happy texts we've been getting in the group text today.

Zara, resident reality TV producer, builds the drama before she answers. "Well…"

"Out with it, or Naomi's gonna have a small cardiac event." Dev's not wrong.

"It actually involves Naomi, just a little…"

"Okay. I will haunt you forever if I expire from this cardiac event before I find out the news that you have kept from me. Since eleven a.m. this morning." I take a sip of the patriotic margarita that appeared in front of me. "Thanks, James."

He squeezes my shoulder and leaves us to celebrate our centuries-old victory over his ancestors. No grudge present.

"I got a job on a new reality show filming here in England!" Zara finally tells us. We're all out of our seats in a flash, crowding around her in a giant group hug.

Zara's had a hard time since she was fired from her first job in London. She's been looking all over the world for the next opportunity, and in the meantime doing temp jobs. And moving in with me, who very much appreciated the split rent. And living with my best friend.

She was even considering going back to the States, but she didn't want to go back as a failure, especially because of whatever happened to make her leave Los Angeles (which she still refuses to talk to me about and I refrain from circling around her for the information like a hungry shark that smells chum in the water because I'm a great friend).

"You lot might have won your independence, but you don't even have universal healthcare," an Englishman drunkenly slurs at us, mistaking the reason for our happiness. Which is rich coming from someone who's enjoying our patriotic margaritas so much.

"Way harsh! And this is unrelated to George Washington, the deeply flawed man who nevertheless kicked your collective tea-drinking asses," Jaya yells back.

"How is this related to me, though?" I ask when we finally disband the group hug.

Zara grabs my hands, probably so I can't escape when she gives me the news. "Well. The thing is. One of my first jobs as this show's field producer is to fix a problem we're having with a contestant pulling out last minute, and the showrunner now hating all the back-ups we had planned."

I get an uneasy feeling in the pit of my stomach, guessing at where this is going, and assuming the worst, most embarrassing outcome of this conversation.

"And I started describing you to my boss, and he sort of loved the idea of adding an American, specifically you, and wants to know if you can join the cast?" Zara gets the request out in a rush, so fast it takes a second to process it.

"Wait. What? Me? Why?"

"I described you because this can be good for you. I know you're thinking about starting your own business as a publicist, and this could be great exposure for you. You can get your name out there. Manage your own post-reality show buzz, or a fellow contestant's, and show everyone how great you are at the job. And then famous people from everywhere will want to work with you."

It would be an amazing opportunity. I've been working at the PR firm for two years, getting promoted from intern to assistant, and I love it. But there's not many opportunities since the company is so small right now.

And my dad keeps badgering me to come home. He's *that* Harrison Richmond, of the New York Richmonds (ew, I know, but an accurate portrayal of how he sees himself) and he has very firm opinions on how I should live my life.

At his company. Living at home. Becoming a mini-him. A terrifying prospect.

He thinks if I'm just getting coffee and arranging schedules for very little money, I should be doing it for the family business.

He's even offered to put me in the marketing department. But I can't work with him. He treats me like a spoiled princess, like any actual work might break me. Anything from doing my laundry or getting my own groceries.

And I let him. Because it's easier to give in than fight over chores. And I hate doing laundry.

Every time I get geographically close to my parents, I let them take over, and I regress to an entitled teenager. But I don't want to be that person. I want to earn my accomplishments. I won't say I'm doing it by myself, because I didn't refuse the financial help for school and some living expenses. I may have pride, but I also need to eat, despite how unfair that is to people who don't have my safety net.

But here, unlike in New York, at least no one knows who I am. I even go by my mother's maiden name, Patel. Every success I have, I'm confident I earned.

Unlike the time in sixth grade, when Dad saw I got a C on an essay, and he went down to the school, yelling and badgering teachers and administration until I got a B on it. And I know I deserved the C. I completely forgot about the assignment until the last minute, when I word vomited something onto the page so I wouldn't get an F.

I worked harder after that, because I didn't want to be known as the person whose father comes and saves her all the time.

But the clamoring from Mom and Dad to come home has gotten louder, and since I'm now in possession of two shiny degrees, undergraduate and graduate, it's harder to push them off. Dad sweetens the job offer every time I see him, and it's getting harder to resist, because I can be weak.

I've talked to Zara about the issue. And about the fact that if I started my own business as a publicist, a successful one, then my parents would see that I can and should be on my own. Bonus: I would be able to afford to live on whichever continent I damn well please.

But still. A reality show?

I love the genre. But they edit those for maximum drama, so I'm sure it's going to lead to some embarrassment. And I don't want to think about what my parents would say if they found out. Which is why I wouldn't tell them till after filming, like the mature adult I am.

"C'mon, leprechaun. I need this, but I think it'll be really good for you too," Zara says, unfairly using the nickname she gave me when we first met, arguing over that box of Lucky Charms.

"I am only seven inches shorter than you, giant," I say without heat, a regular argument for us.

"Do it!" Lucy says. "I wanna be famous adjacent."

"You're the famous author. We're already famous adjacent. To *you*," Jaya says.

"I'm not famous. But if you want to mention my books on the show, that would probably be really helpful for me paying rent in the future." Lucy wags her eyebrows at me.

"I haven't agreed to do this." I remind the table. "What's the show even about?"

"I can't actually tell you that. It's sort of a dating show, mixed with a little bit of competition. A cash prize at the end." Zara is hedging. "You could use the money to start your company."

"A dating competition show? Do you want me to be on *Love Island*?" I'm both terrified and excited about that prospect.

"You wish. No. But it's similar."

"You did say you wanted to get out there and meet more men," Dev, usually quiet during our conversations, says.

I glare at him. "How dare you remind me of my own words? At the most inopportune moment?" It's true, though. I have been avoiding hooking up with the many attractive, accented men I meet on this island. But I've been busy.

And no one quite matches up to a certain man. Who is now an ocean away from me and probably doesn't care about the distance, because he definitely doesn't think about me as much as I think about him.

Dev looks at me neutrally, like he always does when we overwhelm him with our combined personalities. Just like I imagine a little brother would if we were all his big sisters. But he got dragged into this circle of friendship years ago and we're not letting him go.

"To clarify, you want me to sign on to a show where I don't know any of the details, and give an anonymous corporation the rights to portray me however they want on TV with no privacy restrictions?"

"Yes. But if you come in tomorrow to sign a non-disclosure and do some light interviews, they'll give you more details before you have to sign on for good. And there'll be scones." Zara looks so hopeful.

This has the potential to help us both. Or, you know, ruin my PR career before it even starts, forcing me home to an Upper East Side mansion with my tail tucked in between my legs in failure.

I take a sip of American freedom juice and answer, "Fine. But if I look like anything other than an intelligent, professional woman, you have to buy me unlimited Lucky Charms for the rest of my life."

CHAPTER 2

NAOMI

hat did I agree to when I was blinded by alcohol and never-helpful American exceptionalism?

I wake up this morning to a pounding headache and a text from Zara, which is so sweet it puts me off my regular bowl of sugar cereal. And it also means I can't back out of my rash agreement from last night.

She's already left for the office, escaping before she has to face my regret and second thoughts. Her text says she has some last-minute prep to do for the show, but I can read between the lines. She's avoiding me so I can't back out.

I get ready with a low level of dread and anxiety wrestling around in my belly, putting me a little on edge while I do my makeup. Which is why I freak out I hear the loud pounding on my door, almost poking myself in the eye with mascara.

The pounding continues at the same intensity, while I find a tissue to wipe excess makeup off my eyelid.

"This had better be important," I mumble as I stomp to the front door of our flat, tissue still rubbing at my right eye. Because if it is important, I can get out of going to this meeting with the reality show producers.

I open the door, panting at the exertion of my morning rush. "What—Oh my god."

My first instinct is to close the door so fast that I can pretend I never opened it in the first place.

Close it right on the attractive face in front of me, that great smile bracketed by dimples, short, dark brown hair cropped close to his head, and brown eyes looking at me expectantly. I give in the impulse.

"Nope," I say to Nate Williams as I slam my front door shut. That strong jaw is too much to take when I'm not hungover; it's not happening now that I am.

"Come on, Naomi," he says, starting the knocking again. Strong knocks. Just like that cursed jaw. "Just give me a few minutes. I crossed an ocean for you."

My heart constricts, the inconvenient crush I have…no, *had* on him stirring at the words that can't mean what they sound like.

"Why?" I ask through the door.

I hear a deep sigh from the other side of the heavy door. A natural businessman, he tries to negotiate. "I'll tell you everything. But only inside."

"Fine." I can't actually leave by any other avenue than the front door, so unless I get this over with, I won't be able to go without passing him anyway. Because if there's one thing I know about Nate, it's that he's really persistent. A great asset when working for my father, but an inconvenience when I'm trying to avoid him.

I open the door, and his face lights up with that endearing smile again. Damn smile.

I've had a crush on him since I met him five years ago, when I was visiting home from Cambridge senior year and he dropped off some paperwork for Dad to sign at the house. He had just started with the company, and even though he was only seven years older than me, I was a little overwhelmed by his expertly tailored suit and the air of confidence he had while working for one of the most demanding employers in the world, especially in my I-don't-know-what-I-want-in-life phase.

But he's always treated me like a much younger little sister. Which grated when I was in college, angered me when I was a grad student, and never fails to get my blood boiling now that I'm an adult. With *bills.*

As a human, it's annoying. As someone with a crush on him, it's beyond frustrating. He's never gotten over the fact that he was an executive when we met and I was a college student.

"Hey, squirt," he says as he enters my space.

I barely stop the growl that his words produce, hating that he still sees me as a little girl.

"I'm not making you tea." I don't know if he understands how rude I'm intending to be, since he doesn't live in England nor is he Indian, but I take comfort in knowing the grave insult I just delivered.

"No need. This shouldn't take long."

"Great." I sneak a peek at myself in the hall mirror on the way to the living room, making sure all the mascara is gone from my surprise earlier. It is, but now my eyes look uneven. I'll have to live with that for now, since I don't want Nate to be here longer than necessary, even the amount of time it would take to fix my face.

I sit down in the middle of the couch and spread out my arms, leaving the armchair in front of me for Nate to sit in, which he does. "Well?"

"I had a great flight, squirt. The food and wine were decent, and I watched three movies on a screen slightly bigger than my own tablet but with more fingerprints. And I just got in, so my body is still confused about what time zone I'm in."

I roll my eyes. "Yes. I'm glad you had a good flight. Wait, did you wear a suit on an international flight?" The executive life is weird.

"Yes."

"Okay then. But why did you take the flight with the finger-prints on the screen and the okay food, in a suit?"

"I wanted to see how you were doing." Nate gets comfortable in my armchair, sinking deeper in it, despite him saying this would be quick.

"I'm fine. But that feels like it could have been a phone conversation. Or even an email. FaceTime, if you really wanted. Why come in person?" This is a lot of effort to casually catch up with someone, and I'm suspicious. We were never that close, despite all my dreams, wishes and desires to the contrary.

"Well, your dad asked me to—"

There it is. I interrupt him. "I knew it! Now he's sending his executive to drag me back home like an overpaid babysitter?" This isn't even the first time he's sent anyone. He must be getting desperate, though. First it was a junior account manager, then it was senior client services, and then some director.

But now I'm getting full-on vice president gracing my humble abode.

"How can he spare you for such an insignificant job? Is this proof executives don't actually do anything and all the value is made by the workers?"

He laughs at what was supposed to be cutting. "Cute. I do like to think I add some value. But that's how much he wants to make sure you're all right, and to see if you would be open to having a conversation about coming home."

"Don't corporate-speak me. He ordered you to bring me home."

"Technically, he never said the word *order*."

"Well, this has been a giant waste of your time. You should sue him for…making you run personal errands on another continent. Whatever lawyer speak for that is. You should take another flight, this time in the opposite direction, and tell him that."

"I'd rather not."

Yeah, I wouldn't want to give Dad bad news either. Mom can do it; she has Dad-related superpowers.

"Do you really not want to come home? Your dad has a job lined up for you, and a nice apartment. With a view." He looks pointedly out the window to a brick wall and our neighbor's window.

"Hey, I love this view. Mrs. Wu has adorable kittens."

"He would give you anything you wanted if you would agree to live in the same city as him again."

"That's the point." I throw my hands up.

"You hate being comfortable?"

Well, when he puts it like that…

"No, I don't hate being comfortable. He's given me so much, everything I could ever need or want. But I never feel like anything but Harrison Richmond's daughter. I just want to be Naomi. I want to know that everything I get professionally, I earned. I can do that here. I can't in New York."

"I get it," Nate says on a sigh.

"You do?"

"Both my parents are professors. They weren't happy when I decided to go into business. But I was sick of being 'the Professors Williams' kid' and business was the furthest thing to choose. The more classes I took, the more I liked it."

"Wow, that nickname is a mouthful. I don't even know where to start on the apostrophes in there." And it's the first real thing I know about Nate, besides his preferred drink when he comes to the house. I could like this new dynamic, being treated as an adult.

"Yeah. I don't know where they go either. My parents would, though." He shoots me half a smile, one dimple peeking out to say hi.

"You'll be heading back soon, then?" I ruthlessly squash the flash of sadness that he's leaving, cutting short the first time we've been alone together. Even if we're only alone because of Dad, which does make it significantly less exciting.

"Listen. You know your dad." Nate starts in with a smarmy smile, the executive trying to close the deal smile. Not his real one that he gave me after he talked about his parents.

"Yes. I have been his child for a while now." I narrow my eyes.

"So how about I stay for a little bit? Your dad doesn't get mad at me, I keep my job, Harrison doesn't send Stevens to come bring you home. We all win."

I curl my lip in distaste. Stevens is a dinosaur who's been with the company since before I was born, and always finds a way to spray you with food if you're unfortunate enough to eat across from him.

"Fine. You can stay in London. Do whatever, I recommend Hampton Court Palace. I'll tell Dad you were here for what, a week? However long you want to take a vacation. I'll also tell him how forceful you were in trying to kidnap me back to the States. But you were no match for my self-defense skills."

"That'd be helpful. Except that last bit, I think."

"Okay. Decided." I look at my watch. "Actually, I have to run, or I'll be late for an appointment. I hope you enjoy London."

"An appointment on a Saturday?" Nate gets up with me and follows me around the apartment while I get everything I need, including quickly finishing up my makeup. If he wants to see how the sausage is made, I won't stop him. Because I don't have the time to stop him. "What's it for?"

"Something work-adjacent," I hedge. It's technically true. If this is successful, it can help my fledgling career.

"Great, I'll come with you."

"No." I say firmly. "I don't need a babysitter at a work thing. It doesn't really instill a lot of confidence to show up with one." Plus, if he finds out what this particular work thing is, he'll tell Dad and I'll never hear the end of it.

I can picture it now. "A reality show? What are you, a

Kardashian? I can buy you a reality show. What's the profit margin on reality shows? Should I buy a TV network?"

Exhausting.

"All right. How about I ride with you then get out of your hair? I'll pay for the cab as apology for making you late."

I look at my watch again. "I will take you up on that, actually." The Tube stop is kind of far from the apartment, and I'm cutting it close now because of him.

Nate gets his phone out and procures the promised cab. I give him the address and can breathe when he doesn't seem to recognize the building we're going to which houses the network offices.

Since Nate is being chill about his wasted trip, I give him a tour of London as the black cab drives us from Kensington to the South Bank. Tips for things he can do after he drops me off, for the rest of his vacation.

It's nice driving around London with Nate. We have an easy conversation now that he's not badgering me about coming home. Joking, laughing, even some seductive brushing against each other in the unusually tiny backseat.

That last one might just be on my end. This cab is a regular size. Which would easily accommodate two people, except I'm sitting closer to the middle than is strictly necessary.

But Nate doesn't shy away when we touch. It may be my imagination, but he even leans into it? Most likely the delusional ramblings of a sex-starved brain, but I need to take my wins somewhere, since I'm about to have a meeting that terrifies me.

London traffic, usually so ubiquitous, decides now is the time to listen to my pleas to get lost, making the trip short. And now I have to face the producers.

"Thanks for the ride," I say as I get out of the cab.

But then Nate gets out with me. "I'll just wander around. Maybe we can grab brunch after? Mimosas on me."

"A boozy brunch?" The way to my heart. Maybe me being

away from the family is enough to show Nate that I'm not a kid. He must have been impressed with my very adult flat and very adult furnishings (who knew a couch would be that expensive?). Maybe we can have a good time while we're both out from under the watchful eye of my CEO father. "Sure. I'll text you when I'm done."

"Have a good meeting."

I nod at him and turn, fighting the urge to look back to see if he's watching me walk into the building. I try to catch a glimpse of him in the window, but there's too many people on the other side to get a clear image. Then I try to sneak a look back when I open the door and catch him standing there in my periphery. Or someone who could look like him.

I'm about to give in and take a proper look back to confirm who the figure in the suit is when I get distracted by a sassy, messy top bun filing my vision.

"Thank you so much for coming today. You are saving my life. Or career. Which you know are the same thing."

"We need to get you a hobby. Maybe two. Possibly a man."

"I got you a tea." Zara jiggles both cups in her hands. "Healthy or sugar water with a splash of caffeine?"

I look at her without answering, my mind still on the man who may or may not be panting after me like a cartoon character with big eyes and his heart beating out of his chest. Probably not. But it's my imagination and I can dream big.

"Hot sugar water it is." Zara presses one of the to go cups in my hand. "The other producers are waiting for you in a confer-ence room and they are so excited to meet you."

I take a deep breath as my best friend gently strong arms me into the elevator and then down a hall filled with soulless corpo-rate art and ugly carpeting. She drops my arm to open the door for me, and I take a fortifying breath as I walk through the door to face the suit-clad people sitting on one side of a long, glass table.

"Hi. I'm Naomi."

~

"OH MY GOD," I say when I walk out of the conference room. Or gladiatorial arena, which is what it felt like. As a result, I have a pounding headache and also think my body is in shock.

After giving me a few minutes to talk about myself, the producers immediately started asking if I had ever been arrested or done drugs. And then they started in on my exes and my sex life.

At one point someone said I looked beautiful and "exotic," and I think I snarled at him, but someone immediately asked if I had ever gone to rehab and I might have gotten side-tracked from following up on that bit on nonsense.

They didn't even tell me what the show was about, really. Just a general premise of modern people who will be living like they're in Regency Britain, with contestants partnering up in a romantic capacity to complete challenges. And there's some prize.

By the end of *whatever* that was, the producers said they would love to have me, and I think I made a sound of agreement, or it could have been of horror that they mistook for agreement, and they set a 30-page contract in front of me. It had even more horrifying clauses like "no privacy," "hidden cameras," and "producers can hide things from me and edit the footage however they see fit."

I think I said I would consider it, just so I didn't have to tell the scary people no in person. But I *am* leaning toward no. I knew there would be some level of manipulation, just like behind the scenes of my favorite shows, but seeing it in black and white and applied to me is another thing entirely.

Zara stays behind with her co-workers to discuss the show, and I reach into my purse to take out my phone, the contract in there taunting me. I ignore it, and see a text from Nate, letting me know he's walking by the river whenever I'm ready. I text him the address of a good brunch place near here and head in that direction myself.

I get there first and order a mimosa immediately. I deserve it. It arrives before Nate does, and I start drinking while I review the contract I thought I was going to ignore. It was taunting me a little too loudly from my bag.

"Hey, squirt," Nate says as he sits down next to me.

Great. Squirt again. I take another large sip. "Hi, Nate."

"Are you even allowed to drink?"

Just when I think we're seeing each other as adults. "Yes," I say sharply. "In both American and England, although I've been able to do it longer in England." I take another sip, this one out of spite. At least I'm not thinking about the job offer now.

Nate senses dangerous territory and charges the subject like a smart businessman. "How did your meeting go?"

"Interestingly." Would be the tamest word for it.

"What was it for, anyway?" he asks, picking up his own menu.

Might as well tell him now that I'm pretty confident it's going to be a no. "It's wild. I have this friend here who works for a TV network. Anyway, it was for a reality show. They offered me a spot on it."

Nate drops his menu and his lower jaw. "A reality show?"

CHAPTER 3

NATE

I can't have heard that right. "Excuse me?"

Naomi finishes off the liquid in her glass. I don't know how much she drinks, but she's probably going to very inebriated by the end of this brunch if she keeps going so hard at that glass. Especially when she asks for another one from the server. I ask for a few waters with the drink order, sure that Harrison's request to "handle the Naomi situation" includes making sure she doesn't get wasted before noon.

"Zara, my friend, needs someone to be a contestant, and I could use the exposure if I want to break into entertainment industry here."

"That's ridiculous." I blurt the words out before I can think twice about them.

"Excuse me?" Now she's the one to use the dangerous words. With a far more dangerous tone.

I know I've stepped in it, but I'm not sure how to make it better.

I've been uncomfortable around Naomi since I saw her the first time I went to the Richmond house. She was dressed in pajamas, fresh-faced with her earbuds in. And beautiful. She was in college and too young for me, already out of business school and in the working world for a while. I felt even older than her in my suit, meeting her father for work.

That same father found me a few seconds after I almost bumped into her, reminding me that even if there wasn't an age gap between us, she was off limits unless I wanted to lose my job. And as hard as I worked to get to where I am, over my parents' objections, there's no way I'm letting that go any time soon.

"It's just those people on reality TV…you're not like them."

"There's a wide range of humans on television, from attorneys to personal trainers to phlebotomists to construction workers to influencers. What exactly is different between them and me?"

She's using a tone of voice that I've never heard from her: one like steel. A big departure from her usual tone, which is either affectionate exasperation directed at Harrison, or general youthful cheer. When did this tone develop?

Instead of responding to her question, I try another tactic. Mostly because I don't really know how I would answer that without sounding like a dick. "Your father wouldn't be too happy if you were on a reality show. You know how much he worries about image."

I think this was a bad tactic to have chosen. Her eyes get narrower, like she can glare actual daggers at me. At the very least, she's going to give it the old college try.

"I am an adult," Naomi grinds out through clenched teeth. "I can make my own decisions. And they don't have to be whatever Dad thinks is right. Other people are allowed to have an opinion that differs from the great Harrison Richmond."

I feel like I've touched on a sensitive subject here.

"You know what? I'm incredibly busy. What with my new job on a reality show. I should go." She rustles through her purse for some money to drop on the table. She gets up. "Sorry I can't stay for the actual brunch. I'll catch you next time you get sent to interfere in my life."

"Wait…" I try half-heartedly, starting to get up from my chair. But she's already down the street before I can respond.

"Shit." I collapse back in my seat. I take out my phone and stare at the screen, contemplating how I can tell Harrison that his daughter is going to be on a reality show in England without him losing it at me. Not that I should, or want, to be in the middle of this. And even though I wish I could tell Naomi it's her life and screw her overbearing dad, I can't.

None of my options end well for me, so I put my phone back in my jacket pocket. Maybe I can talk to the producers and get them to see what a bad idea this would be.

Renewed with the thought of a task to do, I get up and march to the same building I dropped Naomi at earlier, the address still in my phone as the last trip. When I get there, I realize I have no idea where she went in the building or who she met. I walk to the information plaque, hoping that an office here is named "Reality TV division that wants Naomi."

Unfortunately, things are not labeled that clearly.

Out of the corner of my eye, a familiar Indian woman walks out of the elevators to my right. This is the woman who met Naomi after I dropped her off. She's walking with a white man and woman now, all three dressed in business casual, phones in their hands and heads close in conversation.

"Hi." I step in their path, the future of my job at stake here.

"Is there something we can help you with?" the other woman asks.

"Yeah. You spoke with Naomi earlier today and I need to talk to you about her."

"About Naomi? I can stay and talk to him," the woman from the morning says to the others.

The man waves her off. "You both have things to do before we start shooting. I can take this young man's statement here and fill you all in later. Go ahead."

The familiar woman looks conflicted, but one last glance at

the man has her nodding. Especially since that "go" had all the hallmarks of a boss's order, stern tone included. The man is already guiding me in the direction he came from, taking for granted everyone will listen to him. The same attitude I see in Harrison, this time with an English accent.

"I'll check in tomorrow morning," the Indian woman says.

"There's a conference room down here. If you would like to talk there?" The man directs me to our right.

"Sure."

He leads us to a small space, overlooking a garden courtyard in the center of the building.

"I'm Mark, the executive producer for the show."

"Nate. A fri—" Well, not really a friend. "An acquaintance of Naomi's from home. New York."

"Interesting." He steeples his fingers, channeling a supervillain. Comforting. "I will say, this is a first. So it has my attention, something hard to do. What do you want to tell us about Naomi, Mr. Acquaintance from Home?"

I clear my throat. "I work with her father. Harrison Richmond of Richmond Enterprises, and he would prefer his daughter not be involved in this program. No offense. He just doesn't want his daughter to do something she could regret later. He's a protective father. With a lot of lawyers." I do some light threatening when Mark doesn't look convinced by the first part of my plea.

"Huh. That's not the name she gave us. Lying about her name. A protective father. A young man who travelled an ocean to protect her from the evil producers. Naomi Patel keeps getting more and more interesting."

I see the wheels turning in Mark's head, and I don't like it. I might have made a mistake here. But it's too late to do anything about it now.

"He's a rich man, and I'm sure he would be willing to help out if finding a replacement is a financial burden."

"A bribe."

Well, yes. Technically. But that doesn't sound great. "Not a bribe. Just a payment for any inconvenience. Or for any penalties incurred due to breaking a contract." Everyone has a price. I just have to find this bastard's.

"Hmm. Well, Naomi called us right before we came down and already agreed to be on this show. Since she is an adult who can enter in her own contracts, she has a place on this show when we start filming next week. I have the backing of a network behind me, and your Richmond is an ocean away. However, you interest me. This storyline interests me."

I want to punch the man every time he says "interesting" or some variation thereof, knowing this isn't going to be good for me.

"So here's what I'm going to offer: come in tomorrow for some meetings, and if we all think's it's a good fit, you can be on the show too."

"*Me?*"

"You. You're attractive enough for TV and this backstory will make an interesting plot point."

There's that word again. "I also have a career to protect. I have enough trouble being taken seriously as a young executive. I don't need this making it worse."

Mark shrugs. "It's completely up to you. I'm not going to kidnap you to be on my TV show. Laws and all that. But if you are on the show, you'll have the best chance to protect Naomi, maybe talk her out of doing or saying things that could embarrass her or her father on camera. Better than if you're in a boardroom in America. An ocean away."

Mark sees the conflict on my face with his newest points. "I'm not asking you to decide right now. This is usually a much longer process, months of screenings really, but we need Naomi after someone pulled out last minute. And I can replace one of the male contestants with you, since you present such a unique opportunity. So take the night, but not much longer than that, because we do start filming next week. Here's my card. Tell the receptionist you're here to see me if you do want to meet tomorrow."

I take the card reflexively. "I'll think about it."

This producer is a terrifying man, acting so nonchalant while he's turning my world upside down. And he has all the power since Naomi already said yes to this. I haven't been this off balance in a negotiation in a while. I came into it so confident. As a business executive used to the cutthroat atmosphere of the energy sector, I kind of thought it would be easy to go up against a reality TV guy. Joke's on me for making assumptions.

I walk out of the room, not saying anything after that defeat. I GPS my hotel and decide to walk, even though it's not that close. Maybe the cool air will help me get over the meeting.

It's not just the other executives either. I can't imagine what the Professors Williams will have to say about their son, already a disappointment far from the ivory tower in the messy business world, getting into the even messier, and more public, world of reality TV.

Oh god, Mom will probably write an article about me. Some sociological tour-de-force about the world of reality TV and modern psychology with an analysis of celebrity and probably an anecdote about how I ran around naked at my third birthday party.

Hell, Dad will get in on it too. He'll be comparing the rise of reality TV to the history of the European Levee. And somehow it will also include the same anecdote about me being in my birthday suit on my third birthday.

An anecdote that will then be cited in other academic papers for generations to come, I'm sure.

But if I don't do this, and Naomi goes on this show and gets hurt... I stop walking at the thought, getting rammed in the back by other pedestrians. I offer a mumbled apology and start walking again.

I don't want Naomi to be hurt by this. She's...nice. She doesn't deserve to be hurt.

Or me. I shake myself out of the thought of Naomi hurt. Because I don't want to be hurt either. And if I let Naomi get hurt, Harrison is going to hurt me. By firing me.

And now I've thought the word "hurt" too many times, and it's ceased to have meaning to me as a word.

I guess I'm going to be at that meeting tomorrow.

CHAPTER 4

NAOMI

"*I* can't believe I agreed to this," I say to Zara as she ushers me into a beautiful, historic house that Jaya and Dev could tell me the whole history of. I don't know any of it, but I can still appreciate the beauty that's lasted hundreds of years.

It was a rash decision. I was ready to say no, because the risk of potential embarrassment. But then Nate goaded me and I said I was going on the show just to see the look on his face. But saying it felt right. Scary, but right. I really thought about how it could help my career, and I was excited about the prospect. So I really agreed to do it.

With a boatload of trepidation.

This is the first day of filming and Zara had us chauffeured to the shooting location in the countryside outside of London. The last few days have been a rush of contracts to review, bags to pack, and last-minute push-ups so my arms look as toned as they can be. And checking my phone to see if Nate texted.

He hasn't. And I don't want him to. Really.

"I'm glad you did. You're really helping me out here. Although there is something I need to give you a heads-up about…"

"Will I have to eat something unpleasant? Or skydive? Or go on a roller coaster?" I list all my fears. And all the reasons why *The Amazing Race* isn't a reality show I could ever be on.

"No. None of that. But some guy named Nate came to the offices the same day you had your meeting, and said he wanted to talk about you. He's kind of hot, actually. Anyway, he and Mark went off to talk. I tried to stay, but Mark wanted to talk alone, so I have no idea what they said."

"*What?* Nate's talking to producers? And you are only telling me this *now?*" Although I'm still on the show, so he must not have as much influence in London. I knew I chose this city wisely.

"I've had a very busy few days trying to coordinate this show, which has had multiple emergencies before I even came on board. It's the only reason they hired me last minute. But I'm sorry I didn't tell you sooner. Who is he, anyway?"

I sigh deeply. "Some guy who works with my dad."

Zara, knowing me, says nothing. She can tell there's more. That I haven't told her about because it's been easy to pretend Dad and his world doesn't exist when I'm here.

"I don't know. Nate's attractive, obviously. But he treats me like a child," I mumble.

"Oooh…you never told me about this crush."

"It isn't a crush."

"Isn't it?"

"It doesn't matter. He was supposed to be on a different continent." And I was supposed to be over this little girl crush. I mean, I've hooked up with guys since I've been here; it's not like I'm waiting for him. So what if everything fizzled with the others? It's not about Nate.

"Why is he here now?"

I roll my eyes. "To babysit me. Because I'm so naïve and vulnerable."

"You're none of those things. Not that I would know, because

I am a good friend and I didn't look at the results of your back-ground check for the show."

"Then you missed out on me going to private schools and not getting into trouble. Posting about the books 've loved, my travels, and cute dog photos."

Zara knocks into me. "Boring. Don't worry, leprechaun, we'll dirty that perfect reputation. And then you can rehabilitate it, showing the world you're amazing at PR. Do you have appointments with charities lined up?"

"I already have standing appointments with charities. Because it's good to give back. And you're lucky work let me do this. Because they operate under the belief that any publicity is good publicity. But even with that belief, if I really embarrass them, I'm fired. And I have to work their name in at some point."

We walk through the elaborate entryway, gilt furniture competing for our attention with painted walls and ceiling. Figures mock me from all around—chubby cupids winking down at me from the ceiling, and Venuses coyly trying to cover themselves as I pass. Even a particularly unhappy-looking man in a wig from the wall. Don't know why he's so mad, he's living in a gorgeous space.

The rest of the space is filled with people moving around, carrying modern equipment I assume is to make the show.

Zara stops us in front of a room with a paper sign telling everyone the space is for female contestants. We both look at each other, two sets of eyes, both large in fear. We're both nervous for this show, for different reasons. Zara says this is her last chance after what happened at her old job. And I'm worried this will destroy my reputation with out of context cuts and them catching what I say when hangry.

It's not pretty.

"Ready for this, leprechaun?" Zara asks.

"Always, giant." I pull my suitcase behind me and give Zara a smile I don't feel. I open the door and walk through alone, with

Zara staying on her side of the door with the other busy crewmembers.

The room I walk into was probably a sitting room at one point, or a morning room, or whatever name they gave for a room to receive guests and show off, but now all the elegant furniture that once held aristocratic butts is pushed to the side to make room for makeup stations, clothes racks, and tables of food and beverages.

I'm immediately surrounded by three women. "New girl," an East Asian woman yells out. She's dressed in a shimmery blue empire-waist gown that looks like it's out of a *Pride and Prejudice* movie. "I'm Sarah." She grabs my hand.

"Hi. I'm Naomi."

"Jessica." A white woman shakes my hand next. She's in a similar gown, but in green.

"Hannah." The last woman, a Black woman, takes my hand next. She's got on the same uniform, but in yellow.

"I did not get this memo." I indicate their dresses.

"Don't worry, none of us did. But apparently we're going back in time," Jessica says, pointing at the clothes rack dripping with Regency wear.

"They want us to get dressed up before filming. We're going to a ball!" Hannah claps her hands in excitement.

My inner Cinderella is also perking up in interest, birds on my imaginary princess shoulder chirping in agreement.

Some people (the judge-y ones) will say it's hypocritical that I'm a feminist who wants to make my own way apart from Dad's famous name while still wanting a fairy tale, but they can get stuffed. Feminism is about choice, and I'm allowed to want an independent career and a man sweeping me off my feet at a ball. I can be an executive and a princess.

Cinderella, Chief Marketing Executive. With the most loyal team of mice publicists to do my bidding and a handsome man to come home to, ready to take me out to dinner after a long day.

I'm complicated.

"And then are they going to tell us what we're doing while we're here?" I ask.

Hannah snorts. "Hopefully. I just got dumped, so I'm ready for some romance. I hope there's someone who's a bit of me in there."

"Fingers crossed for fanny flutters for you," Jessica says. I love my adopted home so much, and their way of speaking.

"I quit my job when they passed me over for a promotion for the fifth time. But not the less experienced men," Sarah says. "I just wanted a change from home. Some adventure. And some fun. Maybe some love, too."

"I have horrible luck in relationships, so these lot can't be worse than my own choices. It'll be fun," Jessica says. "I'm also excited for the increase in Instagram followers."

"Yeah, it should be a laugh." I pull a pink number with lace from the rack, the dress with my name helpfully pinned on the sleeve.

"Here's to fun." Jessica pulls two glasses of champagne from the table behind her and hands me one.

"Yes to that." I take the glass and down it, then start the transformation into society lady of olden times.

A few minutes later, Zara comes into the room and winks at me. "Welcome, contestants. At the risk of inciting violence and you all getting my blood on these nice dresses we've rented for you, I have to take any electronics or books you have."

Zara gets a chorus of boos from everyone, me included, but we all give up our electronics. Well, after she pulls them from my resisting hands.

"Be gentle with my babies," I say as she takes my phone and tablet away from my grasping hands.

"Thank you," Zara says dryly to us all, since no one gave up their devices without a small and ineffective fight. "Now I can tell you that we're working on getting everything set-up. When we're done, I'll come get you and then the host will guide you through the rest of the day. Please eat and drink to your heart's content until I come back." With that, she takes our contemporary life-lines with her through the historic wooden door.

For the next hour, I get closer to these women than I've ever gotten to people in this short amount of time. Something about the nerves, alcohol, our certain future embarrassment, and lack of things to do mean that we're now to the level of tipsy friends who just met in a bar bathroom.

In other words, best friends. There's a lot of tipsy women supporting women in this room right now. And doing shots together.

Eventually some hair and makeup people come in and complete the transformation to aristocrats. And mic us up, which I'm sure members of le bon ton didn't have to deal with. They also teach us about the mics, and how to turn them off at night and on in the morning. And for bathroom times.

Apparently, that would be too much reality for reality TV.

My best friend finally comes back. "Zara!" we all yell in unison.

"Well, hello, party people. How about we film a hit show?" She gets a standing ovation like she's the first Indian actress to win a Best Actress Oscar. Even she looks surprised by our intensity, but then she looks at the table of empty wine bottles and it all makes sense. We start filing out of the room.

"Before we go." Zara snags me away from the rest of the pack. "The executive producer said I can't be your field producer since we're friends, so all your interviews and producing will be done by Aiko. She's great." Zara moves forward and covers my mic, lowering her voice. "But don't trust her, or any other cast member, a hundred percent."

"We're not doing this together?"

"I love you. You're gonna look so pretty on camera." I'm not assuaged by that. "Anyway, we have a schedule to keep. To the ballroom!" Zara turns, fleeing to do her job.

"And men to meet!" Hannah grabs the two arms closest to her (mine and Jessica's) and moves with alacrity after Zara. I grab Sarah's arm, and our chain crashes into the doorjambs on our way to said ballroom. But the cameras aren't on us yet, so I think we can call this a win.

"Hi, ladies," a white man with a posh British accent, dressed like Mr. Darcy including pants tucked into high books with a dignified, historic heel, greets us. His clothes are fancier than any of ours, with a velvet vest, a frilly shirt, and a ponytail tossed artfully over his shoulder. To be fair, that ponytail, which usually doesn't work for me, is working when it's framing those sharp cheekbones and light stubble.

"I'm Lewis. Your host for the foreseeable future." He pauses, looking at us until we clap.

"You'll each take a place around the room, looking busy while we film some individual footage. Then we're going to release the men to you! You'll all mingle and get to know one another, and I'll explain what's going to come next on your adventure. The cameras will be turning on now, and they'll turn off in a week."

Hannah whoops. I like her optimism and her enthusiasm for this goal. Even Sarah and Jessica have smiles on their faces, so I belatedly throw one on too. I am happy for this opportunity. Really. I just didn't drink enough to ignore all the dangers of this particular plan.

"But don't get too comfortable. We have chaperones scattered around the ballroom, to protect your womanly virtue."

Ew.

I see a piano in the corner and make my way to it, claiming it before anyone else can or the producers can complain. I took lessons for years, but I haven't played for a while. Stretching my piano muscles will be a nice distraction from what I agreed to.

The other women find spots around the room, by the food table, by some chairs, and by the drinks table.

I start to play while a man in a bright red coat drops a drink off on the piano with a wink, telling me it's madeira. Whatever that is. I smile to him while playing "Hot Cross Buns" to ease me back to the instrument.

A white woman in a muted gray version of what us contestants are wearing approaches me, and introduces herself as Diane, my chaperone for the duration of this show. Her brown hair is pulled tightly back behind a cap, and her non-smiling expression lets me know she will not be allowing any shenanigans, or even light chicanery.

If I have to be on a reality show, so far this isn't too bad.

I've got ample liquor, I'm not in a skimpy bathing suit, my virtue is being guarded by a dragon of a woman, and I'm in a beautiful room.

Gilt flowers pepper the ceiling and the sides of the room, with crystal chandeliers dripping down from the ceiling, dressed with electric candles. Trompe l'oeil paintings cover the spaces between the gold on the ceiling and walls. The room itself is long and narrow, with a gleaming wood floor. The entire room sparkles like the inside of a jewelry box.

Mom would throw up her hands in disgust at the extravagance in this room.

Even though I grew up rich, Mom always reminded me that not everyone lives like we do, since she didn't have any of it when she was growing up before immigrating from India to America in her early twenties. She's adapted very fast to the luxury but kept at least one of my feet on the ground when Dad was buying me a pony for my seventh birthday.

I want to be like Mom. She was already working as a successful lawyer when she met Dad. On opposite sides of a case. Dad told his attorneys to settle the case (although Mom said she would have won anyway and he only settled because of how weak the case was), and then asked Mom out, intrigued by the woman who told him no to numerous settlements before she got almost everything she wanted from him. She said yes that time.

I want to be able to point to my accomplishments as mine, at least with my career. Like Mom and all the cases she's won. So I can know I'm more than a spoiled rich kid. Even if I am also a spoiled rich kid.

My opinion on the reality show dims a little when the camera gets to me, making me self-conscious while the cameraperson films away. And then starts asking me to lift my head to get the best light, and fake laugh, and look like I just saw the love of my life, and stop cursing like a sailor when I get a note wrong. And stop playing; they'll add music in post so I can focus on what my face is doing.

This is kind of exhausting.

"Come on in, men," Lewis yells after the camerapeople decide they're done torturing us.

Despite the fact that I know this is a reality show, and very few people find love on a reality show, my heart still starts beating a bit faster. It's hard to fight against the atmosphere they've created here, and how they were talking up the men during hair and makeup.

A set of doors open theatrically and I keep playing, until I see the first face out of the door, when my hands smash the keys on the piano in a loud cacophony.

Not again, damn it.

CHAPTER 5

NATE

I didn't expect a warm welcome from Naomi, but watching all the blood rush out of her face is a bit excessive. I adjust my too-tight coat and walk across the floor, my shiny boots making a clicking sound with each step.

"Hey, squirt." I get closer to the piano, then lean against it when she doesn't look at me. That's fine. That means I can look at her in peace for once.

She looks amazing in her costume. The pink cloth flows around her curves, shifting like sand every time she moves. Which she's mostly doing to avoid interacting with me. Her hair is done in some intricate braids pinned back, small whisps curling around the tanned skin of her face.

Her red lipstick draws my attention to her mouth, which is stubbornly closed and not responding to anything I say. Her eyes are avoiding me too, although I know they're a deep, bottomless brown from past experience.

Back in New York I would never feel this free to look at her. Mostly because the only times I'm around her, I'm also around her dad, who doesn't need to catch me ogling his princess and fire me. So I'll take this opportunity to enjoy the view, since it's all I'll get.

And it wasn't easy to get this moment. I had to explain to Harrison that I was staying in London for a while longer without telling him why (Naomi is on a reality show and apparently so am I) and for how long exactly. Luckily I've worked with him for a while, and he trusted me when I said I needed to stay here. And Stevens agreed to cover for me while I'm gone.

Naomi can't hold out in silence for long. Just like any time Harrison talks about how she should come back to the States or talks about anything related to the stock market.

"What are you doing here?" she snaps under her breath. But since she's a Richmond, she's able to do it while still smiling for the cameras. I think she's forgotten that she's on mic, and that is undoubtedly going to come across not great if this is included in the final cut of the show. Which means I'm already failing in Operation: Keep ALL the Richmonds Happy and Unembarrassed.

"You wanted to do this. And I went to talk to the producer. About the show..." I try to minimize my involvement in that conversation.

"You ran to the principal like a tattletale and tried to get me kicked off of the show." The smile is gone from her face now, all pretense of not being angry with me dropped.

"I didn't run. I walked with purpose," I say.

A woman I don't know clears her throat and walks in between Naomi and me. She crowds me, until I have to move away from Naomi. Well, I don't like this. But I'm not going to do anything about it since this woman looks like she might have a knife or a small gun with a pearl handle in her purse.

"A gentleman waits until he is introduced to a lady," she says to me archly.

"Yeah," Naomi says over her guardian's shoulder.

"I've known her for years." Not well, but closer than strangers.

"And I bet you still haven't been formally introduced to her." She shakes her head at me in disappointment and Naomi matches it behind her.

Well, probably not. Because who does that?

"This is not a good first impression," the woman says, voice colder than the North Pole but with less Christmas cheer and cute polar bears.

"Terrible first impression." Naomi shakes her head in shame. Again. I think she's starting to enjoy this, if her very faint smile is anything to go by.

The woman turns to face Naomi, her skirt twirling in judgement as it brushes against my leg. "And you should have given him the cut for poor etiquette."

"Yeah, you should have cut me." Wait. That was poor phrasing. But at least the chaperone isn't lecturing me anymore.

"As the chaperone, I will make introductions. Naomi, may I present Nate." She looks at Naomi expectantly.

"Hello, Nate." She has to give me an amicable greeting with scary Mary Poppins looking at her like she's a naughty child, but she's clearly not happy about it.

"Very pleased to meet you." I take her hand and bow over it, assuming that's what I'm supposed to do from TV and movies. And the crash course in the Regency time period that the producers sent us to study in the past few days. A lot of informative videos and clips from *Pride and Prejudice.*

Naomi snatches her hand back from mine as soon as I stand up fully.

"Excellent. And I am her chaperone, Diane. Now, why don't you ask her to waltz?"

"Oh no, he doesn't have to do that," Naomi says, looking a lot less smug now than when I was being chastised.

"A gentleman does not talk to a lady whilst standing about." Okay, I know this woman isn't from the 1800s but she is really committing to the role with her scandalized tone. "You have to ask her to dance. Or to promenade around the ballroom."

"How about it? Would you like to dance or…promenade?" I ask Naomi, only knowing what promenade means and having a general understanding of the waltz because of the Regency training materials we were sent.

She rolls her eyes. "Let's promenade."

"Let's promenade." There's a sentence I didn't think I would ever say to anyone in my entire life.

We start walking awkwardly near each other.

"Don't forget to take her arm," Diane yells after us.

"I thought she was supposed to protect my virtue, not make me touch a strange man," Naomi says under her breath, tucking her hand in the crook of my elbow.

"How were your crops this season?" I ask after an uncomfortable amount of time has passed in silence, hoping to lighten the heavy mood that's descended between us.

"Well, I'm a woman, so no one told me how our crops were because apparently I need to be coddled like I'm a child. Hey, look at that. Nothing's changed in two hundred plus years," Naomi says. "Now tell me what you're doing here."

"You're here." I shrug. "So I'll be here too."

"This can only hurt your career."

I look up at the cameras following us from a slight distance and answer her honestly. Lies would only make Naomi madder. "It's a possibility. I'm hoping an ocean will be enough space that no one I work with will ever see this. It's not like they watch American reality TV, much less the English version. Or spend all day on social media. I don't think Stevens even knows what TikTok is. And if I let anything happen to you, your dad will fire me anyway. So here I am."

"You're doing this for Dad and your job. Of course you are. You always do everything for the job. Well, hate to break it to you, but someone's kid will probably see some viral clips of this on social media and tell their parent in your precious C suite."

I get defensive, but I'm not really sure why. It's not usually considered a negative to be good at your job. Or dedicated to it. But the way she says it doesn't seem like a compliment. And I don't want her thinking badly of me. Not just because it would make my job harder, but because it's Naomi. "It's not a crime to work hard."

"No, it's not. But there are other things in life besides work. Especially if your work makes you do things that are clearly outside of your job description. Like babysitting me. This is probably a labor violation."

"On the list of things Harrison could make me do, getting dressed up in period costume and drinking alcohol while I hang out in historic mansions in the UK isn't the worst." My tone is light, but I'm frustrated too. Not at her, but at Harrison. I shouldn't be the one mediating between them. I am far too attracted to her and far too employed by Harrison.

"That's because your standards are so low after all the time you've worked with Dad."

"I also care what happens to you."

She dismisses me with a wave of her hand, probably noticing I didn't mention that first. I should have mentioned that one first. "Plenty of people go on reality shows, and they're fine."

"People are terrible, and they say shitty things when they're safe behind a computer screen. I don't want you to deal with that."

"They do that when they're not behind a screen as well."

"Then why give them more ammo?"

"Why care? I'm probably going to mess up. Either here or just in life. But they'll be my mistakes, made with my own decisions and not Dad's."

I sigh, because she's right and Harrison is being unreasonable. Looking around the room, the other men I was waiting with in costume and hair seem to be doing a lot better than me, since the women they're with don't look like they want to punch the men. Lucky bastards.

"Contestants!" Lewis yells. "Gather around."

I lead Naomi over to Lewis, and she snatches her hand from my arm as soon as we stop walking. The rest of the contestants are already here, waiting for someone to tell us something about this show.

"By the end of the night, you eight are going to pair off into courting couples. And since we're back to a less enlightened time, this is going to be gentleman's choice. But pick wisely, because you'll be in these couples for the long haul."

Naomi gives me the stink eye, a fact I know because I looked right at her when Lewis made that announcement. And I know it's because she knows exactly what I'm thinking.

Because when I get to choose, I'm going to pick Naomi, if I can. Then I can make sure she has the most boring, wholesome, non-news-worthy time on reality TV that anyone has ever had in the history of the salacious shows.

I also don't particularly want Naomi with any of these other men. I saw them getting into these costumes, and their abs have abs. As someone with just the one layer of abs, abs which sometimes hide under a layer of not-muscle, who used to feel good about himself, it was quite the revelation.

Anyone who spends that much time on their midsection can't have any time left over for treating a woman right. I'm doing her a favor and saving her reputation all at the same time. I'm trying to protect her.

And spending time with Naomi is never a hardship. She's more stubborn than her dad, smart, and beautiful. No, it's not a hardship at all.

Even when she looks at me like she wants to do me physical injury.

"Not a chance," she warns.

CHAPTER 6

NAOMI

Of course I've thought about being with Nate; I'm not a nun. Even nuns would have a moment of weakness at the sight of the man. But I thought there'd be fewer cameras involved, and maybe less aggressively patterned velvet waistcoats (which he's kind of rocking, not going to lie).

But I never thought about it seriously. Because at the end of the day, he'll never see me as more than the boss's daughter. And I can't be around someone who's thinking about Dad when they're with me. Beyond that being ew, it's too common.

Like my high school boyfriend who only dated me to get that internship with Dad so he could put it on his college applications. I found out too late, after Dad, who could see what was happening, didn't give him the internship. Or the college boyfriend who started pushing to meet my family after a few months. I was happy he wanted to deepen the relationship, until he spent the night explaining to Dad why he should hire him after graduation. He did not get a call back. Or the job.

So I'm not going to let Nate ruin this for me. However much I want him.

I turn around and start looking at which of these men I can

trap in an advantageous partnership. Trying to meet any one of their eyes. Everyone is doing the same thing, but the first person I make eye contact with is the man closest to us.

Bingo. I turn and move toward him, leaving Nate without a second look. Because if I did, I would probably change my mind and want to stay near him some more. Him and those dimples that peek out every time he laughs at me or the broad shoulders that even three layers of clothes can't disguise.

I'm about to introduce myself when I feel an attractive presence behind me, board shoulders brushing against me as he moves next to me.

"Strange men need to be introduced to you." Nate reminds me, crossing his arms. Making those three layers of clothes bulge dangerously.

"That's true." Diane, my chaperone, appears on my other side. "Naomi, may I present Amir." She indicates the Indian-British man standing in front of me.

I offer my hand and he turns it over to kiss the back of it. Oh, yes. This is more like it. He looks like a model, and his eyes even sparkle, looking up to me as his lips make contact with my hand.

"Pleasure to meet you," he says, his melodic accent making me feel even more like I'm in Shakespeare.

"You as well."

"Would you like to dance?"

"I'd love to." I ignore the sputtering attractive man next to me, extending my hand to tuck in the smiling attractive man's arm. An arm that is just as firm as Nate's, if I were the sort to make comparisons.

He whirls me around when we get on the floor, narrowly avoiding taking out two other dancers already on the floor. I get a quick glimpse of Nate, who's being introduced to Hannah. Hannah's glowing under these dimmed lights, looking hopefully up at Nate while he gazes down at her like she invented electricity.

Guess he isn't just here for me anymore.

"What do you do when not wearing tight pants in a dimly lit ballroom?" I ask, trying to focus on the man in front of me.

"Just this usually. I'm English, so it happens more than you think." He flashes a one-thousand-watt smile at me.

I laugh. This is nice. Being able to talk to a man without the scepter of my father hovering over me. "See, I'm American, so my life is mostly wearing cowboy hats and declaring my independence from things."

"Monsters." Amir shakes his head in disappointment. "Well, when not going to balls, and again, that does take up a majority of my time, I'm a personal trainer."

Yeah, I could have guessed that. What with the shoulders and the arms and the butt, especially in the tight outfits the show is making the men wear.

I'm about to ask where in England he's from, but a hand comes into view to tap Amir on the shoulder. A hand attached to the very irritating Nate. "Can I cut in?"

Amir looks at me in question. "If she wants, mate."

I don't want to leave uncomplicated. Everything else in my life is fraught: work, missing my parents and appreciating them but also resenting them a little…everything related to Nate. Amir is…none of that baggage.

But I should get this sorted.

"I'll just be a second. Maybe we can dance later?" I offer.

"I'll look forward to it." Amir bows, already in the Regency mood, and then leaves.

I smile at Amir's retreating figure. Nate, a trained corporate executive used to observing his opponent, knows he doesn't have my attention and clears his throat to get it.

I'm contrary, so I give it another full five seconds of ogling Amir before turning to Nate with a very put-upon sigh. "What else could there be to say?"

"Just hear me out. Maybe we can go to the gardens. This is

really public." He turns in the direction of the French doors leading to outside the mansion.

"We're on a reality show. They probably have the garden camera'd up too."

"Maybe. But it's the best chance we have for privacy."

I groan. "Fine. But you only get five minutes."

"Not counting the time it takes to get there. That's acceptable." Always the corporate negotiator, this one.

"Agreed." I give in. One of the things I've picked up from being my dad's daughter is to pick my battles. Because I can't win them all, but I can overall win, if I plan right.

I turn off my mic like the producers shoved us, and motion for him to do the same. I time the exit so that the camerapeople are distracted, using the other couples, chaperones and other camera crews as shields so this conversation doesn't make it on TV. They already got more than I anticipated. It's surprisingly easy to forget we're being watched.

Adaptability of humans, I guess.

We also have to shake our surprisingly astute chaperone. Fortunately for us, Diane is a stickler for manners and didn't refuse when I asked if she could get me a drink.

The French doors lead to a terrace overlooking the garden and we find a staircase on the side down to the verdant space.

The garden is impressive, with stone walls protecting the retreat filled with manicured plants and planned pathways, dotted with benches and statues that have a little bit of moss coloring the white marble. The plants conspire to make private alcoves away from prying eyes, where couples have probably been getting in trouble for hundreds of years.

I walk to the farthest bench, hoping the production team didn't bother putting any cameras or mics that far out.

"I think we've said everything that can be said. You want me to go home, but I've committed to this under pain of contract penalties if I leave. I want you to go home, but you obviously also signed the same contract. We're here, fine. But I don't need to waste any more time with this when I have things to do." I sit down on one of the marble benches.

"Why are you doing this?"

"I want to start my own PR and publicity company. So you see, even if I embarrass myself, I'll rehabilitate myself through a vigorous campaign of heartfelt social media posts from the Notes app, and a very sincere, so sincere it borders on looking insincere, amount of charity work, and people will trust me to handle their PR needs. Or I can do it for the cast member friends I make here. Either way, my name will be out there."

"That's… ambitious. It feels like there are easier ways to start a business."

I scoff. "Not with this much exposure, this quick."

"Why does it have to be like this? Just start a business. Your dad will give you any investment you need and you can slowly build up a client list."

"I don't want his investment! Then everyone will think he just gave me a company."

"Instead he just gave you an education and helps pay rent."

"It's not just about the money. If his name is attached to my company, I'll always wonder if I was a success because I'm talented, or because he used his connections to make sure I couldn't fail. I'll never believe that I deserve it. That's different than getting money to pay for school or living expenses. Or at least it feels different to me. And I don't know why I'm getting flack from the man with two prestigious professor parents and their prestigious professor salaries."

"So much deflection."

"Yeah. I heard it." I sigh. "Wait." I turn to him in urgency, grabbing his arm. "Did you tell Dad about this already?" I look around, half expecting Dad to have sent an extraction team to rappel down into this garden, throw a bag over my head, and drag me back to the States.

"No," Nate says emphatically, with equal horror at the thought of Dad knowing what we're doing. "I just said that you didn't want to come home, so I was going to hang around London and try to change your mind. Then I said the reception was bad and hung up the phone. I hope he doesn't call, because a very muscular man in a too small shirt took my phone, and his muscles glared at me when I hesitated."

I can relax a little, then. Although the fact that I'm still here should have let me know that Dad doesn't know what I'm doing right now.

"So why drag me out here?"

"I want to be okay with you. I know you're not happy that I came, but I don't want you to be mad at me."

"You're not going to try to convince me to jump over this garden wall and run?"

Nate snorts. "In these clothes?" He looks down at his own tight pants, and then back up at me. "You made good points I can't argue with. Contract-based points I wouldn't dare argue against. So I'm not going to push for leaving. And I would like to be on good footing with you while we're here. But you've been varying degrees of mad at me since I saw you in your apartment."

"Why? Why does it matter if I'm mad at you?" I'm beginning to get really uncomfortable in this dress. It's empire waisted, but all the layers on my skin are making me feel a bit warm and constrained. Or maybe it's the emotions Nate inspires: lust (because of everything about him) and inadequacy (because he reminds me that he's only here for me because of Dad).

"I don't know." He sounds sincerely frustrated, but aren't businessmen trained to lie as part of their job? "I like spending time with you, and I don't want anything bad to happen to you. And it's not about Harrison. If anything, he's the reason I *shouldn't* feel like that."

"I...don't...what...?" Nate likes spending time with me...like I sort of like spending time with him? And we're away from Dad's prying eyes for the next few weeks? This sounds simultaneously too perfect and too terrifying. Because eventually those prying eyes are coming back.

"It's not a big deal. Maybe I can put together a business plan to buy a new company to distract Harrison and lessen the blow when I tell him his daughter is on a reality show. And also one of his executives."

I let out a sound that is a mix between a groan and a growl. "You need to stop calling me 'his daughter.' I'm actually a real person beyond my parents."

"Oh. Sure. I can see how that's annoying. Sorry," he says sheepishly.

Nate is an enticing mix of adorable and sexy, confusing my brain and turning it into mush, ensuring it'll never understand the feelings coursing through it right now. But through all the confusion, one thought repeats. A thought I can't shake, no matter how often I tell myself to stop.

So I don't.

"Just kiss me, you idiot."

CHAPTER 7

NATE

es. God, yes. I want that. Still… "There are so many reasons why that's a bad idea." I want to throw caution right into the wind, but it'll be hard to find a job as nice as the one I have. Maybe even impossible if Harrison tells everyone what a terrible employee I am.

And there's the chance that Naomi and I have fun, and I'm sure it would be a lot of fun, but then she'll realize I'm a boring businessman, and that she was only interested in me as a way to get back at her over-controlling dad.

Then I'd be jobless and Naomi-less.

I don't want to lose them both. Even if all I get is seeing her for short bursts when she's home, small snippets of humor and intelligence, I don't want to lose that.

In the dim light, I can see her roll her eyes at me, and I squash the urge to tell her not to. Trying not to act as old as I feel around her.

"Of course you're not going to. You wouldn't kiss me unless it was written in the executive manual that it was allowed."

"I'm not that bad."

"You just had a woman who is, at the very least, of average

attractiveness offer to kiss you, and you declined. Despite the fact that you're single, I assume. And straight. Again, an assumption based on who you occasionally brought to company events. That is indeed that bad."

"I am single. And straight. And you're a bit higher than average attractiveness."

"Well, there's no accounting for taste." She smiles at her own joke and my eyes lock on her lips like they're a report listing the weaknesses of a company we want to acquire. With intense concentration at the gift in front of me.

Oh shit. I *am* that bad.

No, I can change. I love my job. It's stimulating and financially rewarding, but I won't let it make me old before my time.

"I want to kiss you too." I start again, hoping she can ignore everything I said after she ordered me to kiss her. I don't know that I deserve a do-over, but I want it.

"Then do it already," she commands, again.

"Fine," I snap back, not sure this is the best frame of mind for a romantic kiss in a dark, secluded garden.

I reach for her neck with my right hand before I can think too much about common sense and operate solely on desire. I pull her in firmly, my lips meeting hers in an abrupt mesh of skin.

But the second our lips touch, the aggression of the initial challenge fades away. I ease back slightly and angle my head so I'm caressing her mouth, not attacking it. She responds by loosening the tension in her body, dropping into mine on the bench. I take the weight, savoring the proof that she's here, with me, kissing me willingly.

Proof that I'm not too old or boring for her.

Once the battle of the kiss turns into a mutually enjoyable endeavor, I open my mouth to tease her lips with my tongue. She opens immediately, taking my tongue on a groan.

The hand at her neck relaxes into a massage, as my other hand searches for even a hint of the body underneath her clothes.

Her hands come up to my lapels, fisting in them and pulling so I move the last inch closer to her on this bench. And then we're touching from lips to torso. My dick, annoyed to be left out in the seated position, starts to rise in my too-tight pants.

As if that will get him in contact with the attractive woman in my arms.

Actually, contact isn't a bad idea. But before I can make the required adjustments that would make my dick very happy, I hear the crunching of shoes on a gravel pathway. My brain knows I should pull away, but the message gets lost on the way to my lips and hands, which stay plastered on Naomi.

The crunching gets louder, so the messages my brain is sending get more urgent, only to be openly ignored by my own mouth. I remind myself what's at stake here, but immediately after Naomi's teeth brush against my lips and I stop arguing with myself.

Fuck it.

I savor the next few seconds, until an outraged gasp permeates the little sanctuary we've established here.

"You're ruined now!" a voice screeches.

I lift my head at the inane comment. "What?" My lips are still wet from the kiss, and I still have a painful erection. I don't appreciate the interruption.

I see Diane, the chaperone, looking incensed in front of us, with a cameraperson and producer standing behind her.

"Right, we're on a reality show," I whisper to Naomi.

"Ruined! After all my hard work keeping you virtuous, now you're ruined!" Diane carries on, adding some dramatic hand gestures and maybe some tears.

Naomi starts giggling next to me, first demurely behind her hand, but then louder as Diane keeps ranting. She sets me off and now we're both laughing in the face of...whatever this is.

"Why is no one concerned about my virtue, though?" I ask Naomi, sending her into more fits of laughter.

"You're a man." Diane pauses the rant to educate me. "And you've ruined Naomi!"

I try to defend the lady next to me. And myself. "Ruined seems like a bit of an overreaction for a kiss."

"A kiss." Diane sounds as scandalized as if I told her I was getting a hummer on this bench instead of a hot, but still tame, kiss. "Ruined!"

These might be the only words Diane knows now, too shocked at the (fully clothed) debauchery that allegedly happened here.

"All right then. Maybe we should go back to the ball?" I have no idea what it supposed to happen now that I've "ruined" a woman, never having done it before. I look at Naomi, hoping she has any idea what we're supposed to do, but she's still laughing too hard at the situation to be any help.

I stand up, not worried about my penis, which started softening at the first screech of "ruin." I extend my arm out to Naomi, who manages to stop laughing enough to take it.

The producer standing next to the camerawoman gives us a thumbs-up and Diane immediately stops crying. Terrifying.

"Great. We've got that. We can go back inside, but we're going to put you two in a sitting room for a few hours. Part of the ruin consequences. We'll bring you out when it's time to get in a couple." The producer indicates we should follow her. "I'm Aiko, by the way. I'll be producing the both of you."

"Hi. Nice to meet you," I say to the East Asian-British woman in front of me. "I don't usually ruin women in gardens."

That sets Naomi off again, and I have to half drag her laughing body back inside the house.

Aiko drops us off in a sitting room where we can still hear music and conversation from the ballroom. She leaves after she turns our mics on again with a stern warning not to turn them off again until the approved times.

"I wasn't aware there would be consequences for being

ruined. That's…fun." Naomi's voice still a bit breathless from the laughing marathon she just engaged in.

"There were a lot of dire warnings of ruin in the Regency videos they sent us. Apparently we were supposed to take something from that."

She shakes her head in disbelief. "I am so glad to be born when I was."

"Yeah. Also, turns out knight in shining armor is harder than historical movies make it look."

"Knight in shining tight pants, you mean." She eyes my pants. My groin, to be more accurate. Which conveniently forgets that we're here to save the woman across from us, not ravish her. Another word I heard a lot in those informational videos.

Her smile fades as she looks back at my face. "Do you want me to tell Dad that kiss was staged?"

Oh god. Harrison is going to see me kiss his daughter. I hadn't even thought of that, getting too damn caught up in the romantic garden. And her.

Naomi sees my look of disgust and drops the last lingering bit of a smile on her face. A hard look replaces it. "Sorry to ruin your spotless reputation." Her tone does not convey apology in any way.

"It's not that. It's just that—"

"It's just that I'm getting in the way of *your* job, even though I literally left the country, and you came to me. Unasked. To mess up my life for your, and Dad's, convenience. But now *your* life is getting uncomfortable, and you don't like it." She shakes her head at me. "You should have stayed in New York."

Naomi marches to the other side of the room and gets a book down from the shelf. She treats it a little harshly for something that is probably an antique, but I'm not going to be the one to point that out to her.

Especially since I can't argue with anything she said. I did come here to stop Naomi from living her life and drag her back to her father, regardless of her wants and needs.

I still want to do that.

Or at least I need to if I want a job after this is over. Harrison might not have come out and say I would be fired if I failed, but he did joke about the topic. The sort of joke that has a kernel of truth. At the very least, I won't be getting a promotion to head of my department any time soon.

And having Naomi back would soften the blow of seeing me kiss her considerably. Hopefully.

Not having the moral high ground makes an impassioned defense to her accusations hard to muster. Instead, I'll sit in this leather chair and be quiet. Before I sit down, I see a bar off to the side and make a detour, pouring myself a drink with the glass decanter that might be older than America.

I make an extra one for Naomi, hoping she likes straight whiskey since that's all there is here, and set it on the table next to her, not saying anything. Or making eye contact, like the coward I am.

I can't change why I'm here, even though I wish I could.

When Harrison asked me to his office to go over this assignment, I thought the meeting was to give me a compliment on the folder I assembled of information that could lower our manufacturing costs for wind turbines. But instead, Harrison sat me down and told me he wanted Naomi home.

I sympathize with him, to an extent. It seems like he loves his family, and in typical controlling billionaire fashion, he wants his family back with him, now, regardless of what she wants. That part I didn't sympathize with as much.

Then he started suggesting things. Like what if I went over to London and checked up on her. Which then became me going to London to convince her to come back. Which led to me having a booked ticket to London that left the next day, and a muddled confusion as to how things got to this point.

The situation was so ridiculous and fast-moving that I didn't even have the time or presence of mind to tell Harrison it was wildly inappropriate to tell me to get involved with a family issue.

And that I can't kidnap a grown woman who wants to live an ocean away from her dad. In fact, after that conversation, I kind of understood why she would want to live an ocean away from her dad.

But that sympathy won't get me anywhere.

I spend the next few hours in the library thinking about what I can say to make it better, but I come up blank. I'm better with numbers and logistics, so a heartfelt apology isn't coming easily to me.

She does drink the whiskey, comforting me slightly. She hasn't looked at me the entire time, but she took my peace offering. I know she's avoiding me, because I'm looking at her, hoping she'll look up and see the apology in my eyes. Then she can tell me she forgives me without me having to say anything.

It's not all about apology. She's beautiful, even when radiating pure anger in my direction. It's not hard to look at her.

When the door opens and the producer walks in, I've never been happier to be interrupted.

"Hello, my mischievous pair," Aiko says as she opens the door. "Are you ready to face the punishment for a running?"

CHAPTER 8

NAOMI

Do they still put people in public stocks? Because it feels like that's where I'm headed now, with some enthusiastic masses throwing rotten tomatoes at me.

"Does it mean we'll be free of this very comfortable prison? And maybe given some solid food?" I ask, not entirely mad at the liquid diet, but something substantial might be good. To deal with the fact that Nate just kissed me. Mr. Perfect Executive broke every human resources guideline to kiss me. On TV.

And then he had to ruin it by saying, *"It's just that..."*

"Yes. And eventually. We're not going to violate the Geneva Convention," Aiko says, laughing at her own joke and scaring me a bit. She shuffles us out the door and back to the ballroom. Right before we go in, we're joined by another couple consisting of Hannah and Amir.

I gasp. "Did you guys get ruined too?"

"Technically only you and Hannah are ruined. The men are fine. Maybe they get a reputation for being rakes, but they'll be okay in the long run," Aiko says.

"Well. That is not right," I say. Hannah nods in agreement.

"Preach. But we're living deep in the patriarchy, so let's go face the consequences of your wanton lady weaknesses."

Back in the ballroom, the space has been cleared of the extras. Lewis and the rest of the contestants are standing near a stage, everyone turning when we enter the room.

We join then and Lewis sends a dirty smirk our way. "Looks like some contestants couldn't wait for the coupling ceremony."

Oh, for crying out loud. "It was just a kiss." Which they interrupted before it could even become something good. But Lewis here is making is seem like we were naked on the piano, going at it like a sea captain and his mistress, when he's about to ship out to war with Napoleon.

"Suuuure." Again with the insinuation. "But that does mean that they're locked into a couple, at least for now. Consequences."

Damn it. Now I can't even escape my babysitter because I have to date him on a TV show.

Nate got his wish. He gets to monitor my every move for the rest of this trip and I'm going to have the most boring, wholesome time, which won't show anyone I can handle a disaster and the subsequent redemption arc. I might as well not even be here.

Except we did get caught kissing the first night. That's sort of scandalous (for the 1800s at least); maybe I can use it.

Or I can start working on these beautiful messes and swoop them up before they even realize they need a publicist.

"That makes Nate and Naomi, and Amir and Hannah, our first two couples. Let's hope they can let us get through the rest of the coupling before jumping each other." Lewis puts salt in the wound, not satisfied with the initial amount of discomfort he was causing with just the stab itself.

I tune out the rest of the ceremony, vaguely noting that Sarah ends up with a white man named George and Jessica ends up with the last contestant, a Black man named Will. Both men have a lot in common with Amir: fit, muscled bodies, hair with more gel in it than is strictly necessary or advisable, and whitened teeth that get shown off in wide smiles. George can be distinguished from Will by an impressive array of tattoos.

The ceremony takes a few hours of shooting, re-shooting, re-shooting the re-shoots, and getting some B-roll of us pretending to socialize, as well as our couple videos, so I'm sober and hungry at the end of it.

"Now that we're all in couples, I can finally tell you what you'll be doing for the rest of the show..." Lewis drags out the anticipation while cameras film our impatient faces. They really like dragging out news here.

"I hope it's eating our way through Regency London," I say under my breath, my stomach backing up the wish with some well-timed grumbles.

Hannah, who I intended to hear that, gives me a sympathetic smile that agrees with my assessment. But Nate, who I was not speaking to, nudges me in his own agreement. I give him a dirty look for overhearing a conversation that I made no effort to keep private.

Lewis gives me a hard look, so I know he also caught my not-so-quiet aside. I attempt a smile at him, and he moves past me without returning it.

He does smile at the camera, though. "You're going to follow the path of lovers before you in a time-honored tradition. A tradition that will test your devotion, your strength, and your endurance."

What did Zara sign me up for? I peek over my shoulder to see where she is, but I'm blinded by spotlights so she blends in to the anonymous crew members behind a line of cameras.

"During the next few weeks, you'll all be taking *The Road to Gretna!*" He pauses, this time for our reaction.

He gets crickets instead.

"Where?" George asks.

"Like the Scottish Vegas of history?" Sarah asks.

Zara steps forward from the line of crew she was hiding

behind, still avoiding my eyes. "Yes. Back in the day it was hard to get married in England, so couples eloped to Scotland to tie the knot, which had more lax rules, like Las Vegas. Gretna Green was the first town they came to across the border. And you're going to be making that trip, with carriages and stagecoach inns, in period clothes, while engaging in some period-appropriate competitions. This has tested great with the *Pride and Prejudice* crowd. But we do need to film your reactions again and we need a little more excitement this time. Which I'm sure you all now feel now that you know what it is."

She fades back with the crew and Lewis resets. "You'll be taking *The Road to Gretna!*"

This time we all go wild, as instructed, like we knew what it was the entire time.

"Can you believe we're going to Gretna Green?" Jessica asks me, a twinkle in her eye reminding me of the absurdity of doing this again. So much reality in this reality show. So much "refined" reality.

"I'm so excited to take this historic journey." I wink at her in return.

"A trip won't be too bad," Nate says next to me, and I can tell he's content there's going to be more activity and less getting into embarrassing situations drunk by a pool. Ha! I'm sure they'll find ways to embarrass us with alcohol in carriages.

"And the team that works best together through all the obstacles blocking their path, and captures Britain's heart and more importantly, their votes, will win £100,000." Lewis looks directly at the camera. "Join us, Britain, for *Love Island* meets *The Amazing Race*, meets *Pride and Prejudice.*"

That gets some real cheers from us, no producer coaching necessary. I would watch this show with that exciting mix. We'll see if I'm still excited when I'm the one on it.

"That's great. We've got it." Zara moves in front of us again and the cameras lower. "We've got to do some individual interviews for background and first reactions, and then we'll be done for the day. Find your producer and we can get started."

I ignore Nate and head to Aiko. She pulls me away from the group, after telling Nate to go with another producer. She leads me to an upstairs bedroom that has been transformed into an interview space and directs me to a chair facing a camera.

"Can I have food?" I start off my interview by asking the questions.

"After this interview, we'll get you more food than you can comfortably eat in one setting. The American way." Aiko smiles, friendly and open.

That's fair. Or I've already developed Stockholm Syndrome with my producer via a mix of hunger and embarrassment. "What do you need?"

"What made you want to move to London?"

Wow. The big questions right out the gate. "Who doesn't want to move to London? It's an amazing, cosmopolitan city with something to offer everyone." It's my canned answer that I have for people I don't want to tell my entire life story to.

"So is New York. No need to move away for options."

"I do love these accents you all have. So fancy." I smile at her, deflecting.

"I'm glad you lot love it. Makes vacations interesting. But that is real devotion to linguistics, to move away from home and family to be around it. So why the move?"

Does she know why I came here and just needs me to say it? I don't know how she would know, but she looks like she has ways.

I'm so hungry, and I feel like they just want drama, so I'll give it to them. "Right. Well, it doesn't hurt that there's an ocean between me and a slightly over-protective father." It only took them like five minutes to break me. Embarrassing.

"I can understand that. My father didn't let me date until I turned eighteen. So I just did it behind his back," she says with a wink. "What's your dad like?"

"Well, he did background checks on every date I had in high school. Even broke into prom with some suits to separate me from my date, who apparently had a speeding ticket come up on his background check." Once I start talking (complaining) about him, I can't stop.

She puts her hands up. "Okay, he's worse than mine. I heard you might have had a prior relationship with someone on the show."

"I know Zara, the producer. We're close friends and roommates. It's a funny story how we met—"

"But with one of the contestants?"

Ugh. It's been abundantly clear that they know about our past, but until she said something, I could live in my own world where we were successfully hiding this secret. "Nate actually works for my dad." They appear to have all the information already. I might as well give in with grace and get to the eating part of this evening faster.

"Tell us about him."

"There's not much to tell. He seems good at his job, since Dad keeps him around. And Dad's picky." That's an understatement. "But I haven't broken into Nate's annual evaluations to confirm that."

"How is he as a person?"

I shrug. "I don't really know. He's young for the job and Dad has nothing but good things to say about him, which means he's really smart at what he does. I know Dad is always emailing at all hours of the night, so Nate must be a hard worker with no work-life boundaries like him, to get his praise." And he does it while looking like someone right out of my fantasies. Which is so odd, since I usually stay away from anyone associated with Dad's company. Or business in general.

My last boyfriend was a musician, for crying out loud.

I think it's those dimples. Mere mortals can't be asked to resist dimples of that caliber. It's not possible. And that he can look so happy, even after spending so much time around joyless business drones, is impressive.

"He's an attractive man," Aiko says, speaking my thoughts like she gave her soul to some paranormal to be able to read minds. Which does not bode well for me. "Is there anything more than him working with your dad?"

"No," I say flatly, sure she's not going to get me to budge on this point, soulless though she may have gone for that perception power.

"Do you think he's attractive?"

"Sure, I guess he's…symmetrical. If you're into that sort of thing." Oh god, did I just call him *symmetrical*?

"Most people are into that sort of thing. Are you?"

"It's fine. He's good." I don't want to think about how symmetrical the man is. He reminds me of life back home, and uncomfortable family dynamics. Something I can't separate from the man himself, however unfair that is to him. And I don't think he can separate the two either, frankly.

But I can't deny that the kiss was damn good.

If we had met anywhere else, I wouldn't be going through so much strife. Because we would be too busy making out.

"If he wasn't working for your Dad, would you admit he's attractive?"

"Maybe it would be easier to admit."

"Would you pursue something with him then?"

"I doubt I would have met him if he didn't work for Dad."

"But let's imagine. He doesn't work for your dad and you met. Would you date him?"

She's relentless. "Sure. Who wouldn't?" I want to keep deflecting, but I also can't bring myself to lie.

We switch topics, but I don't get a chance to be thankful we're moving on because of how scary the next topic is. "Tell me a bit about your love life."

"I'm single. I've dated casually since I've been in London. Never knew when I was going to move back so I didn't want to get involved in anything too permanent." And I may have compared all the men to Nate. Then I remember I'm supposed to be on the show for love. "But now I'm getting more settled here, making this my home. And I'm ready to try for something more serious. "

"How do you feel about love?"

Wow. We got philosophical real fast. I take another sip. "It's grand. For one day."

"What are you waiting for?" Am I getting a therapy session out of this? Except instead of wanting to heal me, she just wants the juicy details about my specific brand of issues to sell ad space.

"I've spent a lot of time on work and trying to figure out a career plan. And I didn't want to drag someone into that when I was so uncertain and busy. When I didn't have time to get to know anyone properly. It's not fair to them."

"Do you feel ready now?"

"More than before, I guess. And I'm beginning to realize I need more work-life balance." That's true. I don't want to end up like Dad, obsessed with work.

"What are you hoping to get out of this?"

I can't answer that one with complete honesty. It would be awkward to tell them I don't care all that much about this romance competition/ historic cosplay and I want that sweet exposure. "I want to make time to get to know someone, despite the reasons that stopped me before. I don't want to feel like it's too late."

Despite hiding some of my truth, Aiko is getting a surprising amount of truth out of me.

"Maybe some time getting to know Nate? You are his partner."

She neatly backed me into this corner. "I look forward to getting to know all the contestants."

Aiko takes pity on me and ends the interview there. She leads me to a room and tells me that dinner is on the way. "Come down for breakfast at around eight a.m., in that dress, please." She points to a dress hanging on the outside of an armoire.

I look around the room, with all the historic furniture and decorations. My contemporary hard-shell suitcase, anachronistic though it is, sits in the corner.

Phew, I don't have to wear a corset to bed. Or whatever they did in the olden times.

Food comes on a tray, and I demolish it, not knowing when they'll feed me again. After, I feel better about what the rest of this show will bring.

Even though it means more Nate.

CHAPTER 9

NAOMI

My alarm clock, the one modern piece of technology in this room (and modern is pushing it since this alarm clock still looks older than me), does its job interrupting my already fitful sleep, worried about what else could happen on the rest of the show.

I approach the dress on the wardrobe. And the corset. "Ah. Hello, big brother. I don't know how to put this on," I say into the mic, hoping someone is listening.

A few minutes later, Aiko appears at the door to help me dress, without the cameras.

I get to the wood-paneled dining room before anyone else and pile food onto my plate. I'm halfway through my first serving when Nate walks in, looking well-rested and attractive in his tight pants and high boots combo.

And his shirt is rolled up to show thick forearms. Come on, producers. Not fair.

"Hey, squirt." He sits down next to me. "What's the big rush?"

I finish chewing before answering. "Last time they didn't feed me for hours. I don't trust any of these people anymore and I will load up when I can. As god as my witness, I will never be hungry again." I hold up my bag after I'm done imitating Scarlett. "This is now my pastry purse."

"Do you have any room to spare for me?"

"Get your own reticule." I shove the last bit of eggs into my mouth.

"You'd let your partner starve?"

"My partner hasn't even attempted to go to the buffet right there and get his own food. And oh yeah, also my partner *ruined* me."

"This is the most negative reaction I've ever had to a kiss. Hands down."

"Go get your food. These people will use your hunger against you and you'll say things you don't want to in the interviews." Like telling Aiko that I thought Nate was attractive. I blame that entirely on the combination of hunger, desperation, and alcohol.

Nate gets up. "That was intense. Worse than the job interview I had with Harrison. And that's saying a lot."

I track his black pants-covered butt and bright red waistcoat to the buffet table, while I keep eating. Breakfast and a show. So far the first full day of filming isn't that bad.

He walks back to me and sits down, eating while the room fills out with contestants, our producers, and the film crew. I sneak glances at Nate, watching his strong jaw work to eat breakfast. Then I realize that I'm probably on camera ogling him and trying to be sneaky about it, so I face my croissant instead.

After everyone gets fed (and overfed, in my case), Lewis calls for our attention, cameras up and ready.

"Is everyone ready to get on *The Road to Gretna?*" Lewis asks us, hyping us up for the adventure and working the show title in again.

Everyone cheers, very enthusiastically, already conditioned to give the right response or they'll make us do it again and again until they're happy that we've been excited enough.

"You didn't think we'd make it that easy, though, did you?" Lewis teases us, smile like a used car salesman.

Of course not. I wonder what other tortures they have for us, beyond making me lust after Nate from up close.

"The first task for you, as is the first task for all young lovers looking toward Gretna, is to escape your chaperone and get period-appropriate transportation from the village we've set up on the grounds. Each day will have different tasks along with the travel, some individual, and some in groups." He lets the news sink in for a few seconds, while we look at each other with more than a little trepidation.

"Now, yesterday was gentleman's choice, but these couples aren't set in stone. If you aren't working well with your partner, you can kidnap another one, but you only have one steal, and they can decide to go back after at least twelve hours or stick with you. Your old partner goes with the kidnappee's old partner. We are equal opportunity highway-people, so men and women can kidnap, even ruined women."

Whew, that's a lot to take in. I exchange looks with the women I've gotten close to, all of our eyebrows raised in worry at what the next few weeks are going to look like

"Once you get transportation, you'll be given a map, and you're off. You will have a coachman driving the coach, but you'll have to tell them where to go." Lewis indicates large trunks behind him. "And you'll be doing it all in period-appropriate clothes, from these trunks that you'll take with you. You'll have no access to the clothes you brought, but we'll keep them safe for when you're done."

Great. I'm glad I spent so long picking out all those clothes. But I've learned my lesson; I'm not going to ask what else could go wrong with the show.

"I see some overwhelmed faces, and luckily, that's all the new information for now. Each woman is being sent to a different room with their chaperone, and the men will have to find their lady and help them escape. You can wait until bedtime, which will make it easier to get to the women but you might get worse transportation or lodgings tonight, so make haste!"

The chaperones step forward, a group of four very serious, stern-looking women, their plain gray dresses distinguishing them from us contestants.

Diane intertwines her arm with mine as her co-workers take the other women. She leads me to a sitting room, where she drops me on the couch and sits opposite of me, pulling some embroidery out of a table next to her. The camerawoman sets up in one corner, with Aiko behind her.

Ticks from a clock on the mantle fill the resulting silence. I eventually get bored with looking at the room. Although it is a very nice room, with red velvet wallpaper looking like theater curtains and intriguing furniture with a million small details. Which loses some of the intrigue after I've stared at it for a half-hour.

"What should I do while we wait?" I ask the room, practically begging anyone to give me something to do.

"You can embroider," Diane says, clearly biased to the activity since she's doing it now.

I've never done it, but it's better than sitting here in silence waiting for a man. I nod, and Diane gets me set up with the tools and gives me a quick tutorial. The camerawoman is focused on her phone while the camera blinks it's red light on a tripod, so I assume this part won't feature heavily in the final cut of the show. Unless I say something embarrassing.

It makes me wonder how much of my favorite reality shows have hours and hours of boring footage on the cutting room floor, in order to get the few minutes of gold.

For the next hour, the embroidery is actually quite soothing. Then I'm just wondering where Nate is. And why I couldn't be the one to rescue him while he sat here, embroidering in silence with the dragon lady chaperone? Damn patriarchy.

A half-hour later, Nate opens the door. Finally.

I don't greet him with the deference he would probably prefer. "You took your time getting here."

"You, fair maiden, were hidden in the highest tower, in the farthest room. I found all the other ladies before I found you. But I kept looking," he says. Apparently wanting a cookie for staying loyal one day into this coupling.

Diane clears her throat. "How nice that you've come to call, Mr. Williams."

"Yeah. I love coming to call," Nate says awkwardly, bending into the most abrupt bow every performed in this aristocrat's house. "Are you knitting?"

"Embroidering." I hold up my half-completed design, a very basic flower.

"If your father could see you now," Nate mumbles under his breath.

I glare at him for bringing up Dad again. He's not helping me distance myself from the man.

Nate turns to Diane. "I'm having some tea brought up for you ladies."

As if on command, the door opens a second time, a man in livery coming through it with a silver tray in hand, laden with all the trappings of teatime.

"Let me get that for you." Nate takes the tray from the man and sets it down in front of us. He starts pouring tea the second the metal hits the table.

"Really, Miss Naomi should be doing this."

"Ah, well, I'm already done with this round; she can get the next one." Nate hands the cup to Diane before she can expand on a what terrible failure of a young lady I am.

He hands me a cup next, with the right amount of sugar and milk, and I take it tentatively, wondering what's inspired his moment of consideration. I can't imagine any of the stuffy executives that work at Dad's company making a cup of tea for some-one. None of them are that considerate.

Nate gets his own, and then settles onto the opposite side of my couch. "How are you ladies?"

Is he not going to bust me out of here? He should be breaking some windows and grabbing me to rappel down this building. Or at least telling me to run...we can for sure outrun Diane. We've got youth on our side.

"Lovely weather today," Diane says.

I look outside the window, where England's consistently gray skies dominate the view. Don't get me wrong, I like the weather because it's perfect snuggling-into-the couch weather, but it's not the usual application for that phrase.

"Lovely," I say meekly, mostly because I'm in a strange alter-nate universe where Nate wears tight leggings-level pants and serves me tea, and I don't know how to handle it.

"Diane, tell me about yourself," Nate says.

She launches into probably made-up facts about her life in Regency London. I'm impressed at how detailed she gets. But I keep sending looks over to Nate, wondering if he has a plan to bust me out of this prison, or if his plan is to stall so long Diane just falls asleep in boredom and we're last, getting the most uncomfortable carriage.

After the tea is gone, Nate stands up. "Can I take you ladies on a stroll through the gardens?"

I look at him suspiciously; the last trip in the garden didn't end so well for me. It ended great for my promiscuous lips, that loved all the attention they got from Nate. But now I'm a fallen woman, so there is that to consider whenever I see a garden again.

"That sounds nice," Diane decides for us.

"So nice," I say, tentatively taking the arm that Nate holds out for me.

Nate leads us out the back of the house and starts walking

around the labyrinthine green space. I studiously avoid the bench where my virtue died, more because I don't want to remember how it felt to have Nate's lips on mine, than the fact that I believe in some arbitrary metric of chastity.

"Nice sculptures out here," Nate says to break up the sound of the gravel under our feet, looking back over his shoulder to Diane as if she picked them out herself.

Before she can respond, I feel a sharp tug on the arm that Nate is holding onto and then nothing. I look at him and see Nate on the ground, clutching his lower leg with a grimace of pain on his face.

CHAPTER 10

NATE

"Oh, shit. Nate, are you okay?" Naomi kneels down by me.

"I'm okay. I think I must have stepped on these old stones wrong." Is anyone buying the sprained ankle routine? I hold my ankle a little more just in case. And grimace again.

"You twisted your ankle?" Naomi asks, looking vaguely concerned but sounding vaguely suspicious like only someone raised in the cutthroat business world can be. "In those boots? With the itty-bitty heels?"

I'm affronted. "An ankle took down Achilles, and he was a renowned warrior. Plus, they're very old stones. Precariously placed with no regards to regulations. Lawsuit waiting to happen."

"Achilles was taken down by an *arrow* to the ankle." Naomi dramatically looks around. "I don't see any arrows," she says, in case I didn't catch what she was doing.

"Let's try to stand on it," Diane says, so at least someone is taking this seriously. Not my partner, but that's fine. I'm not really injured.

I get up, hoping I remember which ankle was the one I was

holding when I was sitting on the ground. Once I'm standing, I lean on Naomi, not mad at the turn of events that plasters me to her.

I slowly put weight on the right ankle (which is the one I think I pretended was hurt) and then immediately back off it with a grunt of pain. "No. Can't put weight on it right now."

"Can we get some help? He's injured." Naomi is now apparently convinced, if her pleas for help can be believed.

Some of the crew dressed in period clothing rush forward, surrounding Naomi and me. As we had previously discussed, they cut off Diana, pushing her farther and farther away from us.

"Let's go inside. Maybe I just need to be off it." I start the walk back inside, leaning on Naomi enough that Diane knows this is serious, but not enough that I crush Naomi.

It won't help this plan if she gets actually injured because of my fake injury. Not when we're going to need to run soon.

We get to a sitting room and Naomi sets me down on the sofa. "Do you need anything? Ice? Tea? Iced tea?"

She looks worried, a change from the initial distrust. It's a small victory, but I do feel bad that I've caused her any negative emotions. I just want her to be happy. And need her to be happy to make Harrison happy.

"Just sit with me." I pat the couch next to me and she obliges.

More people come in, pushing Diane even farther from me until she's almost out of the door. Then I nod at Dan, the "footman" standing next to Diane, initiating part two of the plan.

"If you wouldn't mind waiting out here, we'll get the doctor in to see Mr. Williams," Dan says to her.

"Oh. Then Naomi can come with me too."

"It's okay, we're all here to chaperone and he seems calmer when she's around. He's in so much pain." Dan's tone is neutral, but he physically moves Diane out of the door by slowly walking toward her so she has to back up or risk a collision.

But it's hard to pay attention to what's happening by the door when Naomi is being concerned about my health by my side. Pressed against me and sending worried looks at the ankle.

"Should we take the boot off? See if there's any swelling?" Naomi asks.

"It's a long boot, it's going to hurt to pull it off. Let's leave it on for a bit." It'll be unpleasant to run through the damp grass without one shoe.

Dan finally gets Diane out of the room and closes the door behind her. Finally! I jump up from the couch, surprising Naomi, who had her hand hovering over my allegedly injured ankle.

"Let's blow this gin joint," I say.

"I knew you were faking!" Naomi smiles the smile of the always right.

"Less celebration, more running." I urge her up with me.

"Now we're in a hurry? Where was this urgency when I was embroidering?"

"It takes a while to organize an escape. Preparation that needs to be done."

"Is everyone in on it?" She looks around to the people still in this room.

"That's part of why it took so long." I hear a series of loud bangs from the other side of the big house. "And that's probably someone else's distraction. Let's hurry to the stables."

"Right. Where are we going?"

"Out the window, squirt. We're on the first floor."

"Technically the ground floor here. If we were on the first floor, we would be jumping down an entire floor length." At least she's walking to the window while she lectures me.

"Just like a Richmond to take time to tell me how I'm wrong during the middle of a time-sensitive situation."

"I am not like my father. Stop comparing me to him."

She is, but the denial is adorable. Obviously, there are differences between them. But she's just as terrifying and smart an adversary as Harrison. Which is why their conflicts can last years and span two continents.

But proving she's *slightly* better at compromise than her father, she pushes the window open. I jump down first and then help her over the low windowsill. I even take a half-second to enjoy the feel of her weight in my arms as she falls into me, before getting back to the task at hand and running away from the house.

Our producer Aiko and the cameraperson Kelly race to keep up with us, mumbling curse words under their breath. I wag my eyebrows at Naomi and she smiles at me. It's nice to see our torturers feel some of our pain with these activities.

"Do we know where the stables are?" Naomi asks, panting a little.

"I do. Because that was some of the preparation I did when you were impatiently waiting for me."

I don't take the time to gloat because we're in a competition and I'm not a Richmond. Instead, I lead us in the direction of the stables, checking behind us every now and then to make sure we aren't being pursued by Diane. No one back there but our production team.

"Well, I had to make small talk with a woman who's babysitting me like I'm a child, giving me Dad vibes."

"Equally arduous tasks all around." I give in so we can get moving faster. To her credit, she's still moving as she berates me, but she could move faster without the talking.

"That tone is so obviously placating, I can't take it seriously."

"Get revenge on that tone by beating me to the stables."

Naomi sighs but moves faster to the end goal. We hear doors slamming from the main house and I look back. Another couple, who look like two shadowy blobs in the distance, start toward us.

"Oh, no." Naomi's competitive side finally kicks in, another family trait that I won't be telling her she's showing, and she runs even faster. She doesn't know where she's going, so I run ahead to lead us.

We get to the stables, breathing heavily and sweating despite the cool temperature of the afternoon. I'm already worn out at the first task, so things are going well.

I frantically look through the stalls to find someone who can give us the information we need to get transportation, while Naomi checks the opposite side. Finally, I find a man sitting in the corner of the last stall I check (of course).

"Hi. Hello," I say, panting. "Can you help us get transportation?"

The man doesn't say anything, and a closer look reveals that he's taking a nap, hat pulled low over his face, bundled up in his coat. With his arms crossed over his chest and his feet kicked out in front of him, he looks comfortable despite how unpadded the chair must be.

Or he's faking it. Because reality TV likes to play fast and loose with the reality part. Our reactions are true, but they do like throwing shit at us and manipulating us to get a reaction they can use.

"Sir. Hello," I say louder. I catch Naomi's attention, and she comes to my stall. I lightly tap the man on the shoulder.

He slowly raises his head, showing me narrowed brown eyes under a wrinkled forehead. "What's all the fuss?"

"We need some transportation." I'm not sure what the producers want us to say or do to get the carriage, but we need it quick.

"And who are you, then?"

"Nate?" I'm not sure how that'll help, but it is an accurate answer. Even if I'm so unsure it came out as a question.

"Who's Nate? I'm not going to give our best carriage to a stranger."

"Oh, me!" Naomi raises her hand. "I'm supposed to live here, right? So this is my carriage too."

"Well, your father's," the man says.

Naomi sighs, and I know she's damning the patriarchy. "Right. And dear old Dad wants me to meet an uncle in York. If we don't meet him there fast, my father, the lord of that manor, is not going to be happy."

That spurs the man to action. "Why didn't you say something, miss? We'll get you sorted right away." He stands and shakes the sleep off. "Wait a minute. Where's your chaperone?"

"She's arranging our bags. We'll pick her up before we leave."

I look to Naomi, who slipped right back into daughter of the lord of the manor role very quickly. The *lying* daughter of the manor.

"Don't say anything," she growls at me, also picking up the subtext.

"I didn't say anything."

"You thought it. Very loudly. In my direction."

I laugh. "If you could read my mind, I'd be in a lot more trouble than I am right now," I say before I can think better of it. Because it's too easy to forget that the cameras are here and that Harrison is going to see this later.

Well, until now. When I reminded myself of everything.

Naomi immediately drops any anger from her face, eyes lighting up in amusement and lips curling in a small smile. "Tell me about these thoughts." Her voice is husky now and she steps closer to me.

"You don't have enough money in that fancy house of yours to buy those thoughts."

"I would move back home, let my dad give me that job at the company, and embezzle money from it just to pay you for those thoughts."

"Well, it is good to know I'm worth it," I say smugly. A little bit of ego-stroking is appreciated now and then.

She got closer to me during the exchange, and I think she feels the same attraction for me that I feel for her. Sure, she kissed me last night, but I've convinced myself it was a spite kiss because of her dad. There's no way I would be lucky enough to actually get her attention, or keep it. She's a society princess, who had an actual coming out in New York as a debutante, and I had academic texts lining my nursery because my parents ran out of room in their home library.

But she's not looking at me like I'm beneath her. Or too old for her. Or an instrument of revenge. Or any of the thousand other reasons I've convinced myself that I should stay away from Naomi.

When she looks at me like this, face upturned and eyes mischievous, those inappropriate thoughts come back, full force.

"Here's your carriage." The man breaks into our moment, indicating we should follow him to a line of carriages in the corner. "Now some off-camera instructions for you. You'll be going with Fred, who will be in charge of the horses. Each day, you'll travel to our pre-scheduled stops, mostly at local country inns and some historic manor houses. We're providing you maps each day, in sections, that indicate the right way and which roads you can legally be on in the carriage, but you have to read them and tell Fred how to get there. Okay, I think that's it. Have a safe journey." He hands us the maps as his assistants load our trunks onto the back of the carriage. "The routes take you on side roads, so please don't direct yourselves onto the A1."

"Don't worry; we'll be with you the entire time so you won't get into too much trouble," Aiko says.

"Unless it's *really* entertaining," I add.

"We'll be in the carriage with you and I do draw the line at hurting myself to get a good shot."

"That's something, at least," Naomi says.

"We'll also have a van that's following us, close enough to carry our stuff and help in an emergency. And to help guide any cars we run into," Aiko says. "Now let's get out of here before we lose this lead. The team that gets there first gets the best room at the inn." She brings her finger to her mouth like she's giving away state secrets.

Despite her words, the crew films us getting in the carriage, and then makes us get out and get in again so they can film it from a different angle. As we get in the carriage the final time and close the door, Hannah and Amir burst into the stables. They're muddy, and I don't want to know what happened to delay them from when we saw them at the house to now.

"Nate, we have to go." Naomi's eyes get wild now, an urgency that only flares up when she gets sight of the competition.

"There's no actual prize for coming in first for tonight," I say.

"Bragging rights are on the table. And the best rooms at the inn. Didn't you hear?"

"You just need to win." I don't say it, but we're both thinking that's a family trait. Naomi looks at me in gratitude, probably for refraining from pointing that out aloud.

"Fred, let's go," Naomi says instead of responding to me.

"As soon as you tell me where to go," Fred says from outside the carriage, already in control of the horses

"Right," I say. I scramble to open the folded map. "We need a light."

I open the shade on the window, but that doesn't let a lot of light in since we're still inside the stables. I start to look through the items already packed in the small space and Naomi does the same on her side.

"Oh, here's an actual candle." Naomi ho ds up a candle with a metal holder attached to the bottom. She looks at me expectantly.

"Do you not carry a lighter with you at all times?" I ask.

"No. Not even some of the times. So make like Prometheus and give us mere mortals fire." She shoves the candle into my hands, making me drop the map.

"He had fire to steal. It already being there is an important component. I can't make it out of thin air."

Naomi rolls her eyes and keeps looking for something to light the candle. I could always say something to piss her off and use the resulting fire in those deep brown eyes to light it, but there's a risk that I'll get burned in the process. That the entire carriage, and all the people in it could go up in flames. But I don't mention that to her.

"Found it!" Naomi holds up a packet of matches like they're an Olympic medal, quickly using one to light the candle in my hand. "Where should we go?" She takes the map from my lap, smoothing it down onto her own.

"North?" I offer weakly.

"We could overtake our producer and get our phones back. Ask Siri what we should do?" Naomi whispers in my ear.

"We heard that." Aiko looks less than amused at the suggestion.

"Ugh." Naomi looks out the window to see the other team getting in their carriage. "Let's just go right, Fred. Right now."

"Right, right now. Got it," Fred says from the front, getting the horses moving.

"Did you just decide that because it sounds the funniest direction?" I ask.

"Did you have any better ideas?" She's still looking at the map.

"Right it is then. Right now."

"Excellent." Naomi reaches into the same drawer she found the candle in and pulls out a blanket. "I think this is all we have for warmth."

"This is going to be a fun ride." I say the words sarcastically, but as Naomi throws the blanket over my lap and hers, I don't think it'll be that bad. Being plastered against Naomi from shoulder to knee isn't a bad way to spend the day.

Even if the air is trying its damnedest to tear through the heavy clothes we're wearing and leave frostbite in its wake.

After fifteen minuets of going in one direction, Naomi lifts the map closer to her face and says to Fred, "Okay. Maybe we should make a U-turn. But then, after the turn, we'll definitely be going the right way."

"Left was the right way all along." I shake my head. "We're going to end up in the Channel, aren't we?" The Channel, which is in the opposite direction from where we need to be.

"Forty percent chance at this point."

I sigh, putting my arm around Naomi. Because of the small space and the cold.

At least if we ride into the ocean, we must be able to go home early. Until then, I can enjoy being close to Naomi.

CHAPTER 11

NAOMI

Despite the excitement of the escape, and of being filmed, a long carriage ride is kind of boring. Especially since I don't have my phone, tablet, laptop, book, embroidery, or anything else to break up the monotony.

For the first hour, we both look out the windows. "Look how green it is here." Most of my time at home is in New York City, and even when we visit Long Island, the greens are different. And since I've been here, I haven't gone outside London very much, so it is nice to see nature.

However, after the first hour, the allure fades. "I never want to see green again." I close the window.

"Don't blame green for this; blame yourself for wanting to do this show," Nate says.

"I thought this was supposed to be about drama. I thought I would be drinking margaritas with, and possibly flinging them at, my fellow cast. I didn't know it was going to be this much sitting around."

Aiko breaks her silence to talk to us, probably because the boredom's getting to her as well. "You'd be surprised. There's a lot of hours of the day that never make air. It's what *The Real World* was like too. Maybe this is a good time to get to know each other a little better?" She raises her eyebrows at us.

I blow a raspberry at her. "Want to play two truths and a lie?" I don't even care what might get revealed on television. I just want some mental stimulation.

I had food this morning and a good night's rest. So now I have nothing to focus on except the long expanse of road. Even though we keep giving Fred directions and then having to correct those directions, we stay on roads for a long time and there's not much to relieve the boredom.

"Sure. You want to start?"

"We're going to get through so many rounds, it doesn't really matter. But I'm game." What to reveal to Nate and the world? "I love Marmite. I have a tattoo. And I've been hit on by three former *Love Island* contestants."

"Are all of them the lie?" Nate asks, confused.

"Nope, there are two truths there."

"Okay, let's take this one by one. Marmite is disgusting. It's yeast paste and I don't understand how anyone could like that when they could just have bread and beer if they were craving yeast. Marmite somehow has none of the benefits of either, despite having similar components," Nate says.

"Wow. We are not winning this after you insulted the British public's favorite food like that." I shake my head in disappointment but then brighten. "But don't worry, I can fix your reputation after the show."

"Their favorite food is curry. Because colonialism." There's his parents' influence. "But also because it's delicious and the other options are mushy pees. Or beans on toast. On toast, Naomi."

"Listen." Nate looks at me in confusion when all he hears is the horse hooves and carriage wheels against the ground. "That's the sound of more people voting against us."

"Moving on. The tattoo…" He looks me up and down. I'm in more clothes than I've ever worn around him, including a chemise, a corset, and a camisole, and *then* the dress on top of that. Although my titties are poppin' right now. I can appreciate the work of this corset, even though it is uncomfortably tight.

I look up and hope he's enjoying the view. Because I want him to want me as much as I want him. I don't want to be alone in this, or that kiss a result of me throwing myself at him and him going along with it because I was there, and the atmosphere of a moonlit garden, surrounded by cheeky statues in suggestive poses/states of undress. Or because it would have been awkward to push me away.

"I don't think you would have a tattoo. Definitely not one that I can see or remember seeing, at any rate. Now the last one, I hope isn't true. Is it true?"

"Guess which one is the lie and I'll explain all." I channel my inner fortuneteller.

"I hope the last one is a lie," Nate finally says.

"I do love Marmite. It's delicious and you're wrong. I *was* hit on by three former *Love Island* contestants, because the company I work for represents them so they're in and out of the offices and they hit on everyone. Even assistants they barely interact with. I don't have a tattoo, even though I want one, because I can't decide on a design I want on me for the rest of my life. And I'm afraid of the pain," I admit. "But I bet I know what tattoo you would get…your phone. Your work phone."

"I do more than work."

I look at Nate through narrowed eyes.

"Not much more, but I have numerous subscriptions to on-demand workout apps. And I have been thinking of getting a puppy."

"And why don't you get a puppy?"

"I'm not home that often." Nate sees where I was going with

that too late to avoid my trap, proving my original point of him working too much. "Point Naomi."

"Yeah, point me. As my prize, I want to know when you date."

Nate squirms. Interesting. "I don't, that much. Maybe sometimes I take people to work events. Anyway, you sound like you enjoy your job, too."

"I really do, even though I work some interesting hours too, with events at night or on weekends. But I love hearing the drama firsthand, and then figuring out how to make it all better. Social media dominates so much of entertainment. It's fascinating learning how to use it and profit from it. Like the way that with adless streaming, companies had to find new ways to reach people, like paying famous people to promote them."

"I never thought about that. But you could do that in New York."

"No, I can't." I give him a small smile. "Not without a lot of interference." I don't say who would interfere, even though it's implied. Seems like I can never completely get away from my family in my own thoughts.

I shake off the thoughts. "Now give me your two truths and one lie."

"Okay. My parents read me custom-made children's books as bedtime stories when I was a toddler. I've travelled to six continents. And I played competitive rugby when I was in college."

"Hmmm." I look him over, trying to see if that is the body of a competitive rugby player. Not that I have any idea what they look like, but he does have a nice body. He travels a lot for work, so the continent one is a maybe. I don't know much about his childhood aside from his parents are professors and opinionated, so maybe on that too? "The rugby one is a lie."

"What? You don't think I can play rugby?" Nate asks, puffing up like I just insulted him gravely.

"I've never heard you mention it. Dad played lacrosse in high school and we never stop hearing about it."

"It was a good stress-reliever in college. But I haven't played in a while."

Hm. I wonder if there's any footage of that. For science. "So which one is it?"

"I've been to all seven continents, not just six."

"I should have known you'd find business in Antarctica; the penguins are already in businesswear."

"It was to track down some scientists who were working on some promising energy research down there. And the penguins were not very helpful, since I kept getting distracted by them."

"I am jealous you got to see penguins. And what about the books? What's up with those?"

"You know my parents are professors, and they didn't feel like the children's books on the market at the time were touching on topics they felt were important, so they decided to make their own. They included academic concepts being explained by small children, that somehow still managed to go over my head."

"Do they still have the books?"

"Yes. Bad illustrations and all. My parents are not artists."

"That's really cool. I want to see those one day."

We fall into more rounds of two truths and a lie, learning about each other's likes and dislikes and life experiences, while shouting directions at Fred. There's also naptime, one of us at a time, so the other can handle directions. During my time to be awake, I get to look at Nate without him knowing, watching his long lashes rest against his skin, and all the hard lines and curves that make up his face relax. A face so serious when he's awake, I didn't even know it could get this relaxed. Then I remember too late that this is all videotaped and he'll see me perving on him later. At least I'm not likely to be around by then.

The producers packed a lunch for us of sandwiches and wine, and then encourage us to use a chamber pot when we stop. I vehemently refuse to do that, so they hustle us into a McDonald's to do our business. The people there don't bat an eye at our clothes, and I wonder how often people show up in period dress. England, man.

Aiko does have to help me pee, holding layers of clothes in a tiny fast-food restaurant stall. Making us way closer than when we started this journey.

I don't think any of that is making it into the final cut, but the horses really appreciated the fries I gave them when I came back. Maybe this will make it to the bloopers. Still better than me squatting over a chamber pot making it into the episodes.

After six hours of travel by carriage for the day, and me developing slight motion sickness, we stop.

"Yes. Finally." I jump out of the carriage, ignoring the irritating, repetitive disembarkment procedure they usually film. And getting sent back into the small space so they can film it again.

"This 'reality' is ridiculous," Nate says.

"I mean, they aren't making anything up. They're just having us do reality a second and third time so they can film all the reality, at all the best angles. They don't want to miss any of it." Despite my understanding words, my limbs protest getting back in the carriage since they were so excited to taste freedom the first time.

Then we're *really* released from the carriage and I take a look at our surroundings. An old building stands in front of us, made of worn gray stone and covered in crawling greenery in the manner of the best small English villages. Small wooden tables sit outside and a distinguished, if old, sign tells me that I'm at a place called the Coach and Horses.

As long as that name is a metaphor and I don't have to sleep in this damn coach, I don't care.

It's gotten even cooler since we were inside the carriage, the sun abandoning us while we were travelling. I shiver a bit and Nate responds by putting an arm around me, giving my bare arm a quick rub and then stepping away again. He's done with the sweet gesture before I can even register what he's doing. Before I can figure out how I feel about it.

I think I would have liked if he had stayed longer, actually.

I don't know that I trust he would ever be around me just for me. But I can take the good moments when they come my way, knowing when we leave this manufactured, historic fantasyland, work and Dad will be his first priority.

I focus back on my surroundings. "This is nice."

Aiko finishes getting her traveling equipment out of the carriage. "Welcome to Buckingham! Not that palace, Yanks." Aiko whispers that to us out of the corner of her mouth. "We've rented the place for the next day and a half. We're the first here, so go on in and get your accommodations for the night. We'll get all your stuff out for you." Aiko has a twinkle in her eye that doesn't bode well for us.

"Sure." Nate extends his arm to me.

We share a look, both of us wary about what twist they're going to throw at us next. "Maybe they're going to have us time travel again and we get our phones back," I whisper to Nate as we walk into the stone building.

"Maybe we'll get sent back even further to caveman times."

I snort, the large amount of muslin not turning me into a proper lady. "You do wish you could bash me on the head and drag me back to New York."

Nate looks affronted. "I would never bash you over the head. Entice you into an unmarked van with the promise of bulldogs and donuts, maybe. It'd be much more effective."

Damnit, that would work. "Would there be actual bulldogs and donuts waiting for me in the van?"

"Oh, yes. You'd sue me for fraud if there wasn't. Plus, if I had them, you would be more compliant over the cross-Atlantic plane ride."

"You've thought this through to an alarming degree. Should I be worried?"

"I came onto this show, so I think you're safe from a recovery kidnapping. For the length of that terrifying contract, at the very least."

Ah, just what every woman wants to hear—I'm with you due to the air-tight legal document I signed.

The space inside is warm, with wood paneling on the walls and low light setting the mood to make me want to curl up in one of the overstuffed chairs in the corner and plot public relations domination over the entertainment world in front of the roaring fireplace.

Nate tugs me toward the front desk, where a woman with gray hair in a bun and a warm-looking sweater further decorates the lovely inn and builds on the cozy atmosphere it's trying to create. "What can I do for you, loves?" she asks with a kind smile.

"We need two rooms, please," Nate says.

"Well, let me take a look at what we have." She opens the leather-bound book in front of her. "What are you traveling for?"

I pause, not sure how to answer that. Aiko's behind us with a camera crew, so we're being filmed. Aren't we supposed to be in character? And back in the day, weren't people judgey about elopers and unrelated young people galivanting about together?

Nate doesn't know what to say either, so we both stand here, confused and silent.

"We're eloping to Gretna," Nate says finally. Okay, we're going with brutal honesty.

The proprietress closes the book with a disheartening thud and a disapproving frown. "I am running a respectable establishment. I can't have an unmarried couple staying here, alone. Causing all sorts of scandal."

"Oh no, I'm so sorry. Nate gets so confused. Silly." I slap him on the arm affectionately. Or I hope it comes across as affectionate and not aggressive. Even though my thoughts are a little aggressive after he almost blew this for us.

"We already got married last year at Gretna, and we're going back as an anniversary trip. Young love. Such fun." I snuggle closer to Nate, who awkwardly puts an arm around me like he's done it a million times, and not just the handful of times we've had contact in the last few days.

"But you wanted two rooms?" she asks, nothing getting past those wise eyes.

"He snores," I say immediately. "Loudly. All night. Sounds like a chainsaw, in a chainsaw symphony of people who want to hurt my ears."

"Thanks, dear," Nate says through gritted teeth.

"You're welcome, sweetheart." He put us in this position by raising her suspicions in the first place.

"Well, thank you for the...vivid clarification." She opens her book up again, trying her best not to laugh at us. "As you are married, even if it was at Gretna, that's a different story. And since you're celebrating an anniversary, I'll give you our best room. Some time together may help you overcome your... differences."

Just one room. Singular. Which makes sense, considering we said we're married and so in love.

"It could be just the thing." I smile, finding some delayed acting skills.

She gives us the key and directs us to our room. We make our way up the creaking stairs as directed, past portraits of disapproving English aristocrats and gentry, like they know we're unmarried and going to the same room. I don't know why they're so disapproving; people have had sex since forever. Their parents had sex to have them, for one.

I ignore the judgement as Nate puts the key into the door with our number on it. He opens it and backs away to let me go in first. I take the invitation, not going to stand out here arguing over who should go in first when I'm exhausted after that long carriage ride. Surprising, since I was sitting all day.

I find a light switch as I walk in, glad there are modern

amenities like electricity and a modern bathroom so we aren't committed to this historic lifestyle.

But then I get past the small hallway, and into the main space of the room. "Oh, no." I stop abruptly, Nate almost running into me.

"What? What's wrong?" Nate pushes past me gently, head swirling to see the danger.

"There's only one bed."

CHAPTER 12

NATE

"Just the one?" My voice cracks on the question. I clear my throat.

"Yeah. Probably because I said we were married. Which I only had to do because you said we were travelling in sin."

I turn to look at her, trying to figure out how she feels about the turn of events. She's looking straight at me, but that doesn't give me any answers. It's frustrating to have all the tools to figure things out, her standing right in front of me looking me right in the eyes, but not be able to have an inkling of what she's thinking behind those eyes.

She's always been a mystery. Her dad is easy to figure out. Most people we work with are easy, too. Harrison and the rest of them want more money, more power, and to win. But I have no idea what she's thinking.

"Thanks, children. That was great." Aiko pushes through us to direct Kelly to take video of the room.

"Glad to help." I take a deep breath now that I don't have to stare directly in Naomi's unfathomable eyes and get confused anymore.

"You guys get comfortable; relax. When the other contestants get here, we'll do a filmed dinner with everyone. We'll get you when it's time."

They shut the door on their way out, leaving us alone in the room that has probably seen its fair share of runaway lovers. Not that we're lovers. Or running away from anything.

"Freedom, finally!" Naomi starts to tear at her clothes, getting my help for buttons on the back of her dress. She removes her mic and turns it off, throwing it on the bed. Then she keeps stripping away layers.

"Whoa, do you want to do that in the bathroom?" I turn around, remembering that I'm not supposed to be looking at the boss's daughter in any state of undress. That doesn't stop me from catching a view out of the corner of my eye on the closest reflective surface. Which happens to be a very obliging mirror over the desk to my right.

I try to force my attention away when I realize what I'm seeing, but my eyes don't listen to me, leaving me helpless to look away.

In my defense, she hasn't actually uncovered very much; it's less than I'd see at the beach. She's doing a variety of entertaining twists and contortions, trying to get to the fastenings of her corset.

"Don't care." She sounds a little breathless and I turn around. To save her, of course. "Get this off of me," she orders, even though I've already turned to help.

"You know there's probably cameras in here, right? And I'm still mic'd up?"

"Don't care." She's more desperate this time.

"Stop twisting, I'll get this corset off..." Then I get a look at the complicated backing of the item of clothing. "It's fine. I'll figure it out," I say more to myself than her. "You weren't uncomfortable this entire time, were you?"

"No." Naomi stops moving and lets me have access to the back of the dress. "It was just mildly uncomfortable, but then it was time to get out of it, but I couldn't, and then it got worse. The same thing happened to me with this silk saree I wore to my cousin's wedding that had to be tied so tight it ended up leaving indentations on my waist. At the end of the night, I panicked when I couldn't get out of it. Ended up tearing through it."

"The twisting probably didn't help," I murmur. I finally figure out the trick to the corset, untying and loosening along her back.

"Yes. Upon further reflection, and with the benefit of hindsight, I can see how that was not an ideal response. However, I was caught up in the moment and didn't have the luxury of focus groups and market projections prior to my decision to panic."

"Grab your front," I say before I loosen the last few strands at the bottom of the corset.

"What?" Naomi turns toward me without following the instructions, as the last few strands come loose, dipping the entire front of the corset.

"I've got it." I surge forward and slap both of my hands on her chest, remembering the cameras that I'm sure are in this room. But I'm too late and the corset has already slipped down.

Naomi reacts as well, throwing her hands up to her chest. Which means that my hands are now trapped between the thin, see-through muslin that was under her corset and her own hands. The thin material does nothing to disguise the soft but firm weight of her breasts in my hands, or how perfectly they fit.

I couldn't make my eyes look away from her; I have no chance of removing my hands. Despite all the valid reasons I tell myself why I need to let go of her, I can't force my hands off. The only hope I have left is her throwing my hands off and kneeing me in the balls. Or at least telling me to get off.

Unfortunately, Naomi doesn't seem to have any inclination to do that. Instead, she's standing still, even leaning slightly into my hands. Her nipples get harder under my palms, and I feel an answering response in my dick. My hands clench reflexively around her breasts, and she lets a small moan out, so quiet that I lean in to hear it better.

Sure. That's why I lean in.

Outside, a carriage rides up to the inn. The sound does what neither of us are willing or able to do and interrupts the moment.

"You've…" I clear my throat and try again. "You've probably got this now." I risk an internal mutiny by slowly sliding my hands down so she can replace them with her own.

"Yeah." Her hands slide above mine and take over covering the see-through cloth.

I expect her to run to the bathroom now that's she free from the I-hope-it's-not-still-whalebone prison. But she still stands in front of me.

"Why do you think they have cameras in our room?" she asks me instead.

"In our contract it said we don't have any privacy, and that there would be hidden cameras." My trunk is in the corner and I go to it to find what I want, the papers I made sure I slipped in there before they took away my modern luggage. "It's all in here." I hold up the document.

"Huh, I remember that. But I didn't think they would put it in here. Or hoped they wouldn't." She looks around, probably for those cameras. "Why do you have the contract with you? I signed it and promptly forgot how terrifying it was."

"To refer back to it, periodically." It's perfectly reasonable to me.

But apparently not to her, because she's shaking her head at me in judgment. "I bet you read the terms and conditions before installing software, too."

"Why would I enter into a contract without reading it?" I ask, but I'm distracted. Because she's still standing there, clothes dripping off her like they're trying to escape.

"Because you should have better things to do besides spend hours reading unnecessary legalese? There's at least four judges who have publicly admitted they don't bother reading boiler-plate. Just sign and deal with a potential lawsuit later. If even lawyers say don't bother reading it, the rest of us should defi-nitely ignore it."

"But what's more fun than boilerplate?"

"Oh, Nate," she says, full of pity. "You need more fun in your life." But at least the unpopular opinion makes her *finally* go to the bathroom, even if she does get the parting shot.

While I stare at the now closed bathroom door, I can't stop thinking about all the ways I want to have fun. Unsurprisingly, they all involve Naomi, and her clothes falling the rest of the way off. And then putting this only one bed to good use.

Instead, I focus on unsexy thoughts. A bad day for the stock market. Another company finding a way to store clean energy more efficiently before us. Being in a board meeting and not knowing what I'm going to say. That same boardroom, but now empty with Naomi naked on the conference room table, me between her legs.

No! That last one is not helping me.

Maybe prune juice. And grandpas drinking prune juice. And Naomi spilling prune juice on her white T-shirt.

Damn it. I'm fucked.

A FEW HOURS (and one masturbation session in the shower) later, we're having a surprisingly nice evening in the room.

The producers took the TV and radio out of the room but left the wires to taunt us with what we could have had. Which left Naomi and me to fend for ourselves. We'd already covered facts from our past in the carriage today and I was about to suggest naps when Naomi decides to start playing a game where we tell a story, one line each at a time.

We construct a story where a successful businessman quits his job, invents a product, saves an attractive woman from a corporate takeover, tries to sell his company, and elopes with the woman to the Amalfi Coast where they start a dog rescue inside an old castle.

And then the heisting begins.

It's obvious who made each part of the story, but I appreciate that Naomi only rolls her eyes at me and my hapless corporate executive a few times. By the end, I'm the one to suggest the heists, and she seems suitably impressed by that action outside my comfort zone.

I'm getting involved in these characters' lives, flexing creative muscles I didn't even know I had and laughing with Naomi, when Aiko interrupts us with a firm knock on the door.

"Hello, team." Aiko enters the room. "I hope you got to relax a bit, but everyone is here now and we want to do a group dinner soon. Please get back in formalwear," she says after she sees we're in nightclothes. "Also, we're sending some food up because we would appreciate if you didn't eat at dinner. Chewing sounds gross on mic. But feel free to drink as much as you want, now and at the dinner downstairs." Orders given, Aiko leaves the room.

"Fake food?" I ask Naomi, raising an eyebrow at another hit to reality.

She defends her reality-plus reality show "The food isn't fake. We're just discouraged from eating it. And you better hurry so we have time to pre-eat before dinner."

I raise both eyebrows now at the ridiculous statement.

She grabs some clothes from her trunk and disappears into the bathroom, with no response to my reality show criticism. Because she knows this entire situation is absurd, just as much as I do. But unlike me, that doesn't seem to bother her.

I can admit that parts of this experience are more entertaining than I thought they would be. Maybe even fun, I could go so far to say. Quietly. To myself.

Naomi finishes getting ready when the food arrives and leaves the bathroom in her elaborate outfit with more layers than I would have thought possible to wear at once. And even though she's more covered than I've ever seen anyone, I'm still turned on by her.

"More time in the corset. Fun." She eyes the chair and absently rubs her corset-covered abdomen.

I mumble an agreement, feeling bad that she's in pain, and worse that I'm enjoying the view so much, her boobs offered up to me in a sentiment I doubt she echoes. I comfort myself with the fact that she looks amazing without all this too, so I'm an equal opportunity ogler. And I would prefer that she was comfortable while I was ogling, so I'm still an okay person.

"Do you want me to loosen it for the meal?" I try to keep the hope out of my voice, because the last time I played knight and shining armor and helped her, it ended very well for me. I'd love to help again. Because I'm so…altruistic.

Not because I'm so horny.

"Nah. It'll be worse to get back in it after the food." She sighs, and I wince in response.

"You can have first pick of the meals they sent up." My clothes might be a little tighter than I would prefer, but they aren't that uncomfortable. So at the very least, she should eat what she wants.

"I'll take you up on that." She uncovers the dishes, picking fish and chips for her, leaving me with a steak pie. "Even though this is going to make the clothes hurt more, I'm really glad they went with pub food. I have a huge soft spot for English pub food."

"But there's so much better food in London to choose from! Great Indian food, for one."

"I mean, yes. The Indian food here is great. Close to Mom's, but not better. Be sure to mention that when you tattle to my parents." She pauses to level angry eyes at me, still not over why I'm here. Fair. "But there's nothing more comforting than fried food, and carb-heavy food, and food drenched in sauce and salt." She indicates the food in front of her, which checks all the boxes she described. Her eyes have gotten less angry now. That's good.

"I support you in your quest for greasy carbs." I cheers her with a fork full of my own greasy carbs.

I finish my own food quickly so I can transform back into a man from the nineteenth century. I change just in time for another knock on the door.

"Ready for the dinner party?" Aiko's voice asks us through the door.

Naomi smiles at me, a smile that says we have an inside joke because we're sharing this weird experience that I still object to.

But even if I can't have anything else with her, I'll always have the time we eloped for the entertainment of the masses.

CHAPTER 13

NAOMI

$\mathcal{N}$ate offers me his arm to lead me down the stairs. Acting like a lord of the manor must be getting to him and soon he'll grow a small ponytail or take up going to male-only clubs for lunch. Or whatever lords do.

But I do take the offered arm.

Apparently I'm adapting to the lady of the manor role, and I'll have to work on my embroidery and ignoring my husband's many affairs.

On second thought, no thank you. It'll take a lot more than wearing a corset and riding in a horse-drawn carriage for a day to make me accept that.

Not that I think Nate would cheat. I sneak a look to his profile, trying to see if he has the look of a cheater. But then I get distracted by the one dimple I can see, which leads me to the lines of his strong jaw. A very nice picture.

Which is moving. Shit, that's embarrassing. What's he saying?

He turns to me, and I nod, hoping I'm not agreeing to something terrible like giving this up and going home. Or taking the job with my dad. But the risk is better than asking what he said and admitting why I was distracted. Which is because of how pleasing I find his face.

He doesn't say anything else about it, so I shove that firmly into my Problems for Future Naomi folder and concentrate on the scene in front of me. Aiko leads us to a room off the lobby area, and we're the first ones in the space.

A large wooden table, set for the fanciest of dinner parties (and I know my dinner parties that to my extra father), dominates the room with damask-upholstered chairs arranged around it. The table presents a feast for the eyes with sparkling silverware and vibrant, lush floral arrangements. And apparently my eyes are the only part of me that will be feasting in this room, since we've been instructed not to eat, but to feel free to go through the motions of eating so it looks natural.

The crew found more disapproving Englishmen to hang on the walls, just in case we were thinking of having amorous thoughts in the sensual room. It's not working, though, because the contrary person inside me just wants to have sex on this table, preferably with Nate, just so the stuffy bastards can get offended one more time. Because I know they've done worse in their day; they just don't want me, a woman of color, to have any fun.

Nate pulls a chair out for me, and I get so flustered thinking about sex with him on this table that I awkwardly sit down, almost missing the moving chair entirely. But I cover it with a cough. Naomi Harrison, super smooth sophisticated lady over here.

Jessica comes in next with her partner, Will. She gives me a hug and sits in the chair next to me. I'm relieved to see her. Not only because she seems cool, which she does, but because it means there's going to be other people around and I don't have to only focus on Nate.

Because since I've been spending all my time with Nate, I'm realizing that he's a lot more interesting than the soulless corporate executive I've painted him as in my head, as well as being too attractive for my own good (well, that part I already knew).

"How was your trip?" I ask Jessica, ignoring my newfound revelations about Nate.

"We got lost. A lot. Apparently, street signs are a luxury that most country roads can't, or won't, afford. This is what comes from leaving London."

I'm about to commiserate with her when the last two couples enter the dining room.

Sarah and George are out of breath and disheveled, hair out of place and clothes rumpled, and Hannah and Amir look upset. My drama senses home in on Hannah's face and I feel a little push in my brain to find out what's happening.

My drama senses, or as Dad calls them, my penchant for meddling, is one reason I want to work in PR. I genuinely enjoy rooting out all the drama around me and hearing all the juicy details before I make everything better. I like those clients even better than just getting a client's name out there, unless they've done something awful. Maybe because I like the challenge, maybe because I'm messy.

Mom says it's curiosity born of an intelligent mind, but Dad says I'm nosy and she's biased because I get it from her.

Before I can make subtle inquiries, Hannah flops down at the table. "Did you guys get rooms here?"

We all answer with some affirmative word or noise.

"Yeah, we didn't. We told the lady at the desk we were unmarried and she started throwing a fit. We're staying in the carriage. Which is also the smallest and least cushioned," Amir says.

"We almost got kicked out for that, but we lied through our teeth to backtrack and she let it go. I'm half convinced she got confused because of our American accents," Nate says.

"At least we can use the bathroom inside all we want, but no shower," Hannah says.

"I figured there was going to be some patriarchy bullshite, so we lied about being a couple straight away," Jessica says.

I throw a considering look her way. If I was concerned about winning this show, this would be the team to beat, with that level of competitor. Good thing I'm here for ulterior motives.

Without permission, my head turns to Nate, who's picking at the food that the crew brought to him. I sympathize; this looks, and smells, much better than the food upstairs, even though that was good.

"Hello." Lewis walks into the room with Zara, and I perk up. I haven't seen my friend in a while.

But I don't get any time to catch up with her, as Lewis continues talking and Zara scurries behind the wall of cameras. "I hope you are all enjoying the food. But now we're going to have some fun. Since not everyone got to meet at the party…" Lewis winks at me, then at Hannah, the ruined women. "We're doing some speed courting. First arrange yourselves with couples sitting next to each other. Then men, please get up and shift over one woman, so you're sitting with someone new."

I glare at Zara over the news, letting her know how I feel about this show so far with my eyes, and she avoids my gaze like she owes me money. That's right, strain your neck to avoid seeing me, you traitor. Who I love, but that's beside the point.

Amir sits down next to me, changing my glare to a genuine smile. "Hi, Amir. Bad luck on the sleeping situation."

He snorts. "It's less than ideal. It's been fun otherwise, though."

"It is. Surprisingly. Not even too embarrassing yet."

"There's still time. Famous last words and all that."

"If I've jinxed us all, I apologize. I should know better than to tempt fate." I've read *Oedipus Rex*.

Amir effortlessly guides us into conversation about life outside this reality show, and we find out that we're both Indian, which leads to bonding over auntie horror stories, comparing and contrasting the American and British varieties.

Like apparently British aunties just drop by. No call, no text, just a knock on the door that you have to be ready for at all times. I know it comes from a place of love and community, but this American introvert would turn all the lights off and hide behind the sofa to avoid that.

Amir's as charming as he is gorgeous, but even though he has all the points on the pros column and none in the cons, there's no spark. He's maybe too pleasant? It's too easy? I don't have the same feelings around him that I get whenever I interact with Nate. Those have nothing to do with comfort or pleasantness. Those are demanding, even when I wish they would go away.

Maybe because the man himself is so demanding. Demanding my attention from across an ocean when I want to ignore him, demanding I see him as more than my father's employee. Is it because he's so wrong for me? Soulless businessman just like Dad...workaholic just like Dad.

But I can't imagine anyone else at the company dressing in a velvet waistcoat and following me around England, with cameras involved.

I sneak looks at the man, who's busy talking to Jessica. Smiling at her, but more of a polite smile. I prefer his exasperated smile that only I get, the one he gives like he thinks he shouldn't be smiling but can't help himself. Because I'm just as wrong for him. One fight with me as his girlfriend and it's going to be an awkward day at the office with my dad. Or one fight between me and Dad and Nate still has an uncomfortable day, stuck in the middle of it.

I try an experiment, even though science was never my favorite subject in school. I reach for the water pitcher in front of Amir, brushing my arm against his wrist in the process. A slightly awkward move, since because of my gloves and his coat, it's the only part of our bodies exposed, aside from our faces.

Nothing. No spark. No goose bumps. No tingling. No out-of-control desire to touch him more. All things I get with Nate.

"Sorry. Just trying to get the water," I say when Amir gives me a questioning look.

That's an interesting reaction, anyway. Or an interesting *lack* of reaction, I guess. Informative, either way. And unfortunate.

In an attempt to avoid Nate, I look at Amir, and in my periphery see Hannah, looking at Amir wistfully. And he turns around a couple of times in our conversation to check on his partner. It's a good thing I didn't feel anything, because I don't think I'd stand a chance with those two sending longing looks at each other. Good for Hannah. Her breakup sounded hard and Amir is nice.

I, on the other hand, can't get a look or a caring check in from my fiancé. This elopement is going grand so far.

Before too long, Lewis comes back in and tells us to play musical chairs again.

"Hi, I'm Naomi." I extend my hand to the new man next to me, another physically perfect specimen, this time with tousled but still gelled blond hair.

He takes my hand. "George. Nice to meet you."

Apparently it's nice to meet my breasts propped up by the corset as they are, because that's where he's looking when he says the words. I fight the impulse to tie my napkin around my neck, instead just clearing my throat and hoping he gets the hint. Nate would never be so obvious. Although that's probably more to do with who my parents are than chivalry. Or maybe he finds the quality of my breasts lacking. Hmm, I hope it's not that one.

In the meantime, someone takes our food and replaces it with a dessert that we're also not allowed to touch. Which is very rude. Because it's sticky toffee pudding. And I love sticky toffee pudding. In the four years since I've been here, I went from never having it before to being obsessed with it. And after being trapped in close quarters with Nate all day, I'm not enthused to deny myself more delicious things.

My mood isn't improved by the current company. George mostly talks about himself. Himself being a builder from Leeds. Himself and the gym. Himself and his protein supplements. Himself and the meal prepping. It's all clearly working for him, so kudos, but hearing about every step in his fitness regimen is a bit much. Especially since I haven't been able to get a word in with him at all, so I might as well be a cardboard cutout sitting next to him. With breasts. He does acknowledge those.

I realize too late into this speed courting, that if I wanted to escape Nate and make my own way on this show, I should be talking up all the other men in the hopes that they'll steal me. Or seeing who I can kidnap and convince to stay with me.

But when I think about that arduous task, I just drink more wine. I'm enjoying my time with Nate, away from Dad. I don't think I want to leave him, even if he is a saboteur sent to ruin any chance of independence I have.

I meet Will next, a salesman from Manchester. He keeps his eyes above my décolletage, but he does try to sell me on his supplements, making me question if I'm doing adequate vitamin consumption in the process. So well done him.

Zara comes in to interrupt the longing looks I'm sending my pudding. "Thank you, everyone. That's it for the dinner. We're going to do our daily interviews now, one at a time with your individual producers, women then men, and after you're done for the night."

Aiko comes in and grabs me before I can yell at my friend for getting me into this, taking me to the hotel room that's been set up for interviewing while sending Nate to our room. Inside the interview room, the crew pushed the furniture to the sides, with all the recording equipment focusing on one chair, which Aiko tells me to sit in. I don't know when or how they got this all set up, but I'm impressed.

"Exciting day, huh?" Aiko asks.

"Yeah. I've never ridden in a carriage, so that's been fun."

"How about Nate? How do you feel about him as a partner? Don't forget to answer in complete sentences so they can edit my part out later."

"Oh, sure. I can't complain about Nate as a partner. We haven't gotten seriously lost and we got a hotel room for the night. A resounding success, so far."

"Do you feel like there's a connection forming?"

"We already came with a little connection, since I knew him before." I try to evade the question, not wanting it recorded for everyone just how much I'm lusting after my partner.

"But a romantic connection?"

"Um, it's only been a day that I've actually spent any time with him beyond a surface acquaintance. I can't possibly know if we have a romantic connection in a day."

"But you can know if you're fantasizing about him."

I don't have a pithy response to that. Instead I just stare at her, mouth clamped shut. Maybe if I faint, I can get out of this interview? I start breathing heavier to set the scene for a believable faint.

"Can you see him as your boyfriend? He's considerate, smart, attractive. Everything I'm looking for in a guy," Aiko says, as I try to clamp down on the sudden jealousy that flares.

"Sure, he's all those things. He would make a good partner for anyone." Even if I hate the thought of him with that anyone.

"And for you?"

"I don't know. I would need more time to see." I know I should say no and shut this down. There's no harm in not being into someone. I've said how great he is, and sometimes things just don't click.

But I can't exactly bring myself to say that out loud, on camera, putting it out there in the world and forever documented. It's so...final. And every time Aiko asks if I can see a romantic relationship, I do start imagining what it would be like. After a pleasant day of good conversation and working together well, I could see us working together to do other things, like cooking dinner or putting together IKEA furniture.

But even in my daydreams, the happiness doesn't last long until Dad calls and Nate leaves me alone sitting in a pile of wood boards and nails, one Allen wrench my only weapon in the battle for Swedish building mastery.

"You should seriously consider it. I've seen you guys together and you have a spark that shouldn't be wasted. I felt that once and I let it go for work. I regret that."

"Hmm." I'm noncommittal at that. She doesn't understand, and I don't want to tell her, about all the reasons we wouldn't work.

Aiko finally moves on from Nate. "What about any of the other contestants? Do you feel a spark with any of them?"

"No, I don't feel a spark for any of them." I answer immediately and without hesitation to that question. "They also seem like solid guys." Well, one of them does. "But I don't think we're suited to each other."

"Thanks, Naomi. That's all we need for today. Please send Nate over, and I hope you get some rest."

Her tone is amused, making me feel her parting shot is more warning than genuine hope, but I'm so relieved to be set free that I run without following up on it.

"You're up," I say as I walk into the room. Nate is lying on the bed, fully clothed except for his boots and coat, which are in a pile by the bed. He opens his eyes and sits up, the loose shirt shifting and moving to caress those damn muscles.

"Is our interrogator in a good mood?" He leans over to put the boots back on.

"She's in a mood, but I wouldn't say it was good for us. She wanted me to say I loved you and we'll fuck in the carriage so she can make great television and was very disappointed when I wouldn't do any of that."

"Ah, well." Nate clears his throat. "Stay strong in the good fight." He gets up and draws my attention to the bed he was lying on.

"When you come back, I'll probably be asleep, but I'll stay on my side of the bed so feel free to take the other," I say awkwardly.

"No. I'll take the floor or the chair in the corner." Nate puts his jacket on.

"We're adults. You shouldn't have to sleep on this wooden floor, where you'll probably get a splinter in your unmentionable places." Despite me not being able to ment on those areas, I am thinking about them now.

Plus if he gets splinters in his ass, I'll have to help get them out. And if I find out he has those dimples on his lower back to match his face, I will lose the will to keep myself away from him.

"Here." I get a blanket off the chair. "I'll sleep under the covers and you can sleep under this. It'll be fine."

"You get comfortable. I'll worry about where I sleep later."

I shrug. "It's your back."

"Do you want me to help you with ties before I leave?"

"Yes, please."

He helps with the fastenings of the outer dress and then after I get that off, he gets the ties on the corset. I breath in and wiggle every time he brushes against my back with his large hands to try to avoid contact, wishing he was someone else so I could breathe out and wiggle into him to get more contact. Or that I could jump him outright without all the extra baggage we have.

"All done." He pats my shoulders and is already walking to the door before I can crane my neck to say thank you.

By the time I turn, all I can see is the muscles in his broad back filling out his historic jacket as he walks out the room until the door closes behind him.

I take a quick look around the room to see if I can find these allegedly hidden cameras that Nate is sure are here, but I don't, so I just make sure to be clothed as best I can, assuming they're everywhere.

Thanks, ninth-grade swimming in gym class, for making me a champion at changing out of a wet bathing suit under a towel without flashing anyone my, well, bathing suit areas. Everything else is a breeze after that.

After some stealth getting ready, I slip into bed, leaving the bathroom light on for Nate. I don't expect to be able to fall asleep until I know where Nate will sleep, but the long day catches up with me, and I have to fight to keep my eyes open.

Because I want to know what Nate's going to do.

CHAPTER 14

NATE

By the time I get back to the room, I'm so tired that I could sleep on the floor, on the chair, or leaning against the dresser. Hell, I could probably lie next to Naomi and not have to worry about the torture it would be to sleep next to her without getting to touch her. Because I'm that exhausted.

When Aiko the Interrogator didn't get the answers she wanted out of me, she kept repeating the question with slightly different phrasing until I would have told her I loved *her* if she would let me out of the room and let me sleep.

Instead I just said progressively flattering things about Naomi. Which I now realize she'll see at some point. Me, complimenting her independence and her intelligence and maybe her butt. Definitely her face. It's a good face.

Nothing I can do about that right now.

I open the door to the room and close it quickly behind me so the light from the hallway doesn't disturb Naomi. We might have gotten some sleep in the carriage, but it was uncomfortable and I kept waking up every time the horses went over a rock. I doubt her sleep was any better.

The light in the bathroom is still on, saving my knees from

bumping into every sharp furniture edge in this room, and also letting me see Naomi. She's on her back with her hair settled wildly around her head like a chaotic crown for the pretty heiress, one leg peeking out from under the covers and the big nightgown riding up her golden-brown thigh.

The soft glow illuminates her face, mouth hanging open and slight snore coming from her. It's adorable, and I'm glad she's getting rest.

I quietly get ready for the night, then grab the spare pillow from the bed along with the blanket Naomi laid out earlier. I take them both and set up a makeshift bed on the floor.

After an hour of tossing and turning, my earlier statement that I was so tired I could sleep anywhere is now a lie. And it's gotten colder to boot. Naomi is still asleep, but she's burrowed deeper into the sheets in response to the drop in temperature.

I should go up there. To keep her warm. I can't bring back her frostbitten form to Harrison, asking why I couldn't be bothered to save her adorable fingers and toes.

I get my coat and drape it over Naomi so she has the extra warmth (and another layer between us). I slide in bed with the spare blanket over me, keeping what I hope is a respectable distance from the other occupant of this bed. Not that I know what the appropriate distance is when sharing a bed with someone forbidden.

I'm still stiff being this close to Naomi, but at least now it's not because of a hard floor. This should make it easier to fall asleep. I hope.

"YOUR CHAPERONE IS HERE! You need to leave now," a voice yells from the other side. Angrily. Urgently.

My eyes shoot open and my head snaps up to look around in confusion, no idea where I am for a minute. "Wha…?"

"Five more minutes," Naomi growls, pulling the pile of sheets and my coat over her head.

Right. That's where I am. Curled around Naomi, in a hotel bed. On a reality show about historic elopement. But with at least one layer of blanket separating us. I slowly move my arm that somehow found its way under Naomi's head. Without my permission. Then I remove the arm on top of her, hoping that I can get rid of the evidence of my illicit late-night cuddles before she wakes up.

"Oy. You two! I know you lied to me and now your chaperone is here to take you back to London, so pack up and get caught or pack up and flee, but you'll need to get out of my inn. You've got fifteen minutes, or you'll be going back to London with your chaperone." She bangs on the door one more time for good measure, and then harrumphs very loudly as she stomps down the hall.

Naomi's eyes flutter open just as I get my hands away from her and onto my agreed upon side of the bed, like they behaved themselves all night. I have no idea if she saw my hands, but I'm not going to bring it up if she didn't.

"What's happening?" she asks, still groggy and comfortable tucked into bed.

"We've got to flee." I put even more distance between us by getting out of the bed and throwing things in the vintage suitcase they gave us. "We're being hunted."

"So I spend years running from a controlling parent trying to drag me back home just to wind up on TV, running from a controlling chaperone trying to drag me back home? The irony is a bit much before coffee." She slowly puts a bare leg out from under the covers and then back in when she feels how cold the morning still is. "Is it even light out?"

"Just barely." I open the blinds so she can see proof of light and toss her socks so she has something to warm her feet as she gets up. The early morning sun comes through the window, making Naomi's old-school nightdress a little see through.

After the initial shock, where I blatantly stare, mesmerized by the image of her dangerous curves backlit by the soft light, I force myself to turn around and get back to packing.

"It sounded urgent. I don't know exactly what the penalty is for getting caught by Diane, but we better run before we find out that it's sleeping outside or walking the rest of the way, or whatever new torture they make for us. At the very least, it sounds like a delay."

"All right. All right." The words make Naomi hurry, closing the door to the bathroom on my creeping peripherals. She finishes quickly, coming out without the makeup she usually wears, but still beautiful as always. And younger than usual, actually. Reminding me that we're in different places in our lives.

Almost exactly fifteen minutes after the innkeeper knocked to wake us up, we open the door. Aiko and Kelly are waiting for us, camera out and red light blinking ominously at the ready.

"I'll get the trunks." I turn back to the room.

"Don't worry about it; we've got that covered." Aiko waves us along to get the drama going.

I'll take her up on that. It's not that the trunks are too heavy, but they're both longer than the length of my arms and I had no idea how I was going to get both of them down this narrow, winding hall and down the stairs, without dragging them and possibly wrecking this historic floor. Which I'm sure would lead to a lawsuit.

Actually, the businessman inside me is wondering if there are contract clauses about liability for any damage the show inflicts onto the property. But I'm not mentioning that to Naomi, because the last time I brought up contracts she made fun of me for it.

Meeting up with two other groups at the top of the stairs, we rush down them, three teams of contestants and production crews running down the stairs together. If one person falls then this show is going to be over soon or changed drastically. Real Housewives of the Hospital Closest to the Inn.

Sarah and George get down the stairs and out the door first, followed by us and then Jessica and Will. The first team gets in the first available carriage, which was ours from yesterday, and we get in a less ornate one, with less padding on the seats and thinner walls, making it colder inside.

Hannah and Amir are already in a carriage, poking their heads out when they hear the racket of us racing out of the inn. They're still in their nightclothes, and they have confused expressions on their faces, so I guess they didn't get the wild wake-up call that the rest of us did. Or the noise of us coming out is supposed to be their wake-up call.

They still have the least ornate carriage with a torn roof and a rough-looking exterior. That's going to be another uncomfortable ride. But one that I'm glad I won't be having, even though I do feel appropriately bad for them.

Right as the crew gets done securing our luggage behind each of our carriages, we hear a loud noise from the entrance of the driveway. More carriages are coming, most likely carrying the chaperones we're supposed to be running away from.

Although this could just be a normal thing in England, to travel around in your carriage. I've only ever been to London before, but this could be something they do in the countryside to honor their heritage or whatever.

"Good morning..." I tail off when I realize I don't know the new driver.

"Joe," Aiko whispers to me.

"Hi, Joe. Can we please go extra fast?"

"As soon as you tell me where to go, the horses and I will beat everyone there."

"Right. Let's head down the driveway, then we'll tell you which way to go. Where's our map?"

Naomi is already riffling through our stuff. "I don't know." She sounds panicked as we hear the carriages coming down the long drive, getting closer as we sit here. My heartbeat gets faster as the thundering of the horses' hooves get closer. There's movement outside the window and one carriage is already heading down the driveway, passing the chaperones as they leave.

"Where is it?" Naomi asks herself, still searching. "Should we just leave? Follow someone else?"

"Then we could all be going the wrong way."

"Getting lost and doing a U-turn might be better than them catching us. Who knows what happens if they get us?" Naomi's voice is muffled as she leans over and searches the floor.

"What could happen? We have to escape them again? I can maybe put some NyQuil in Diane's tea."

"NyQuil definitely hasn't been invented yet." Naomi can multitask searching and sassing me.

"Then laudanum, I want to say?"

"Pockets!" Naomi yells, lunging at me without warning. She crashes unto me and we both hit the wall of the carriage, sending the carriage rocking in a worrying sway. But I can't be too stressed about it, since I have Naomi in my lap.

"Yeah," I say in response, focusing more on feeling her soft weight on me than the show.

While I'm imagining what else we could be doing in this position, forgetting about the cameras and inching my lips toward hers, she's digging around my clothes and making small sounds of frustration.

She doesn't need to try so hard; I'll take them off if that's what she wants.

"Eureka!"

Yes, that's what I would say with her hand inches from my dick. But then she pulls away, leaving me dazed and disappointed.

CHAPTER 15

NAOMI

I ignore where my hand is located, because if I don't, we'll never leave this driveway, and Diane will see something that will seriously shock her delicate Regency sensibilities. Maybe even some of her modern ones.

Nate's penis, however, doesn't have the same consideration, since I felt it twitch when I grazed it to get into his pockets. Who put pockets so close to the groin anyway? Someone with a sick sense of humor. Or someone who was super horny.

And the producers get some of the blame, since they didn't put the map in his outside pockets, but the ones closest to said groin.

I clear my throat and retreat back to my side of the long seat. "I found the map." I hold it up, somewhat unnecessarily.

Nate clears his throat. "Yeah. That's good." His voice is still husky and he clears his throat again. I appreciate the signs that he wants me as much as I want him.

I open the map with shaking hands, flattening it on my lap. "We're here." I point to the pre-marked spot on the map. "And we need to get there," I point to the marked point at the top of the page.

I move the map after I say that, when I notice that I can still see the outline of Nate's erect penis, the same one I accidentally touched a second ago, out of the corner of my eye. I hold the map out in front of me in an unnatural angle to block the sight, not caring how awkward I look.

Nate looks confused as to why I'm holding it up but twists his head at an equally awkward angle to look at it, without mentioning it.

"Did they have compasses in this time? Can we get some compasses?" I ask Aiko.

"I have an accurate one on my phone that hasn't been invented for two hundred years," Nate mumbles.

"Wait! I think I saw one in here when I was looking for the map." I rummage in the side pockets again until I find one again in the extra blankets and candles. "Yes! Found it!"

"Before you start navigating, we have to stop midway, at this circled spot." Aiko points at a spot on the map.

"Twists and turns in this world. Twists and turns," I say while the compass does its own twisting and turning.

"Let's go right," Nate says when we get to the end of the driveway.

As I look back at the inn, head sticking out of the window like an eager puppy, I see there's one carriage still stopped in front of the building. The chaperones have gotten to the inn, and a woman is opening the door to the stopped carriage. She's dragging Will out, while Jessica hops out to save her fiancé.

Before I can enjoy that too much, the other chaperone carriages fly past the scene and turn to head down the road that we're on. Chasing after us.

"Make haste! Please!" I pull my head back inside.

"And at the next roundabout, please take the first exit," Nate says, looking at the map. "We should be on that road for a while."

We watch the carriages for a while, realizing that they're all following us. "Are we just going to be single file all the way up to the next spot in… Nuneaton. Nune-aton? Nunnie-ton? Nun-eaton?" I look at Nate and then Aiko. "I can't say that word. I hope a lot of voters for this show don't come from there."

Aiko and Kelly are laughing at me, so I can go ahead and assume that none of my pronunciations were right. "You are pronouncing it noonie, which is a word some on this island use for a vulva," Aiko helpfully says.

"Fantastic." At least if I become a meme for saying that on television so many times, people will know my name.

Nate mercifully changes the subject before all the blood leaves vital organs to congregate in my useless cheeks from blushing so hard and I faint. "I hope they do follow us. It'll be a buffer from the chaperones."

"That's true."

After the rush of getting dragged out of bed and then the race to the carriages, I'm still keyed up from the excitement. Except now I'm going to be sitting until we get to the mysterious circle on the map.

"Was there anything we missed about each other yesterday?" I settle in, getting this carriage's blanket out and spread over Nate and me. Which has the added bonus of hiding his too intriguing junk from me.

"Here you guys go. If you want something else to keep you warm." Aiko pulls out a box of wine from her bag and pours us some.

"But will you let us out to use the bathroom?" Nate asks.

"Excellent question." I support my partner, even though I've already started drinking. Whatever. I'll pee in these woods if it comes to that.

"Of course." Aiko sounds offended and I roll my eyes. "We live to keep you happy."

I snort, but don't debate it.

"My favorite food is Greek. Especially gyros, which are amazing at any time. Dinner, lunch, a breakfast gyro. I'll eat them all," Nate says, getting back to talking about ourselves to fill the time.

"Hmm. Indian for me. Reminds me of Mom. And any dish, I'm usually not picky about it. Except for yellow dal…it's so bland, even when it's spicy. It's a very confusing dish." My stomach grumbles thinking about the food. "Maybe we shouldn't be talking about food, actually," I say.

"Are we getting food soon?" Nate asks Aiko.

Aiko gets out some bread, cheese and fruit from her giant backpack. "You get this for now. But more in due time," she says mysteriously, the immediately snaps into a concerned mother persona. "Unless you are really hungry, then we can stop. But that will make you behind."

We look at each other, communicating in raised eyebrows, tilts of the head and scrunched noses. "We'll wait," I answer for both of us and Nate nods along in agreement. I'm a little scared that we've progressed to the point of wordless communication in the few days that we've been fake engaged for television.

Which is yet another absurd sentence I've thought since I've been here.

But I can't knock the feeling of closeness between us. Despite the reality that awaits us in New York.

"Let me know if you change your mind. Just enjoy the ride 'til then," Aiko says.

"I'd enjoy it more if the camera was off." I smile sweetly at her.

"Cute." But the camera's red light stays on.

Seems right for this show.

"I think bulldogs are the best dog breed," I say into the silence. "They have so much personality. And English or French is good with me, which I realize is a controversial statement in England."

"But consider the noble husky."

"But they love to run."

"Yes," Nate says, both agreeing with my premise and clearly disagreeing with my view on it, all with one word.

I push up my sleeves, or I would if they weren't so tight, and throw myself into this fight.

∼

"We're here," Aiko says, loudly.

Since it was my turn to nap, I'm not happy about the second interruption to my sleep today. Yawning, I shift the thin curtain aside and look out of our carriage window.

"Where are we exactly?" I can't see anything outside our carriage but rolling green hills. Some pretty wildflowers. No people. All in all, an idyllic body dumping ground. Back inside, the red light of the camera is still on. There's no way they can murder me on a television show. They might show more skin than American television, but I think they draw the line at murder.

Just in case, I scoot closer to Nate. He tightens his arm around me, and I hope that squeeze means he'll protect me from any imminent attacks.

"Other side of the carriage," Aiko whispers conspiratorially. Her English accent is somewhat comforting. No one that posh would stoop to murder, right? Then again, there are about ten thousand shows where people with posh accents commit murder in the English countryside.

Damn.

To distract myself, I lean over Nate, who doesn't sink back into the cushions with the move. Which means I'm pressed up against a lot of hard muscles. And not complaining about it.

"An obstacle course?" I'm excited at the prospect of getting out and moving after being cooped up in this tiny box all day.

"Obstacle course?" Nate asks, responding to the news with disappointment instead of my excitement.

The crew has set up a course in the open field, with walls,

monkey bars over some water, and mini-carriages with two wheels, that only have room for one person.

"Obstacle course," Aiko and Kelly confirm, gleeful again. This is the first I've heard from Kelly, who prefers to stay quiet behind the camera, so I know this is going to be some entertaining combination of difficult and embarrassing. But I'm just so grateful to stretch my legs that I'll worry about how I look later.

"You can get out and explore for a bit before everyone else gets here," Aiko says.

We're only first thanks to Sarah and George making a wrong turn a few hours ago, but I'll take the moment of calm before the chaos begins again.

Nate gets out of the carriage first, stretching and elongating his body in a way that captures the attention of all three of us women in the carriage, and then turns to help me out. We don't get much of a break since the other carriages are careening our way as I get down from the steps.

Lewis is already waiting, sitting in an ornate gold and upholstered chair between two tents made of embroidered cloth. Any other man would look ridiculous sitting on elaborate furniture in the middle of a field...and so does Lewis. He looks like he's in an ad for expensive watches or cologne, maybe.

Nate grabs my arm and helps guide me through the grass with its potholes and small piles of dirt. A task harder than usual since I'm wearing too many layers of clothing.

"Welcome to my tents." Lewis extends his arms out to encompass his domain.

"Thank you for having us," I respond automatically, even though I might come to regret being here, depending on what we do.

The rest of the contestants get here one right after another, almost immediately after us. Which lets us watch everyone go through the same look of confusion and wariness when they see the setup. And then feel superior because we're already accepted our reality.

"Now that everyone is here, I can tell you why we stopped you in the middle of nowhere," Lewis says, drawing it out by looking at each one of us, to see our reaction like we're on a soap opera and everyone gets a reaction shot.

"Get on with it, mate," Amir says.

"Since you asked so nicely, you're going through that obstacle course, as a team, in Regency swimwear."

CHAPTER 16

NATE

They couldn't resist getting us in swimsuits, could they? I look over to Naomi, already imagining her in a swimsuit. I don't think people wore bikinis in the Regency time-period, but I can't stop myself from imagining Naomi in one. I can't figure out if I'm happy she'll be covered on the show or if I'm disappointed that I won't be able to see her body.

Lewis doesn't let me dwell, giving us more instructions. "We're simulating your carriage breaking on the way to Gretna, which happened during the Regency elopements and would have been an obstacle in your path. But it would be boring if we made you simply fix a carriage, so instead, you're going to overcome this *obstacle* by doing an *obstacle* course." He looks around to see if we're going to laugh at his pun.

We all laugh loudly, mostly because we don't want to film the reaction again. I laugh the loudest. I just want him to stop saying obstacle before it stops registering as a word to me.

"You're going to change in those tents, one for the men and one for the ladies." Lewis indicates the tents on either side of him. "And then you're going to work as a team to get through the course. The activities are based on what was done in the Regency time such as pig running but with puppies because that's cuter, Nerf gun stuffed goose shooting, horse riding with no horses, carriage pulling, and charades, all mixed in with some modern physical challenges of getting over walls, crawling through mud and doing monkey bars over shallow water, as well as a partner carrying sprint in the end. Sorry to the Americans, but there won't be any actual weapons involved in these games."

"I think we'll live." I'm too focused on everything we have to do to let the insult get me too much. Also, it's a fair point.

"The team that finishes first wins a delicious, multi-course meal that they can take in the carriage on their way. Everyone else gets the same meal, but they have to eat it here once you finish the course. So the faster you are, the more time you have to get on the road and nab the best room tonight." He indicates tables decorated with silverware and centerpieces off to the side to show where the losers will all be eating. "And the last team may not get a room at all."

Lewis rubs his hands together. "All right. Let's get changed!" He releases us to the tents. "Go! This is a competition," he says when we just look at him, still processing all the tasks.

"See you in a second," I say, heading off to my designated tent. Naomi waves me off and disappears into the other tent.

Once I enter my own, I contemplate walking right out again, and right off this show. All the way back to Heathrow if I have to. Because along one corner of the tent, there's racks of old-style bathing suits. They're all one-pieces that look like a T-shirt with buttons at the top, attached to long shorts, with a nautical blue and white striped pattern throughout. The material doesn't look like it'll be flattering in any sense of the word.

The other men, in perfect shape that they are, throw off their clothes like they're on fire, making me wonder if I can do some pushups before I go out there. If that would even help.

But this is a competition and I can't stay here forever, or we might have to sleep in the carriage tonight. Or worse. I push aside the insecurities and change. I'm worried and grateful that there isn't a mirror in the tent. I can see the other men, though, and there are too many bulges. Everywhere.

I throw the tent flap open, standing with the other contestants to wait for our partners. Women's clothes are a lot more complicated, if what I've helped Naomi with is any indication.

Naomi is out of the tent first, and I can't help the laughter that bubbles out of my chest. "You look ridiculous. Still cute. But very ridiculous."

She's in a long-sleeve blue dress that ends below her knee, with pants underneath. She's matching me with white nautical stripes around the collar, wrists and waist of the dress, and has a giant wide-brimmed hat on her head. "Why did you even bother changing?"

"Excuse me?" she asks, with great dignity for the amount of blood rushing to her cheeks. "I am wearing two less layers than I was five minutes ago. And I ditched the most painful ones." She twirls in her newfound freedom. Adorable.

After her spin, she starts laughing herself, looking me up and down, eyes catching on my awkward bulge. Which she does stop laughing for, thankfully, or I would have shriveled up and crawled back into the tent, a broken husk of a man. But I do wonder if I can offer to carry something for her, something that could go right over my dick.

Not that my penis *wants* to be hidden from her, but even he knows this is not a flattering look for us.

The moment is broken by Sarah coming out of the tent, and she and George running to start the race.

"Let's get this over with," I say. We run toward the first challenge.

The first stop is a large pen, with four muddy puppies lounging on the ground. "Pick a color and both of you try to catch the dog with that color collar and lift him off the ground. This is a simulation of pig running," Lewis shouts out at us.

"We've got purple," Naomi yells. "He looks the fattest and hardest to lift but maybe also the slowest," she whispers to me, seeing which dogs are left after Sarah and George have already picked red.

"That seems as a good a reason as any." I approach the puppy from one side, as Naomi approaches him on the other.

"Hi, baby. Aren't you so cute? I just want to love you and kiss you and give you food. You just have to stay still and let us give you a hug," Naomi negotiates with the dog.

But this dog doesn't like Americans or doesn't trust us specifically (which is solid since we can't even get food for ourselves), and he bolts when we get close, going through my legs. I try to stop him, but I slip and fall in the mud on my side instead.

I pop back up and chase after him, almost catching him but my hands slip on his muddy coat at the last minute and I fall again. This time face-first. Naomi, not helping at all, laughs at my misfortune.

"He's just a little puppy," she says before I can get mad at him.

"He's a full-grown dog, just a small one."

Naomi waves my opinions away. "Dogs are puppies forever, despite age or size."

"You try getting this puppy then. He's frisky."

Naomi trots after the dog. "Come here, little baby. You just want to play, huh? What if I gave you this annoying hat? Do you want this annoying hat, little puppy?" She unties the hat and dangles it in front of the dog. It works a little too well, and catches the attention of all the dogs, who rush her. She falls back, landing on her butt, with four dogs crawling all over her, getting their teeth into her hat as they track mud all over her. She gets glares from the rest of the groups, whose dogs all abandoned them for Naomi.

The dogs have impeccable taste.

"Well, this works." I pluck the dog with the purple collar off her and hold him tight to my chest. "We've got him," I yell to

Lewis and move out of the way as Jessica almost takes me out when she slips trying to get her puppy away from Naomi.

"Naomi and Nate, you can move on to the next task."

I set the dog down and he goes back to chewing on Naomi's hat. We run on and stop at a table, with four Nerf guns set up.

"For this activity, you're going goose hunting! Our crew are the 'beaters' and will drive game to you by throwing stuffed grouse in the air. You then take them down with your Nerf gun. Each partner has to shoot one before you can proceed," Aiko says to us over the noise of frustrated contestants begging puppies to come to them.

"Do you want to go first or should I?" I ask Naomi.

"You go ahead. Hunt, gather, etc."

"Are you going to cook my goose?" I tease, picking up the brightly colored plastic gun.

She snorts. "With my cooking skills, you probably wouldn't be able to tell the difference between a stuffed animal and actual cooked poultry."

"At least we can thank Harrison for teaching us to shoot at his country estate." I ignore the fact that Naomi is close to being the society lady that she's playing right now, with a rich dad who has a country estate. I've never felt more like a commoner reaching beyond his station than right now.

This isn't even real, but I look over my shoulder to make sure Harrison isn't going to jump out of these trees to take me out for daring to think of being with his daughter. He's never implicitly said I couldn't date his daughter, but he's warned away other business associates who got a little too comfortable leering at her.

Naomi rolls her eyes. "I'm not telling him that." But she has a smile on her face. An improvement when mentioning her family.

"Yell 'drive' when you want me to toss you one!" our crew says.

"Drive," I yell back.

The crew tosses a stuffed bird up, and I take my shot, missing spectacularly.

"The sights on this are terrible," I say as an excuse and a warning for when Naomi's up.

"I believe you," she says seriously, holding up her hands, but with a slight smile she keeps trying to squash on her lips.

I try again, but with a little more effort this time, after my initial failure. The groups around us aren't having any more luck. "Drive," I call out.

It takes me three throws before I finally shoot the stuffed animal, which gets handed to me like a prize, Nerf dart still stuck to its butt. It only takes Naomi two tries, and she accepts her goose with a smug smile to me over her shoulder.

Next is riding with stick horses, in a trot/skip, going through a mini-obstacle course within our obstacle course with turns and small jumps. Naomi's dress snags on one of the jumps, and I drop my stick horse and catch her before she can fall and break anything. We lose some time in that one, falling to second. But Naomi gives me a wide, genuine smile for catching her, and I get her in my arms. Who cares about the competition after that?

Next comes charades, with each of us alternating acting out a word until we collectively get five. Which is harder than it sounds.

"What are you doing? Why is your body moving in that manner?" Naomi yells as me as I attempt to hoe a field without any equipment.

I get on all fours and dig up some dirt, then get up again and pantomime using a hoe, then doing those two motions over until she gets it. "You're hoeing!" She points at me when she says it.

I stop what I'm doing and look at her. "Yes. But phrasing."

It's equally as difficult for her, as she pageant-waves, nose in the air and adjusting her imaginary crown periodically, to be a queen. Okay. That one was easy, but she looked adorable doing it, so I let it go on for a little longer than was strictly necessary. At least until she started to get mad that I wasn't getting it and the adorable just became grumpy.

We get bow (with me trying to be Robin Hood, even if she did call me Cupid first), newspaper, and bouquet, with me skipping pelisse for a two-minute penalty, because I don't know what that is (a short jacket, Naomi tells me).

We're solidly in the middle of the pack now, with all the physical challenges to go. Since every other man here has the body of a movie superhero, I don't think this is going to end well for us.

We run to the first physical challenge, the seven-foot wall.

"There's no chance this is happening. Can we take a time forfeit, maybe?" Naomi asks.

"We've got this," I say confidently instead. "Let's get you up first." I get down on one knee and make a foothold with my hands. "Put your foot here." I give the interlocked hands a shake.

"I can't do that."

"Just put your foot here, squirt, I've got you." Out of the corner of my eyes, I see couples already over the wall, or getting over it.

"You'll drop me!"

"Never," I promise solemnly.

She still looks uncertain, but she puts one hand on my shoulder and takes a deep breath. "If you drop me…"

She puts her foot in my hands and I push up while she grabs the wall on top. Her hands reach, but she doesn't get far, hanging from her position.

"What now, genius?"

"I didn't drop you, did I? Trust the process." I stand up and consider. The most efficient way to do this is probably one no one in the Richmond family will like. "Do you want me to get you over the wall by any means necessary?"

"Yes. Get on with it." Her feet squirm a bit, trying to find stability.

"Okay." I put my hands on her generous butt and push, easily getting her to the point where she can pull herself the rest of the way up. One of the most enjoyable jobs I've had to do in a while. I get myself over next, thanking my parents for the height they gave me.

"For the carriage pull, the ladies will be doing the pulling," Lewis says.

Naomi looks at me, probably gauging how much I weigh, and I feel picked apart in a very unpleasant way.

"You wanted to be on this," I say.

I hurry to the small carriage to avoid her response, almost tripping over the wheels before sitting in the small one-person space.

I've had fun with her on this absurd obstacle course. She's stubborn and intense with competition, but she knows how to laugh at me and herself; she doesn't dwell on any setbacks. If I wasn't doing this with her, I would be too wrapped up in where I was in the game, a side effect from being in business maybe, but today I'm enjoying being with her.

Naomi, however, may be having less fun with me, since she's having a lot of problems lifting the two long wooden bars that she'll use to pull me along.

"Are you okay out there?" I risk my head to ask.

"Can you think less heavy thoughts for a second?" She's out of breath.

"Yes," I answer promptly. "But I don't think it'll help."

She grunts, finally getting me up. Hannah seems to be having some problems as well, probably because of all the muscle Amir has. Take that, Hulk.

I have to force myself to sit still while she suffers through this alone and get out the second she passes the line. "You did it!"

She glares at me response.

"Yay," I say weakly.

"Let's just get through the rest of this." She's still breathing heavily from the exertion, but she's got a bit of a smile on her face.

We crawl through the mud without incident beyond being uncomfortable in the cold, wet ground, and then it's time for the monkey bars.

"Not another arm-strength one." Naomi sighs, shoulders drooping.

CHAPTER 17

NAOMI

My disappointment is a lie.

I over-exaggerate it, throwing out another sigh to really sell it. I pretend like I don't know that Nate is going to help me through this, and I'll have his hands on some part of me. If I was the puppy we had to catch earlier, I'd be wagging my tail, I'm so excited.

Because Nate feels as strong, as capable, and as warm as he looks filling out his boring suits. I was hoping it was a fluke, or a trick of fabric perpetrated by an expensive, expert tailor to make businesspeople look more imposing in negotiations. But his hands on me, pushing me over a wall, don't lie.

This whole experience is making me look at him in different ways. New ways. Not just a boring suit, an attractive face, or a larger-than-life executive who is only concerned with deals, but someone I could spend time with outside of this forced togetherness. Because not only is he strong, he's been surprisingly easygoing about this whole situation. Having casual conversations with me, that produce no profit, about the man behind the executive. Not checking his phone every minute.

Although maybe that's because the show took the phone away from him.

Nate goes first on the bars, getting across without falling and then coming back to help me over. I restrain myself from throwing my arms out like a child waiting to be picked up, instead patiently waiting for his help.

"Do you want to get on and then I'll help you across?"

No. I want to be lifted like a dainty fairy lady in his big strong arms, damn it. "Sure." I climb onto the platform, then grab the first bar with both hands. "Okay, ready for that help now."

Nate grabs me around the thighs, and grunts as he lifts up and takes my weight. Rude. I'm going to try to hang on the bars a little more.

The grunt is soon forgotten, pushed to the back of my mind to focus on the chest my legs are snuggling. The hard, muscle-bound chest that I want to tear the old-timey swimsuit from and maybe lick a little.

Funny how one and a half days on a reality show can make me forget all the perfectly good reasons I have for not lusting after Nate. I know they were valid and important, and they helped my shallow crush from getting deeper before, but I don't remember, or maybe I don't care right now, about what they were.

The bars are conquered a little too quickly for my taste, and I have to let go at the other platform. One team is ahead of us, so we're not going to be first, but we won't be last either.

"One more and we're done," Nate says.

"Then food!"

"Hop on and let's finish this." He turns and bends his knees, arms bracketing his broad back, ready to catch my legs.

Finally, a command I can obey. This is much better than him ordering me home. This show is good for Nate.

I jump on his back and close my eyes, pretending we're on a picnic in a park or he's carrying me in the rain through the streets of London, or some other adorable date and not an attempt to babysit me until he can get me back to New York.

It's very nice here in my imagination. I would like to stay a bit longer, but Nate gently gives me a bump and then slides me down his body at the finish line. I shiver from the sudden lack of touch, and Nate misinterprets it (which I'm okay with), asking Aiko to get me a jacket.

"Nate, Naomi. Welcome to the finish line! You're second after Hannah and Amir," Lewis says.

"Not bad!" I say.

"It's first loser," Nate immediately says.

I roll my eyes. "Okay, Business Barry. In the real world, you can enjoy a job well done and a fun time even if you aren't number one."

Lewis interrupts our burgeoning argument. I guess there are some arguments that are so boring even reality TV doesn't want them. "You can change back into your clothes and then take one of the place settings and relax. We'll get started serving you whenever you're ready."

We go back to the tent and change, then sit at the table closest to the carriages. Helpful crew immediately place plates in front of us while we watch the last two teams get through the obstacle course.

"This is surprisingly tame for a reality show," Nate says.

"Are you not aroused by this?" I get up and indicate my corseted figure covered in layers of clothing. "Sometimes, when I move real fast, you can see ankle." I lift my dress to show off the aforementioned ankle, then the other, for kicks.

Nate laughs. A laughter that is fast becoming my favorite sounds in the world. It's so different from the efficient, straight-laced man who works at one of the most successful companies in the U.S.

And much better, obviously.

"You hussy. I'm supposed to be stopping this kind of wild-woman behavior."

"Come over here and make me cover these ankles…these ankles that just want to see the world and be seen! To taste freedom! And air!"

I twirl some, ankles loving the freedom, but my entire torso wishing I could rip this corset off me so it can enjoy some of that freedom too. The tightness in my chest increases as I spin around, breathless with laughter and the effects of all these layers.

Suddenly I'm stopped from spinning by Nate wrapping himself around me. "You're sounding a little breathless there." Nate's eyes go to my bosoms with laser focus.

My heaving bosoms.

Not from lust! From all the physical activity. And maybe a little lust, if I'm being completely honest. "Clothes," I say succinctly, not mentioning all the reasons I'm breathless, because I've decided radical honest is entirely unnecessary.

"Just don't pass out on me." He leads me back to my seat, and I enjoy the second-place victory food while poor Will slips off the monkey bars and lands in the water below. He gets up, looking like a very angry lion, with his hair sticking out at all angles and a roar ready to come out.

"While we're here…" Nate starts. I get so lost in his deep chocolate eyes, my hungry stomach taking control of my metaphors, that I'm shocked at what he says next. "You're strong enough to be independent in New York. You can be close to family and friends, and you wouldn't let Harrison take over your life."

Disappointment crushes into me, chipping away at my new-found liking of this man like it's the Colorado River and my feelings for him are whatever stone was there before it was eroded and became the Grand Canyon.

I thought we had moved past his job. Or at least put it on

pause while we get through this. So it takes me a second to respond, and when I do, I'm more honest than I would like to be. Because I want him to understand. "I'm not, though."

"You're a lot stronger than you give yourself credit for."

"You don't get it. It's so easy to let him take over that I always let him. He's not a bad guy, and it would be fine, however he arranged things. It's why he's such a great businessperson…he always knows what to do. But I'll never know if I found what's right for me, or it's something that I settled for. And then I'll never be content because I'll always wonder if it was right for me or if I deserve it. I just want to try to find my own thing, maybe something that can make me happier than working in energy."

"All right." He holds his hands up. "You'll tell him I tried, when this is over? Multiple times."

"Sure. I'll even make sure to put it in an email." The only language Dad really understands.

Nate cuts his eyes away from me and looks at the now empty obstacle course. He can probably feel the sudden coldness coming from me in the already cool English day. And if he can't, it's not from a lack of trying on my part

"Much appreciated," he mumbles. I hope it's because he knows the biting manner which my statement was intended.

We eat the rest of the meal in silence, forks scraping on plates the only sound filing the empty space between us.

This would be a nice date, if I wasn't trying to eat the meal so fast as if there's a competitive eater championship title on the line. But the table is nicely set in an idyllic location, and the food tastes amazing.

What little I get to taste of it in between quick bites.

And I suppose, if one were to point a Nerf gun at me, I could admit that the company is okay too. Occasionally. When he's not talking about Dad, or home.

"We're ready for dessert," I lie, both of us still finishing the last few bites of the chicken entrée. But it's honest by the time the crew brings the dessert.

Dessert is a delicious banoffee pie, which I'm truly sad I don't get to savor. We could have skipped it, but who knows when we'll get food next, so we compromise and eat fast.

We finish before the other teams, heading to the carriages as a side ache forms, telling me not to run so fast after eating so much.

"You lot did that too fast. That was our mealtime too." Aiko jumps into the carriage with us.

"Put us in a car, with a heater, for the rest of the trip, and we'll eat as slow as you want us to," I negotiate with our keeper.

"I wish we could." Aiko zips her jacket up even higher as the carriage lurches forward.

Banter with our producer aside, I wonder if I can drag Kelly into some conversation. The camerawoman is usually so quiet, but I would really like to talk to anyone but Nate.

Nate thwarts that by trying to draw me into conversation first. "This is kind of a good time. And it may be the first real vacation I've had since starting at the company, aside from visiting my parents on holidays and the few days I usually take to be tourist on business trips."

"That's…sad. Really sad." I can't stay mad at him after that statement.

"There's always something to do at work." Nate shrugs.

"It'll still be there when you get back from a two-week vacation. I've had like twenty vacations since I've been here and it's only been eight years." That's probably the European influence on me.

"But someone could close deals while I'm off eating English desserts and chasing puppies in the mud."

"There will be other deals. A whole world of deals. You're here now, aren't you? And once you get back, you'll see that you were fine, and you can pop right back into the office. Maybe even more refreshed."

"I may not have a job after I get back. I didn't tell Har….my boss that I was going to be gone for quite so long. Or on TV."

Nate stopped himself from saying Dad's name at the last second and I appreciate the change. Work is a big part of Nate's life and I want him to talk about that if he wants. But I don't want to constantly be reminded about Dad when I'm with Nate.

It's a start.

CHAPTER 18

NATE

"This not-really-a-vacation-vacation aside, where would you want to go on a real trip?" Naomi asks.

"I haven't thought about that in a long time. The last time was spring break and I went to Cancun."

"Wooooooow." Naomi's eyebrows are raised in judgement.

"We can't all have access to a private jet."

"Kind of harsh. We never really used it because it was always busy doing business things. But I take your point. Even though it doesn't matter where you go, you can have a nice time road-tipping to the next city over. Or staying in your own city and seeing it with new eyes." Naomi pours herself another glass of wine that Aiko handed us when we got into the carriage, topping mine off too. There really isn't a lot more to do in this carriage but drink. Smart producers. "We have some time now. Think about where you would go if you weren't a sad workaholic, letting life pass him by while he gets paper-cuts from really big contracts."

"Hey. I like big contracts and I cannot lie. Plus contracts are digital now." I wink at her.

Naomi laughs. "Carpal tunnel then."

"Mexico was fun. I think I would want to go somewhere tropical. Beaches, outdoor activities, and fruity drinks with the little umbrellas. Where would the travel expert suggest?"

"Oooh. I do love planning vacations. Hard-earned vacations, just so you don't think that's all I do. Because I can balance work and life."

"You work very hard," I say, because it seems important to Naomi for me to acknowledge that. She doesn't need to worry; I know she works hard. She wants to work so hard she escaped the cushy position she had lined up for her in New York. It's the whole reason I'm here.

"As long as we're clear on that. Now, if you liked Cancun, maybe you'd like Bali, or Bora Bora, or the Caribbean."

"But will I get a chaperone?"

"Oh, yes. Diane's never letting you go. You and your virtue. She'll protect it forever with her embroidery needles."

I shiver, not because of the chill in the air, but because of the horror of imagining trying to kiss a woman and having Diane's face pop up, slapping me on the nose with a newspaper like a misbehaving dog. And yelling about ruin.

"Hopefully she's so devoted to the bit she'll refuse to get on a plane because it's an anachronism and I'll be safe."

"Oooor she's so devoted to the bit she'll experience the plane like a Victorian woman would, hitting the flight attendant with a parasol when the poor woman tries to do Diane's seatbelt and asking why the metal bird is going so fast."

I laugh at the image and see the map out of the corner of my eye, noticing we need to make a turn or we'll be lost. At least the obstacle course separated the teams a little, and we aren't all bunched together anymore.

I'm surprised how much I want to win. I knew Naomi would get into the competition no matter what she said she was here for, but I want us to win now too. Maybe we're both similar in the competitive department. Although she is a much more graceful loser than me.

In the carriage, Naomi plans my next six trips for me. I don't know if I'll have time to take any of these elaborate trips, but they do sound fun. Maybe just *one* couldn't hurt…

By the time we get to the marked spot on the map, she has me imagining the vacation, sitting in the sand somewhere with a drink in my hand and the waves tickling my toes. Wearing a shirt with some obnoxious pattern that Naomi would insist on, and I would let it happen because her laugh is worth it.

Then I remember that this is the only vacation that Naomi is likely to join me on and try to get her out of my fantasy. It doesn't work, though. She always finds her way back in. Whether it's to put sunscreen on my back, or drop themed novelty hats on my head.

Or to push me into the pool when I take a work call she doesn't approve of. Good things phones are waterproof now.

I get out of the carriage and help Naomi out. We're at another quaint inn, but this one looks more like a country house than the pub with rooms above it like the first one. Giant windows dominate the façade of the three level, gray stone building, with greenery and wisteria crawling along the wall and spilling out to the driveway.

"Go on inside and get checked in before anyone else gets here," Aiko says.

"Looks like we're still second," Naomi whispers, jerking her head at the carriage already parked in the drive.

I open the door for her, entering the grand space. The inside is just as much of a change from the inn we were in last night. This looks like where rich douchebags have hunting weekends, where they drink expensive whiskey and shoot guns in the vague direction of animals. I can say that, since I have too much experience with those rich douchebags.

There's velvet and gold everywhere, the entire lobby out of a museum, complete with paintings of old wigged men and statues of naked young men, overseen by a crystal chandelier.

"Good evening," a posh voice says from behind an antique desk.

"Hi. We need a room for the night," I say. "We're a married couple. Happily in love and very legally bound in the church." I share a wink with Naomi. I learn fast.

"Excellent." The man writes something down in the notebook in front of him and then hands me a key. A much smoother process this time, with the lies. And accepting that we're only getting one room.

Aiko and Kelly follow us up the stairs, repeating the process from yesterday of filming us from all angles going into the room. In the meantime, the crew bring in our trunks.

When I get back home, I'm going to build a shrine to whoever thought of putting wheels on suitcases, because these don't look easy to move and maneuver.

"Got the footage. Dinner is in a few hours, as long as everyone gets here. We'll send pre-dinner soon and there's some wine and beer in the corner, so have fun!"

The door closes on a soft click after Aiko, Kelly, and her camera go, leaving us alone in the room. Or as alone as possible, since I'm still convinced they hid cameras in this room like the perverts they are.

"Do you want to change out of the corset for the next few hours?"

"Yes, actually. That would be great," she says in relief. She takes the top dress off with my help, the laces and heavy material making it a struggle for both of us, with accidental but appreciated touches as I get the clothes off. Standing in her corset and under dress, she turns around and pulls her hair over her shoulder.

The move reveals the smooth curves of her golden-brown neck and shoulders, an area that I wasn't aware I was so attracted to. But it's the only parts of her, outside of arms, face and the cheeky flashes of ankle, that I've seen since yesterday. In that time, I've gotten hungry for the slightest look at her. So hungry I'll take any bit of crumbs that I can get and treat them like a feast.

I clear my throat and walk to the trunks. "Let me get something to cover you with when I undo the corset." I remember what happened last time.

"Yeah, wouldn't want to flash Great Britain. Again." But she doesn't sound like she cares all that much. Probably more concerned with breathing.

Which is a fair concern.

I get one of her nightdresses and hand it around to her front. She takes it while I get to work, untying the corset at the top. I loosen the strings down her back, watching her breathe a little deeper in relief with each level released.

In contrast, my breathing gets shallower with each inch of skin revealed. Even more so when the back of my fingers accidentally graze that same skin. They tremble a bit the farther they go, and outright refuse to move from her when they finish the task. Or maybe it's the lack of blood, which left every muscle to rush to my dick.

"Are you done with the corset?" Naomi asks, an understandable question since I've taken longer than is reasonable to do the job.

"Just one more tie," I lie, instead of admitting I was getting a little lost at the sight of her back. I've already signed up to be on a reality show; I don't need additional embarrassment. I fumble around with the ties so they get even looser, for cover. "All set."

"Thanks." She goes to the bathroom without looking back at me. A good thing, because I currently have yet another erection in these skintight pants, and it would be too awkward if it was acknowledged.

One thing going right for me is that Naomi takes a long time in the bathroom. When she comes out, I'm back to normal, blood in all the right places.

"Your turn. Although if you plan on changing out of those pants, it would be a shame." Naomi sends a flirtatious look over her shoulder at me, stopping me in my tracks with the compliment.

Just like that, calmed body parts flare back to life, begging to show her how they look in those pants.

Instead of taking that as in invitation, because I studied when people were having normal human interactions, I awkwardly laugh, deciding it must be a joke. Easier to ignore it that way.

We're allowed mirrors and modern lights in the bathroom, so I can look at myself in the eye while I lecture myself about keeping it professional with someone I'm supposed to be protecting from bad decisions.

Like getting involved with someone who works for her father, which can't be anything but too complicated. I need to stop this. It's gone too far with kissing her and enjoying accidentally grabbing her breast.

No. I can come back from this. I haven't gone too far; I just have to keep things professional from now on. And stop getting boners every time she's near.

How hard can that be?

I leave the bathroom, sitting as far away from Naomi as I can get in the small room. I make small talk like she's a prospective business partner, avoiding any topic like my pants or her back. Or those ankles. Anything dangerous.

Aiko saves me from stilted conversation and questioning looks over the change in my behavior after my time in the bathroom. "Everyone got here without too much issue, so dinner will be soon. And I come with the pre-dinner food you can eat."

"Sounds good," Naomi says, eyes already locked on the food and not paying that much attention to Aiko's departure.

We eat the dinner, me so distracted by Naomi I don't even taste it, and re-dress for the night's activities.

"Are you all right?" Naomi asks.

"Yeah. I'm fine. Great. Why?"

"You just seem different. Weird. Quiet. Since after you went to the bathroom." Naomi is too astute to not notice the change in my attitude toward her, and too much a Richmond to let it go.

"I'm fine." I add a smile to sell it. "Just getting my head around seeing everyone again. And whatever surprise we'll get tonight."

"It's a lot to take. Thank you again for not snitching me out to Dad and letting me do this my way. Even if you don't agree with it."

"You're welcome." I give her my arm to take her downstairs, instead of what I want to do, which is kiss her.

Because that's not professional.

CHAPTER 19

NAOMI

What could possibly have happened in that damn bathroom? There's no window. I don't think a criminal mastermind could get in the room and give him a brain transplant, replacing the real human I've been traveling with a bland corporate zombie. A hot one, but still.

Was it the comment on his pants? It was a compliment. One I thought would be well received, since his hands were touching my back every chance they had when they were taking off my corset. Not just touching, they *lingered.* I know I wasn't imagining that.

I want the Nate from before back. He was fun. So much fun I was going to see if we could enjoy being partners…in a way that only needs one bed in a hotel room.

But I guess reality must have intruded a little sooner than I anticipated, which I would have thought would be when the filming ended. Maybe Dad found a way to carrier pigeon a cell phone into that windowless bathroom and sent a strongly worded email about Nate enjoying himself a little too much.

Dad has Spidey senses about people in his life having too much fun.

Maybe it's good that Nate is putting boundaries back up. I should have kept mine up, but instead I was swayed by this manipulative show. With its romantic long carriage rides and physical challenges and Nate holding a puppy. And Aiko telling me how great he is every chance she gets. And all the wine, that encourages me to think about things that aren't prudent when it comes to Nate.

I don't even have my friends to vent to, which is making this whole process even harder. For two years I've had the support of an amazing group of people to help me when life got irritating and it sucks not having them now. Even Zara is too far from me doing her own work to take on best friend duties.

But Nate and I are back on even ground now. He's here to make sure I don't embarrass the family name, and I'm here to get my name out there, however I have to do that.

Which I should be focusing on. I haven't done anything to stand out here, although I have no idea what the others are doing, and I might be the most interesting person on this whole show. Probably not, but positive thinking is important.

We walk through the elaborate house, its luxury not affecting me as much as it normally would. Because I'm too busy thinking about Nate, and then trying to think about my goal to get Nate off my mind. Which makes me think more of Nate…it's a vicious cycle.

We end up in a dining room, the only thing really registering through all my denial being the gilt on every surface.

I pour myself a glass of wine, waiting for the rest of the group and avoiding the man next to me. A task made easier by the fact that the man won't look at me. I don't like that, despite how much of a hypocrite it makes me.

The rest of the groups come down a few minutes later, breaking up some of the awkwardness.

"Hey, everyone. Did you know they're still doing the thing that if you got here last, there's no room in this inn and you get to sleep in the carriage? Or the stables, if we can sneak in there later," George says as he blows into the dining room.

My first instinct is to turn and share a look with Nate, both of our eyebrows up in relief that we got a room. Even though I'm *supposed* to be ignoring him and not sharing special moments or looks that carry on a conversation with the man. My brain has conveniently forgotten that in its excitement. I force myself to look at anyone else.

"That sucks. I guess the show really likes making one team rough it every night. For entertainment," I say.

"Our pain sells well. And be careful with the carriage because it gets magically smaller at night," Hannah says, already well acquainted with the carriage sleeping arrangements. "But the sneaking in is a good idea. We didn't even try that."

"You do get an inadequate blanket that somehow makes you colder because it reminds you of warmth without actually providing any. And a hard pillow," Amir says.

I wince in sympathy. The crew serves us some food in costume, which again looks better than what they gave us upstairs. Inconsiderate.

"How was the obstacle course for you two?" I ask Jessica, who's sitting next to me. We were all at the same event, but I wasn't paying attention to anything else, too focused on winning. And Nate's thick biceps helping me through it.

"Muddy. And tiring. How about you?" Jessica asks.

"Same."

"Hello, beautiful contestants." Lewis bursts into the room and pauses for adulation. Which we all give because we don't want to film this again. Like Pavlov's dogs, we can be trained.

"Great. What are we going to have to do now?" Nate asks under his breath.

"Probably make us joust, or become a coal miner," I respond before I can stop myself.

"Do you know what people did in the Regency period?"

"No one knows what happened in the Regency period. Everyone who can contradict me died."

"What about historians?"

"No one believes those nerds. It's why we keep repeating history in such a devastating and avoidable manner." Then I remember Dev and Jaya, my favorite history nerds, are going to see this eventually. Oh well, they know I love them.

"Anyway…" Lewis says loudly in our direction, over our side conversation. "We're a couple of days in, and I just wanted to remind everyone that you can change partners anytime you want, and the kidnappees can choose to return or stay after twelve hours."

The group laughs, nervously looking at each other to see who's ready for some kidnapping.

"What the hell?" George booms as he stands up. "I want to kidnap someone." He announces with all the pomp and circumstance of someone who just announced they won the Nobel Prize. "I want to kidnap—"

"Hold on, hold on. We need a little more drama than that," Lewis interrupts. "Ladies, can I have you all stand up and move to the side of the room? Well, Sarah, you can stay seated," he says solemnly.

I roll my eyes, dutifully getting out of the chair to stand in the assigned area.

"All very beautiful women to pick from. Who do you want to be your new fiancée on your road to Gretna?"

Please not me. Please not me. Please anyone in this room but me. This sideboard, maybe? There's an image of a naked woman on the front of it, inexplicably. That's got to appeal to George.

Who am I kidding? Golden boobies appeal to everyone, even if they are on furniture.

But I still don't want this narcissist to pick me. I can only hear about his hair product and workout routine so many times while he leers at me.

"Such a difficult choice." He walks back and forth in front of the three standing women, looking us up and down like livestock at a state fair. Ew. I turn away from him slightly when he looks at me, not wanting that look full force.

"So many beautiful choices. Not that Sarah isn't also a beautiful option," Lewis says to the sulking woman at the table.

"I want to kidnap…Hannah."

Hannah curses next to me, looking like she just got picked last for dodgeball. Except she got picked first, but she still might have balls flying at her face if she's not careful.

George holds his hand out to Hannah, who takes it wearily. "I have to do this for twelve hours?" Hannah sends a longing look back at Amir. Those two seem to be progressing along nicely, which makes this suck even more for her.

"Yes. We're handing you a kidnapped clock." A crewmember hands her a pocket watch. "As soon as the time is up, whenever that is, you can exercise your ability to return to your partner, or choose to stay with your bold highwayman."

Hannah snatches the clock out of his hand and stares at it, probably willing time to speed up. When it doesn't, she sighs, going to sit down next to George, but her eyes are still on Amir. He's gone rigid next to me, not liking the development either.

"Now Sarah, you and Amir will be partners," Lewis says.

"Actually, I want to kidnap as well," Amir says into the silence.

"Yes! We have heads turning tonight! Remember, you can only steal once! But if you know what your heart wants, who are we to stand in the way of true love?"

Lewis motions for Amir to come stand in front of us. Amir complies, making us feel less like cattle when he gets up here. A gentleman.

"I want Naomi."

CHAPTER 20

NAOMI

What? No. Why? No. But…no!

"What?" Is the only word I can get out. I look around, wondering if there's another Naomi that joined the show and no one told me about it.

"You." Amir smiles at my confusion. "I want to kidnap you. If you want. Although I guess you don't have a choice for the next twelve hours. Sorry about that."

"Nope. This isn't going to work for us. We need to do this again, with more drama. You can't just shout out the person's name, we need to get shots of everyone anxiously waiting, and then the reveal and reaction shots of everyone involved," Lewis says, waving everyone back to their original positions.

"Um. Okay then," I say, not having forgotten any part of it. But I do avoid looking in Nate's direction, not ready for what I'll see there. It'll give me time to think about if I even want him to be upset at losing me. Or fake losing his fake fiancée. Although I guess it's more accurately: real losing his fake fiancée.

This is all very confusing.

I turn to Hannah, who looks like she wants to cry. I try to mouth *I'm sorry*, not caring if they get it on camera. She gives me the saddest smile I've seen on a person, and I want to slap both George and Amir for doing this to her.

In the meantime, Lewis warns us that we have to pretend we don't know what's going to happen.

Amir stands up again, going through the same movements as before, but much slower this time, with the requested drama. The shock hasn't left me, so it makes it easy to bring it back to my face when he says my name.

I half smile at Amir and sit down next to him, hoping this night of thefts and uncertainty ends soon.

From this position, I'm facing Nate and have to see him, unless I awkwardly contort to avoid him. And I've been awkward enough for one night. He's gone blank, which I assume means he's upset, but I can't tell from the lack of facial expression if he's upset I was torn from his muscular, flowy-shirt-clad arms, or if he's just upset that I won't be around to babysit and am free to get into shenanigans away from his watch.

Sarah sits next to Nate, not happy about getting abandoned twice in this dinner; once by George, and then once again when Amir, her new fiancé of thirty seconds, chose me.

Her emotions aren't so hard to figure out; she's glares at me. I try mouthing *I'm sorry* to her too, but she doesn't accept my apology. Instead, she starts rubbing Nate's arm. Now I glare at her.

Damn it. That's *my* confusing situation to deal with. And I didn't even ask to be kidnapped by her thirty-second fiancé. Although that does sound like a good name for another reality show.

"Good thing we're prepared for everything and I have another kidnapped clock on me." Lewis reaches out to a crew member who gives him another pocket watch. He hands it to me and I take it with a nod of thanks, my eyes glued to the instrument to make one more woman obsessively watching the hands of a clock slowly move.

"Why don't we let the new couples get some quality time

together? We'll set up some rooms for you to dine privately and get to know each other while we have the women's things moved to your new rooms, which stay with the men. Unfortunately, this does mean Hannah doesn't get to enjoy the finest room she won," Lewis says.

Oh great. Another reason for her to hate me.

Amir leads me away, but his eyes linger on Hannah, going the opposite direction from us out of the dining room. Mine *aren't* looking at Nate, since he's been chilly to me since before dinner.

Aiko leads us to another room, dropping us off while crew rushes in to set a table of show food we aren't allowed to eat. And lighting candles to make a romantic mood.

"So, why me?" I ask immediately when we sit down.

Amir laughs. "A flattering first question to start our engagement."

"No, I *am* flattered. But I thought you and Hannah were really finding something. Or the start of something to be explored later after the cameras and corsets go away."

"Yeah. I thought so too." Amir hangs his head.

"She didn't look happy to be kidnapped. And she didn't really have a choice. You can't blame her for that."

"I know. I think seeing her walk away with George messed with my head. She's the opposite of what I thought I wanted on paper, but I've had so much good chat with her. And I have so much chemistry with her too."

"You didn't pay enough attention to her. Or you would have seen her sad puppy face. And you would have snuck into her room to steal her back, twelve-hour rule be damned!" I work myself up, getting invested in this romance. I do love a good romance.

"You really think she wants me?"

"You guys are making eyes at each other like that bulldog couple on Instagram that got married in that castle in Scotland."

"That can't be a thing."

"Oh, it is. One of the few good things humans have done. Definitely one of the few good things on the internet."

"It has been nice getting to know her," he mumbles.

"Mmmhmm." I nod. I hope I get to be a bridesmaid out of this. If Hannah can forgive me and they defy the odds of every reality show couple. Or better yet, they'll let me do the publicity for their televised wedding.

"She even makes sleeping in an uncomfortable, cold carriage fun," Amir says.

"See, now I know you're delusional with infatuation." I might be interested in Nate, but I'm not gonna be happy sleeping in the carriage with him.

"It doesn't matter anymore. She's going to be so annoyed about this kidnapping. But I just wanted to see if I could feel that infatuation with someone else. And you're great, so if it was going to be anyone here, it would be you."

"Well, I *am* great." I tuck my hair behind my ear.

"How about you? Have I ruined things for you with Nate?" He wants to avoid the topic of Hannah, which is respectable.

"No. I knew him from before all this, but it's not like that."

"Are you sure it's not like that? He didn't look happy when I stole you."

Everyone here is a CIA-level interrogator. Where do they get the training? And the nerve? Asking me questions I don't want to answer. "That's just his face."

"Could anything happen?"

"No. There's too much history there." Then I realize what that sounds like. "Not that we dated in the past. But he works for my father, who I'm trying to get some distance from. It's a whole, boring thing."

"Sounds complicated."

"Yeah. And uninteresting. Let's plot Hannah's second kidnapping of the night." I clap my hands, buoyed by having a plan to sort out someone's life. Even if it isn't my own.

Especially since it isn't my own.

~

"Pssst," I hiss at the window, wondering how I ended up with the worst position in this caper. My natural compassion, probably. A real Achilles heel. "Hello," I whisper-yell. "Is anyone there?"

Shivering, I look at cameraperson assigned to document my misery. I shiver extra hard, hoping he'll find me a coat, but he stands like a rock behind the ominous equipment, that red light the only sign I'm not looking at a modern statue on this historic estate. See, if I was still with Nate and therefore Kelly, she would have gotten me a coat.

Then again, if I was still in my former couple, I wouldn't be in this situation.

"Could someone just come talk to me?" I have no idea if this is even the right room, but I find some pebbles next to the wall and pick one up. This works in the movies all the time.

I toss one at the window I think I need, but since the last time I played a sport was right field in fourth-grade softball, it hits the wall somewhere between the second-story window and the ground. The mice in the walls who have lived here for generations will know I want to talk to them.

"Naomi? What are you doing out here?"

"Ahh!" I scream, abandoning the loud whisper I was keeping my volume to. "Why are you creeping around the mansion, trying to terrify me?" I put my hand over my pounding heart.

"I'm taking a walk," Nate says. "Now you. Why aren't you getting to know your new fiancé?"

"I am part of an epic quest to win back his ladylove, and you are not helping me right now." I give up the entire plan without much provocation. "What about your new fiancée?"

"She's really pissed that two men rejected her in one night, and everything I say is making it worse, so I left to give her some space." He notices me shivering now that the initial shock is over, and without a word but with a deep sigh, he takes his jacket off and puts it over my shoulders.

I'm cold enough to not deny the gesture. And it's still warm with his body heat, so no force on earth could compel me to return it, especially not embarrassment or me not wanting his usually traitorous help. Traitor's warmth is still warm.

"Thanks," I say begrudgingly.

Nate brings me back to the original topic. "What's your part in this epic quest?"

"Amir is really into Hannah and we're double kidnapping her."

"How are you going to double kidnap her?" Nate asks, crossing his impressive arms over his impressive chest and shaking a little in the cold.

I open the jacket and throw the edges over his shoulders, sharing his own clothes with him.

"I'm the distraction, if I could get George to come down here." My voice is muffled by his shirt, which my face is buried in.

"You're going to have him meet you out here, alone, in the middle of the night?" There's judgement in his voice, but he wraps his arms around my back and rubs it. For the warmth, probably. Can't return an icicle to Dad. For the record, it's working, and a resulting warmth is being created in me.

"I have producers and camerapeople and everyone in this house to protect me. Now go away while I try to use my wiles on an unsuspecting man." I take the jacket off, regretting the move instantly, but still double down and shoo him away.

Because the only thing that I would choose over my own comfort is facilitating a love story. And pizza, maybe.

"Fine, but I'm staying close. He doesn't look like the kind of guy who'll take rejection well after you blow him off when the distraction is over."

I roll my eyes at him. George is so self-involved he won't even notice I'm rejecting him, because then he'd have to acknowledge the fact that there's a woman who doesn't want him. And who does Nate think he is, making assumptions and assigning himself to be my protector? I don't need a protector. I've survived how many years without him?

He's so irritating.

And I'm not going to let him get away with that without a little payback. "Who says I'm just going to blow him off after the distraction?"

CHAPTER 21

NATE

I recoil in disgust. Naomi? With that asshole? He doesn't deserve her. He can't see anything past his meal prep schedule for the next week. How is he supposed to remember her birthday or to celebrate once she gets her business up and running, or when her dad's been an ass and he'll need to get her some comfort crème brûlée? Her favorite.

"You want him?"

"I could," she says, but she flinches.

I can't stop the jealousy that expands to fill my chest, even though that flinch keeps me from Spider-Manning up this wall and punching George in the face for getting her interest while all I get is anger associated with her dad. Which is why I twist the knife in a little more.

"Are you ready to carry his towel at the gym?"

She frowns.

"Or to throw out all carbs because he's gone carb free?"

"No," she responds immediately and with horror, and then smiles when she realizes I got her. "It'll be fine. And when I help Amir with his love story, I will be a bridesmaid/ publicist at their televised wedding extravaganza."

"Do they know that?"

"It would be rude not to humor me, since I got hypothermia making it happen."

"Do they know they're going to defy the betting odds and get married from a TV show?"

"It could happen. It's worked a time or two."

"A time or two out of hundreds of reality show couples."

"They just need to open themselves up to the experience. Unlike you right now." She lightly slaps me on the chest, and then maybe lingers? That could be my imagination. Or my dreams.

"Because this isn't real. And anything that starts here in this fantasyland doesn't have a chance in the real world."

"It could! People meet everywhere, and most of those relationships will end. You didn't marry everyone you met at the bar or the gym or at school. When considering how many relationships end anyway, reality TV's stats probably aren't that bad. We just see them more."

"Did you just make your point by saying that all relationships are doomed?"

"Not all. Just a lot. The majority. You have to kiss a lot of frogs."

"Oi, are we still doing this?" Amir pops his head out a window next to the one I'm trying to siege.

Naomi gets back to the whisper-yell. "Yes! Just get ready to talk to your lady." She turns to me. "Can you please shoo now? I have to single-handedly save this love story."

"Hey! What about me?" Amir asks from his window.

"Will you get in position?" she yells, rolling her eyes.

"I'll get out of your way. But first…" I pick up a small pebble and throw it at the window next to Amir's, hoping it's the right one and I don't get billed for fixing anything that breaks. With my luck, it'll be historic glass that's no longer made and will cost five hundred times more than regular glass.

The pebble hits the window, and a few seconds later the

curtains are moved aside. Hannah peeks her head out. "What's going on?" she asks.

"Can I talk to George real quick?" Naomi asks while she pushes me away. I comply, but only moving so far as to go behind a large shrub.

"Take him," Hannah says, disappearing from the window without asking for an explanation as to why a young woman wants to see her fiancé alone, late at night. That relationship must be going well.

"Thank you," Naomi calls after the retreating figure.

"Hi Naomi. You all right?" George's voice comes down from the window. I can't see him from where I am, but he sounds self-satisfied and not even a little surprised that a woman is asking for him under his window like a reverse Romeo and Juliet. Probably not even the first time it's happened.

"Can you come down here for a second? I want to talk to you." Naomi tries to sound enticing and not reluctant, but she doesn't succeed. Maybe he won't notice.

"About what?"

A pause from Naomi as she looks at me. Did she not think this through? Did she think a man was just going to leave his room and come down to meet a hot woman in the woods? Okay, it's fair to assume that would have worked without further plotting.

"You want to talk about the gym," I whisper from behind the shrub under George's window.

She looks at me in gratitude. "The gym. I had burning questions about a comprehensive workout routine."

"Compliment his muscles," I say. Hell, who am I to stand in the way of young love? I'll help Hannah and Amir as much as I can. But I'm not budging if George comes down here. I'm helping Naomi too.

"You know, since you have such a great body. I would love any tips you have on fitness. I couldn't sleep, so I wanted to see if we could go over those tips and maybe make a weekly plan. Down here. Right now, if you're not busy."

I hear some commotion from inside George's room, the sounds of a door opening and muffled voices.

"Who's there at this hour?" George asks.

"It's probably Amir trying to get Hannah, just a little too early," I whisper at a confused Naomi.

"What do I do?" she asks, panicking.

"Keep him at the window."

"How?"

"Ask him about moves for your butt. That should keep him glued to the window." It would keep me glued to Naomi, no matter what was happening in the world. Flood, fire, plague of locusts, everything around me could be falling apart, but if Naomi wanted to talk about her butt, I would ignore them all.

Hell, even if she wanted to talk about her lower back, or upper thighs. Butt-adjacent would do it for me too.

"George! What are some moves for a firmer butt? I need some work here." Naomi commits to the bit, turning around and sticking out that same ass toward the window. Since I'm directly below the window, I get a full view of the presented body part.

I send out a thanks to whoever planted these shrubs high enough to hide the erection I'm sporting because of Naomi's… diversion tactic. I'm less enthusiastic about George getting the same view, even if it is part of the diversion.

"Right. I see." George sounds so lascivious I escalate the imaginary punch to an entire fight, with multiple strikes from different body parts. "But you look like you have no problem in that department." He sounds close again, Naomi's plan to get him back to the window a success, apparently.

"Oh, you. Thanks for saying that." Naomi giggles. Flirtatiously. I roll my eyes at her in an exaggerated movement. She sees it and scowls at me before smiling back up at the window.

"I could just use some tightening right here." She turns around farther and lightly rubs the sides of her own butt through her many layers, still glaring at me out of one eye.

"Damn it, stop that," I whisper. I can't have an erection on television. I can't have an erection on television. Thinking about baseball, and England, and prunes now.

"I'll be right down to work on your ass. Some tips for your ass." George's voice sounds muffled near the end of the sentence, like he turned around.

"No!" Naomi yells. "This is good. Just tell me from here."

"I thought you wanted me to come down?" he asks, but louder. Like he returned to the window.

"Say you're into Romeo and Juliet," I say, wanting George to stay up there as much as Naomi does. Plus, the plan might have initially been to get him down, but now Amir might still be stealing George's fiancé at the door.

Naomi doesn't respond to me, but she does say, "I'm feeling the Romeo and Juliet thing that's going on right now. You know, so romantic."

"The best romance in the world," George says.

"Does he know they both died?" I ask Naomi.

"Shove it!" Naomi whispers to me. "So those exercises…"

"It works better if I can show you in person. Guide you through some of them. I'll just come down."

"No!"

"It's fine, Hannah said she had to do an interview." He's too distracted to notice Hannah left with Amir, not a producer. Naomi is doing such a good job with the distraction that even I've almost forgotten there are cameras here and I'm acting out Cyrano de Bergerac.

"What do I do now?" Naomi whispers at me.

"Isn't this what you wanted? Wasn't this the whole goal? Did you not plan *any* of this out?"

"We barely had enough time to decide to do a person heist, much less adequately plan one out."

"Not to be a boring businessperson, but maybe you should have spent some time on the planning portion."

"Then the moment would have gone."

"And this is better?"

"Sort of. Maybe. Obviously hindsight is twenty-twenty. And maybe you would have planned everything out and made a PowerPoint with four contingency plans before you got to this point, but we can't all be you."

I'm about to respond with a defense of planning when I hear a noise and flatten myself against the wall behind the shrub.

"Who are you talking to?" George asks as he rounds the corner.

"Producers," Naomi lies. And they don't correct her.

"You want to learn some exercises to tone the butt?" George asks, ignoring the transparent lie. Because Naomi was facing away from the producers.

"All of the exercises. Why don't you tell me about them?" Naomi sits on the stone bench to her right, patting the space next to her.

Which turns out to be a bad idea. George advances on Naomi so fast I'm around the shrub and halfway to her before I know what I'm doing. But Naomi is off the bench before I get close and shakes her head at me. I stop where I am, but don't go back behind the shrub. George has his back to me now, so I'd rather be closer, just in case.

I don't trust anything about this guy.

"Why don't we go inside and find a comfortable room? We can go through some of those exercises together," George says, still advancing toward me.

I move, putting the bench between us, which stops him. "That sounds like a lot of effort. Maybe let's just talk them out and work up to practical exercises." I jerk my head in the direction of the crew, implying blame on them for not wanting to follow his creepy self to the anonymous room and not just self-preservation or common sense.

"All right, we can play this your way. For now." He shoots me a look I'm sure is meant to be seductive, but instead makes me gag a little. I cover with a shiver; it is really cold out here.

Beyond George, I see Nate throw his hands up and go back behind his shrub. I breathe a sigh of relief. Nate looked surprisingly ready to physically defend my honor. I didn't think they taught that in business school.

I would have thought they taught some non-violent negotiation skills in that degree. And step one would be to not look like the flames of hell are trying to come out through his eyes and his fists.

Despite the situation, it kind of works for me. He looks bigger, like he's flexing every muscle in an attempt to be ready for whatever. He strains against his already tight clothes, and I send some thanks to the ghost of Beau Brummell for his influence on the male fashion world.

The intensity in his dark brown eyes is also a turn-on, even though he's locked on to George and not me. Where was he hiding all this passion our entire acquaintanceship?

He's doing a lot more for me than George, who is getting ahead of himself for thinking that we're going to fuck even though I just invited him out here to discuss my fitness journey. Or more accurately, to distract him so Amir can get to Hannah.

This better work, after all this effort.

"Well, you should probably start with your diet. You can cut out carbs." He looks at me, considering.

I glare at him. I don't know if he's trying to be get back at me because I won't go to a room with him, or if he thinks he's genuinely being helpful. It's not cool, either way.

"Let's table the carb discussion 'til a later date." Like never. You will drag pizza out of my cold, dead fingers. "Maybe just tell me some exercises. Squats, etc." I keep my voice even, though I'm still fuming about the thought of pizza being taken from me.

George doesn't pick up on the subtext, happy to talk about his favorite subject after himself: working out. He launches into a long monologue so boring I sit down to keep myself from falling asleep standing up. Something about complexes that I'm sure would be super successful for my butt if I had the determination to work out regularly.

So much time passes that Amir could have gotten a good head start fleeing with Hannah the rest of the way to Gretna. It's still dark out, so nature rudely suggests that less time has passed than it feels like to me. Maybe I just entered a fugue state and an entire day has passed, meaning this is the second night we're here discussing the benefits and drawbacks of using dumbbells versus body weight movements for beginners.

I nod and make a sound of agreement in the back of my throat, since I haven't made any movements for a while. Not that my lack of response has deterred George. Carb shaming aside, he probably makes a good trainer with his wealth of information. An insufferable ass, but knowledgeable enough to give me muscle that can be used to pop him in the face once or twice when he suggests I give up chocolate.

I raise my eyes to Nate, sharing this moment, to find he's watching me with a slight smile. His eyes have the same intensity as he had earlier when he first saw George, but gentler now. I don't feel like there's any danger he's going to give anyone paper-cuts with a contract full of unfavorable terms or clobber someone with a laptop.

But thinking about exactly what he could do with all that intensity is an intriguing thought. One that distracts me from whatever subject George has moved on to now.

I try to listen to him, hear something about protein powders, and tune back out to focus on Nate again. With a nod so George still thinks I'm paying attention, and a yawn that I can't stop but hope I stifle. George's voice doesn't change or slow, so I guess it worked.

Back at Nate, he's raised an eyebrow in the short time I was paying attention to George. I return his slight smile and nod at him, telling him I appreciate him being around still, even though any danger has long since faced to boredom. He tips his head back at me.

Finally, after eons pass, Amir coos down from the second floor (or first floor for the contrary Brits). After the pre-approved sign that the kidnapping is complete and he got Hannah to decide to break the rules and stay with him, I don't waste another second before I cut George off mid-sentence.

"Thank you so much for your time," I say like we're in an

interview for a candidate that won't be getting the job. I refrain from adding that I'll contact him if I'm interested. "But it's getting a little late." I fake a yawn that turns into a real yawn quickly.

Nate yawns from his position behind the shrubs, but George doesn't. Guess we know who the sociopath is, and more importantly, who isn't.

"Oh, yeah." George stops sheepishly, a first for the usually self-confident man. An interesting sign of vulnerability. "I can get carried away with exercise stuff."

"No, it was very helpful." Or it would have been if I was paying attention and/or was interested in fitness. "You're very knowledgeable in your field." Okay, we're back to the job interview dynamic.

"Thanks. I could help with some cardio now if you want to get started with your exercise goals." He leers at me.

And there's good old Georgie again. Not one to linger in anything less than one hundred percent self-confidence. Still. "No thank you. I did a lot of running today at the obstacle course, so I think I've fulfilled my quota of cardio for the month. Plus, it's hard to work out in a corset." I deliberately misunderstand his invitation, smiling in thanks that's he so concerned for my health.

George is taken aback by the response, probably not expecting anyone to miss the subtext except sweet innocent grandmas and people who flat out just don't understand the language, much less innuendo.

"Maybe later?" Not to be deterred, this one.

"Hmm. Let's get back upstairs. We should sleep when we can to get ready for whatever they throw at us next." I break some rules by talking about the show and get two pairs of stink eye from the producer and cameraperson for my crime.

We trudge up the stairs, and I leave George at his room before heading to mine down the hall. I open the door, desperate for news on how our kidnapping went. But I enter an empty room, so I'm thwarted from getting any answers. Logically, I know that must be a good sign since Amir is out with his lady.

Although he could also be brooding on a moor like Heathcliff, which is less than ideal. Are there even moors here? I suppose any field can be a moor when you're broken-hearted.

I'll sit here and hope for him until I can find out the gossip. But if he makes me wait until the show airs to know, I'm never helping him in an epic quest again.

I'm thinking about how I'm going to get this corset off without my usual Nate-shaped lady's maid, when someone knocks on the door.

"Finally. Tell me what happened and then you can go back to your woman and—" I stop when I open the door and see Aiko.

"And do what? And more importantly, who's going to do it to who?" Aiko has her terrifying producer face on.

"Nothing. No one." I clam up. I'm no snitch. "Nothing exciting here."

"Mmm-hmm." Aiko purses her lips, not believing any of that. "We need to do our day's interview. Which I guess we can do here." She looks around for my new partner. My partner of two and a half hours, I calculate as I check my kidnapped clock.

"Great."

"Don't sound too excited." Aiko smiles at me, but it doesn't put me at ease.

I stiffen my spine, knowing what to expect in these interviews now. And Aiko doesn't deviate from the script. She spends the next forty-five minutes telling me how amazing Nate is, pointing out every one of his amazing characteristics, and probing how I feel about being kidnapped.

I admit that Amir is great, but I would prefer to be back with Nate, and that's what I'll do when the twelve hours is up. She doesn't know (or maybe she does since she's scary good at her job), but Amir isn't really going to be an option after these twelve hours are up, so I better smooth things over for myself now by being team Nate.

Getting me to admit I miss Nate is unexpected.

But it's what I was feeling when I walked into this room and Nate didn't come in behind me, so we could commiserate at how absurd our lives are right now. And how I was feeling when I realized that Sarah would be watching him get ready for bed tonight instead of me, all those mundane tasks performed in the intimacy of a shared bedroom.

I don't like the feelings, and I might have said something about missing his muscles in my weakened state.

It's those silences that get me. Aiko looking at me, waiting for me to fill them, and I comply because even though I know what she's doing, sitting in silence is still beyond awkward.

Aiko finally gets all the blood she wants from me tonight and leaves. I breathe a sigh of relief, but then I start thinking again about the logistics of getting out of this dress and corset alone. I'm turning in circles trying to reach the back like a dog chasing its tail when I'm interrupted by a knock on the door. I was about to run down the hall yelling "help," so it's a welcome interruption.

"Was Mission: Probable a success?" I ask as I throw open the door, but again, it's not Amir. I really need to check who it is before I open my mouth.

But I don't spend too much time regretting it, because standing at my door is Nate. Bathed in soft light from the flickering LED wall sconces, his skin glows where the light touches it, giving him an ethereal presence. Not that he would appreciate being told that.

"What are you doing here?" I ask.

CHAPTER 23

NATE

"Hey," I say instead of a response, not sure how to answer her question.

I hadn't planned on being here. I was going back to my room after watching Naomi and George walk upstairs together, even though that felt like I had eaten something my stomach violently disagreed with. Then I was going to get ready for bed and hope my really kidnapped, fake fiancée decided to come back to me in the morning.

But the angry pit in my stomach wouldn't go away, so I told Sarah I was going out for another walk, and dodged Aiko when she tried to find me for the daily interviews. By dodged, I mean I lunged behind a cabinet and cowered there, hoping she wouldn't find me. She did walk past me without noticing, making it worth it even if I felt like a teenager sneaking in past curfew.

I hope it wasn't caught on camera, but considering how desperate and unflattering it was, I doubt I'm that lucky.

When I was sure Aiko had moved on to look somewhere else, I got up, ignoring the tingling in my left foot from the position I was hiding in. Then I went straight to Naomi's room.

"Hey. So what are you doing here?" she asks again.

"I wanted to make sure you got back all right," I say, not entirely sure if that's a lie or not. Because I don't know why I came here, beyond that feeling in my stomach. But seeing her face is right. Unfortunately, that would make me sound creepy, and saying it was because of my upset stomach is weird, so I go with chivalry. If the velvet, paisley vest fits.

"Oh. Thank you. I did."

"Good."

"How is Sarah? I can't imagine she's happy to be passed around from fiancé to fiancé, and then abandoned for most of the night."

"Oh no, she was angry." I settle into her doorframe, leaning against it and crossing my arms because I have no intention of moving anytime soon. Unless she tells me to. Her eyes drop down to my chest, and I enjoy the attention. It's only fair, since I can't stop looking at her. "I get it. It's not great to be rejected three times in one night and then know it's going to be on TV."

"Yeah. That sucks, now and later."

"Where's Amir?" I ask.

"I have no idea. He hasn't been back since I got to the room. I hope that means he's having a romantic night somewhere away from the cameras."

I lean forward. "I still don't think that's possible."

She leans in too. "I'm still pretending it is, so I don't stress too much about it."

"I won't bring it up again, then."

"Cool." She clears her throat, probably still confused as to why I'm still here. "I guess I'll see you in the morning."

"Yeah. And you'll have to decide if you want to come back to your boring, old, business fiancée."

She rolls her eyes at me. "You're not old, you drama king."

"But I am boring?"

"I haven't decided yet. It's only been a few days; I'll need more data." Her eyes sparkle at the gentle dig she gets in. I do love my data.

I nod. "Fair enough. Have you decided yet if you're going to un-kidnap yourself?"

"I won't have much of a choice when Hannah decides to un-kidnap herself and Amir welcomes her back with open arms."

Ouch. No one wants to be chosen by default. But I smile neutrally at her, because I am her dad's employee, and I have no right being upset that I'm not her first choice. It shouldn't even be a surprise that I'm not her first choice since she spent the first night yelling at me.

Well, and kissing me.

"You could kidnap someone. Equal opportunity kidnappers, remember?" I shouldn't be pushing. But I want to be her choice.

"I do remember that." She stops there, making me suffer while I see if she's going to expand on that and tell me if she wants anyone else. She doesn't for an uncomfortably long time, staring at me instead like she's trying to read my mind.

I sincerely hope she can't. I've had enough inappropriate thoughts about the woman in front of me that I should lose my job over them. And since the bank likes their mortgage payment every month, I better not lose the ability to pay it.

"Well?" I say, again not able to control my mouth. Not that my mind even tried; it wants to know.

"No, Nate. We're going to be engaged again in…" She checks her pocket watch. "About six and a half more hours."

I nod, absorbing the information. Wanting my own kidnapped clock so I can count down the seconds in private.

"Well?" It's her turn to ask. But I'm genuinely confused why I'm being "welled."

"Well what?"

"*Well*, are you happy about that, or are you going to use that kidnapping rights to get someone else?"

I am incredibly, over the moon, ecstatically happy about that fact. "No. No more fiancées. I'm not supposed to be here for fun." I realize what I said right after the words are out of my mouth. My eyes widen and I try to backpedal. "I didn't mean…"

She surprises me by laughing in my face. "Calm down, Nate. I get it. You're a serious business-boss-bitch and you don't need any frivolous enjoyment in your life."

"But I do have fun with you. Even though that's not why I'm here. Squirt."

"Same. Old man." She still has laughter in her eyes, so I know she's not mad at me. That's a relief. For a lot of reasons, and not just because she can smooth things over with her dad. "Listen, since I'm alone, it's hard to get out of all this." She indicates her clothes. "Would you help a girl out?"

I am here to help Naomi. Harrison said help her stay out of trouble and being strangled by her own clothes while she's sleeping would be trouble. "Of course."

She steps back from the door and I enter her room. I fidget once I'm in, nervous even though I don't know why. I've been alone in rooms with her for days now. Maybe because I shouldn't be here. Or at least the show thinks I shouldn't be here. But I have an invitation from Naomi, and she's the only opinion that matters.

Naomi starts the now-familiar ritual, presenting me with her back so I can tackle the buttons on the dress. She takes that off and then presents me with the corset. I take my time enjoying the view, my hands lead weights with a hundred balloons tied to them. Both wanting to touch her but knowing when I'm done with the ties I'll have to leave again, so trying to draw the moment out.

They settle on a compromise, loosening some fast, regretting it, then a few slowly, then regretting that, and then repeating the process. I savor every small patch of tan skin that's revealed. My hands get clumsier, knuckles brushing against her skin that is as warm as if it holds onto every bit of sunlight that has ever touched it.

Beautiful.

"Well, thanks," Naomi says as she turns her head before I'm done.

Her voice breaks into the world where it's just me and the miniscule amount of skin I can see of her back. "What?"

"Beautiful?" The half of her mouth I can see quirks in a smile.

Shit. I said that out loud, destroying any chance of being an impartial observer only here to look out for everyone's best interests. Can I do anything to make this better? Backpedal a little? Maybe say I was talking about the dress, or the curtains, or the bed? No. Whatever I do, I shouldn't mention that inviting, soft bed next to us.

Because I shouldn't jeopardize my job, my entire livelihood, the only thing I have going for me, by getting involved with the boss's daughter. But my body disagrees with me. Vehemently.

I settle for the truth, my mouth siding with my tense body and ignoring common sense. "You are."

She twists and turns her long, graceful neck the rest of the way, looking me fully in the face, but doesn't say anything. I wait, hands still on the small laces at her back for what she'll do next. Slap me? I deserve it. Jump me? A man can hope.

She doesn't do anything, just searches my face for… I don't really know what she expects to find. But she doesn't turn away.

She turns without responding to my compliment and shimmies out of her corset, since I already undid it enough that it slides down with her movement. A lot of hip movement.

She steps out of the circle of the corset, standing in front of me in her mostly see-through under-dress. Then time slows a little as she takes that off too, this time without my help. She's left in her underwear, braless. And any thoughts of common sense are firmly packed to the corner of my mind and ignored for a later date.

Maybe I'll keep on ignoring it. She's beautiful. And I feel more excited now than I have in a while. I want to hang onto that feeling for a while longer. Or as long as she'll let me.

I suck in a sharp breath, eyes and all my attention locked on her breasts. So much I get bereft when she bends and blocks the view. When she stands back up, completely naked, my mood perks up.

Now that there's no clothes in the way, I can see miles of her perfect curves. I regret that last breath I let out so emphatically, because I can't seem to take another one, can't seem to make my lungs work again.

"Beautiful," I say again, all other words too mild or outright wrong to describe her. She's so beautiful I'm still frozen, even though there are a thousand things I want to do to her right now.

Not all of me is frozen, though. All of my blood has rushed to my penis, and the resulting erection wants me to get a move on and find out if she's as soft as she looks.

"Well, thanks," she says again. But she has a smile, so I don't think I've blown it yet. Whatever is happening.

She approaches until she's right in front of me. "What are you going to do about it?"

CHAPTER 24

NAOMI

The silence is not an ideal response to my question. In fact, only a few things could be worse. Him laughing at me, throwing up at the sight of me, running away in horror, screaming so much he looks like that Edvard Munch painting. All would be much worse, if I'm trying to make myself feel better.

And he has an erection, so I know he's not unaffected by me.

It seemed like a very logical thought process at the time. His hands were warm on my back and I wanted them on more of me. So I got naked.

I did imagine that we'd be on each other by now, though. Instead, I'm starting to think of all the reasons why this was a bad idea. All the reasons that were pushed out of my head by lust earlier. Chiefly, the fact that I can't get away from Dad if I'm fucking one of his closest employees. This is a step away from independence, away from everything I've done in the past nine years.

Oh god, what if the kisses are all flukes? What if he was humoring me as part of his babysitting assignment, softening me up so I'll go back home without a fight? But sex is too far even for him and he's trying to figure out how to get out of this room without embarrassing anyone more.

Right, even years of being Harrison's child isn't enough to get me through this attack of self-confidence, Nate's erection notwithstanding. The wind is firmly taken out of my sails, and I'm getting a little cold in the English night. Reality is creeping in, uncomfortable and embarrassing.

"Okay, then. Silence is an answer." I reach for my chemise when Nate's hand darts out to catch mine.

"No. I…" Nate doesn't finish the sentence, even though I would give everything I own to hear his thoughts right now. "Let's go to the bathroom. Less chance of cameras."

Well, that's a good point. The perks of being with someone who's always thinking of the bigger picture with that business brain. "Yes."

Once in the thankfully large bathroom, Nate takes off his outer jacket, then his flowy white shirt, while maintaining eye contact. I rapidly forget why I was upset. By the time his boots and skin-tight pants are off, I don't even remember that I was upset. He takes a visibly deep breath before removing the last of his clothes.

"Hi, old man," I whisper, to break the silence as we stand there naked.

"Hi, squirt," he replies in his own whisper.

"How's your family's crop yield this year?" I ask, repeating the same thing he asked me the first night on the show.

It gets the reaction I want, and he laughs. He swoops me up in his arms and keeps charging until he gets in the shower. I can still feel his laughter against me as he sets me down, keeping me close while he starts the water.

"Excellent," he replies, looking down at me with a smile. Then he's kissing me, his mouth covering mine and our tongues battling. We're constantly moving, my skin striving to touch all of his and then getting disappointed when it isn't enough, so it keeps shifting to get more.

I hitch one leg over his hips, body ravenous but rational enough to realize it *really* wants at the skin between his legs and moves once more to get it. His penis rubs against my clit and the shock of pleasure races through me, causing my hips to involuntarily jerk toward him and even more contact with Nate. It's not enough, so I reach down and put my hand under his penis, increasing the pressure on my clit as he keeps thrusting his hips to slide between my legs.

Any worries I had about him not wanting me or this being a bad idea are history. Replaced by the swirl of heat and electricity that comes around Nate but a hundred times more intense now that we're naked together. The steam from the hot shower envelopes us in another world.

Nate raises one hand and lightly grabs me by the neck, pushing me back against the wet, slick tile and holding me there. Like there was the slightest chance of me moving from this spot. His thumb strokes the side of my neck in time to me firmly stroking his penis against my folds.

He makes me come from the movement, makes me break apart while standing in the shower, water raining down on me. He keeps thrusting against my wet thigh until I push him away. He looks at me, confused and sad. I keep up the pressure on his chest and he stumbles back and past the shower curtain, the dazed expression still on his face.

I keep guiding him until we're lying on the rug in front of the shower, me on top.

I work my way down his body, kissing and licking his warm, wet skin, but stop when I reach his erection. I drag my nail lightly over it, watching it jump and move in reaction to my touch.

"What are you doing down there?"

"Inspecting the goods, like a good businessperson. Now hush and let me work."

"You do know how to talk dirty to me." Nate rests his head on the large rug.

I laugh, watching as my warm breath hits his penis and it grows a little more in response. "Only a truly messed-up person would think that's dirty talk."

"That's me. Messed up. Now go back to the inspect—" He breaks off on a groan.

Because I take his penis into my mouth before he can finish the sentiment. I grasp the base and lick up his still wet shaft, reveling in his grunts of enjoyment and the way all of the muscles I can see are tense.

Reveling in the fact that I caused it. Am causing it. And that he wants me to continue causing it, if the impatient tugs on my hair are any indication. I take his penis completely in my mouth and suck, getting the loudest groan from him yet.

I continue working him until he tugs insistently on my hair, the sharp prickles sending pleasure through me like his hand on my neck did. "I'm going to come."

"So come." I'm about to get back to blowing him when his next words stop me.

"I want to be inside you."

Damn. I want that too. A lot. So much I don't even have the presence of mind to be happy that he wants me as much as I want him; there's only need. "If you insist."

Nate gently moves me aside and onto my back. I willingly go and close my eyes to focus on the coming sensations, but when I don't feel him on top of me, I sit up.

"Hey, where are you?" My nipples are hardening more as the cold hits them when they should be hardening because of the hairs on Nate's chest rubbing against them.

"Getting this," Nate says through the open bathroom door, bent over and showing me his amazing ass while he rummages through the coat he took off earlier. He straightens and turns, depriving me of the sight of his muscular ass, but gifting me with more views of his perfect, erect penis.

He holds up a condom that he unwraps and puts on his penis while he walks back to the bathroom.

"How—" I start, but then stop when he gets back on top of me, blanketing me with his firm body. The multiple sensations of the warmth of his hard muscles, his soft body hair, the residual water on his skin making us slide against each other, and the hard floor at my back make me forget what I was going to ask.

Nate kisses me again, further scrambling any remaining coherent thoughts I had. He enters me slowly, turning me from a woman with thoughts and ambitions into a bundle of happy nerve endings whose only goal is to get more touch.

He thrusts a few times and then pauses, breathing roughly over me while our foreheads touch. He lets go of my hip with one hand, tracing my body until he reaches my clit. He starts rubbing, and my muscles react by pulling him in deeper with each stroke, tightening as I get closer to a second orgasm.

When he's in as deep as he can go, my body succumbs again, waves of pleasure crashing over me as I contract around his penis. The orgasm was great before, but there's something even better about coming around him.

Nate quickens his pace now, thrusting in and out with furious strokes, until he comes as well. He collapses next to me while my racing heart gets back to normal.

For once, I don't have a flip comment at the ready. I can't think about being flippant right now. Or I don't want to be. Because what happened here feels…serious. Important. Like something has changed, even though I'm not sure I wanted anything to do with this man beyond the physical.

But that was not just physical.

I turn my head to see Nate's broad back as he gets rid of the condom and then returns to give me a half smile and a light kiss.

He bends down, drawing me into his arms and picking me up. I don't know where he's finding the strength, but he carries me back to the bed and gets us under the covers.

I yawn. Maybe I'll figure out exactly how I feel about this a little later.

~

THE NEXT MORNING, I stretch under Nate's muscular arms and turn so I'm facing him. I'm lighter than I have been in years, and happy. That could be because I'm cocooned in warmth in a soft bed.

Or maybe it's all the orgasms.

Nate's still asleep, features highlighted by the soft morning light streaming in through the window. Who would have thought *Nate* could give me this feeling of contentment?

Someone who's happy to spend most of his days around Dad. And therefore, by proximity, represents the controlled lifestyle that I want to avoid.

But I don't feel controlled right now. That lightness is enough to give me the power to float to the stars.

"We better get up," I whisper to the man sleeping so peacefully next to me. I don't want to disturb him, but whatever this is, I don't want the cameras to catch us, if they haven't already. And I'm still choosing to believe there aren't cameras here because I can't see them and it would be a bummer if they caught this and put it on TV.

His face scrunches up in response to my whisper. Adorable. Not an adjective I would have chosen to apply to the serious man, but one that fits in this private little escape we have here.

"Nate," I whisper again. This time caressing his face because that strong jaw must have magnets in it that are specifically calibrated to attract my hands.

His eyes slowly flutter open, confusion filling the dark brown depths initially. He looks around, taking in me, the ornate decorations, our state of undress and then back to me again. He doesn't have confusion in his gaze anymore. Instead it's clear, but there's not exactly happiness, peace, or contentment in it.

"Oh, shit."

CHAPTER 25

NATE

Naomi flinches like I just hit her and I curse again, this time to myself. If only I had that much foresight before. "I didn't mean…" I try to repair the damage I did with my half-asleep words. In my defense, I was surprised. I didn't think that I would ever be here with Naomi, after an amazing night together. And it was amazing.

But now reality is here, brought in by the morning sunlight. The reality that this was probably videoed, and even if whoever is in charge of morals in this country edits it to keep out the steamiest parts, the United Kingdom is a lot less puritan than the United States and they'll show more than I'm comfortable with. Enough to understand exactly what happened here.

And then the reality that Harrison will watch me defiling his daughter on this reality show and I'll be fired.

But still, I don't know how to finish my sentence. How to make it better that my first thought after our night together was to curse? Because it was.

Naomi saves me from having to finish the sentence by getting out of bed.

"Whatever." She gets out of bed, flinging my arm off her in the process of flinging the covers off. "You better get dressed and get out of here before they catch and film you."

"They most likely already have." I fall on my back and look around the ceilings, trying to see if I can spot the expertly hidden cameras.

She pauses in the act of running away from me but doesn't look back. "Guess we'll both just have to live with the fallout then," she says, sharply. Coldly. Then keeps going the rest of the way.

"Damn it." I get out of the bed and pick up clothes along the way. "Naomi," I yell as I knock on the bathroom door. I hear movement from the hallway, and curse again.

"I'll see you later today? We'll talk," I say, much quieter in deference to whoever might be in the hallway.

Naomi grunts her assent from the bathroom and turns on the water for the shower, cutting off anything else I might have wanted to say. A shower I have very good memories of.

I sneak out of a room for the second time in twelve hours, this time making it back to my room without having to jump behind any furniture.

Sarah ignores me as I walk in and get ready for the day, not even a good morning or asking me where I was last night to break the silence. Another woman who's not a big fan of me.

Join the rapidly expanding club, Sarah. I'll have membership cards printed up soon.

After getting ready, I shove the clothes from yesterday and this morning into my trunk along with my toiletries. Just like that I'm packed up.

Sarah's left by the time I get out of the bathroom, so I go downstairs, and some helpful crew direct me to the dining room.

Naomi and Sarah are already in the room, along with Hannah and Amir, sitting close to each other and looking very infatuated. I fix myself a breakfast plate from the side table and choose a seat next to Naomi, even though she's ignoring me along with Sarah.

The silent breakfast is made less awkward and a little less silent by Hannah and Amir's whispering to each other. They must have had a good night, since he never came back to his room with Naomi. The atmosphere in the room gets a little lighter when the rest of the contestants come in, except for how uncomfortable it is when George comes in, glaring at Hannah and Naomi.

"Hello, beautiful contestants," Lewis sings as he dances into the room. Whatever he's taking to make him that happy must be dangerous for his liver in large doses. He's completely unaware of the drama that unfolded in the house last night, or a better actor than I give him credit for, because he doesn't look at us like frisky zoo animals.

"It's time to check in with some kidnapped fiancées." He gets a good look around the table. "Although maybe some of these decisions won't be much of a surprise." He winks at the original couples, sitting together. "But first everyone sit by your current partner so we can get some footage of the morning."

We move while the cameras flutter around us, back to silence with partners we don't like.

"All the kidnapped ladies," Lewis sings to the tune of "All the Single Ladies," laughing to himself at his joke, and then pausing until we all do. "Please stand next to me."

Hannah drops a quick kiss on Amir's lips when walking past him, and Naomi smiles at the couple as she moves to the stand next to Lewis.

"Give us some suspense," Lewis says. "Just a little." Hannah continues to smile down at Amir and Lewis sighs. "Or we can edit some in later. Let's start with Naomi. You've had a full night with Amir."

No, she hasn't, thank you very much. And it surprises me how much I want to jump up and set that record straight. Only years of training with Harrison's boring and sometimes rude associates helps me stay in the seat.

"And now you can choose to stay with Amir, go back to Nate, or do a little kidnapping of your own. What do you want to do? And please explain why."

Even knowing she can't stay with Amir and she doesn't like anyone else here, I still start to worry. Maybe it's the way Lewis is dragging this out, not letting Naomi respond right away. Or the way he ordered her to look at every man like they were a viable option. She's either too good an actress, or me messing up this morning is making her reconsider every man in this room in a last-ditch effort to get away from me.

And then she looks at me. No hint of a smile, but no frown either. Just a lot of intensity. I don't know what that means.

I audibly swallow, the sound like an explosion in my own head. I hope no one else can hear it, making it obvious just how affected I am by Naomi.

"I choose—"

"Don't forget to drag it out," Lewis whispers at her. "And smile!"

Naomi plasters a fake smile on her face and starts again. "Right. Well…" She pauses, as instructed, adding even more drama by giving us mere mortals a last look. I imagine that she lingers on me just a little longer, but that may be more wishful thinking than any actual desire on her part.

"I've enjoyed my time with him as my partner more than the other men, so I choose Nate."

I vaguely hear our castmates cheer as I feel the relief coursing through me. This show really does a number on emotions, if it can take a choice I thought was going to be solidly in my favor and make me doubt it.

I can see why people think they fall in love during these things. The excitement, the crew hyping love up, the constant alcohol, the competition, nothing else to do or think about. All potent when combined to mess with heads and hearts.

That explains why after the show ends, so do most of the relationships. It's hard to sustain a relationship into the boring calm of everyday life when this was a couple's introduction, every emotion amplified by the situation. Another reason to remember that this, whatever is between us, isn't going to last. But my job will. Hopefully.

Naomi makes her way back to the table and sits down next to me without saying anything.

"Don't be shy. You two are reunited after a cruel separation. You can celebrate. Don't mind us," Lewis says.

Naomi keeps the fake smile on her face and gives me a tepid one-armed side hug. One that is over before I can react fast enough to return it. It's a disappointing change from the passion of last night. Understandable, but disappointing.

"Deny us what we want, you coy contestants. We'll catch you when you least suspect it."

Naomi adds a fake laugh to her repertoire, one tinged with a bit of hysteria. Now we're both thinking about last night and wondering how much of it will wind up in the show.

Lewis laughs lasciviously, like a perverted old man thirty years his senior. Maybe an ad executive from the sixties fresh off a boozy lunch. Then he thankfully turns his attention to Hannah and goes through the exact same process with her that he did with Naomi.

Except it takes a lot longer, since Hannah is eager to pick Amir and not doing a great job building up the suspense. She does have a lot more complimentary things to say about Amir, especially compared to Naomi's short speech when she picked me. Which doesn't affect me at all. Not one bit. While Lewis tries to make a show, I turn to Naomi, shifting to catch her eye and commiserate about this with her.

She avoids me, focusing on picking at food she can't eat.

Finally, the crew is satisfied with what they have and Lewis releases us, letting us race to the carriages to determine who will be stuck in what for the next twelve hours. Naomi lingers to grab some pastries for the ride while I focus on getting the best carriage. Because we do make an excellent team.

"I, for one, am glad to see you two back together," Aiko greets us as we pant next to the third-best carriage I was able to secure. "Can't break up this dream team that is going to win over the voters of Britain. Even if you are damn, dirty Yanks."

"Good to see you too. Limey, tea-drinking bastards, etc," Naomi says, much better equipped to handle British-American relations after her time here. But she doesn't admit to being happy to be back with me.

And she still doesn't look at me when I help her up into the carriage. I doubt she would have even taken my hand except the cameras were rolling and it would be a bigger deal if she refused. This bodes well for the relationship. The fake, TV relationship, I mean.

"You avoided me last night for your interviews. We're going to have a lot to cover tonight," Aiko says to me. Her tone is light, but I feel threatened.

I try to change the subject. "Went out to explore the place. You guys make good houses."

"Rich pricks exploiting the masses made this house," Aiko says from across us, while the cameras set up. She feels a lot freer to give her opinions now that the cameras are off.

I'll take it. I would much rather talk about the exploiting landed aristocracy than what happened last night. Hell, I'll even agree to eat the rich, despite the fact that I would have to eat Harrison. And maybe gnaw off my own leg as well.

"Where are we going today?" Naomi asks when she's settled in the carriage, blanket thrown over her and map already open. "Bakewell." She looks up at Aiko. "Did I pronounce that one right?"

Aiko laughs. "Yes. And you didn't even allude to genitalia this time."

"A rousing success then." Naomi puts on an accurate English

accent, to this American, at least. Then back to her Yankee roots, she asks the coachman, "Good morning. Can we go right when we get to the second roundabout?"

"Morning. Yes, we can."

"Great, we should be on that road for a while. Time for a nap." Naomi still doesn't look at me, turning away from me to rest her head on a bunched-up cloak she uses as a pillow against the carriage window frame, eyes closed.

That makes her thoughts on talking about last night crystal clear. Not that I want to have that discussion with the camera pointed at me, but I don't like that she's mad at me. That she might have been hurt by something I said.

Not only is it my job right now to make use she doesn't get hurt, I personally don't like seeing her hurt, and feel worse that I caused it. And not having any way to make it better makes me uncomfortable in this seat. More uncomfortable than just having to sit in this carriage for hours on end.

The first hour is nothing but the sounds of horse hooves on a road, taking us farther north, and the occasional times one of us speaks to give directions. We're in the middle of the grouping of carriages, since we all left at roughly the same time.

"You lot are extra boring today. Don't you know I have a show to produce?" Aiko says to break the tension.

"So sorry that we're boring. Would it help if I tear off all my clothes and go streaking in the English countryside?" Naomi asks.

"It doesn't have to be that dramatic. But if you feel so moved, I'll never stop you from tossing a drink at one another. Maybe flipping a table if you want to emulate a classic moment. Or maybe a make-out session."

I flinch when Aiko talks about throwing drinks, like the liquid is coming toward me. Naomi would be only too happy to deliver that piece of drama. And even though I deserve it for getting involved with her and hurting her this morning, it still won't feel great.

Despite the suggestions, Aiko doesn't get the excitement she requested. After a lot more silent hours, including a short bathroom/food/stretch break, we stop at what looks like a small village with charming stone cottages. With no cars around, and us in period clothing, it's easy to imagine I really am in the Regency period.

"Is this our stop?" I ask when I get out of the carriage. Usually they try to isolate us in the middle of nowhere, like we're going to an elaborate "The Most Dangerous Game" scenario where killers will hunt us while we evade them using our meager survival skills.

On second thought, that might be easier to handle than this show.

"Yes, but it's not the final task of the day," Aiko teases, enjoying her power trip.

"Of course not." Naomi knows Aiko just as well as me.

Aiko continues, "We have some adventure for you before you can go to sleep."

CHAPTER 26

NAOMI

Oh, joy. More adventure. Not like having sex with Nate wasn't enough adventure. Or this whole show idea isn't enough adventure. An absurd idea I don't even know is working because I haven't been able to check my social media follower numbers.

"What's the plan now?" I ask.

"You know I can't spoil the surprise for Lewis. We need real reaction shots because none of you are great actors, to be honest. But we'll serve you tea, including all the champagne you want, while we wait."

"With sandwiches?" The eggs from earlier are a distant memory.

"Finger sandwiches. But yes," Aiko says. "And scones."

"Fair play." At least there will be food. I won't ask what else can go wrong, because that would be an invitation/challenge to the universe for all sorts of nightmarish possibilities.

Aiko drops us off in front of the cutest little cottage in a village filled with adorable stone cottages that look like they belong in a movie where Reese Witherspoon meets Tom Hardy in a fisherman sweater at a grocery store while she's holding a can of spotted dick, confused as to what it is.

A movie I would watch, actually.

Inside the cute cottage, Nate and I sit down and a woman in period dress, but a little plainer than what we're wearing and probably easier to move around in, sweeps in and efficiently puts an entire spread in front of us: teapot, teacups, and a three-tiered stand with savory sandwiches, scones, and sweets.

And the champers. An entire bottle left at the table.

"This experience really isn't all bad." Nate picks at a sandwich that looks comically small in his giant hand. A hand as skillful as it is physically appealing. Unfortunately for me.

I look at him while taking my own little sandwich. "I guess."

"Yeah. Nice clothes, nice houses, nice food even though there could be more of it. A little rushed at times, but still good."

"Nice bathrooms," I blurt out before I can stop myself. Because I do want to force him to talk about last night. I thought I wanted to ignore what happened after Nate's first words this morning were a curse. But I can't stand being confused and angsty about it for much longer.

If I have to suffer, he should too. It's his fault; I woke up feeling great before he spoke and ruined it.

Nate is equally surprised by my question, if his sudden choking on a bite is any indication. I almost feel bad, but then I remember someone in the crew must be a medic and take another bite of my own sandwich. And chew appropriately so I don't overtax our medics.

He finally stops coughing and takes a sip of his tea. I get distracted again by that strong, capable hand holding the tiny, delicate porcelain. So much that I almost forget I'm grilling him. Like Aiko usually does to us.

This time it's me asking questions, and I have no mercy just like Aiko. I'm not motivated by the profit margin on the show or the production of art, but by something way stronger: righteous indignation.

"Well, that is a strange reaction to the thought of…the bathroom." I take a sip of champagne casually, slowly like I don't have a care in the world and not like his response is more important to me than the next meal I'll get. An unpredictable occurrence on this show.

Nate swallows a few more times. "I'm sorry. I had a really good time with you. And then I got nervous, thinking about the show and real life. It was all too much. The high high. *Very* high high. Highest of highs. But then thinking about everything else. It just came out. I didn't mean it."

That is slightly better. As far as apologies go, I'm moving from there's-nothing-he-could-say-to-make-this-better, to eh-this-isn't-the-worst-apology-I-suppose. I'm still mad. Or maybe I still want to be mad. But I'm on the downward curve of anger. If anger could be graphed.

I sigh, deeply, to convey that I still have vestiges of anger. But I begrudgingly say, "It's fine." When he looks at me in doubt, a look that gives me a whole conversation without saying a word, I continue. "I will be fine. We'll be fine."

"I respect that and I'm glad we can get to fine," he says.

I nod, going back to the business of demolishing the food around me. The rest of the groups filter in, getting their own table.

After we've been mostly fed, since we never get an entire meal without some sort of shenanigans interrupting the otherwise pleasant times, Lewis shows up. "Hello, beautiful runaway lords and ladies. You've made it almost halfway to Gretna!"

I cheer along with everyone else at the tea shop but can't help the slight jolt to my stomach at the thought that this fantasy with Nate will be over soon. Even a quarter mad at him, I still want to spend time with him. Maybe get to zero percent mad and be able to enjoy the time before he leaves and I carry on in London. Alone.

"You've had a lovely day, if uneventful, so we're going to shake things up a bit!" Oh, grand. "Your carriage has been beset by highwaymen while you've been enjoying tea!"

I turn to the door as if I could see the remnants of our carriage, stripped bare by thieves, but all I see is green ivy crawling up the wall of the stone building opposite us.

"That means, of course, that you don't have any clothes, especially not wedding clothes, or any other luggage. You do have money, since you were smart enough to keep some on your persons. You'll need to take the list we provide you, and go shopping on the high street, getting the necessary supplies, with the money in the pouches taped under your tables. Budget and make a plan, because the faster you finish, the faster you can get to the inn for the night."

I exchange looks with Nate. We know what that means now. Last one to the hotel gets the crappy room. Or no room at all.

"On the count of three, get your list from your producer right outside and you can be on your way. One." He looks around at each of us, building suspense for the cameras. "Two." He smirks and pauses again, before *finally* saying, "Three!"

We all scramble up, chairs overturned and precious porcelain rattling at the force of four teams pushing away from their tables and sprinting out the door. Amir and George have a cartoon moment where they both go through the door and get stuck, before Amir wiggles his way out first, leaving George in a close second place.

Nate and I are in a respectable third place when we find Aiko, who throws a list at us and makes shooing motions. I open the list as Nate counts the coins, naturally falling into our team dynamic.

"This list doesn't look too bad. Wedding gown, a formal gown, a casual dress, all the under things, hats, shoes, toiletries, and for you, formal and regular pants, shirts, coat, and pocket watch. And two wedding rings. And one book each, for entertainment." That last one is very welcome for these long carriage rides.

"How do we know which stores are open for us?" Nate asks.

We look right and left from the tea shop, at the rows of stores in each direction that make up the high street. A lot of gray stone, green plants overtaking man made construction, and thatched roofs.

"There are people in period costume standing in some stores. And the rest look closed, actually," Nate says as we walk a few shops down.

"Let's just go in one then." I take a breath as I walk into the first store on our left. And right into a wedding wonderland.

CHAPTER 27

NATE

I didn't think I had commitment issues. I want to find someone I love and marry them. I want to make a home together and sit next to them on the couch, fighting about what to eat for dinner and what to watch next for eternity.

But this store is a bit much for even me. There's white everywhere, more shades of it than...well, more than fifty. There's silky white dresses and fluffy white dresses. And then there's the accessories, whose only qualifications seem to be that they're sparkly.

It looks like the show took over the space, putting up a sheet halfway and setting up the racks with vintage wedding dresses.

"Is it too late to leave you at the altar?" For a second I think I said that, but the voice is softer than mine, and to my right. It's scary when we have the same thoughts, since we don't agree on much.

"I think it may be too early," I say. "I have to be in sight of the altar before you can leave me at it."

"Ah. Helpful distinction. Then this would just be leaving you, without the extra cruelty of public humiliation."

I smile. "It's all getting a little too real for you?" I ask know-ingly. Because it's a little too real for me in this store.

"Yeah. As real as a reality show can be. I guess being engaged, even wearing a ring, wasn't as big a deal as seeing the dress. All the dresses."

"Let's grab one and then we can get out of here and to the inn." I reach out and grab the closest dress to me.

"Ahh. About that." Naomi looks at the dress in my extended hand, her lips curling in disgust.

"What?" I look at it but can't see what would make her have that reaction. It's poofy and white and I think that means it checks all the boxes. Are there other boxes I don't know about?

"I have to wear this, I assume. On television."

"It's not going to be your real wedding dress."

"No. But it will be on TV, making it more real, and long-last-ing, than any other dress I'll ever wear. Including my actual wedding dress."

"Right." This may be beyond my ability to care about, since I've just got black pants and a white shirt to worry about. "You should pick one you want." I replace the offensive (not that I know why it's offensive) dress back on the rack.

"Well, if you insist." She looks gleeful and attacks the racks with vigor. She piles dresses in her arms, until her face is obscured by the mountain of white cloth growing in her arms.

"Let me help." I still want to make it up to her for the shitty comment this morning. I hold my arms out to her, and she dumps the entire pile in my arms, freeing hers for more dresses.

"I want to support you finding a dress you like. But I also want to sleep in a bed tonight." As if the universe is on my side, the door to the shop opens, and another team comes in.

Naomi looks too, and grudgingly puts the top two dresses in my pile away. "I think they would have made me look lumpy anyway."

The words make me look at her reflexively, even though I

don't need the visual reminder since I'm not likely to forget her body. Ever. People don't just forget one of the most stunning sights in their lives.

"I sincerely doubt the dresses have the ability to change reality." But I'm glad the pile got smaller.

"Let me try these on." Naomi ignores the compliment; the only sign she heard me is the slight red in her cheeks. So I also ignore the compliment. Because we still have time constraints.

We walk to the back of the shop, where a helpful employee (or cast member cleverly disguised) opens the door for Naomi, who grabs half the dresses and disappears with that crew member behind the door to change. The rest of the crew set up next to me, to take turns filming the closed door and me sitting down.

This must be the parts of the show that get cut later in the process. But I smile so they don't have unflattering footage of me to use out of context later.

After a while of waiting, the only sounds being me sipping champagne and the urgent whispers from the other team that wandered in, I start to get bored. "Are you going to come out and show me any of these dresses?" Seeing her in anything, really, is better than staring at the door and wondering which state of undress she's in.

"No. It's bad luck for the groom to see a bride in her wedding dress," she yells back, sounding a little out of breath. What is she doing in there?

"But we're not actually engaged."

"We're partners. It could be bad luck for the partnership for you to see me in the dress."

"Fine," I say, exasperated. "But can you at least describe them to me? That should be entertaining and not offend the luck gods."

"Well, this one is white. More of an eggshell, if we're being precise."

"Precision is very important in these matters."

"Ha! The more pretensions you try to sound, the more you

sound like you're doing an English accent. Coincidence? I think not."

"I've no idea what you're on about," I respond, in what I think is the height of posh English people talk. "And that can't help win over Brits and their votes, calling them pretentious."

For the next fifteen minutes, I get helpful updates on the dress situation, like:

"This one has lace. Just on the top, though."

"This one has lace everywhere."

"This one has layers of lace. Multiple kinds."

"Oooh, this one has no lace. Rebel."

To which I reply, "Get the one with lace."

Finally, Naomi comes out of the dressing room. Not in a wedding dress, which is kind of disappointing after how invested I got in the descriptions.

"How much should we spend on it, do you think?" Naomi asks.

"I have no idea what a shilling is or its purchasing power, so I say let the employee take what she needs and we'll pray we have enough. We don't have time to price everything then go back to every shop and buy."

Naomi follows the employee to sort out the payment, making me stay behind so I don't see the dress. She returns with nothing in her hands, and I give her a questioning look.

"It's being delivered to our carriage."

"Then onward." We leave the team in the store, Jessica taking longer to find a dress she likes than Naomi while Will gets more frustrated.

We go to the next store, which carries non-wedding women's clothes. She doesn't try anything on this time, saying she wants to make up time and that the sizing and cut look the same as the wedding dresses. It's my turn at the next stop, and we find me a few outfits quickly.

Naomi is fun to shop with, even though this isn't an activity I usually spend too much time on. I even reach out and hold her hand. She refuses to look at me, but her fingers tighten around mine with no hesitation.

It starts to rain somewhere between the clothes stores and the bookstore, forcing us to huddle together. I hear a curse from Kelly, one of the few times she's spoken to us. Or around us, since I think it was directed to her camera.

I let go of Naomi's hand to take off my jacket and hold it over her head.

"I won't melt," she says, but doesn't make a move to get out from under the jacket. She does move my right arm across my own head so I'm under the jacket too. And then she snuggles in closer to me.

"I know you won't. But you would be slightly uncomfortable. And that's not necessary."

"I'm wearing so many clothes I don't think I'll even be damp after this. But thank you, anyway." And she stays under the jacket. We walk into the bookstore, me losing my excuse to be near her when she smiles in thanks and drops out from under the jacket umbrella.

"Chivalry says I have to." I smile despite my disappointment that she's not plastered against me anymore.

"Chivalry said you have to walk in front of a lady when going up the stairs and follow when going down. So maybe it's just a bunch of nonsensical, patriarchal rules." She lifts the book she opened, one on rules for gentlemen, and points to the rule she just read.

"If that's one you picked out at random, I'm afraid of what else is in that book."

"Probably best not to read any more of this." She shuts the books and replaces it on the table. "I'll probably go for some Austen. Classic." She wanders around the small shop, darting in and out of old wooden bookshelves, the smell of paper permeating the space.

"What should I get?" I keep my eyes on her as she moves around, and not on the perfectly acceptable books on the shelves that can't compete with her. Sorry, literature.

"Austen, too. Duh." She shoves a book at my chest that I grab on reflex.

"I've never read Austen."

She scoffs at me. "Of course not. Because society has told you that books by and about women are frivolous and lesser, especially if they're about relationships. As if so many people aren't spending time and money trying to find a partner, via friends, the internet, or random bar hookups. Either for forever or for a night. But if a woman writes about it, heaven forbid."

Naomi gets more animated the longer she talks, clearly a topic she's passionate about. Fire sparks from her brown eyes and her whole body gets into the subject, arms waving and feet shifting like she has too much energy that can't be contained.

"I'm excited to read this," I answer meekly, because she's right and I'm guilty of not reading many books by or about women. In my possible defense, I don't have time to read at all. But I don't think she'd be receptive to that defense, the way she loves books.

"Are you one of those people?" She opens a book and skims it as she asks me the question.

"One of who people?" I ask to clarify before I shoot myself in the foot and admit to things she hasn't asked about. Amateur mistake.

"The people who are trying to find a partner, via friends, the internet or random bar hookups?" She still doesn't look at me, so I can't tell how she feels about the question, not with her neutral tone. I don't know if she's eager for the answer or if she just asked to fill the time.

"I guess? Maybe not actively. It's hard to be dedicated to the search when I'm busy at work. But I'm open to meeting someone if it did happen organically. What about you?"

"Kind of the same. It's been a lot of hours at the office, plus lots of odd hours in evenings and on weekends working events for clients, meaning I only meet clients and people associated with them. But I do want to date someone."

Is Naomi hinting that she would be open to dating me? Is that why she brought it up? Do I want to date her? Obviously, she's beautiful, intelligent, and so snarky it hurts. But do I want to take the risk? It would be against the recommendation of any HR manager, even though she isn't the one I work for.

It's not that I think she would be petty about anything. I don't think she'd go to Harrison after an argument over who should have done the dishes, but if she were to get upset at me and Harrison saw it, of course he would want to make it better. Which would mean punishing me.

And it's not like I'm planning to fuck up, but even the strongest relationships have their tough moments. Knowing my job is on the line every time I interact with my girlfriend would be unnecessarily stressful on the relationship and my job.

All valid points telling me I should back away from whatever this is. It was spectacular last night, and she's amazing, but it's a lot to risk. More than the average broken heart or broken phone, from one particularly vengeful ex-girlfriend who didn't like the time I spent working.

"Ready to finish up this shopping trip?" I change the subject. Because I don't want to say that I'm backing away out loud, or that we should put the breaks on whatever this is. I want to spend time around her, trying to keep a distance while still getting to soak up her sunshine until I have to go back inside.

CHAPTER 28

NAOMI

Why is this man so frustrating? On paper, Nate's the worst possible partner for me. But here in this fantasy world, it *is* working. But this is going to be over soon, and then we'll both be back in the real world where Dad dominates everything. Like he always does.

My whole reason for moving away, I have to remind myself yet again.

I can be nice to Nate. I can be Nate's partner. Maybe I'll even have another go at Nate, if we're off camera at any point. But I'm going to command myself to stop wishing for a future with him. Immediately.

It's not exactly the best strategy to command myself to stop feeling things, as it hasn't really worked in the past, but maybe this time will be different. I'm very motivated this time.

"Yeah. Let's go," I say.

I take the list back out as we leave the bookstore, making sure we got everything on it. "We still need toiletries and the rings, and then we're done." The rain falls on the list, smearing the text.

"There are still teams out shopping, so we should be good on time."

"Yeah." We duck into what looks like a general store and they have everything else we need.

I get a little wary when we try on rings, trying very hard not to get affected by the sight of a ring on my finger.

Especially when I find the perfect one. It has a large center stone and tiny stones around it, looking like a flower. There are even little leaf imprints on the band right next to the main setting. I love things that look like flowers but aren't, because flowers die, but this flower never will. It's exactly what I want to wear on my finger for the rest of my life.

I clear my throat. "This is fine." An understatement, but I don't want to dwell on how perfect I think it is on my finger. I take if off quickly and try not to imagine the time when Nate's going to put this on me.

Because I like that thought too much.

I quickly move on the toiletries so I don't stare too long at Nate trying a wedding ring on. "Success!" I say, holding up random soaps and brushes like a prize belt. We walk to the counter and I slap it all on the table, already imagining how good the bed is going to feel tonight.

"You don't have enough money for this," the shop employee says, pissing on my parade.

"Excuse me?" Nate says.

"It's four shillings. You need five more pence," the employee says.

"Okay, I don't know what that means." I turn to Nate. "Were we not budgeting?"

"No. I was busy finding the shops and general directing."

"I was checking the list. Sometimes twice." I hold up the paper as evidence.

"Someone should have found out the value of this money before we started spending it."

"Hindsight. What do we do now?" I ask Aiko.

"Debtors." Aiko shakes her head in disappointment. "We're going to send you to debtor's prison."

"*Prison?* For five pence? Doesn't that seem excessive? Cruel and unusual and all that?" Not that I know how much that is. Could be a million dollars, although for that price I hope the soap is made out of a giant diamond, however uncomfortable that would be to use on my soft bits.

"Them's the rules in this universe we made up, loosely based on history," Aiko says. "Come on, criminals. We've got jail all set up for you over by the teashop."

"By a teashop?" I ask.

"They need to go somewhere. And this is England; there's a teashop on every corner." Aiko walks us back to the teashop.

"What, no cuffs?" I ask on the way, still salty about being sent to jail.

"Nah. You lot look trustworthy. Plus you have no phones or money. So I think we're good."

"Excessively rude."

We get to the teashop and Aiko walks us past the entrance and then right at the next intersection. She leads us to another anonymously cute stone cottage building. When we walk inside, however, the adorableness ends.

Abruptly.

Because the inside of the cottage has been transformed into a prison. The main room is divided into two cells with metal bars, with two cots in each cell. The bright, floral wallpaper of the cottage clash with the austere furnishing, because this is probably a holiday home when it isn't rented out by sadistic reality TV producers. The windows are boarded up, so we don't accidentally forget we're in a jail being punished in a very serious matter.

Over five pence. I genuinely have no idea how much that was worth in the Regency time period, but if that is anything close to five pence now, or even fifty pounds with inflation, this seems like a waste of resources.

Before we're shuffled into the cells, Lewis walks into the room, followed by Jessica and Will and their producers.

"Are you criminals, too?" I ask.

"Apparently it's a crime to be poor," Jessica says. Truth, lady. Then and now.

"Attention, debtors," Lewis says. "You are here because you couldn't complete the challenge with the money you had. We're putting you in debtor's prison for the duration of the night as punishment, while the rest of the group is going to the inn down the road. Tomorrow, you'll all leave at the same time, your sentence served. For tonight, you'll get a simple meal and then tomorrow, you'll be sent off with the items you bought. All teams will get some extra clothes thrown in beyond what you all bought, from the charity of the local parish vicar who heard about your plight and wanted to donate."

More like they don't want us to wear the same clothes for the rest of the show. I'm catching on to these producers' shady ways in search of aesthetics and drama.

"Let's have Naomi and Nate in this cell." He indicates the one on the right. "And Jessica and Will, you can take this one."

We move where we're told and I take a look at my new home for the night.

"This is cozy." Nate looks around the small space. "And co-ed."

"Any chance to film more couple drama, I guess."

"Double the couple drama this time," Jessica says from next door, proving that physics is still operating as it should and sound can pass through the bars that separate us.

Although not exactly groundbreaking information, it does bring home the fact that there won't be any hanky-panky tonight. I'm surprised at the intensity of my disappointment, considering how ambivalent I was about the man for most of today. But there's nothing ambivalent about how sharp the feeling of sadness is.

"We'll serve dinner in a bit and whenever you want to use the bathroom, just let us know and a producer will escort you. And while you're in here repenting or rehabilitating, or whatever debtor's prison was supposed to do, feel free to drink as much as you want." Aiko slides a bottle through each of our cells.

Ah. Our producers are consistent, if nothing else. But I am here with no TV, no books, and no social media. I take the bottle and offered glasses, pouring the wine out. I hand one to Nate and offer a cheers, and then one to our cellmates when I see they've wasted no time either.

"How did the rest of the teams avoid this fate?" I ask.

"Hannah and Sarah made Amir and George take time to look at all the shops and ask a shopkeeper about prices before buying anything. I saw them and thought they would be last for sure. Joke's on us," Jessica says.

"What do we do now?" Will asks.

"Sit in silence? Think about much-needed prison reform? Drink ourselves into passing out?" Nate says.

"Those are our only options, aren't they?" I say, a little hysterical.

"You could play a drinking game. Never Have I Ever or Truth or Dare," Aiko helpfully says, cameras rolling behind her.

I give in with exasperation. "Might as well."

"Great, but can one of you suggest it so we can get it on camera?" Aiko asks.

"Drinking game, anyone?" Will asks. I hope they can edit out the sarcasm, because it's coming through crystal clear on this side of the cameras.

"Sure. That sounds like a fantastic idea you just had," I say, also not able to keep the sarcasm out of my voice.

"You guys are great, really." Oh, now Aiko's trying sarcasm out. This must be the time in shooting when everyone cracks under the pressure.

"Never Have I Ever, anyone?" Jessica asks, with no sarcasm, but a little too much laughter in her voice.

"Let's do it." Nate is the only one of us who sounds normal. Who knew he would have the best acting skills out of all of us? Must be all his years in business, keeping a straight face while the people he worked around made even more outlandish demands. Like Dad loves to do.

"I'll go first then. Never have I ever had a threesome." Will ups the stakes immediately, and then drinks, showing he has done it and wants to know who else has. He doesn't get any juicy secrets for his sacrifice, since none of us drink.

"I'll go next. Never have I ever peed in public. Like not in a toilet." Jessica brings us back down to a different level of playing, a non-sexual one.

Nate and Will drink, and Jessica laughs. "That always gets the boys going."

"They deserve the drink. After some of the bathroom lines I've waited in, I wish I could have just gone in an alley. I'll go next. Never have I ever gone skinny-dipping," I say the first thing that pops in my head, even though I'm dragging us a little closer back to the sexual topics.

I don't even see if our cellmates drink because Nate takes a sip. "Nathaniel Williams! As I live and breathe!" I put my hand over my heart.

A light dusting of red appears on his cheeks. "I was young. It was a hot night and there was a pool but we didn't have bathing suits. Things happen."

"But didn't you have a merger to complete?"

"It was the time before mergers in my life."

"Sounds like you were a wild guy before the mergers took over."

"Not that wild."

"I've never been naked in public. So you're wilder than me."

"My turn." Nate changes the subject. "Never have I ever..." He pauses and I wonder if he's going to keep the game saucy or go back to being sensible Nate. I would put my money on sensible

Nate, youthful, naked, indiscretions notwithstanding. He'll probably say something like never stealing pens from work or never working less than a fifty-hour week.

"Never have I ever lived in England." He takes a safe route and makes us all drink in the process.

"Dick," Will says good-naturedly, raising his glass to Nate for a distanced cheers. "Never have I ever had sex in public." And then he drinks.

"The point of this game is to get others to drink and to not drink yourself," Jessica says, watching her partner with wariness.

"Where's the fun in that?" Will's confusion at the prospect of not drinking is probably very genuine.

Nate takes a drink as I do too. "You?" I ask.

"You?" he responds.

"Strict parents. Creepy, top-of-the-line security systems. Had to make it work," I say. "Now you," I demand.

"Not as strict parents, but they were a little *too* supportive of budding sexuality. And they worked from home a lot. Had to also make it work."

Hidden depths to this man. Frisky, wild, top-button-undone depths. Maybe Dad should check the company pen supply after all.

We keep playing, getting another bottle of wine from our jailer Aiko. I somehow don't think this is exactly what debtor's prison was like back in the day, but I can't complain since I'm also positive this is an upgrade.

After a few hours and a very plain chicken dinner, although who knows if that's punishment or just English cuisine, Aiko dims the lights in the cottage/ jail. "Lights out, prisoners." Then she laughs. "Just kidding. Do what you want. We'll leave some wine and someone will be on call if anyone needs the bathroom. We also have simple nightclothes if you want to change for bed." She slides the clothes through the bars and then leaves the room, giving us the illusion of privacy.

"Okay, I'm off to bed." Because again, and I don't mean to jinx myself even though that's exactly what I'm probably doing, who knows what this show is going to throw at us tomorrow.

"I'm out too," Nate says

"We'll try to keep it quiet." Will opens a new bottle.

"Sure." I won't hold my breath until that happens. I will go change into this nightgown that looks like it was made out of a burlap sack.

And hope tomorrow brings boring, uneventful calm. But I'm not holding my breath for that either.

CHAPTER 29

NATE

After changing into a scratchy and uncomfortable nightgown, I hope for the millionth time that they don't have cameras where we sleep. It's bad enough that Naomi is going to see this. Because this cut can't be flattering. Like Scrooge in *A Christmas Carol*. And I'll probably get tangled up in it at night.

"Ready for bed?" Naomi asks as she gets under the blanket on the cot. Then she turns around. "Oh wow. We match." She laughs at me.

"I would prefer us matching in anything else but this." I extend my arms out, the excess material hanging off my arms and making me look like a wizard. But one who can't afford the flashy silk, like Mickey in *Fantasia*.

"Got it. I will put in the order for matching Santa onesies for Christmas."

"You think that's supposed to scare me, but a soft, comfortable onesie sounds great right now." I sit down on my cot and itch my arms where the material chafes. And my cot is too far away from Naomi's. Why are they adding beds now, when we had one this whole time? I guess it's the punishment.

Especially now that we got past my unfortunate choice of words this morning, I want more. When she rightfully started acting cold, I got a taste of life without Naomi, and I hated it. I don't want to stay away from her when we're this close, and it's exhausting to go against what every part of me wants more than anything. I want to keep getting to know her, keep enjoying being around her. Keep avoiding any conversation about the future.

And then maybe later, we can decide if we want to unleash the can of worms that would be a real relationship, not a fake engagement on a reality show. Once we know this is something we both want, and that it would be worth the complications that would come with it.

But these cots, and all the distance between them, aren't the best way to use the rapidly diminishing time we have together. And since I'm under the influence of many glasses of cheap red wine and exhausted from all these activities making my will weaker than usual, I pull my cot over to hers, until it's right against hers.

"In case you get cold, I'm here." I answer her unasked question when she looks at me with raised eyebrows. "It's chilly for the summer."

"Thank you for that offer. But this burlap sack has done its job keeping potatoes warm in its past life. I should be okay."

"Then I'll stay on my cot. But the offer stands if this historic cottage doesn't have the best insulation." I pat the side of the cot touching hers, hoping she decides to roll over and right onto mine.

"Thank you."

I settle into the hard cot in my itchy nightclothes and wish I could go back to this morning. Waking up in a plush bed, my arms surrounding Naomi. I would stop myself from cursing, instead kissing her and then we could have had sex again.

Just like that, I'm grateful for the heavy, uncomfortable material on top of my dick. Because the erection that's springing up thinking about last night and what could have happened this morning would be really embarrassing to see on TV later.

I turn to the side anyway. Just in case.

THE SENSATION of itchiness on my face wakes me up. I try to deal with it, but my hand is blocked by something warm and solid. And soft.

I open my eyes to find that I'm grabbing Naomi's breast again. I move my hand quickly and take in my position. At some point in the night, one of us moved on to the other's cot, I started spooning her, and she accepted it. The cause of my itchiness is Naomi's cloth-covered shoulder, which my face is snuggling despite the discomfort.

My other arm, the one that was not copping a feel, is under Naomi's head, and I slowly remove it while willing my morning wood away.

Luckily, I'm the only one awake. Will and Jessica are asleep on their respective cots, and I can't see any producers trying to get our embarrassment in high definition.

The movement wakes Naomi up, and I slip the rest of my arm out quicker, without any regard for stealth now that she's already awake.

"Morning," I say, hand tucked under my side innocently, like it isn't warm from her body heat.

"Morning." She turns her head to take in the same scene I just saw.

"Still in jail. And on this reality show," I say.

"Hmm. For a second I thought this all might have been a very strange dream."

"Hopefully not a nightmare." She's lying next to me; I might have to take that personally.

Naomi pauses, as if that wasn't (mostly) a joke and was a real question. "No," she says finally after consideration. "Not a nightmare."

It's a testament to this how show is affecting me that I get excited over that small bit of praise, as if she's given me a pot of gold *and* the rainbow.

"Are you ready for freeeedom?" Aiko sings as she walks back into the former living room/ current jail.

"Yes," we say, in equal states of excitement. Jessica and Will groan from their cell, apparently just woken up by Aiko's entrance.

"Don't trample me when I let you out." Aiko unlocks us first with a wink, perk of her being our producer, and then frees the couple next to us.

"Now that you're free, we've got breakfast in the dining room, and when the groups at the inn are done eating, we'll send you all off."

Aiko leads us into a dining room I hadn't seen earlier, and it's a big change from the meager furnishings in our cells. We take seats at the table, the food already laid out for us. The crew brings us fresh clothes that we all take turns changing into. To my disappointment, Naomi and Sarah help each other with their complicated dresses.

After her trip to the bathroom, Naomi sits next to me in another dress that boosts up her breasts and cinches her waist. I do feel bad that I find her so attractive in what I know causes her pain, but my penis has too much blood in it and there's no room for empathy right now.

"Well, I feel a little better. The corset is preferable to the terrible cloth from last night. At least for now."

"I never thought I'd hear that," I say. "But you do look great it in, even if I do feel appropriately bad about the pain it causes you."

"Don't feel bad for enjoying it. I certainly don't have the high ground; I'm looking forward to you getting back in your tight pants." Naomi rests her head on her hands and looks at me with mischief.

I have a moment when I can ignore what she said, which is the safe, responsible option. Or I can engage with her in the flirting that I started, frankly. While my brain is thinking this out, making a pros and cons list, my mouth forms words. "Just my tight pants? My chest is jealous. It even did some push-ups for you this morning."

Really, man? Push-ups for her? My chest has emotions now? Its own backstory? But it's already out there, and I can't take it back, so I just smile my way through it.

Naomi chokes on her eggs and beans. I wince because I'm still not convinced that's a good combination, even though she got a hardy helping of both, looking at me with judgement when I settled for a bean-less breakfast.

After she gets some water in her, she segues into a laugh. That's good. At least she can go out on a happy note, if she's still in danger of choking. And I'm the one who made her laugh. My chest, subject of so much recent attention, puffs up in pride.

"Nathaniel Williams, any time your chest needs some appreciation, you bring him to me, and I'll make sure he feels good about himself." She dips her eyes to said chest, which flexes before I can stop it.

Not a bright body part, since she can't see anything under the thick dressing gown I'm in.

"Noted." I catch sight of Will coming out of the bathroom. "I'll be right back."

When I lock myself in the bathroom, I take a moment to breathe in the small space. Then I give myself a pep talk in the mirror.

"What are you doing? Flirting? Like a teenage boy with his first crush? Get some self-respect."

"Yes, I know she's very beautiful. But you can still have some self-respect," I tell my reflection, which didn't actually talk back to me.

"Okay, just a little respect, buddy. We'll settle for not throwing ourselves at her."

Footsteps sound outside, and I silently tell myself that getting caught talking to myself will not help me in my quest for self-respect.

I finish up changing, glad to be out of the uncomfortable clothes into slightly more comfortable clothes. Back at the dining table, I get more food in case the show decides to withhold our next meal until we do gymnastics through rings on fire in costume.

I never could do a cartwheel.

"Hi, Fred. We've missed you," Naomi says as she gets back into our carriage. The most stable home we've had in the past few days.

"Hiya. I heard you were in prison last night, so I'll take that with a grain of salt." He winks at her.

"Did you get to sleep in the inn?" Naomi asks.

"It was shit," Fred says, voice a little uneven.

"Lies. But thank you, anyway." Naomi opens our map. "It looks like we're headed to…" She pauses, and then points to it and looks at me.

I look blankly back at her. "What's up?"

"We're going here." She looks at me expectantly, picking up her finger and pointing to the mark on the map a few times.

"She wants you to pronounce it because she's afraid of being made fun of by an entire nation. Again," Aiko helpfully says when I don't get it.

"Ah. We're going to Burnley. That wasn't even hard."

"I never know with these names. Do you know Cholmondeley is pronounced Chomly? Why are there so many extra letters if you have no intention of pronouncing them? It's wasteful."

"To separate the Yanks from the rest of us," Aiko says.

Naomi sniffs. "I thought you tea drinkers had manners."

"No. We just use a pleasant tone and big words when we say mean things, so you Americans get confused."

Naomi sniffs. "Left up ahead, please," she says instead of responding to the bait.

"Another long trip today?" I ask. Not because I need to know. I could just look over her shoulder and see how far we have to go. But I like talking to Naomi.

"Always," Naomi says. "But since every time we stop, we get tortured, I think I'll enjoy the down time in the carriage for as long as possible."

"This is why you're the thinker in this partnership."

"Take the second exit on the next roundabout, please," Naomi yells to Fred out of the carriage window.

"What should we do today?" I say after a few minutes of silence.

"Didn't we buy books?"

"Yes. They were the last thing you bought before you descended into destitution," Aiko says, rubbing salt into that wound. "They should be in your bags."

"If we each read our books to ourselves, we'll be finished in half the time, but if we read to each other out loud, it'll take twice as long," I suggest, more as an excuse to keep talking to her than any real concern about boredom.

"Can't we just switch books when we're done with ours? Then it'll also last longer."

She's too smart for my own good. "Yes. But that's slightly less entertaining."

She opens her book. "Fine. We can do your way. I'll go first. 'It is a truth, universally acknowledged…'"

CHAPTER 30

NAOMI

"*I* can't read anymore." My voice is getting scratchy after the hour I've been going at this.

"I can take over," Nate says.

"Are you even paying attention to what's happening? Your eyelids are drooping and I think I heard a pre-snore."

"I was resting my eyes. But I'm still awake and aware of what's going on." He sits up from his position stooped on my shoulder and stretches in the small space.

"Okay. Your turn then." I push the book into his chest, which he accepts.

"What do you think our torture will be today?"

"I resent that you keep implying there will be torture. We just want you to have fun," Aiko says, compelled to break the rules since we're impugning her character.

"What character building/team building activity do you think they'll subject us to today for the entertainment of the masses?" Nate asks.

"Maybe sell flowers to a curmudgeonly old professor who takes us in and teaches us elocution and pervs on us, but still can't be nice to us? Beyond that, I'm not sure what else Regency people did."

"I think *Pygmalion* is a little later than the Regency." Nate impresses everyone in this carriage (or at the very least, me), with his knowledge of literature. Must be the parental professor influence there.

"But do they know that?" I give a meaningful look at Aiko and Kelly.

"Disrespectful cast. I'm doing shows with animals from now on, exclusively. Penguins, preferably," Aiko whispers to Kelly.

"You'd miss us," I say.

"Maybe we have to invade another country and take all their resources while employing racism to keep the local populace down," Nate says.

"Ooooh, Nate coming hard with the truth." I put my hand on my mouth and look back and forth between Nate and all the British people in the carriage, seeing how they'll react.

"Don't look at me. My parents came here after the height of all that. And I'm leaving this in the final cut of the show," Aiko says.

"I think I would have a hard time with instituting the racism. What with my Indian family probably jumping out of nowhere to give me a chapere for the disrespect." I pantomime a slap so the non-Punjabi speakers understand what my family would do to me. "And it just being flat out wrong to do a racism."

"I don't think my Scottish ancestors would be too enthused about it either, so we may have to lose that challenge," Nate says.

"It's more important to take the stand. I'm glad we're in agreement."

"Read your books," Aiko says. "Or better yet, have a cuddle or get in a fight or do something equally interesting."

Nate picks up the book quickly and starts reading where I left off.

"WE ARE at our destination for the night," Aiko says when I tell Fred to stop in front of the building indicated on the map.

"That's it? We're done for the day?" I ask, wary and distrustful.

For good reason, because Aiko says, "No. We're going to have a group dinner and some friendly competition once everyone is here. So please enjoy the time to relax before you have to get ready for the night."

"Oh, joy." Nate helps me out of the carriage.

"All the joy," I say.

I look up at the building we're staying in for the night, a big house surrounded by a bigger, wild countryside with trees as far as I can see. I never thought I would get sick of all the beautiful, quaint, stone buildings, but after this mad rush through England, I'm more excited about what's inside (a warm shower, food, the ability to stand) than the outside. Even though there's a perfect amount of bright multicolored flowers and emerald ivy growing up this inn, along with a vintage sign making it a particularly cute example of the genre.

We check in without any mishaps, knowing now to lie through our teeth about our marital status to get a room for the night. But every time I say we're married, I see us as a couple a little more, and it makes my heart skip to think we're getting closer to Gretna Green, and closer to the end of the show.

And then we won't be pretending to be together anymore. We won't even be in the same country anymore.

"What should we do with our limited free time?" Nate asks when we get in our space, starting the fireplace in the corner of the room. The room with one bed. Which has not lost its ability to annoy me, unlike the fading luster of the stone building. This time it's worse, because I know I won't be able to resist him.

"You know, I was thinking of popping across the channel for

some macarons. Or maybe going on over to Rome for some gelato on a suspiciously cheap flight." I collapse on the bed to get my shoes off.

However, I forgot that I'm wearing a corset, so I can't even bend to reach my knees from this seated position, much less my feet. I drop my arms to the side and sit there, deflated emotionally but physically very rigid because of said corset.

"Those plans sound fun, but I think you've probably just got time for a shower. And maybe a very efficient nap," Nate says, bending down in front of me and lifting my foot to rest on his knee.

"You don't have to…" I start, but then I stop, because really, if he doesn't, it's not happening.

"It's fine. If I don't help you, you'll be stuck here the entire time and your attempts to get free would just make me sad." He undoes my shoe ties and slips one off, then goes to work on the other.

"Maybe," I half concede. Other words are beyond me, since the light from the fireplace is flickering over his hair and skin, making him glow like he's being fucking blessed by the heavens. Like those medieval paintings where angels send down rays of light on one figure, so the peasants looking on, both those in the painting and those of us outside it, know who's important. I'll hear trumpets soon, tooting out an ode to his wonderfulness.

I don't need any of it, universe. I get it. He's a catch. A catch any women would be lucky to have. Even knowing I'd have to sacrifice any semblance of freedom to have him, he's still tempting. Tempting enough to throw away the last six years of my life, making running to London entirely pointless.

"Corset time." He stands up gracefully, an impressive feat with his large body.

"Right." I stand, turning around to let him help with the outer dress. He undoes the ties at the back and slides it down my body until it pools at my feet.

Then his hands brush against me as he loosens the corset. I don't know how people with lady's maids weren't constantly horny, because being so carefully undressed is one of the most erotic experiences I've had.

Maybe they were. I don't know what people got up to back then. But if someone had taught me that in school, I think I would have remembered. Or maybe lady's maids didn't pack quite the same punch as Nate does.

The corset falls away and this time I don't do anything to stop it. Neither does Nate. Instead I turn and he doesn't move back. Before I can overthink it and overanalyze it to death, I kiss him.

Nate kisses me back, his arms getting tangled in my thin, wispy chemise. I rip his coat off as well as I can since half of it is trapped between us and he can't move his arms. Then I get frustrated, a small whine escaping into his mouth as my hands change course and untuck his shirt at the back.

I will take this defined, muscular back, if I can't have this defined, muscular chest.

Nate lifts me up onto the bed, my legs getting caught in the chemise and my mouth making another sound of frustration when I can't get as close to him as I want. Nate growls in response, ripping his mouth away to finish the job of undressing me. My hands are free as well now and reach for his clothes. He thrusts his erection against me, each movement scrunching my chemise up a little at a time.

Someone knocks on the door and we freeze, hands gripping each other's clothing. His dick is less discerning, the only thing that's moving as it throbs against me.

"Hullo," Aiko says from the other side of the door. "Hope I'm not interrupting."

The way she says that makes us both look at each other in horror. She sounds like she knows that she's interrupting. Was she watching this from some creepy control room somewhere?

Our hands fly away from each other like our clothes are on fire but we don't move apart.

"Everyone has arrived early, so we're planning to do the group dinner in twenty minutes. Please change into some formalwear and meet us in the drawing room."

"Right. We'll be there," Nate answers for the both of us, voice low and rumbly. A voice that I can feel the vibrations of with him pressed against me.

"I'll just wait outside the door to get some shots of you leaving and to show you where the drawing room is," Aiko says.

"Great," Nate says through gritted teeth. More gracious than I can manage, since I'm ramming the back of my head into the wooden bedpost and mouthing the word *fuck* over and over again.

"Do you think we still have time?" I ask when I'm done silently yelling fuck, going through every derivative I can think of.

"Probably not," Nate says. "And she'll be out there, listening."

"Right." I put my hands on his shoulders for one last squeeze before I move away.

"Do you need help getting dressed again?" Nate asks.

"Probably." Right now, looking at Nate's shirt all askew, I regret signing up for this show. But, to be fair to this show, if it wasn't for them then there wouldn't have been anything to interrupt. So I guess I only half regret this idea.

The sensation of Nate's hands dressing me is bittersweet; I love the feel of them but know I can't do anything about it for at least too many hours. And then when he's done with his task, I'm back in my multi-layered prison.

"How many chimneys do you think they have in here, just in case we have to sweep them?" Nate asks when he extends his arm to escort me to dinner.

"Too many. At least these aren't my clothes. In case I have to crawl around in soot."

"I know you don't want to hear about the man, but I can't not point out that Harrison would have a heart attack if he saw you sweeping chimneys."

The sound of my dad's name from his lips doesn't send me into a rage anymore. It's just two people who are semi-close, talking about family. I don't know if that means I'm growing as a person or starting to trust Nate to not be Dad's tattletale.

Either way, I like the easy way we're interacting now. I'm even regretting all the time we missed where we could have had this all along. But then again, I doubt this chill feeling will last once the show ends and Nate leaves, or when I visit and we get in the same room as Dad. It's a little different here in the past, hundreds of years before Dad is even born.

Who would probably be happy if I had something to tie me to New York. And then he would sneak in with that cushy job offer, after he lets me get bored with unemployment and demoralized by the job market. And I would take it, because I'm afraid that deep down, I am that spoiled princess who lets her dad and then her husband take care of her.

I really don't want to be that girl.

Mom, on the other hand, will just be happy I found someone. She doesn't bother me about moving to London, aside from complaining it's too far and she doesn't see me enough, but she does think being in a relationship is the optimal state. On that front, she is the stereotype of a Desi parent.

Not that I'm in a relationship with Nate! We would have to have a discussion for that to be true, and we definitely haven't talked about that. By design.

Even aside from my family, Nate's a big-shot executive and I'm barely out of being an intern. I would be expected to get up and leave, moving back to New York so he can have his job. His career. And all the contacts I've made would be useless.

Which is why I'm going to keep avoiding any relationship conversations, please and thank you. Until Nate gets on a plane.

Then I'm going to get a new phone and a new phone number so I won't have Nate's number and he won't have mine.

At any rate, that's a problem for the future. Now I just have to worry about what this show is going to do to us tonight.

CHAPTER 31

NATE

Damn this show. Damn them for throwing me in close quarters with Naomi. Damn them for putting me in impossibly tight pants that don't hide an erection. Then damn them for interrupting my time with Naomi.

Yes, that is damning them for both putting me in contact with her *and* for interrupting that time. Damn them for taking logic from me!

Or maybe the last is the effect Naomi has on me. Not the best for my mental state, even though my reckless side likes it. Like cocaine, probably. I wouldn't know because when my roommate offered me some in business school I said no, because I'm a nerd who can't stop thinking about consequences.

Even though right now, Naomi is doing a good job making me ignore potential consequences. Making me want to ignore them.

Aiko, a professional, doesn't let on that she knows what happened in the room. She does have a knowing smile, but it's no different than her general, I-like-to-make-you-suffer smile. It's not a particularly gleeful, victorious one that would show she's got juicy material for the show. She leads us along the labyrinth of hallways in the old house.

Finally, she walks through a door and tells us to wait as she closes the door behind her.

"Okay. The cameras are rolling and you can open the doors and come through. Maybe laugh like Naomi said something funny and also like you two are infatuated with each other."

"Enhanced reality," Naomi says, smiling and shrugging.

"It'll look better on the screen." I nod, now an expert in reality show production. "No one wants to see a boring room entrance."

"Heaven forbid there's a boring room entrance."

"Is there a specific way you want us to walk through the room? A specific speed you need us to go?" I joke to cover my embarrassment at how I'm already infatuated with Naomi and don't need to fake anything on that front.

"Slow enough for the camera to capture it but not so slow that it looks unnatural, or like you're trying to do *Reservoir Dogs*. Try to glide," Aiko says, taking the joke seriously.

Great. Even when I try to tell a joke no one believes me. Further proof I'm too stodgy for Naomi.

"But will you add some epic music to the entrance in post?" Naomi asks. She's much better at this joke business.

But Aiko defeats her as well. "Probably something orchestral. It'll be great. Now stop stalling, other couples are waiting to come down and enter."

Aiko opens the doors slowly with a partner, staying out of view to enhance the drama.

"Is this a glide?" I ask out of the corner of my mouth as we move.

"She's not yelling at us, so I'm going to go with my philosophy that if no one's yelling at me I'm a resounding success," Naomi whispers, keeping her debutante smile. Not that I know if she did the whole debutant thing. But considering her father…

As much as I hate to admit it, the drama of the doors opening before us like we're royalty is a nice feeling, making me feel more important than I actually am. And then when we get in the room, the royal sensation only increases. There's gilt on everything: the walls, the sculptures, the chairs, all glittering and winking at us with knowledge of what we're about to do. Like they know what it is, and how amusing it's going to be at our expense.

Aiko directs us to the table, and we watch the other groups go through the same drawn-out process to get inside, every one of us getting the Cinderella experience.

"I'm worried they haven't fed us a fake dinner yet," Naomi says, drinking the very real wine they did see fit to give us.

"That's a good point. What do you think they're going to make us do? Eat spiders?"

"I'm not doing it," Naomi declares imperiously. "I don't care if they put me back in debtor's prison or make me sleep in the carriage or walk naked through the English countryside the rest of the way to Scotland."

I choke on my own drink, my throat forgetting how to swallow mid-way through that sip at the image burrowing itself into my brain.

"I'll eat your spiders, if they let spiders transfer." Unless the penalty really is walking around naked. Then any chivalry I have would flee for the hills, leaving the douchebag that just wants to see her naked again, any way he can.

"Can we expand that to any insect or strong cheese or just anything I find distasteful?"

"Sure. I'll eat whatever you want."

Naomi rewards me with a smile. My chivalry, still here because there's no present opportunity for nakedness, swells in pride. Along with other, less chivalrous parts of me.

"I'm so glad to see you guys again. I was worried when you weren't at dinner last night," Hannah says when she sits down.

"We were in jail. We're hard now," Naomi says in the most princess voice I've ever heard from her.

So hard.

"I heard they had wine on demand at that jail," Amir says, his arm extended across Hannah's chair, looking very cozy.

"It was very cheap wine," Naomi says.

"That is not helping your argument in the way you think it is," I say.

"Hey, I'm harder than the man with the penthouse in Manhattan and the shoes that cost more than my rent," Naomi says.

"They go on your feet, Naomi. The feet you walk on all day. It's an investment in my health," I say with as much dignity as possible.

I don't think they're more than her rent, but I also don't want to start talking figures and find out if I'm close. London is so expensive, I don't see how I can be. I'll concede my shoes could be rent, especially if one has a roommate, in a less expensive market.

"Contestants." Lewis walks into the room with the most dramatic entrance out of all of us. "I've missed your beautiful faces."

"Missed harassing us, more like," I whisper to Naomi, mouth close to her ear.

Her shoulder brushes my mouth as she laughs silently, body moving up and down.

"Wait, I want to do a steal!" Sarah stands up, looking nervous to have all the attention on her.

"That's the spirit!" Lewis looks happy at the development. "We always have time for a steal. Come on up here, Sarah. Men, you come up too."

He waits for us all to get in position and for the crew to get the footage they need of us looking nervous.

I'm not faking my nervous look. Because I don't want to be stolen. I want to stay with Naomi. I don't like this feeling at all.

Lewis clears his throat when the crew gets enough footage of us. "Now, which of these men would you like to steal?"

CHAPTER 32

NAOMI

ell, I don't like this development. My heart is beating like the poor racehorses at the Kentucky Derby who have to run for a living, my palms are sweating like I'm a rich person who just got a call from the IRS, and I'm hanging on Sarah's words like she's about to tell me if I'm going to be drafted for war.

I'm uncomfortable, physically and emotionally uncomfortable, at the thought that she might pick Nate. It's just that we have things to do. Like oral. Just more sex in general. And I also want more of that grade-A cuddling Nate gives.

None of which can happen if he's stolen from me by this attractive nuisance.

Lewis makes Sarah draw out the tension by looking at each man in silent consideration while the crew films us all, and I find myself falling victim to his drama tactics, barely refraining from yelling, *"Get on with it!"* at them. This is my future they're talking about.

My future next few days, at least.

"I want to steal Will."

Oh, thank god. I breathe out deeply, still clutching the arms of my chair as my heart starts the process of returning to beating at a normal rate. I clap along with the rest of the group while the cameras catch each of our reactions.

"Will, here's your kidnapped clock. We'll check in with you tomorrow. In the meantime, enjoy getting to know each other," Lewis says.

Jessica rolls her eyes as she sits down next to George. Yeah, good luck to her. I scoot a little closer to Nate. This brought up a lot of feelings I wasn't prepared for, chiefly how much I don't want to be apart from Nate anymore.

"Now that the excitement has passed, it's time for more excitement," Lewis threatens us with a smile. "I bet you're all anxious about the events of the day, so we have a real treat for you today…savory *and* sweet." He laughs as his own joke, not realizing that none of us know what he means, so none of us can be in on the joke.

Lewis sees that and pushes on. "We're doing a full, real Regency dinner. With authentic recipes from the time period for you to enjoy." He looks at us expectantly. The look we've all come to know as the indicator that we need to emote or he'll keep pausing until we do to his satisfaction. Then they'll edit out the pause later.

So we cheer. I'm getting good at this fake excitement. I should try for an acting gig if PR doesn't work out. But then I wouldn't be allowed to have as much candy as I eat.

And that's a dealbreaker.

But I do wonder what's the big deal about this dinner. I don't think they ate spiders back then, so this should be better than what I was worried about. How bad could just regular food that rich people ate be?

"You'll each have to eat all the food you're served, which will be replaced with the next course as soon as both members of the team are finished with their plates. No sharing among partners; each person has to eat an entire meal. Then you'll leave tomorrow in the same order that you finish the food tonight. Unless any member of the team quits, then you get an even larger time penalty and won't leave until hours after the last team."

This shouldn't be a problem; I love eating. Especially during this show when they don't let me do it as often as I think they should.

"Let's get started." Crew members dressed in livery come in to serve us dishes as Lewis talks. "As England colonized, they brought back food they hadn't seen before. One of those new foods were turtles, which they made into a very expensive turtle soup. Also known as your first course," Lewis says.

I gasp and look at Nate in horror. Little turtles? We're going to eat them? Like that old turtle that was having adorable slow sex to repopulate his species or the ones who adorably poke out of their shells to eat some lettuce and then take the daintiest little bites? Those adorable turtles?

Well, now I know how they're going to torture us.

"Then we're going to keep bring dishes, until we get to twenty! We're going to serve you pigeon pie, fish, mutton, beef, jellies, custards, salads, cheeses, puddings, nuts, fruits, and ice cream. All historically accurate. Don't worry, the portions of each are small. But they will add up."

I exchange another look of horror with Nate. Pigeons? Also, twenty courses? Will the torture never end?

"This might violate the Geneva Conventions," I say to Nate, whimpering a little.

"I haven't read it in a second, but probably not."

"Well, if we're being honest. But I don't want to be honest, I want to not eat turtles or pigeons." I choose to ignore the amount of food I have to consume, to focus on the details of what that food will be. Because I don't think I'll be able to handle the thought of how much I'm about to eat.

"You eat other meat. What's really the difference? People eat all sorts of meat." Nate tries to help me get through as the servers uncover the dishes they placed in front of us when Lewis was talking.

"I'm used to the other meat."

"Those cows can be really cute too, you know. Mooing happily. Frolicking slowly with their little calves. Munching on grass. Emitting greenhouse gasses. And you tear them away from their families and put them between some buns."

"Fine. I'm a monster. And a hypocrite. But you won't make this any better."

"Let's just get through this and not think too much about the origin of the food."

I look at the uncovered plate in front of me. "They serve it in the shell. That seems cruel," I say. And there's no way to ignore what it is now.

"Maybe it's just using all parts of the animal. That's good. No waste."

I pick up a spoon and look around to see how everyone else is handling this. Everyone's reaction is pretty much the same: horror, resignation, and one interest (George, who I now think is a monster).

"We should start now," Nate says.

"Yeah." But there's no real need; everyone is just looking at the dish and no one has started eating.

"We don't even know how it'll taste. It could be fine," Nate says, more to himself than me. And he hasn't taken a sip yet either.

"Then taste it and tell me."

Nate looks at me and then takes the leap first, taking a tentative sip. "It's not bad. Just don't think of Crush from *Finding Nemo* when you eat."

"Great. Now that's all I can think about. Duuuuuude."

"Hmm. It's an interesting texture, like if beef were as chewy as calamari." He takes another big spoonful, warming to it.

I look around again and see everyone else starting to eat. I don't want to be the weak link in this relationship, so I dip my spoon in.

Well, he's right. Maybe I won't put this in the rotation regularly, but it's not too bad. I'm doing a lot of chewing right now, but at least one part of my body is getting a workout.

We finish that dish first, my natural competitiveness taking over.

"Pigeon now. As a New Yorker, it feels very wrong to eat this. I've seen what they eat," I say.

"I doubt they pick random pigeons off the street in some pigeon hunt on Fifth Avenue, so I think we'll be okay."

Nate takes a bite out of the pie first, his spoon breaking into the flaky crust to get some of the meat below. He raises it to his lips. Full, enticing lips that almost make me forget what we're doing.

"Hey, this tastes like chicken," Nate says as he digs in with relish.

"Sure, Jan." I take my own bite, more forward now that the turtles are behind us. "Actually, it does taste kind of like chicken."

"It *is* poultry," Nate says with a full mouth.

"We're going to win this," I say with an equally full mouth. Because Sarah is still very wary about the pigeon and is taking her time on the first bite. I shovel some more in as she considers the bite on the spoon in front of her.

"Wer gona bin so har." Conversation becomes increasingly difficult as Nate shoves more food in his mouth. Despite the picture he's presenting with his mouth full and a little piece of pigeon stuck to the corner of his mouth, he's adorable.

I reach over with one hand and flick the piece off, continuing to shovel food with the other one. Because this team wins, grossness aside. "Fr sure."

"Bring on the next course." Nate bangs his fork on the table. How quickly he's turned into the spoiled lord of their manor, in only a few days pretending to be a spoiled lord of the manor.

The crew keeps bringing food, while we get fuller and fuller. There's nothing as unique as the turtle soup and pigeon, but the sheer amount of food is getting to me.

"I can't eat anymore," I say, holding my fork as a barrier between me and the food at somewhere around the tenth dish.

Nate immediately puts down his utensils. "We can be done if you want. We'll take the penalty and it'll be fine. Much better than you feeling ill."

I know how much the man needs to win, so to have him admit that he would give up so I can be comfortable means a lot.

"Yeah, give up!" George and Will both shout.

"Oh, hell no. We're not losing this," I say, pushing my fork back into food in front of me.

"If you want." Nate starts eating again. "But don't hurt yourself. We can stop anytime you want."

"Eat, Williams!" I yell with a full mouth.

He listens, and we power through more dishes than I thought possible.

Everyone is in different stages of the competition, and some are eating while their partners rush them from the sideline. Mostly the women, who are tied into corsets, are having a hard time eating. Everyone looks miserable, despite how good everything tastes individually.

Wait, the corset! I can't do this in the corset.

"Nate, untie me." I get up and bring a plate with me as I present Nate my back.

"What? On camera?"

"I'm wearing a million layers. Just unbutton a few buttons on the dress and loosen the corset a little."

He obliges quickly, and I feel immediate relief when he gets the first few ties undone.

"Yes! A little more!" I can already feel more room for food and dig into the plate I'm holding with renewed ferocity.

The other teams notice, and rush to copy us, the women giving me a nod in appreciation of the idea.

Nate finishes loosening my corset first, and we sit down to dig back in as the servers keep bring a never-ending supply of new dishes.

"This is your last dish," the crew member serving us whispers as he drops it on the table.

"Thank god! And it's Christmas pudding." I clap my hands together in joy as the server puts a plate with an individual serving in front of me, which is on fire. "Thank you. I've been wanting to try this since I've been here but haven't had a chance yet." I blow out my desert, excited even though I don't know how it is physically going to fit in my stomach.

"More eating. Less reminiscing." Nate's is already not on fire anymore.

"I can do both." I take my first bite. The sweetness of the desert and the sharpness of whatever alcohol they use to make it explodes on my tongue in a fight for my attention, and I moan, closing my eyes. I open them again when I swallow and look over to Nate to find his fork halfway to his lips, his half-full mouth hanging open to show me...too much.

"Get to eating." I use my finger to close his open mouth. We could win this. And then we won't have to worry about anything tomorrow. I take a few more bites. "I wish I could eat this later, when I could appreciate it more."

"Get frough t'is forst."

I roll my eyes but eat food as directed. As I get halfway through, I begin to regret my initial excitement. Although this pudding is delicious, it's the density of lead and each bite, albeit starting out as a party in my mouth, turns into a rock in my already full stomach.

I take another drink of the brandy in front of me, hoping it'll dilute the contents of my stomach, instead of just adding to it.

"Don't fill up on liquid." Nate's mouth is empty for once during this meal. He must be feeling the amount of food too.

"I've eaten so much food."

"We can't be defeated by the thing that tastes the best. Not when we're so close to the end," Nate says.

"Yeah. But there's no room at the inn." I clutch my stomach as it uses pain to tell me enough is enough and I'm a glutton.

"Then find a manger."

"I'd find that funny if I wasn't in too much pain to laugh."

Nate drops his fork back onto the plate. "You're in pain? Don't keep going if you're in pain."

"We've already covered this; we're winning." I'm already in pain, and if I ate turtle for nothing, I will be incensed. I take another bite in rebellion, the angriest bite I've ever taken. Then an equally angry one after that, with particularly violent chewing. Nate picks up his own fork with a sigh.

I tune out all the sounds around me, continuing to put bite after bite into my mouth with a singular dedication.

The last few bites are the hardest, so close to the end but still a few dense, delicious obstacles in my way. I conjure the image of Dad in my head, paying off a producer to have the rest of the food disappear for me.

No. I chose to do this, and I will complete this challenge without any help. I shovel the last few bites in my mouth, washing them down with a healthy swig of brandy.

"Done!" I yell, throwing my fork down dramatically, a gift I got from my mother, who is obsessed with Indian soap operas.

"Seconded," Nate says right after me, his shoulders hunched, presenting a much less victorious picture of victory.

"Naomi and Nate win first place." Lewis moves to stand behind our chairs and lift our arms like we're prize fighters, who somehow both won in a fight. My stomach protests the quick rise of my arm, which jarred the poor organ, and I just barely keep from puking all over the table.

But, on the other hand, my vomit would make it harder for the rest of the teams to finish or would even make them give up completely which could give us extra time in the morning.

But, on the main hand, it would be kind of gross. And immortalized on television.

Since we're done, Aiko tells us what time we're leaving tomorrow and we're dismissed. We hurry out of the room to get as much sleep as we can tonight. Or try to, until we get out the door and my stomach moves past protest and the food gets even closer to coming back up.

I slow down immediately, clutching the abused area. "Nope. Sorry. This is my one speed right now."

Nate looks relieved and slows down. "Well, if you need to go slow, squirt." He gives me a paternal nod of the head, telling me this is all for me.

"On no. If you need to go faster, by all means, you go. You can use the bathroom first." I wave him on.

"I shouldn't leave you. There could be highwaymen in the hallways." He tries to look noble but grimaces in discomfort.

"*In* the hallways?" My mouth is undisturbed by the pain in my stomach.

Nate shifts his eyes back and forth and everywhere that's not meeting my own. "You never know with this show. And you know they just want to say Hallwaymen. They love a pun."

"Everyone loves a pun, Nate. They're wonderful. "

We walk back upstairs and I've never missed elevators more. Whoever invented the elevator is going to get Googled by me and then they're going to get the largest statue built in their honor that they've ever seen. It will include moving parts that mimic an elevator's movement.

As soon as I digest this meal. And get my phone back. Who knows which will happen first.

Nate gets to the door and opens it to let me in. I walk through, and almost (but not completely) forget about the pain in my belly.

Because we're back in our room. The same one we were in when we were interrupted earlier. Making out.

But there won't be any more interruptions. At least not tonight.

CHAPTER 33

NATE

heave a sigh of relief as I close our door. Another day of this show down and one day closer to being back at home, with no moral quandaries to navigate.

Unlike right now, when Naomi is tempting me by existing.

"Do you want the bathroom first?"

"Take this corset off me," Naomi says at the same time. "My stomach is about to explode." She paws at the buttons on the back of her dress.

"That must feel terrible. Let me do that." I move behind her to finish the task I started downstairs. My own stomach hurts when my loose shirt brushes against it, or when I think about it too hard. I can't imagine how much pain this corset is causing her after that meal, even partially untied.

I make quick work of the rest of the ties, not even enjoying the task of undressing her like I normally do because of how much I know she's hurting. I get the last tie and drag the corset down, faster than the first time when she was panicking because she couldn't get it off.

"You're good," I say. Not that I need to, because she's already halfway to the bathroom and then inside it in another second.

"Do you need me to bring in your nightclothes?" I ask the closed door.

"Yes, please." She turns the shower on.

I dig into her trunk and find the article of clothing for her. "I got it."

"I'll grab it in a second."

"How are you feeling?" I sit down on the bed, night clothes in hand.

"Like bad decisions and regret."

"But we won," I say weakly.

"At what cost, Nathaniel? At what cost?"

"A steep one." I hear her groan through the door. "Is there anything I can do?"

"Build a time machine and stop me from being a glutton for winning."

"That is beyond my skill. But I could put out some feelers and hire a team who might be able to tackle it."

"Useless managers."

I don't take offense to it since she's in too much pain to be taken seriously. Managers have value. Lots.

"I'll be out here if there's anything I can do."

"Thanks," she says, getting weaker sounding with every sentence.

Isn't she supposed to feel better over time? Is this a sign of something more serious happening? Should I be reporting this to a producer...and a medic?

"How are you not miserable?" she asks.

"I don't feel great. But I wasn't squeezed into a Regency device specifically meant to put more tension on my stomach."

"Patriarchyyyyyyy!" she yells, but still weakly. And I know without looking that she's shaking a raised fist to the ceiling. She's done it before.

Naomi finishes up in the bathroom and then trudges out.

"Hey." I don't want to ask her how she's doing again, because the answer doesn't look like it would be any improvement from when I first asked.

"Your turn," she says before collapsing on the bed. On her back.

I ignore my own pain and go to the bed. On the way, I get a blanket and toss it over her, glad I can do the task before my stomach rebels. I walk slowly to the bathroom, one hand on my stomach.

When I come back out, the only light is from a lamp on one of the bedside tables. The light covers her like the blanket I put on her earlier, drawing my eyes to her features. Perfect hair flowing around her head like a halo, perfect nose to look down at me, her dad's boring business executive, perfect mouth to…well, probably best not to dwell on what her mouth can do.

I walk across the room, trying not to make any noise. Which means I find every creaky floorboard in this room.

Miraculously, Naomi doesn't wake up. I ease myself into the bed next to her, turning the lamp off. I feel momentary regret that we can't finish what we started earlier, but my stomach and hers are not up to the task.

I turn so I'm facing her and fall asleep wishing I had the confidence to do what I want and take her into my arms for the night.

AN ALARM BLARING from the decidedly modern clock by the bed wakes me up way before I'm ready to be up. And I can't even turn it off, because it's on Naomi's side. "N'omi. Alarm." I bury my head into the closest soft spot…which is Naomi's shoulder. My arms found their way around Naomi during the night, and they're very comfortable there, despite how angry my ears are.

"No," she says, burying her head under her pillow.

"You need more time in the bathroom."

"That's sexist. I will not brush my teeth if that's what it takes to get extra sleep time."

I take my head away from Naomi's warmth, the new position not helping block out the music. "If we don't get up now, all that eating to leave first was for nothing."

Naomi takes her head out from under her pillow. "Excellent point, and since I've been raised to respect my elders, you go first, old man. You'll need the extra time to get to the bathroom." She dismisses me with a wave of her arm. "Get those older joints going."

"Your joints are going to get old one day too." I'm offended by how much older she thinks I am. I can see how annoying I was at the beginning of all this, when I would comment about how much older I am. All seven years. "And we're not that far apart, age wise," I say. I've drastically changed my opinion on our age difference, especially after we've had sex.

"You're still older." She closes her eyes again, getting comfortable for our last few minutes before the rush.

I sigh. "I'll take one for the team since I'm so responsible." I get up and stretch, taking my time to get to her side and turn off the alarm. Okay, so I might be a little petty, along with all the responsibility I have.

As I go through my morning routine, I can't stop thinking about how nice last night was. Not the excruciating pain; that part sucked. But just being with Naomi was comforting. Even with multiple trips to the bathroom for both of us. Despite how unpleasant and uncomfortable it was, just being with Naomi made the bad situation a little better.

But it does mess up the idea that we're doing a very casual, sex only, no feelings, won't blow up my life kind of thing. Because feelings would be a problem. Feelings would have to be dealt with, either by denying them, or telling Harrison I want to date his daughter.

But after this time together, I'm starting to think it'll be worth it. And I've watched Harrison make a CEO of a Fortune 500 company cry. It was funny at the time but takes on more worrying implications at the thought it could be turned to me. And he could fire me, along with making me cry.

I need to hold the course for another few days with our casual whatever. That's it, and then the temptation Naomi represents will be an entire ocean away from me and all I'll have is the memories of how amazing she is.

Just a few more days.

"WHERE ARE WE GOING TODAY?" Naomi sing-asks Aiko when we get down the stairs for the second time, so it was appropriately filmed. She's in a great mood, what with all the extra sleep she got cuddled into the warm bed while I went out in the cold to get ready for the day.

"We've got a treat for you two...ta-da!" She steps to the side and holds her arms out.

"Is that...a real vehicle? With an engine? And maybe some heating?" Naomi walks up to the SUV to poke it, as if to test if it's real or if it's a mirage brought on by our mutual tiredness and all the food we haven't fully digested.

"Yes. And we're even going to let you use it," Aiko says, waving us on.

Naomi pauses getting into the vehicle. "What's the catch to all of this?" she asks slowly.

"We can't tell you that, it would spoil the surprise. And will knowing really help any?" Aiko asks.

"The ball of anxiety eating through my stomach would go away," Naomi says.

"Then you'd just have the anxiety of worrying about what's coming," I say. "Could be just as bad, depending on the activity."

"How far are we from Scotland, again?" she asks, getting into the vehicle.

"Not too far now." Aiko hurries us into the SUV. It's already running and warm, so I'm more than willing to be shuffled into it.

"Fred, would it be considered rude if I tried to take over this car in a semi-non-violent manner and drive us to Gretna myself, probably on the wrong side of the road?" Naomi asks, hoping to avoid whatever they have in store for us.

"Depends on what a semi-non-violent manner is." Fred is used to us by now.

"Just some mean taunts. But low-grade mean taunts," Naomi says, getting comfortable in the back row of this SUV. Aiko and Kelly settle into the middle row, and Fred is in the front.

"Hmm. No. I'd be able to withstand that."

"Damn it," she whispers. "What do you have?"

I accept the box of breakfast from Aiko, which has a warm sausage roll. They're definitely trying to spoil us for some horror later today. "Nothing. I'm going to enjoy being treated like a human and not a product for a few minutes."

"Our standards have been lowered," Naomi says sadly, but accepts her own boxed breakfast. "At least with this modern horsepower, whatever we're doing should happen faster than if we were with the other horses. But less cute." She mumbles the last part. Classic Naomi.

As predicted, we go faster than we have for the past six days, and it takes me a second to adjust to the new speed. This must be what people felt like when they first tried cars. Well, maybe they were a little more awed…and moving slower.

About an hour later (which I can tell because I see the car's digital clock, a wonderful invention I will never take for granted again) and a drive through a big city, which gives me some cultural whiplash after the small country villages and isolated inns/mansions we've been in the last few days, we get to our destination.

The car stops near the water, in a busy port with multiple full slips and too many people in normal clothes. We get out, and immediately get stares. I almost forgot we're in period costume. Easier for me to forget than Naomi, I guess.

I slide a look over at her, and remember, very fondly and with some guilt over how much I enjoy something that causes her pain, all the times I've helped her out of her torture chamber.

Some people have already taken pictures, but some official, muscular people in black shirts and slacks with humorless faces keep anyone from getting close to us. Not that anyone is trying too hard to find out what's happening. Maybe people dress up in period clothes in England more regularly than I previously thought?

"We're here. What misery do you have for us?" Naomi asks, taking in the scene in front of us like she's trying to find out what the next task will be.

"Maybe we'll have a pleasant day on the beach, where they bring us ice cream and we build a sandcastle with period tools?" I ask hopefully. It's a beautiful day. Fluffy, cotton candy clouds dot the blue sky, and despite the crispness of the air, it would make a nice vacation.

"There's fireplaces that need cleaning out by the sea too," Naomi says with a meaningful look.

"None of the above. But I do have a fireplace if you're so keen on cleaning one out before we're done," Aiko says, reminding us that she's heard almost everything we've said since this started. "You're going on that ship."

CHAPTER 34

NAOMI

"The what now?" I ask. I just got used to the slow horse-and-carriage bit, got put back in a car, ruining all my progress with accepting a horse and carriage as transport, and now I have to go on the water?

If I wasn't here with Nate, I might have broken before now. His business cool and occasional moments of levity have really helped get me through this. And I would have been so embarrassed to have a melt-down, fueled by a lack of food and too much stress, broadcast on TV.

Even if getting though my own PR was the purpose of this entire show. Hopefully my castmates use me and then tell everyone how great I am at image repair.

And even though I haven't really seen what the rest of the cast gets up to, I know at least George will need slight image repair, and Will and Jessica will need publicity for their businesses.

Aiko sighs. "If Lewis were here, he would tell you that your carriage and all your belongings was stolen when you stopped for a comfort break and your chaperones are close behind on your heels, etc. So you got on the first transportation you could find, which is a ship. Unfortunately, you don't have much money.

Fortunately, the captain has agreed to allow you to work in exchange for your passage. Lewis isn't telling you that because you're all getting here at different times, so he's filming this explanation separately for the viewers."

"And with a lot more enthusiasm and pagentry, I bet," I say.

"I'm going to let that go because I know what's on the road ahead for you. Or the sea ahead, in this case. Feel free to pick one of these." She points to four large sailing ships, white sails fluttering around tall masts as they bob up and down by the dock.

"Are one of them faster than the others? Like more aerodynamic? Or would that be naut-odynamic?" I ask, wishing I had paid more attention when Dad went on about boats and regattas. To be fair, who would have thought regatta knowledge would be helpful in daily life? It seemed like a solid bet that tuning him out would have no consequences.

When Dad sees this and has his inevitable tantrum, maybe he'll calm down when he realizes he can say "I told you so" about sailing. He loves saying "I told you so." He might even have so much fun he'll forget I'm having carnal thoughts about one of his vice presidents. And not imaginative, wishful, carnal thoughts. *Reminiscent* carnal thoughts, of a very real past.

"I can't help. Not because I'm trying to protect my producer integrity, but because I don't know anything about boats," Aiko says.

"Do you have any ideas?" I ask Nate.

"We should pick the best-looking one," he says.

Apparently he didn't listen to anything Dad says about sailing either. "Yes. We're going with the prettiest one."

"Pretty is subjective, so I'm going to need you to give me more details. Or really, just walk to one and we'll follow." Aiko shoos us, getting behind Kelly and the camera.

"Which one do you think is best-looking?" I ask the person who suggested this metric.

"I don't know. I sort of hoped you would have an opinion

about it, and I would graciously follow whatever you said. I was going to get points for it." Nate looks chagrined.

"What are these points?" I say, deciding the closest ship is the prettiest. And also has the added benefit of being the closest. In addition, the figurehead is the best. It's a lady with her bosoms out. I don't know why anyone thought that needed to be at the front of the boat, but they are nice breasts.

"I thought maybe they could be redeemed for cool prizes from you later. Like a Chuck E. Cheese situation. Like maybe you would have to use the bathroom first in the morning."

"Keep dreaming. If there was a points-for-prizes situation in adulthood, everyone would be a lot happier about the whole situation." I stop in front of the first boat. "This boat. This lady. She beckons me."

"I'm okay with this." Nate raises his hand.

"Do we just walk up this, or…" I point to the moving wooden plank with ropes on the side, from the pier to the deck of the ship. It doesn't look secure.

"Yes. Hop on." Aiko looks happy in her sadistic way.

We walk up carefully and are confronted with what Captain Crunch would look like if he was live action. Mostly it's the facial hair, a handlebar mustache that he must spend hours twirling to get it in that shape, and an oversized hat that must taunt birds to poo on, along with the shiny medals on his chest. I mean, I would take all that as a challenge if I was a bird.

Standing next to him is another sea-fearing type, this one more humble. His face is grizzled, in a way that feels like he's been battling the sea his whole life, and the sea is winning with the lines it's etched on him.

Probably because he didn't moisturize. You have to fight the sea with more hydration.

And behind them is a group of men and women who look like extras in a *Pirates of the Caribbean* movie.

This is daunting.

"Finally! The guests of honor get here," the elaborate one says, sarcastically. "We've already waited too long for you to arrive. Now change, and we'll assign you some jobs so we can get underway." He indicates a rack with clothes hanging on it. A rack full of pants and shirts and no corsets in sight.

"Cool." Out of this corset and into pants? Yes, please. I might just run off with the clothes, and they can keep the dress. "Where should we change?"

"Through that door," the leader says, kindly. Then he remembers he was cast to be an overbearing captain and treat us like worthless peons. "And hurry, scallywags! You're paying for this trip in work, and I'm getting the full value out of you." He looks us up and down. "If there is any there to get."

We grab clothes off the rack and run away from the group to the room we were directed to. Inside the dark and small space, door safely closed behind us to make it darker and smaller, we look at each other in shared amusement.

"Are they going to make us walk the plank?" I ask.

"Aye, matey. Argh. And where's my parrot?" Nate asks

"Less talking, more changing," a stern English voice says from outside the door. We look back at each other and laugh, this time a silent laugh that shakes out shoulders.

The room is bare except for two makeshift changing rooms made with hanging curtains. I take the one closest "room," getting inside and closing the curtain before I realize the problem.

"Actually…" I step back out.

"Yeah. I was waiting for that."

I turn around when I get in front of Nate, presenting him with my back and the buttons. When he gets done with that row, he unties the corset without taking the dress all the way off. Disappointing, but understandable because Captain Serious is right out there.

"There you go." He pats me on the back and then lingers.

"Thanks," I say. "You have a great career as a lady's maid if this whole business executive thing doesn't work out."

"I'll get the business cards ready." Nate winks and turns to go to his changing room.

"Yeah, do that." I'm distracted by the playful gesture. Like I always am when Nate shows me some of that more human than executive robot behavior. Or when he does anything that Dad would disagree with.

I change into the sweet, sweet freedom of pants and flats and a loose shirt, dancing around the room when I get out of my changing room. Nate comes out mid-move, making me freeze in embarrassment.

I don't know why my body thought that freezing was *less* embarrassing for me than just continuing to dance, but I give my muscles a stern talking to, forcing them down to be a normal human person in a normal human stance.

He lifts an eyebrow, judgment very unnecessary in my opinion. "You liking the new clothes?"

I raise my chin and lean into it. "Yes. I'm going to leave this engagement, adopt a peg-legged parrot, and take to the seas in a life of piracy."

"Argh," he says again. "Will there be cameras on the high seas?"

"There won't even be mics on the high seas," I say as I pass him.

"This isn't a pleasure cruise. You're here to work. The tides won't wait for you to have a bath," Captain Meanie-Pants yells at us when we get out of the room.

"I haven't had a bath in years. What am I making a Naomi soup?" I ask, not able to take the yelly-man seriously when I grew up with Harrison Richmond.

"None of your sass!" Captain Frustrated yells.

Yeah. That command didn't work for Dad, and it will not work for Captain Amateur Hour.

"Will the tides wait for you to chastise us, or should we get to that work now?" I ask.

I feel Nate shake next to me, but don't take my eyes off of Captain Angry and in Possession of a Sword to confirm if Nate's silently laughing at me or shaking his whole body at me in disappointment.

"Get to work, sailors!" Captain Yelly…yells.

"What work should we be doing?" Nate tries to get us back on course.

"You're going to start off where all the sailors do: swabbing decks." Captain Cruel points to the side of the ship, either starboard or port, definitely one of the two, where there are some mops and buckets of water. "During this trip, the crew will do the same tasks as you, so if you need help on how to do something, just follow them. But I hope you can handle mopping."

"It'll be a toss-up with this one," Nate says, and I slam my elbow into his gut, earning a grunt back.

"Let's get to work." I walk over to the tools, ready to prove him wrong.

CHAPTER 35

NATE

A few hours into the deck swabbing, I regret making fun of Naomi. Because she's going strong on this task and I'm wishing we could go back to eating unusual things or sitting in an uncomfortable place for a long period of time. And it's not just the physical exertion of working out taking its toll on me, but the mental exertion of failing in front of the woman I'm interested in.

"How are you still going?" I ask, wiping sweat from my brow. I'm over here sweating and smelling like a farm animal and she's glistening like a model on a cover shoot. How does she look that perfect? Even disheveled, she's perfectly disheveled.

"Kickboxing, Pilates and weights. It's the best combination of workouts possible." She literally swabs a path around me.

"Apparently." I pant, leaning on my mop.

"No breaks!" the captain yells at us.

"Hey! There are labor laws against this sort of thing," I say.

"Maybe you can give them a seminar on those labor laws. That haven't been passed yet." Naomi smiles at me.

"I don't think they can afford my prices. I don't take payment in bottles of rum."

"Yanks. Too much talking. Not enough swabbing," the captain yells.

"Yes, this work is so important that we could just wait for a large wave to come and do it for us," I mumble, satisfied with the laugh I get out of Naomi.

We keep working until we get assigned another task, this time coiling rope. Which at least we can do sitting down. The other sailors leave us alone, letting us chat while Kelly walks around to get the best shot. It's gotten surprisingly easy to forget the camera is there.

"Time to scrape rust from the chain cables," the captain instructs, leading us to a large pile of chains.

Naomi frowns, looking less excited about the work now that she's already mopped and coiled. "About the payment for this trip, I think I remember my credit card number, if that would help steer us away from these tasks."

"What's a credit card?" The captain maintains character. "I won't be taken in by your flim-flam. But you can take a break and eat some bread and cheese, because we wouldn't want you to pass out from the strain of all the work."

"Bread and cheese. No rum?" Naomi asks, surprised. Fair, since the show usually gives us enough alcohol to drown a horse.

"No. We can't give you alcohol before what we're going to make you do later. Legally speaking. And morally."

Naomi takes the offered food from the crew members and eats gingerly. "What are they going to make us do?" she whispers at me.

"Steer this ship?" I take my own plate of food. I hope it's nothing more intense than that.

"That doesn't seem extreme enough. Why would they tease us so far in advance? It just seems cruel."

"It makes better television. If we're miserable."

"I bet you can't argue with that market analysis." She sighs.

"I wish I could. It's going to make them so much money."

"Sucks being on this end of corporate exploitation, doesn't it?"

"We do sustainable energy," I mumble.

"Hmm."

We finish lunch in silence, enjoying the gentle rolling of the ocean and how good food tastes after that much physical work. After, we go back to scraping rust. While continually looking around worriedly for what the next task will be and tensing every time someone walks by us.

Finally, the captain decides to put us out of our misery by walking over.

"You've done decently enough." He drowns us in praise. "For amateurs."

"We did so well you don't need anything else and we're going to dock soon, before the other teams, and you're going to give us a shiny medal?" Naomi asks hopefully.

"No," the captain says, giving a surprisingly straightforward response to the absurd question. "One of the sails isn't working correctly, so we need you to check the rigging."

"Oh. Sure, where is it? Are we going to have to sew anything? I'm not a great sewer, but I think I can make something passable." Naomi looks around, trying to find the sail.

I see the captain pointing up, at the tallest damn sail on his damn ship. "I don't think he means down here." I nudge her so she looks up.

And up. And up.

"Are one of you going to get it down for us? Is there a button we can press and it'll bring itself down, or…what?"

"No. You're going up. We'll harness you in. And there's barely any wind."

We both watch the captain's hat feather swing in the breeze. And bob up and down with the movement of the sea.

"You'll follow one of my sailors up, and once you get to the top of the tallest mast, you'll recover a flag up there to show you checked out the right part, and then you're done. Once you get back down, you can relax with all the rum you can drink 'til we get back to port."

"How do we get up there, though? We can't just fly." I think Naomi's in the denial stage of grief.

"Climbing. The rope ladder. You have all the time you need. But if we get to port before you finish, you can't leave the ship until you're done."

"And what is the policy on doing a quick shot of rum before we get up there?" Naomi asks.

"We're very against it. For safety reasons."

"But wouldn't that be the sailor way? Irresponsibly ignoring safety standards for the pursuit of a buzz that makes me feel invincible and then doing dangerous maneuvers?"

The second in command laughs, and then covers the laugh with a cough.

"Here's your harnesses." The captain ignores the question and indicates the equipment at the foot of the rope ladder. "We have helmets too."

"Is this period appropriate?" Naomi gives in but with sass, like I knew she would.

There's nothing she can't do. All the stubbornness of her family line, but she does it with a smile and a snarky comment. She has fun while getting her shit done. Something I forgot was possible somewhere along the way.

I love her.

Oh god. I break out into a sweat at the thought. But it makes sense. Why would I, someone who lives for the risk-averse, sensible choice, who does risk analysis in his job, keep spending this much time with the absolute wrong person?

When she said she was going to be on a reality show, I should have walked away. Or maybe tried to talk to the producer and then walked away. Those were the sensible choices. Harrison would understand that I couldn't control his daughter; he certainly can't.

But I didn't want to leave her. Spitting fire at me, telling me she's going to be on a reality show, damn my opinions. Then I got myself invited on and agreed to it. Just to be around her more. Especially without Harrison around.

Because I love her.

What am I supposed to do with that?

"Nate. Are you okay?" Naomi, the woman I love, is right in front of my face, looking intently into my eyes. "You're sweating."

"No," I say reflexively. Denying what is probably a verifiable fact. "I'm fine."

"If you don't want to do this, we can take whatever the penalty is. It's not a problem." She still looks worried.

"Let's just get up there. The waiting is the worst part of it. The anticipation," I ramble. But now that I know that I love her, it's very stressful to look at her face. This can only end with a firing or a broken heart. Or maybe both. And I'm going to have to do something about it, to try to be with her, because this inconvenient love won't let me do anything else.

Mom will love her too, though. And Dad too. They'll appreciate her make-Nate-work-less-and-make-fun-of-Nate-more approach to life. The holidays are going to be brutal with all of them ganging up on me. If I can even get her to love me back.

This is making my stomach hurt a little. Isn't love supposed to make me feel invulnerable? Because now I have a stomachache.

Naomi is still looking at me, making everything worse.

"I'll go first," I say, more as a tactic to get out of this conversation than a desire to be the manly man who does the dangerous thing first.

I pull on the harness and the helmet, looking at the rope ladder that can't possibly hold the weight of one man, much less three grown humans.

I take a hold of a rung and put my foot through another.

As I make my way up along the mast, my mind calms. The extreme physical discomfort of climbing this rope ladder is helping, because it gives me something to think about alongside my newly acknowledged love.

Pretty soon, keeping my balance as the ship tries to toss me off of it is all I can think about. I'm doing okay, maybe I can be a sailor if Harrison fires me. As long as he doesn't try to kill me and fire me at the same time. He can multitask.

My mind calms to the point I can look down at the woman I'm agonizing over without having a panic attack. "How are you doing?"

"This is…" Her face does nothing to give away the rest of that sentence. "Amazing." Her face breaks into a smile. "The sea air." She takes a big breath. "The gentle sway of the boat." She sways a little around the rope, causing me to sway and terrifying me at the same time. "And the exercise to justify all the rum and bread I'm going to consume once we get back down. How are you doing?"

"Good," I lie. Technically, I suppose I'm okay with the climbing, which is what I think she's talking about. My emotions are not good, but that's a different story she didn't ask for.

We continue the climb until we get to the top of the mast, where there's a horizontal wooden plank and ropes to hold up the sail. Our guiding sailor stops. "Climb over on this horizontal part, the spar, with your feet on the rope part and hands on the wooden part, and then take in the view if you want. You deserve it. When you're ready, grab the purple flag and we can start the trip down."

I move across the area as instructed, carefully not looking down to avoid the terror of being this high up, and not looking behind me to Naomi, to avoid the terror of the emotions she evokes.

"This is beautiful." Naomi's head is on a swivel to take in all views from her position.

"Yeah. Beautiful." Or I think it would be if I wasn't so terrified of the height. And if I wasn't so terrified, I would say the same thing when looking at her, because she is. But there's no way I'm taking my eyes off my hands clutching the wooden...whatever this sailing thing is.

"Don't you want to look out to see the shore? It's right there."

The ship gives a particularly violent lurch, making me clutch the wooden part in front of us even harder and close my eyes to my surroundings. "Not particularly."

"It's really pretty. And I've got you. See." Naomi threads her arm through mine, and I open the eye closest to her.

Well, that is adorable. That she cares. And that she thinks that this arm will prevent us from falling to our deaths if the ocean decides we aren't respectful enough.

"Look. And if you don't take my very strong arm as valid safety equipment, you're in a harness." She tugs on the fabric at my waist.

"I'm looking. I'm looking." Anything to stop her from jostling me again. I pry open my eyes through sheer will alone and focus on the wooden bar I'm holding onto, seeing everything else in my periphery. When that doesn't tempt fate, I expand my focus, looking first at the ship below (nope, that was as big a mistake as I thought it was) and then out over the horizon.

"How many people get this view?" she asks, head up, confident. She's a lot braver than me when it comes to risks and enjoying them.

"Not many people, because they're sane enough to stay on the ground," I say. "But I guess they're missing out on a spectacular view." The ocean goes on and on in one direction, the blue of the sky layered atop the blue of the ocean, making me feel small on top of this giant ship. And in the other direction, I can see the coast, hills of green rolling down into the blue water, buildings dotting the shore of this seaside town.

Calmer, I unclench one hand from the ship and slide it

around Naomi, drawing her in closer until her solid weight is against me. This is much, much better. Even up here.

We stand on the top of the world for a little longer, until the sailor with us interrupts. "Just so you know, we're going to dock soon, and you have to change back into your clothes before you leave. If you want to leave the second you can, we should head down now."

"Good call. Thanks," Naomi says. She goes down first. I follow, slower, and we make it down without major incident.

We get back in our regular (or as regular as they can be when they're still historic) clothes and are ready when the captain lets us off the ship. It's a toss-up as to who looks more relieved that we're leaving.

"Bye, Captain Way-Harsh."

"Goodbye. You make terrible seamen." The captain weaves us off.

Naomi snickers at the use of the word *seamen*, making me laugh at her. The captain rolls his eyes at both of us and gestures to the ramp.

"What now, Aiko?" Naomi asks.

"You guys are really going to enjoy this next part..." She smiles her cheshire cat smile, the one that never bodes well for us.

CHAPTER 36

NAOMI

"Out with it!" I demand. "Please." What more could there be? The sun's already gone down and we've been working the entire day. In that same sun. Or what passes as the sun in England.

Aiko laughs at us. "No, you'll actually enjoy it. We're going to drive you to the hotel, where you can have room service. We've got enough footage for the day."

"Oh, thank fuck. Your sadist smile is just how you smile." I'm so ready for a real hotel.

"But rest up. Because tomorrow is the last push to Gretna, and we're going to have a long day before you get fake married."

"Yay," I say weakly.

"Now, the public votes are most important for winning, but the first couple who accomplishes the Gretna wedding will get some points added to their votes as a prize. And then we're going to give you back your phones and modern clothes and set you up in hotel rooms for the night. And a flight back into London the day after. You'll still have to show up at the reunion where the winners will be announced, but you'll be free until then."

"Yay!" I say with genuine excitement at the prospect of

returning to modern life. I am going to roll around in my leggings, maybe do some high kicks, while I look at all the social media I missed in the past week. Oh, and I'm going to sit and watch TV. I need to know who's feuding with who on the new season of *Real Housewives* that started airing right before I left.

Then I look at my partner to share all the things we're going to do when we get away from these restrictions, and immediately feel the glow of excitement fade a little. Because I won't be seeing Nate anymore. I'll go back to work in London, and Nate will be back to his work in New York.

I'm not ready for this to be over. I *finally* found someone I like spending time with romantically, someone who's easy to be around. Or at least he has been in this isolated world, galivanting around the English countryside.

And even though I know it has to end, obviously, I don't want it to end *now*. Not for the first time, I wish my friends were here to talk to.

London and New York aren't even that far apart. Maybe we can keep this up a little. He'll take some much-needed vacation and I can show him some of my favorite spots around London, and even England, or Europe. I won't go to New York, because that's just asking to get caught by Dad or one of his nefarious spies.

It'll be fun. More of this bantering, more of his abs, more of his amazing penis. And then when we get each other out of our systems, he goes back to his life until the next time we both have an itch to scratch.

A perfect arrangement. Now I just need to survive our wedding day, and I can propose living in sin with him.

"THIS MEAL IS THE BEST MEAL." Nate clutches his stomach in

gluttonous satisfaction on the bed, all that's left of his giant cheeseburger is one lone, unwanted piece of lettuce.

"Food tastes better without a corset. And when there's no camera on you," I say. All that's left of my fish and chips is one full portion of mushy peas. Because peas are gross enough when they aren't mushed, England.

I'm glad there aren't cameras around to catch me disparaging peas.

We're both in comfortable night dresses, enjoying the room and the privacy. Aiko made us do some individual interviews, but she did them on the ride back, separating Nate and I into different cars. She didn't press that hard, for once. Or maybe I'm getting better at thwarting these manipulative producers. Or worn down and worse at noticing I'm being manipulated.

And then we got back into the room, which has hot water and a room service menu, as promised.

"I still maintain there's cameras somewhere in this room, catching our every move." Nate looks around like he does every time he mentions the possibility. He hasn't found one yet, though.

"I still hope, a lot, that you're wrong. Like in *The Amazing Race.* They leave the contestants mostly alone in the rest periods. I'm going to live my life under that assumption."

"I think this is going to be a *Love Island* situation, where there are definitely cameras in the bedrooms."

I point at him as I gasp. "You *have* seen the show!"

Nate blushes charmingly. "I never said reality TV wasn't entertaining to watch; I just said it's embarrassing for the people on it, which you were trying to become."

I shake my head as I pick up the cake I ordered for dessert. Eating with Nate in a companionable silence as we enjoy modern conveniences is nice. This is what it could be like if we continued on after the show: hotels, and good food, and hopefully good sex.

Sex that I would like to have now.

"So," I say. I don't really know how to get from here to sex without being awkward.

"Well?" Nate asks when I don't follow up with anything.

If I wasn't being too affected by the Nate-ness of Nate, then I would be able to think of something that isn't awkward to say in response. Maybe we could talk about the bees, adorable pollinators. Or maybe about the birds. They can fly. How cool is that?

Damn it, even my subconscious can't think of anything other than sex around Nate.

Maybe I don't need to say anything at all.

I stand up abruptly. Nate sits up, not sure why I'm moving around, but ready to react. I walk toward him, mind quieting from all the chatter and worry about the future the closer I get to him. He looks up warily since I still haven't said anything after the *so*.

I grab his hand and find no resistance as I lead him to the bathroom. Nate follows without question, but I answer the one that he must be thinking, about why I'm dragging him around. "In case you're right, this room has the least likely chance of secret cameras."

My eyes focus on his lips, ignoring everything else about him like I'm ignoring all my maybe, potential, not-acknowledged, feelings right now.

In a further attempt to not think of anything, I kiss him. It works, and soon I'm in a world of heat, comfort and pleasure with wonderful, responsible Nate. He doesn't ask any questions either, kissing me back. His tongue reaches out to caress mine, and I burrow my hands under his nightgown to reach more of that warmth, pulling it up until I access skin.

Everyone should wear dresses and skirts constantly. The access is amazing.

My hands are about to reach his penis on their journey up his lightly hairy thighs when he pulls me all the way down and onto my back. I land half on a soft rug on the floor and half on the cold tile. I jerk up to avoid it, having the added benefit of rubbing against Nate's body. I don't stop to put anything down to cover the cold tile.

Another thing I'm ignoring.

Nate pushes my nightgown up, tearing my underwear off and replacing it with his mouth. My back arches off the floor again, this time in pleasure, pushing my clit harder against Nate's tongue. He accommodates the move easily, angling his head to save us from an awkward trip to the emergency room.

I writhe under his expert tongue, driven wild with every swipe of it. I can't decide if I want this to last forever, or if I just want to have my orgasm already. Ultimately, Nate takes the decision out of my hands and raises his read, my pelvis chasing his head until it remembers it has dignity.

Just barely. And only because Nate sat up and is too far away.

"I'll be right back," Nate says, walking back out to the room.

I prop myself on my elbows to see what he's doing and watch that amazing ass bend over. He has no right to look this good in a nightgown. He stands up again, holding a condom. Right. It's good one of us remembers basic safety, because the effect he has on me makes me forget common sense.

He takes off his clothes and pulls down his boxer briefs as he walks to the bathroom, releasing his jutting penis to lead the way. To me. Once back, he closes the bathroom door and tosses the condom packet beside me. He grabs fistfuls of my nightgown and raises it over my head.

He raises it over my head and says, "Oh."

"What?" I look around for what could have made him say that now, of all times.

"The tile floor is cold. Are you sure you want to…"

"Don't care." I motion for him to get back on top of me. "Worry about it later."

"Okay." Nate looks unsure, but then he turns us until I'm on top.

I kiss him again, until we're back to where we were before he got the condom.

The only thing I want to think about, is Nate. Warm and velvety skin painted over hard muscles, the soft smell of bergamot from the shower he took earlier filling my nostrils. A playground for my senses.

He picks up the urgency, his erection rubbing against my slit, which gets wetter with each pass. Finally, *finally*, he enters me. He slides in, and his fingers pick up where his mouth left off earlier on my clit as he thrusts in and out.

In an embarrassingly short amount of time, he gets me back right where I was, close to the edge of orgasm. The sounds of his grunts fill the air along with the sound of our skin sliding against each other, and on the hard bathroom floor. A floor whose chill is forgotten in our passion.

I can't hold out for much longer, the pressure building higher and higher even after every time I think it's gotten as high as it can until I don't feel in control of my own body anymore; I'm just a giant mass of pleasure reacting to Nate's touch on me. And then I snap, convulsing around and over Nate as pleasure washes over me.

Nate holds out for an admirable four more thrusts before he comes. Breathing heavily, I collapse next to him, the cold floor now a nice cooling sensation against my overheated body. Nate moves next to me, I assume to get the condom off, but I can't turn my head and see for sure.

"Naomi…" He says my name like a fucking benediction, but I can't handle that and take the coward's way out by closing my eyes, feigning sleep. On the bathroom floor.

"Okay, squirt. If that's what you want." He kisses my head and tosses my nightgown over my front. Then he lifts me into his arms to carry me through the dark room to the bed.

My heart beats out an entire metal song at my nickname, and the easy way he got me off the floor. Once we're on the bed, I snuggle his back. It's a lot easier to deal with the man when I don't have to look at his face.

"LAST DAY, CHILDREN," a voice yells while knocking at the door. "Get ready. Get excited! I need you up and ready in twenty minutes."

I bolt up in bed, looking around to see where the attacking army is. Because there should be no other reason to wake someone up in such an unpleasant and abrupt manner unless an entire horde is invading.

"That woman is the devil. She doesn't look like the devil, but I hear that's how he gets you," Nate mumbles, face still in the pillow.

"You get ready first." I try to lay back down, but Nate's already stolen my pillow.

"I got ready first last time. Your turn." His thick forearm tugs my pillow tighter against his head.

"But chivalry," I say, already shivering in the chilly British morning just by sitting up.

"I would never insult you by implying you need a man to take care of you."

"Insult me," I say, looking longingly at the combination of the warm blankets, pillows and Nate.

"Never. My mother raised me better." I can see a half smile from the part of his face not under my pillow.

"Damn feminists," I grumble, hating mornings more than misogyny, apparently. This is something I should probably work on.

I get up and rush through my morning routine, minus the actual getting dressed since I can't do that alone. "Your turn." I pull Nate out of bed. The second he's up I steal his vacated spot. It's still warm from his body heat, and I snuggle in.

"Hey, you didn't finish dressing," Nate says when he walks out of the bathroom and sees me tucked in bed with my nightgown still on.

"My lady's maid is late for the job." I get up with dignity, sniffing my nose at him, the crappy lady's maid in question.

"Five-minute warning. Get down here. Trust me, you don't want to be late," Aiko yells at us from the hallway.

I roll my eyes, but I'm grateful for the interruption. Aiko has made sure that this morning, in fact she's made sure *many* of my mornings with Nate, aren't uncomfortable and awkward. We have no time to feel awkward until we get to the carriage, and by that time, we're already worried about what Aiko's going to throw at us next. And the cameras.

I get out of bed and Nate helps me into the million layers of clothing I have to wear for the show.

"Finally! I was going to have the proprietor burst in if you were late. To check on you for your health, of course," Aiko says. There's a slight frown on her face when she sees me, but then it's gone, replaced by her cheerful, professional demeanor. It was probably the lighting.

"Lies. You were hoping to see something interesting," Nate says.

"Was there something interesting to see?" Aiko perks up her producer head.

"No," I say without looking at Nate. "Absolutely nothing. So what's the plan for today?"

Aiko just laughs at me. Not that I expected an answer. I roll my eyes at Nate to show what I think of Aiko. He winks at me, because he knows what she would have found if she burst into the room this morning—snuggling. I blush in response.

Aiko leads us to the dining room and frees us to get food from the side buffet. The rest of the cast and crew follow soon after, looking as tired and worn down as we do. Zara's in the tired group, and she gives me a short wave and small smile before focusing on her couple. The last day is getting to all of us, even though we've only been at this for a week.

Lewis lets us eat in peace, worrying me even more about what he's got in store for us. When we're done and chatting, he makes his grand appearance.

"Beautiful contestants. Can you believe this is the last time I'm going to see your faces over breakfast? I wish we could keep this going forever." Lewis is dressed in his best Regency suit and looking like he got more sleep last night than we've had in the past week.

We all laugh, but a bit manically. Because I can't do this for much longer, and even without the romantic tension, I don't think the rest of the cast can either.

"But all good things must come to an end." Is this speech ever going to come to an end? It's not good, but I still want him to get on with it. "And as a treat, since I've come to care for you all so much, I'm going to tell you what this day holds for you."

This really can't be good, if it's so intense we need an itinerary.

"First, we're going to walk over to the local courtroom to play a little game. After that, it's a race to Gretna Green! You'll have to stop at Carlisle to arrange a priest and a venue, and then straight to Gretna to get married in the clothes you bought back in Bakewell. The first couple to get married wins an extra two thousand five hundred votes added to their totals, which could make a difference, or not, depending on how popular you all are."

He pauses while we digest all of that information. "I see you've already eaten. Let's head over."

Well, that was not enough time to process.

I sigh, begrudgingly getting up and following the producers wherever they want to lead us. Not like I have any options unless I want to end up at a real courthouse, being sued for breach of contract. True to Lewis's words, we don't go far, ending up at a building a few doors down from our inn. The producers usher us into a courtroom with all the desks, chairs and walls in wood, with the occasional marble accent thrown in for variety.

"Let's get Naomi and Nate up to the witness stand first," Aiko says.

I have a small heart attack at the mention of our names and at the fact that we're going first, at whatever this is. The producers don't make it any better since they haven't told us what's happening and it takes them another half hour to get us all seated where they want (me and Nate in some box and everyone else facing us in another, longer box) and the cameras set up. The suspense increases every second we're there, the other cast facing us and equally confused. And just when I thought I was used to this show.

Finally, Lewis sits in the highest seat, the one lording over us all with the most elaborate decoration around it. Columns and an entire wooden backdrop were made just for it, and it has comfortable-looking green leather–covered padding. I shift on the wooden bench we're on, assuming that Lewis got the judge's seat.

"Cameras ready?" he asks. At a producer's nod, he turns on, smile wattage increasing and his voice going from normal human to excited like only a TV presenter can be. "Our cast has been living in the nineteenth century, which comes with pretty dresses, grand houses and a slightly slower mode of transportation. But one thing hasn't changed: gossip. Today, we're going to play *Guess the Gossip*. The producers have written some headlines that might appear in the papers due to the scandal you've all caused with your elopements. Each couple will be read ten different headlines, and they will guess which couple they're about, or if it's about themselves. Remember, it might be about a couple that was only together for one kidnapped night. The team who answers the most right will leave first, a head start on the day's travel."

Lewis looks at us from his perch. "And first up is Nate and

Naomi. Let's get started." He puts on some certainly fake glasses and holds a newspaper in his hand, looking very seriously at us. "Headline number one: Quality couple shocks quantity when they're caught in a compromising position, under chaperone's not-so-watchful eye."

I turn to Nate. "That could be us or Hannah and Amir. From the beginning."

"Us," Nate says out loud. "We should bet on ourselves," he whispers to me.

"Yeah. Us," I say.

Lewis lowers the paper with a sigh. "Well. Then we're off to a…" Then he changes his entire face with a smile. "Great start. Because that's right!"

Competitive spirit kicking in, I high five Nate.

"They will get harder," Lewis says.

Over the next hour, the crew film us answering questions and the reaction shots from the rest of the cast. And I learned some very interesting things about my cast mates, like Amir almost got arrested for picking some flowers for Hannah and trespassing to do it. And that George fell in a stream during a pee break (with the heavy implication that Sarah might have pushed him in when they were partners). Jessica got caught saying her partner had the personality of drying paint.

One of the headlines that gave me the most difficulty was, "Lord looks at his lady with very unfashionable affection." That was apparently Nate, and not Amir as I had guessed. In the end, we got six out of ten, and we're released out of the hot seat.

Hannah and Amir are up next, and their first headline is, "Old lovers create enough heat to set fire to the wooden carriage they're riding in." Which apparently was me and Nate. A fact that Hannah knew.

I laugh it off, scoffing at the thought of us making heat that others can see. It's *Nate*. All right, we might be in lust, but it's not like we make eyes at each other all day.

And even if we do, it's because who else are we supposed to look at? We're discouraged from looking at the camera. Maybe they just caught us looking constipated and confused the two.

Then with Sarah and Will: "Lady tries hard to hide emotions but doesn't succeed in hiding the moon eyes she has for her lord."

This must be Hannah. There's no one else here that besotted.

"Naomi and Nate," Hannah says.

"That right!" Lewis says.

What is going on here?

I look at Nate and replay every interaction we've had over the past week. The long talks, every time he made me laugh, every time he made me come. Him talking about loosening up, when he tries to take care of me, even though he knows I can take care of myself.

Oh god. I *do* have moon eyes for him. I do love him. But I don't want to!

I'm still looking at him, but with eyes more panicked than moon-like. Because the panic is filling every part of my body and I can't imagine I can keep it out of my gaze.

"What's the matter?" Nate asks when he notices I'm staring at him with a mix of horror and panic.

"Nothing," I say, shrill even to my own ears. I try a placid smile, even though my entire body is in crises right now. Heart pounding, palms and armpits sweating, feet twitching toward the exit. I'm ready to flee.

This is going to be a very difficult day.

CHAPTER 37

NATE

What happened to Naomi during this game? I look around for possibilities of things that could have freaked her out so I can help her. But I'm coming up blank. There's nothing too embarrassing being revealed in the game, and not much in the room that would cause panic. It's not like Harrison's here.

Maybe it's slightly embarrassing that the producers think she's making moon eyes at me when we're just hanging out and having sex surreptitiously. But nothing she can't come back from.

Lewis reads Jessica and George the next headline. "Couple caught in the marital way on the way to be joined in marital bliss."

I snap my head to the witness box, eyes wide to take in what's going to happen even though I can't do anything to stop it. Is this show going to tell the world I'm having sex with Naomi?

Of all the ways that Harrison could find out about us, this would be the least ideal. I'll have to tell him immediately after we stop filming. Maybe before. I wonder if we'll pass anyone with a phone today.

It won't be ideal to tell Harrison I love Naomi before I tell

Naomi, but that's what I'm going to have to do if this headline is about us. Because Naomi isn't ready to hear that at all. I need more time to ease her into the idea. And get used to it myself.

"Hmm," Jessica murmurs. "I know it's not me and George. So that's one couple out of the way." She looks over us, considering. So much consideration she's doing Lewis proud for making some dramatic tension. And we're squirming, just like when Lewis does it to us.

Actually, everyone is squirming. I can see that in my peripherals. I tear my eyes off the witness stand to look at my fellow cast members, but no one will look at me, everyone more focused on the two people in the witness stand.

Naomi looks surprisingly Zen. Her eyes are locked on Jessica and George like everyone else, but she's not leaning in as much as the rest of us. She's interested in what's going to happen, but she's not depending on it for her well-being. She looks like she's thinking important thoughts, not related to the game.

Jessica and George whisper to each other, the hushed tones not loud enough to figure out what they're saying. It's not helping anyone with their anxiety.

"We think it's Hannah and Amir," George finally says.

Step one down: they don't immediately think it's us. But there's still a step two: them getting this right. Now it's up to Lewis to give the answer that's not us, and then we're golden.

But it's Lewis. He savors the moment at our expense, doing the reality show host thing and drawing it out.

"Why do you think that?" Lewis asks instead of giving us the answer, his shit-eating host grin on his face.

"They seem like they get along with each other, and we have to say someone," Jessica says, diplomatic 'til the end.

"Amir's horny for Hannah. We can all tell." George is less diplomatic.

"The answer…" Oh joy, another long pause. "Is correct!"

I'm ashamed at the relief that flows through me, knowing that this isn't great for Hannah or Amir. I look over and Hannah has her head in her hands, red staining the bits of her cheek I can see between her fingers. Amir, on the other hand, is frozen, eyes wide. His cheeks are getting redder the more we all look at him. He belatedly realizes his partner is in distress and rubs her back.

This is mildly embarrassing for them, but at least this isn't the actual Regency time; they'll be fine if people know they're having sex. Unlike me if Harrison finds out.

Just when I get my breathing back to normal, Lewis speaks again. "Although there were other answers that would have been acceptable." He leers at all of us but doesn't single any team out. Letting future audiences speculate freely.

My heart responds by beating so hard I think I just ran a marathon. Or took one of Mom's cardio classes. The woman believes in strengthening the body and the mind. I might need to go to some of those classes with her when I get back, because my body and mind are not holding up well to the intrigue and physical exertion of this show.

"Thank you all for playing," Lewis says like we had a choice. "The winners with the most points are Hannah and Amir. Then it's Naomi and Nate in second, Sarah and Will in third, and Jessica and George in last place. See your producer and they'll tell you when you can leave and from where. Good luck, couples, on the road to Gretna." He smiles placidly into the camera for an unnaturally long time.

"Cut," a crew member I don't know says, and Lewis loses the smile and wanders off without another word to us. "Let's just get some extra reaction shots," the same crew member says.

The crew makes us shoot reactions for another half hour before they let us go, calling out emotion after emotion we have to show until they're satisfied, like a Regency improv class.

Aiko comes to get us. "Are you ready for this to be almost over?"

"Yes," we both reply with no hesitation.

"I'm hurt by the speed with which you both said that. But on the bright side, look at what a beautiful team we made. You've passed all your challenges and you're ready to go out into the world. I'm like a proud mum right now."

"I don't think mums are supposed to film their children making bad decisions," Naomi says.

"My children need to learn from their own mistakes. And I'm providing them with HD quality footage they can review to help make better decisions next time," Aiko says.

Aiko leads us to our carriage and I help Naomi into it for one of the last times. I ignore the pang in my chest because this is near the end of our time together. Because once this show is over, I have to tell her how I feel, and she gets to decide if she *wants* to keep spending time with me. As opposed to being contractually obligated to spend time with me like she is now.

I hope she wants to keep seeing me. I want to keep seeing her, despite her geography and family complications.

We sit in awkward silence for another half hour, not moving.

"Feels like we could have waited somewhere else," I say.

"We're already cleaning out your rooms and the courtroom," Aiko says, looking at her phone.

A weight leans over my left shoulder. "I miss my phone so much," Naomi whispers in my ear, her longing eyes looking at the phone in Aiko's hand, not me.

"I'm going to spend an entire day in bed with my phone when I get her back, and I'm never going to take her for granted again." A day is how long it'll take me to catch up on all my work emails, which dims my excitement somewhat.

I remember being so excited about getting my first work phone. It felt like I had achieved something. Despite my parents not understanding why I wanted to be a "corporate monster," and after how hard I worked at business school, when I got my first executive job and they handed me that shiny phone with the cling wrap still on the front, it felt like a sign that I had made it.

Then I realized that it just meant that my boss could call me whenever they wanted. Weekends, vacations, middle of the night, whenever.

This is the first time I've been fully away from my work phone since I got it. It hasn't been bad, surprisingly. The itch I usually get being away from work faded soon after the first night with Naomi.

Because she makes me better. Or at least makes me take more breaks, which makes me better.

"Did you just refer to your phone as a she?" Naomi asks, dragging me from the past and right into the present. The one in which we're imitating the past.

"Yes. If I'm going to spend that much time with something, I would prefer it to be a lady."

"Did you name her?"

"No. I'm not that attached."

"Of course not. Do you love to fondle your lady? Love wrapping your hands around your lady's curves? Whisper into your lady's…microphone?" Naomi smiles to herself, the humor of a teenage boy on full display.

I lift an eyebrow in response. "Are you done?"

Aiko interrupts our conversation. "Okay, we can go."

"One more," Naomi promises both of us. "Do you use protection with your lady or do you go naked?" She attempts a leer for a half second before she dissolves into a fit of giggles. Even I have to crack a smile for that one. Because she's fun. So much fun.

Naomi is still laughing when she pulls the map out. "Let's go straight then take the first exit at the third roundabout. Hey, this map ends at Carlisle." She shows me the paper. The thick, printed stars that have been guiding our journey this whole time from London stop at the city of Carlisle.

"You'll see," Aiko says smugly. I roll my eyes in response to that.

I settle in for a long ride, casually putting my arm around

Naomi. I hope it was smooth, but since this is caught on camera, the only thing I can hope is that it's better than the yawn-and-stretch-into-a-cuddle move.

But it's too late to worry about it now. And I want to squeeze every second of fantasy out of this show before it airs and ruins my life. With people making fun of me on the internet and Harrison yelling at me off the internet.

Unfortunately, this show chooses today to let us out of the carriage quickly, after a short hour and a half long ride.

"Welcome to Carlisle. Find an agent to help you book a wedding venue and a priest. And we use the word priest lightly. Here's some money." Aiko shoves a pouch with coins at us while we get out of the carriage.

"Where do we go?" I ask. Not that they've ever made it that easy, but a boy can hope.

Aiko just laughs at us in response. It's a good thing she found her niche manipulating and torturing contestants on reality TV, because otherwise she would end up in jail for some serious felonies.

"Comforting," Naomi whispers to me as I help her out of the carriage.

We're outside a train station, with a long row of men dressed in priest's robes standing around the platform. When they see us, they explode into action, and my first instinct is to turn around and flee. Maybe even knock Naomi between us as a sacrifice, to give me a few minutes of a head start.

I'm not proud of it, but the sight of twenty priests gunning for me seems like an appropriate reason to abandon all self-respect.

And they aren't slowing down as they get closer.

"What a fine-looking couple!" one man yells at us.

"You look like you need a priest," another says, elbowing the first one aside.

"You look like you need the best priest. This is quality we're looking at," a third says.

"What is going on?" I say as I hide behind Nate, who keeps moving to avoid being a shield, Aiko and Eelly at our backs recording this ambush.

"We found the priests," Nate says.

I get close to his ear and whisper, "Let's just pick one then." I feel him shiver at the close contact and smile over the fact that he's still affected by me, even though we've already had sex twice.

"Yeah. But *which* one?" he says.

They do eventually stop before they knock us over, continuing their own in-fighting and jostling right in front of us.

"Who has a venue?" Nate asks.

Good thinking. That's one way to weed out some of them.

"I have the blacksmith's shop. A classic."

"I have the local tollbooth. It's the closest."

"I have the Gretna Hotel. Where people truly got married in

Gretna, historically." He gives the stink eye to the priest from the blacksmith shop. "And it's classy."

"I have a back room at the Bulldog Public House. I'll throw in two pints for the newlyweds."

This hasn't weeded out any of them.

"Who can do this for…" I take out the pouch and pocket some of the coins to save them. I'm not going to debtor's prison again. "This much?" I hold the rest of the bag up, jiggling the money for effect.

"The Gretna Hotel would be happy to host you for that amount," the priest dressed in silk says. Okay, he must be the fancy option.

"I can do it for a few coins less than that."

"I can do it for half."

This didn't help either.

"Let's not waste time on this. Do you want to get married in a pub or a hotel?" I'm not getting married in a tollbooth, which is a weird option, and I'd rather not get married in a blacksmith's shop. I don't want soot in my wedding photos. In my fake wedding photos.

"Pub, to be honest. How many people can say they were married in a pub?"

"Still not you, even after this." I remind him this isn't real. Really, I'm reminding *myself* that this isn't real. And each task we do today, every second of this day that passes, we get one step closer to the fantasy ending.

"How many people can say they've been fake married in a real pub?"

"Right. We'll take the pub," I say to the masses.

I think that'll be the end of it, but all of the priests throw in a last-ditch effort to win us over. All at once.

"She wants the pub!" Nate roars, done with the loud voices and harassment. Which I appreciate because they're giving me a headache. I also appreciate it because stern Nate is doing things to me. Things I like.

The pub priest looks smug, and he shoes the other priests away. "I'll arrange everything. You two lovebirds make your way to the Bulldog, and I'll meet you there. Payment up front, though."

"Small deposit up front, the rest when we get to the pub and see a real fake priest there," Nate snatches the coin purse out of my hand before I can hand it over to our priest.

Untrusting businessman. But probably smart. I mean, these "priests" were just standing around trying to get marriage business instead of like, praying or whatever.

It's a good thing Nate's here with me.

"Would a man of the cloth lie to you, there?" Our priest looks offended.

"That is not the defense you think it is, from our particular time," I say.

"Fine." He snatches the money Nate pulled out of the pouch. "Here's a map to the pub. I'll be ready when you get there." He shoves another map at Nate.

"Fresh meat," one priest yells. They all swarm us again, this time passing around us like we're rocks in a fast-slowing stream. Once they pass, we turn around and see that they're congregating around Sarah and Will.

"Let's escape while they're distracted," I whisper to Nate, saluting Sarah as we pass the crowd around them.

She mouths *help*, and I respond with, *I'm sorry* and keep going. It'll be fine. I'm pretty sure all these people are part of the cast and are instructed not to hurt us. Embarrass us, yes. Any physical pain, no. It would interfere with the filming schedule.

"I wonder if the team ahead of us is already on their way to Gretna?" I ask.

"Probably. Unless they got really lost. We saw the next team, so I don't think the show made a big gap between us all."

"I hope they got lost." Uncharitable as that thought it, I really want to win. "Just a little. Not like stuck in quicksand lost. Just maybe they go the wrong way and decide to have lunch at Nando's."

"What's Nando's?"

"What's Nando's? What's *Nando's*? You've never had a cheeky Nando's? You sad, deprived American. Missing out on that Peri-Peri." I shake my head in disappointment.

"Why, or maybe how, is it cheeky?"

"If you don't know, you don't know, Nate. Maybe we'll get some before you go back to New York, which sadly still does not have one."

"We got the Americans to talk about Nando's. The U.K. is going to love this," Aiko whispers as she raises her hands in thanks to a higher power.

We get back to the carriage, and Nate helps me into it for what is probably going to be the last time. Maybe we can get lost and go to a Nando's right now. Extend my time with the man that I love, or whatever, before Dad ruins this.

And he will. The second I see them together, reality is going to beat up this love I'm feeling with weapons of awkwardness and frustration. And then Nate will side with Dad over something insignificant, and it'll be ruined completely.

I take the map from Nate and contemplate saying we should go left when the way to Gretna is very much a right.

"Which way, navigator?" Nate asks.

"Left," I say before I can weigh the pros and cons of saying either direction. "Shit, no, sorry. It's a right."

"Final answer, ma'am?" Fred asks.

"Yes. Right is the final answer," I say, kind of hating myself for not sticking with left.

Except that would just delay the inevitable, and I have these butterflies in my stomach that are punching my bladder. Best to end this show early so we can get to the moment we have to decide what's going on with us and I'll know what's happening, so I can stop worrying.

Plus, I really want to win those extra votes.

The carriage jerks ahead, sending us on the (right) way to Gretna.

"Whatever happens, I've really enjoyed being your partner," Nate says over the clapping of horse hooves.

Is this a goodbye? Or is he just trying to make conversation?

This is not the love experience that I thought it would be. This is confusion and strife and when do I get to feel the waves of euphoria? I was promised waves of euphoria. But here I am, analyzing every word he says for clues that he wants to stay with me. How do people in love get things done?

It's just so time-consuming.

I peek over to Nate, but he's looking out the carriage window at the passing scenery. No help at all. Why he isn't spontaneously announcing his feelings for me, I'll never know. It would make my life considerably easier, to know I'm not alone in these feelings.

The rest of the ride goes as excruciatingly slow as the first ride to Carlisle. And not just because we're in a carriage. Because there are things I want to say but I can't make myself, and every few minutes I hype myself up to say something but then chicken out. After another hour and a half of anticipation, Fred stops the carriage at Gretna Green.

"This is it," Aiko says, opening the carriage door for us. We exit, but Aiko makes us do it again, but this time with more excitement on our faces. Apparently, exhaustion and confusion don't play well on TV.

"Is this going to set us back? Because that's not cool." I decide to focus on the winning and not the feelings.

"Then emote correctly the first time, and we won't need to do things repeatedly," Aiko callously says. Good thing I won't need this advice for much longer.

We pulled up directly in front of the Bulldog, our wedding venue for the day. I don't take my usual time appreciating the buildings, only noticing we're in front of a building that is made of stone, and it has a roof. And it looks old.

We rush inside (filming way too many takes of us rushing into the building, because apparently it was *too* fast the first time) and look around for anyone who looks even vaguely like a priest.

"Priest," I finally yell, looking around the room and ignoring any details that aren't a priest-shaped person. "Where are you? We want to get married. We have money." Mom would pay so much to see me now. And all she has to do is subscribe to whatever gets her British television in the States.

"And fast!" Nate adds.

A man saunters out of the back room. "Hello. Is this the couple my partners found in Carlisle? What's the rush? Are you in a family way?"

"Yes. Just excited. No. I do. He does. Are we married yet?" I ask, ready to turn around and declare myself the winner of this show.

"A few more steps than that, love. First change into your wedding outfits, and the priest will be here when you're ready." The unnamed man opens the curtain to a back room and reveals our trunks. I don't know how they got them from the carriage to the back of this pub without us noticing, but I've stopped questioning the power of the reality show crew.

"Okay then. Ready for this wedding, fiancé?" I ask my fiancé, who will only be my fiancé for another few minutes. Not because we're getting married but because this is going to be over.

"I've been ready for this day since I ruined you in a garden," he says, smiling. Bending his face toward mine.

"A little under a week ago," I whisper back.

"A very long week. A real year of a week."

"It's been busy." We both stand in the pub, talking when we should be changing so we can win the extra votes. But then I remember all of this is on camera, and I need to hurry or I'll come across looking even more lovesick than I already apparently do. And that would be embarrassing on top of me being vulnerable, which would be the lemon juice on my paper cut.

"Where can we change?" I focus on the last obstacle standing between me and getting away from these cameras so I can feel my feelings in private.

"Toilets are past the bar. Ladies to the right, gents to the left."

I move first, getting the dress from the chest on the floor, and rushing past an antique wooden bar. If the world was a kind place, someone would be at the bar handing me a very stiff drink of some good scotch, being that we're in Scotland now and all.

This show is trying to keep me surprisingly sober now that it's the penultimate moment.

"Wait, I can't do this by myself." I look to Aiko and Kelly, who followed us down the hall. That's a loaded statement. But while it works as an emotional plea about marriage, I mean getting dressed.

"We've got you covered. You found a lady's maid who's willing to help for free because she loves love." Aiko moves out of the way for another woman to follow me into the bathroom.

The woman works silently, unfortunately, so the sound of my heartbeat pounding in my ears is even louder. But I can't think of any small talk at this particular moment to drown it out, so I try to pretend it's just the sound of the ocean.

Finally, dressed in the clothes that might have put us in debtor's prison and a full face of makeup which is why I think they want me to have a lady's maid for this day, I exit the bathroom at the same time that Nate comes out of his changing area.

"Ahh, you can't see the bride! It's bad luck." I duck behind my lady's maid, cowering down under her superior height.

"For a fake wedding?"

"Yeah. Maybe we'll confuse the universe by getting dressed in wedding clothes and saying we do, and it'll still give us the bad luck." I feel silly at my reflexive reaction, but now I'm stuck with it.

Nate sighs, then I hear some rustling. "I'll leave first."

"He's gone," Aiko whispers to me after a few minutes. "And he's in position at the makeshift altar. We're ready for you." She hands me a bouquet that I didn't notice before now and I take it.

"Okay. Walking myself down the aisle," I whisper to myself. "Mom is gonna be pissed." Because she has definitely demanded to co-walk me down the aisle, with Dad. Who is also going to be pissed, but for different reasons.

I turn the corner into the main space of the pub to see Nate and the priest standing directly across from me. I smile as I see Nate, despite everything that's happening. Because he looks good as the lord of the manor. Regency suit, vest, tight pants and tall boots all outlining that perfect body. Reminding me I've already had the honeymoon.

And he's got a smile on his face so bright it's lighting up this ancient, dark space.

Aiko and Kelly follow behind me, capturing the moment. And then doing it again to film me from behind. Finally, I get to Nate as the faint notes of "Here Comes the Bride" finish.

This venue, even though it's a pub, is surprisingly nice. Instead of cramped, dark, and depressing, it's more intimate, historic, and cozy.

I put my hands on top of Nate's, his fingers curling around mine to lock them in place. Standing in front of him, this feels more real than any of the relationships I've had in the past. And it's completely fake.

Well, I guess parts of it aren't fake. Like the sex. And neither is the look in his eyes, the fire in the brown depths warming me inside as effectively as his hands are warming my cold fingers.

The priest is done letting us have our moment. "We are gathered here..." the priest drones on. So much that I tune him out. But then he gets to the important questions.

"If anyone objects to this marriage, speak now or forever hold your peace." The priest pauses longer than I think is necessary and looks to the door. I raise an eyebrow at Nate, who shrugs.

"Stop this wedding," a voice booms from the pub entrance.

I freeze in horror. I know that voice.

A little too well, as it's been yelling at me since I was a child.

CHAPTER 39

NAOMI

What is he doing here? I'm unsure if I'm having a nightmare or this is real life. Because to be honest, Dad bursting into big moments of my life and yelling that they need to stop is a reoccurring fear I have.

"Damn it," Nate curses under his breath.

I don't blame him, Dad looks furious. The man would rather cut enemies down with a crushing verbal blow than a physical one, but he looks like he could make an exception right now. I'm not exactly sure who he wants to punch, but he's sending unhappy looks at the producers and Nate, so they must be the targets of this anger.

"I knew I should have kept a closer eye on you. Going on a reality show. Ruining any chance of protecting your reputation. Your mother was wrong to let you run wild in a foreign country."

"I am an adult!" I yell back, before realizing that adults wouldn't even get dragged into the argument. I go on the offensive. "What are you doing here?"

"Trying to stop you from making a giant mistake by being on this reality show. Like Nate was supposed to be doing. But he can't do his job, which we *will* talk about later." He sends another threatening look at Nate before turning it back on me. "At least he had the good sense to tell the producers about me. They contacted me."

"The show is over. They brought you on to make more drama, which you're doing, harming my reputation more than any show could. Congratulations, *you* got manipulated by them." I thrust my bouquet at him to make it crystal clear who was manipulated.

"The show is over?" Dad looks around, looking taken aback for the first time since he stormed in here.

"Last day of filming. In fact, we were almost done with the fake marriage, so it's about five minutes from being over. In fact, I do. Nate, say I do," I snarl.

He looks concerned but mumbles, "I do."

"There, now we're married and it's over. "

Dad shifts his priorities and starts harassing Aiko. "We are going to talk about the editing of her footage before it airs."

"Dad, I am not a child. I can drink. I can fight for my country. I can take out a mortgage. I can rent a car!" I yell louder with each task I can do. "I don't need your protection. If I make mistakes, which I promise I will, I'll deal with the consequences. If I make really big ones, I will ask for your help. Well, most likely just Mom's. But I am an adult, and I have the right to make my own choices."

"I need to protect you!" Dad yells at me.

"No, you don't! I need to live my own life. And you know what, if I'm ever going to walk off a literal cliff because everyone's doing it, then you can step in and grab my arm. But you're not stopping me just because I make decisions you don't agree with."

"And you." I turn on Nate, snatching my hand out of his. "You told the producers about Dad? You knew they were going to use that against me at some point in this process, and you knew I moved all the way to London to not be Harrison Richmond's daughter. But you told them and now here I am, going to be known as Harrison Richmond's daughter on yet another continent."

"Wait—I didn't know they would—it was before—"

"I don't know what I thought. I've known from the beginning that you work for Dad, and of course you care more about him and your job than me. It's your livelihood. I'm the idiot that forgot that."

"Just listen, it's not—"

"No. There's nothing for you to explain. I was the one who should have remembered who we are."

I toss the bouquet onto the bar and back away from both men. "There's clearly no point in sticking around here." I turn, my dress making a satisfying swish as I do, and march out of the pub. I hear both men try to call after me, but with all the crew following me out to get my exit on camera, they can't reach me.

Never thought I'd be happy the crew was around.

The tears come next, of frustration with both of them and for what could have been with Nate. I think the crew gets them on camera, but it's beyond me to stop them. In fact, thinking about how this is going to be on TV later just makes me cry harder. So less than ideal, all around.

When we get outside, the British weather mocks me with its unusually clear blue skies. Can't it read a room? This is one time I would appreciate some rain so it can disguise the water already on my face. But no, the sky is still bitter about 1776 and is punishing me for it.

"You should go back and confront your dad. And Nate." Aiko looks uncomfortable with pushing me, but still does it. She's gentle but firm with the opinion, reminding me that even though she sees I'm in pain, she's still going to do her job.

"No. I don't want to."

"If you end it like this, he'll always see you like a child. Running. You need to stay and hash it out."

"And it'll make great television," I say bitterly.

Aiko shifts and clears her throat. "It can be both."

"No. You don't know him. I won't be reduced to a child in front of the world." This much is bad enough.

"But—"

"The answer is no."

Aiko sighs. "Fine. But we need to do the interview."

"Are you kidding me right now?" I'm crying on the side of the road, life disrupted, and I still have to do the interview?

"If we get it done now, then once you get to the hotel, I can let you have some privacy. We'll do it in the car, even." Aiko dangles privacy in front of me even though it should be a basic right. Not if you've signed it away apparently.

"Fine." I wipe the tears from my face as the car comes and Aiko speaks to someone in a walkie-talkie.

In a few minutes, I'm speeding away from the pub. The one pub in this whole country that I hate, even though I usually love their atmosphere and had found great comfor in them for some after work drinks or a nice night with friends. Roaring fires in the fireplaces, comfy chairs to sink into, and the smell of fried foods surrounding me.

Now even that is all ruined.

I start the interview. "Did you know he was coming?"

Aiko sighs. "Yes."

"Right." And she still joked with us all day. She's very talented. Or lacking in any empathy. "Did Nate know?"

"No."

I nod. That's something. I don't know what. But something. "You can start now."

"Great. Tell us why you're so mad at Nate?"

I run different responses in my mind but settle on the truth. I've already had a breakdown on TV; nothing can be more embarrassing than that. So they get brutal honesty now.

"It's one of my lifelong fears, that I'm noting more than successful businessman Harrison Richmond's daughter. I grew up privileged and I just wanted to know that I could be my own person; I wanted something that was just mine. Specifically, a career that I built. Not something that my daddy got me. And I was doing that here, in London. And it hurts that Nate told the show about Dad, and that led to him coming here and destroying what little independence I had left. And I was even madder when I realized at the altar that Nate was never going to think I'm more important than his job and by extension my dad. I've always been in Dad's shadow and I'm used to it. But I can't accept it with the person I've come to…care about."

There. That's the fragile heart of me, put on display for everyone to judge. Even if I did downplay how much I care for Nate.

"Do you think you can forgive Nate?" Aiko asks.

"I don't know. I'm not really mad at him because I should have known better than to think he would choose me over the career he's worked so long for. Not that I even want him to, because it's a bad spot for him to be in. I'm more disappointed and mad at myself for forgetting that and letting myself get close to him anyway. That I let my guard down."

"Do you think you can move forward with him if he wanted to continue being with you? He looked gutted when you walked away from the altar."

I shake my head. "Nothing's changed. It would still be an awkward position for him to be caught between me and my daddy issues. I don't think we can get over that." The thought leaves me even sadder than I was when I stormed out of the building, and I feel the tears coming again. I scrunch up my face to keep the tears in, but that just pushes them out faster. Aiko hands me a packet of tissues she had at the ready, probably happy she's finally getting to use them and get some good drama.

"Would you be together if it wasn't for your dad?"

"Probably. But I also probably would never have met him if it wasn't for Dad, so there's that."

"How do you feel about him?"

"I care about him." My tone is final. I'm not giving more than that.

"Seems like you care about him a lot."

"Hmm."

"Do you love him?" Aiko is done beating around the bush.

"I can't possibly know that. It's only been a week."

"Don't forget to answer in a full sentence," Aiko says.

I sigh but comply so they can get edit they want. "I can't possibly know if I love him. It's only been a week."

We stare each other down in the moving vehicle, her wanting me to say more and me willing her to ask the next question.

Aiko blinks first and moves on. "How about you and your dad?"

I roll my eyes, the tears abating for a second to express exasperation. "Dad is Dad." I shrug. "He's just doing what he does: taking over. I'm not even mad, just resigned."

"Are you going to be able to forgive him?"

"Probably. Eventually I'll forgive him. But I may also move even farther from New York. Maybe Italy this time. Or India. Except I only know a little Punjabi, which could be a problem when everyone assumes I can speak the language since I'm half-Indian."

Aiko nods at Kelly, who turns off the camera and puts it down from her shoulder. The red light goes dark for the last time, at least until the reunion show.

I breathe out a sigh of relief and soon we're pulling up to a serviceable and uninspiring modern hotel. An airport hotel, if the planes flying overhead are anything to go by. I walk through the lobby with Aiko, who leads me directly to my room. A clean and anonymous room that could be any hotel in many cities around the world.

No more cozy and inviting inns or extravagant stately manors for me now that the show is over. Good.

"Nate and my dad won't know where I am, will they?" I ask Aiko before she leaves.

"Well, Nate is coming here too, but to his own room. I won't tell them your room number if you don't want me to. You can call down for food, drink, or whatever you want on the company tab," Aiko says, nodding to a binder on the bedside table. "I'll come back in the morning to pick you up for your flight back down to London."

"Is everyone going to be on the same flight?" I ask tentatively.

"Probably. I can get you to the airport early, though, if you want to try to change your flight and leave earlier than anyone else?"

"Yes, please." That is the first good news I've had in a while and even gets a weak and somewhat shaky smile.

Aiko points to the corner of the room. "There's your luggage from before filming, so you can get back into your own clothes. And all your electronics are in there too."

I look at the luggage in surprise. I forgot I was getting my phone back today. This is the longest I've been without it since seventh grade when I got one of those Nokia brick phones and couldn't stop playing Snake on it.

Aiko helps me with my corset and I swallow back tears at the fact that Nate won't be helping me get dressed and undressed any more.

Aiko starts to leave the room then. "Do you want to know if you got married fastest and won the extra votes?"

"Sure. I guess," I say, the emotions of the day taking over my usually overcompetitive side. I hadn't even thought about winning, because I already feel like I lost.

"You guys did get married fastest. Hannah and Amir got lost after leaving the courthouse game," Aiko says with a slight smile, like she knows it won't be the comfort she intended it to be. Then she leaves.

Oh joy. I raid the mini-bar before getting in my PJs and

crawling into bed with my booty of three mini-bottles of alcohol and overpriced M&Ms. I turn the TV on and let the soothing voices of the *QI* guests telling me trivia be the soundtrack for my sadness.

Or try to, but a knock on the door interrupts me while the TV is talking about spite houses. I contemplate ignoring the knock, but it gets stronger and I worry whoever it is won't go away until I answer.

I wipe my eyes in the full-length mirror next to the door and look through the peephole, not sure who I'm expecting, or dreading.

But it's Zara, so I open the door and throw myself in her arms. "I know, leprechaun. Aiko texted me as soon as she dropped you off." She moves me into the room, backing me up until we're back at the bed. "I'm so sorry. I feel responsible," she says when we're both sitting.

"It's not your fault. It's my family drama."

"But it wouldn't have been on TV if it wasn't for me. I had no idea they planned to bring your father in. I didn't even know they knew about him."

"It's okay." I clutch my friend, turning my head into her shoulder to cry some more.

"Do you want to talk about it?" she asks.

"No," I say, sniffing. "But if I did, I would just say that this is all so typical, and I'm sicker of it than I was when I first moved to London."

"I know your dad is…difficult." Understatement alert. "But I've been sneaking views of some of your footage like a good friend and I think you should let Nate explain before you dump him-dump him."

"He works for Dad; he's never going to be my partner."

"He already acts like your partner. The way he looks at you when you aren't paying attention and tries to find you whenever he's in the same room, it's sweet. I don't think he's concerned about what Harrison thinks or wants, at all. Just about what Naomi wants."

"It's too hard," I wail. "I'm never going to think I come first. It's his career."

"It's all up to you, of course. Either way, I've already assembled the Ex-Pats, and they're waiting to pamper and love on you when you get back to London tomorrow. I didn't tell them what happened, that's up to you. But they'll be there to offer general comfort."

"Are you coming back too?"

"I need to do some work up here, shoot some B-roll. Then I'll be down with the biggest comfort package I can find, to shower you in love. And Lucky Charms. The all-marshmallow box with none of this whole grain crap getting in the way."

"Thank you," I whisper.

"Now. Have you eaten?" Zara helps herself to my room service menu.

AIKO GETS me early the next morning, as promised. I leave Zara in the room, surrounded by half-empty plates of food I said I didn't want until they showed up and I got hungry, and entirely empty bottles of wine. I snap a quick picture before I leave, to go in her future wedding slideshow.

I deserve it.

Stepping out of the lobby with modern makeup and sunglasses, I'm ready to have this moment videoed, but this is the one time I won't be on camera, and we get to the airport with minimum fuss (and no Nate).

"Take care of yourself, my favorite contestant," Aiko says as she hugs me in the departures area.

"I bet you say that to all your contestants." I know her manipulative tendencies, but I hug her back. It's been interesting.

Aiko sniffs. "I mean it every time I say it. In the moment." She's surprisingly honest now that we're done. "Anyway, have a good flight back, and I'll see you in a few months for the reunion."

Shaking my head, I go to the empty departures desk, changing my ticket for an earlier flight. It could have been because they had space on an earlier flight, or it could have been because they wanted to get the sad lady hanging by a thread out of their airport before she cries on them, but either way, I avoid seeing any other cast members.

I also avoid checking my phone. It kept buzzing last night, until I put it on silent, but I know I have missed calls, texts, and emails from Nate and Dad. And I will continue ignoring them until I feel...not like this.

A short flight later, I land home in London. Feeling very "Treat Myself," I get a cab instead of taking the Tube. I'm fragile and as great as the public transportation is here, I just want to be home as fast as possible.

The lights are on in my flat when the cab pulls up, but I don't immediately freak out. Probably the Ex-Pats, at Zara's instruction, who have a spare key for emergencies and housesitting, making my sad homecoming better with comfort food and beverages.

"You lot didn't have to make sure I'm—"

Shit.

CHAPTER 40

NAOMI

Dad is half-standing in my living room, probably in the act of getting off the couch, looking like an awkward burglar surprised by the owners coming home early from a vacation.

"What are you doing here?" I ask, dropping my bags and pushing my suitcase inside the door and leaving them there.

"You did ask us to co-sign the lease. So the landlord was only too happy to give me a key." He holds it up like proof he didn't climb in through a window. Like Harrison Richmond would climb through a window; he'd pay someone to climb through a window and then unlock the front door for him.

I check in with myself to see if I'm going to cry again, but I think I'm still dehydrated from all the previous crying, so my tear ducts stay dry for the moment.

"That's *how* you got in here. But *why* are you here?"

"You were upset. I didn't want to leave the country without talking to you." The usually confident man sounds more subdued than I've ever heard him.

"Did you tell Mom?" I don't think so, because it's been more than twelve hours and if Mom knew, she would be here by now, ready to slay dragons for me. Or at least she would have blown up my phone, and none of the calls or messages have been from her.

"No." Dad scoffs. "Then she'd yell at me."

"Because you did something wrong."

"I still don't understand why wanting the best for my child is wrong."

Of course he doesn't. He never acknowledges any mistakes. "Because even though I'm your child, I'm not a kid. I'm an adult. And I am capable. I can do things for myself."

"I'm your father!" Dad roars, frustrated by this argument. Again. "If I can spare you pain, then I'm going to do it. What's the point of all this money if I can't take care of my family, the people I love? If I can't make their lives easier?"

That's the nicest thing anyone has ever yelled at me. When my shoulders sag, letting go of a tension I didn't know I had, I finally admit that I was a little worried he was only so protective of me because he didn't want to hurt his image, or the family's image. But if he is overprotective of me because he loves me…I can deal with that.

Well, I can deal better than if it came from a place of keeping up appearances.

"And I love you for that!" I yell back, equally as aggressive. "But I'm not a family pet. I'm an adult and I need to make my own decisions. I need you to respect my decisions. Or this time, I will move to Australia!"

Dad sighs, taking in what I just told him. But not liking it, from the look on his face.

"Well?" I'm going to need some confirmation that he's hearing what I'm saying.

"Yes. Okay. I will try, very hard, to give you space." He looks like he ate expired sushi from a gas station but the words are what I need to hear. "And I'm sorry if I ever made you feel like I thought you were less capable."

Well, that's more than I was anticipating. I don't think I've ever heard him say sorry to anyone. Ever. For any reason. "Come again?"

He sighs, looking more pained than when he said it before. "I'm sorry. Nate yelled at me after you left, and he made me realize how my actions made you feel. I never thought about it before. And I've had time to think about it in the last day, and I don't want you to feel like that. I want you to feel like the fiercely independent, smart, capable woman you are. If anything that I'm doing is stopping that, then I need to change."

"Wait, Nate yelled at you?" Perfect employee Nate? Corporate drone Nate? Guy who lives for his job, yelled at his boss? For me?

"Yes." He glowers into the corner at the thought of this yelling. I'm sorry I missed it. "Lucky for him he's a great employee." Then he turns back to me, looking less like he wants to do physical violence to someone. "And he was right."

I'm still a little frustrated with Dad and hurt he tried to inter-fere again, but I'm not ready to go no contact yet. Only time will tell if he actually lives up to his nice words, but I can give him that. This is the most we've talked about our issues, and it is a good start.

Still need at least an ocean between us, though. But maybe just one will do.

And now I'll have something to rehabilitate—instead of the image of me being a wild child, it'll be to rehabilitate the image of me as a daddy's girl. I'll be my own first client after all.

"Even though Mom didn't find out yet, you know she's going to see what you did when it airs," I say, getting a little bit of revenge.

He pales. "Are you sure you don't want my lawyers to bury this footage? We can get out of it." He looks hopeful and I know this time it's because he's worried about himself when Mom sees this.

I crack a smile. "It's too late now. I signed a contract."

Dad shrugs. "I can get you out of that. Do you know how many lawyers work for me?"

"We just talked about this," I say in exasperation.

"Fine. Stick with your predatory contract. I won't do anything. Even though I could."

"Yes, you could. You're the most vicious businessman."

Dad doesn't pick up on the condescension. "Good," he says, clearing his throat. He shifts, and I've never seen the man look so uncomfortable. "So. About Nate—"

"Nope." I interrupt before he can say anything. "You aren't going to fire, suspend, demote or even talk about this with Nate. He wouldn't even have come if it wasn't for you asking him to do things way outside the scope of his duties. He will have grounds for suing you and I will testify on his behalf." We probably won't win because Dad really does have the best attorneys, but it'll be embarrassing for everyone before it dies.

"But you were upset at him." That wasn't what I expected him to say. "He hurt you."

"That is none of your business, remember? We just discussed this!" Is our tentative peace going to be over so soon?

"But…it…ugh, fine. You're right. I promised I would work on this. So this is me, working on this and letting it go." He doesn't look like he's letting it go, but as long as he leaves Nate alone, it's fine.

"He was only doing what you told him to, as your employee. And it was inappropriate of you to ask in the first place." Nate and I might not work out, but I don't want anything bad to happen to him. Especially after he apparently stood up for me.

"Fine." Dad sighs. "Now that this is settled, do you want to go get some Nando's?"

I don't know that it's settled, but I haven't eaten a decent meal in a while, so he can have this one. "Always," I say. "Now if you did want to use your power and money to cater to my every whim, you'd open one in Manhattan."

"Noted," Dad says, calling the car.

"I'm paying tonight, though." I'm testing out my new independence.

Dad laughs. "All right. If that's what you want."

See, it's a start.

After a nice meal where I catch Dad up on what the show was about, without giving him any information about what happened with Nate, I give him a hug goodbye and watch him get a car outside my flat.

It's a surprisingly nice meal with Dad, one where I'm more relaxed than I've been since I was in elementary school. I've missed getting to simply be with him, without worrying about my independence or his overbearing tendencies. He did look at me with judgment in his eyes about getting two different varieties of potatoes with dinner as my sides (fries and mashed potatoes), but he didn't say anything about it.

The night was a good start.

I sigh deeply when I close the door, exhausted by all the emotion of the past twenty-four hours… really the entirety of the last few weeks. I fall into bed and sleep the deep sleep of someone who *finally* isn't going to be interrupted in the morning.

One Month Later

I elbow my way through a crowded restaurant for dinner with the Ex-Pats. I haven't seen them in a few weeks, which isn't unusual, but I also haven't texted much with any of them in those weeks, which is. I'm excited to be back with my London family.

I told them about the show and Nate when I got back. They rallied around me with their usual brand of love and support, and it helped. They helped me stay strong when Nate texted, a few days after we got back. His first communication after all the calls and texts from our disastrous wedding night.

All he said was *Hi*, but it set me off feeling miserable and needing my friends. And then he made one more effort, when he sent me a bouquet of chocolate-covered strawberries. I didn't even open the letter that came with them, but I did eat the fruit. He got the message and stopped reaching out, which was even worse. I really needed my friends after that.

But then I started to avoid them a little because they kept giving me sad looks and texting to ask how I was. It hurt too much to think about the show. About what I can't have, even though I've discovered that Nate's basically perfect for me. But I also miss them, so I'm done avoiding them.

I've put this night off as long as I could, telling them I'm busy at work, setting up my own PR company. I've been genuinely busy with the minutia of starting a business and figuring out the immigration rules, so I haven't had time to be overly sad. Is this why people throw themselves into work? It's surprisingly reliable as a distraction from a messy personal life.

I reached out to my castmates, and got interested responses from Jessica, George and Hannah. Now this show has to be a hit and I can grow this business even more. I've already started to see an increase in social media followers as the first episodes have started to air, for myself and my cast mates.

I've tried to avoid the show; living it was bad enough. But sometimes I can't help but watch along with the rest of the country. Watching myself fall in love with Nate is too hard, knowing how it ends. But I can't look away either. It's almost like falling in love with him all over again each episode when I see how he was toward me, and how we were together. And then another heartbreak when I realize he isn't next to me, and he never will be.

To capitalize on the show's momentum and to distract myself, I've organized a charity football/football game where we're going to play both American football and rest-of-the-world football in one day. Since athleticism isn't my thing, this should be fun. But I did get some former and current contestants from *Love Island*,

Geordie Shore, and *The Only Way Is Essex,* so it should be entertaining. And the charity of course—they'll get plenty of money out of this and we'll get the great publicity.

I'm even in early talks to get George to represent some protein powder.

And I made business cards.

With the busy schedule, I had gotten down to only thinking about Nate once every few hours (more when I torture myself with watching the show), which I feel is a vast improvement over constantly, the amount of time I was thinking about him when I first got back from filming.

But now, as the reunion draws closer, my anxiety and the thoughts about Nate are slowly increasing again.

This is a very frustrating development. I was banking on any feelings that I felt during this show being a lie. Just a manufactured delirium that was the result of the challenge/game atmosphere, the copious alcohol offerings and the devious, manipulative producers.

But a month apart and my feelings are not going away. Making me acknowledge that they might not be the result of producers' machinations. Not the most comforting realization.

"Sorry, all, I lost track of time," I say as I find the group. All seated with drinks in front of them.

"Oh, I see, Hollywood leprechaun. I make you famous and now you show up everywhere late?" Zara asks, clearly already into her cups.

I roll my eyes as I take the empty seat at the table.

"The show's only aired a few episodes," Lucy says. "Which means she's probably late because she was thinking about Nate, and not because she's gone full influencer diva on us. Or she has gone full influencer diva in record time." And there I go, falling right under the path of the oncoming bus she pushed me under.

"With friends like you…"

"I ordered you a margarita," Dev says, not as comfortable mocking his friends as the rest of us are.

"Thank you, only real friend at this table," I say pointedly.

"Speaking of Nate—" Zara begins.

"I wasn't." This is why I avoided these people I love. I just sat down and they've already started, speaking the truth that I don't want to hear.

"*Speaking of Nate,* how is the reunion going to go?" Zara asks, not unkindly, even though the question feels like a stab.

"I'm going to give Aiko and all you evil producers exactly what you want and cry a lot, probably."

"I think you should talk to him before the big day. You've gotten on better terms with your dad and if you can do that, you can figure out a way to have Nate and deal with the complications," Jaya says. This is a coordinated attack.

She's right about my dad. He's only brought up moving home once, and he stopped immediately when I said no, and in return, I'm calling more. Mom is thrilled, even if she doesn't fully understand what happened. Still, it wouldn't be the same with Nate. It wouldn't be as easy, because him being at work with Dad would be a constant issue, as is our geography.

Even if it was pretty easy to be with him on the show. But that was a fantasy.

I sigh. "I've wanted to text him so many times since I got back."

"What's stopped you?" Lucy asks.

"I don't think he'll pick me next time there's an issue between Dad and me. He gets paid to agree with Dad." But it's been hard. Especially since social media is in love with Nate and Naomi right now. Since I have to be on social media for work, I can't avoid posts about how adorable we are together and how we're restoring one viewer's faith in love.

Wait 'til you get to the end, @born_to_nap10. We won't be #goals then.

But it is hard hearing from everyone that we should be together, and trying to explain (to myself) why we wouldn't work. I sound less and less convinced every time I have to do it.

"But that was before the show. After spending time together, don't you trust him more?" Zara asks.

"I want to," I say finally. "And that's a big step for me."

"Is this any better?" Dev, the man who's usually quiet when we vent, butts in with some truth. "Don't you already feel bad?"

"Et tu, Dev-us? I thought you were the nice one."

"I'm just honest."

I sigh and think back to the first few days after I got back from filming, sitting in a cocoon of blankets while I ate through enough food to give a bodybuilder a food coma. "Yeah, I do already feel bad."

"And as someone who might have peeked through some of the footage, I think you guys built something that could last," Zara says.

My head snaps up. "The footage."

Zara looks wary, rightfully so. "Yes. The footage we took of you guys. From that camera that followed you around for a week."

"Do you feel bad about what happened to me, that was your fault because you wanted me to be on this show as a favor? To you."

"Well, yes." Zara shifts uncomfortably in her seat. I know that was below the belt, but I need to soften her up before I ask for what I'm about to ask for.

"Then let me see the footage of Nate and me before the reunion. Right now, if possible. I need to see it." My words come out fast and my tone is high pitched in desperation.

"How would that help?" Zara asks carefully, knowing I'm asking something that can get her fired. And I know it too.

But I need to see Nate from an outside perspective. I'm too close to this, but maybe if I can see our whole relationship through the eyes of an impartial camera, it'll help me see things without the lens of my issues. Or maybe I'm already so far gone I'm just looking for any excuse to see Nate again.

Not many people can get this chance to see their entire relationship, but I have it and I want to take it. The show's already been airing, and I've seen some of our early interactions. If I'm being perfectly honest, seeing Nate and me together like that has been weakening any argument I have against us.

Because the couple in that footage is strong, damn it. Strong enough to deal with anything that comes their way, whether a Regency chaperone or an overbearing modern father. As long as they have the courage to decide to make a go of it.

But I need to see the unedited footage. I want to know if it's us or the editing making us into something we're not. Lulling me into a false sense of security because I want to believe we're strong and they added the perfect orchestral music to our scenes.

"You don't have the time to go through everything. We have days' worth of footage," Zara says, but she's already getting her purse and coat.

"Thank you." I get up as well. I reach for my wallet, but Dev waves me off.

"We'll get this. Do you need us to come with you?" Dev looks like he wants the answer to be no. Jaya and Lucy look interested, though.

"No. I think I need to face this by myself." I smile at the group that's been my family in London. "And we might be doing a crime, so it's best to keep it to the absolute minimum, people-wise. But think non-prison thoughts for us."

I follow Zara out of the door, hoping I find something in the video to give me the answers I still don't have.

THIS IS LESS James Bond than I thought it would be. I insisted we go home and change into all black, but Zara just laughed at me and said it's fine. She took me to the same office I had my interview in, where multiple people are diligently staring at screens, ignoring us completely.

While I appreciate the ease, this can't be good for the show's security.

Zara leads me to a desk I know is hers, because it's covered in pictures of our London group and her family. She enters her log-in information to her computer, but before she pulls up the footage I want, she turns to me. "I'm doing this because I love you, and in return, I need you to not tell anyone about this. Because if I get fired, I will not be able to pay rent and that will affect you too."

"And I love you, too. Also, I do not want you to be fired. Don't worry, I'm an expert at the producer manipulations and can avoid giving you up. Now can I see it, please?"

She looks doubtful, which is rude, but as long as she moves, I'll be fine. She sighs while turning back around to bring up the footage. "There's a lot of this, and you don't have time to go through it all."

"Okay, okay. Then stop cutting into my viewing time." Done with the delay, I gently push her to the side and click play on the file she brought up.

And am immediately confronted by my own face on the screen. I'm still not used to it, and I have to fight the urge to close the window, except then the camera pans to Nate. Now a smile fills my face, and I barely hear Zara dramatically sigh again, before she walks away.

Good, now I can get to the important stuff, without judgement. For the next few hours, I laugh when past me does, fast forward through a lot of silence with longing looks, my heart races when past Nate looks at past me, and I fall in love with him all over again.

And then I get to the last scene. I fast forward through me storming out of the pub, not needing to see that again, and slow it down to regular when I'm gone.

Oh. Nate looks mad.

He defended me. He yelled at his boss. In a choice between me and Dad, he did choose me. I don't have to worry about what would happen if we were together and I got into a fight with Dad, because it's already happened, and Nate chose me. I didn't believe it when Dad told me or when Zara told me, sure they were exaggerating to make me feel better, but they weren't. Nate is livid and he is not holding back.

Looking at us from this chair, on the other side of this computer screen, we are working. And Nate is an adult. If he wants to risk his career for a potential relationship, that's his decision. Although to be fair to Dad, he has been calm since the show, even after getting yelled at by Nate.

All I can control are my own decisions, and I want to try. I want to get back to laughing with Nate, teasing Nate, having new experiences with Nate, and loving Nate.

Because I'll take a little bit of him, for however long we last, over no Nate. And if the worst happens and we grow to resent and hate each other, at least letting go of him will be easy. In the best-case scenario, we're deliriously happy for the rest of our lives.

Now I just have to tell him that.

CHAPTER 41

NATE

ne Month Later
I'm nervous as the car drops me off at the same country house where we started filming the show, the place where I "ruined" Naomi, where we escaped her chaperone to elope, and where I began to realize there was more to life than work. I was nervous when I first stepped through these doors, not knowing what I was facing being on a reality show and how Naomi would react to find me on the show.

Now I know what it feels like to have the cameras and producers following me around, but I'm still nervous about seeing Naomi, considering how mad she was at me for how the show ended.

"My favorite contestant!" Aiko says when I walk into the building. She's waiting for me by the front desk with Kelly, who has a camera up on her shoulder and already rolling. They're not wasting any time for this reunion.

I look at her suspiciously. "I'm on to your methods now."

Aiko rolls her eyes. "I'm cursed with far too perceptive contestants to produce."

I snort. "Do you have any popcorn to go with that butter…ing up?"

"Come on, cynic. We made you and Naomi look good this season. I think I deserve a nice box of chocolates. Or a gift certificate to a spa."

"I'll get right on that," I say dryly, my entire experience flashing through my memory. I have no complaints for most of the show, surprisingly, but the last two months since our disastrous wedding left some things to be desired.

And this woman knew Harrison was coming. Knew it was going to hurt Naomi. And I can't forgive my part in that, by letting the producers know how big their rift was and who Naomi's dad was.

Maybe I'll give Aiko some of the six-month-old Halloween candy I'm sure I have pushed to the back of my pantry. That feels like a fitting gift.

Aiko gets me settled in my brightly lit dressing room with snacks and drinks. While the crew gets me camera ready with makeup, I wonder if Naomi is angry at the way we were presented in the show.

It wasn't bad, really. The only part that isn't great, besides whatever the end is going to look like, is that there *were* cameras everywhere, and even though the show didn't air us actually having sex, they aired enough of the pre-sex moments of us escaping to the bathroom for even the most oblivious of viewers to know we did it.

We weren't the only couple that did it, so at least there are multiple scarlet letters for this group to distract from ours.

Or maybe I can't be mad at any of the show because I get to see Naomi, something I don't get in real life. And aside from a few glares in the beginning and that ending, she was happy to be with me on the show.

Social media hasn't been particularly revealing. Naomi's been all smiles and busy days on her Instagram and Twitter, getting her business started. But that's social media and who knows how true that image is.

I tried reaching out a few times, but with no response, I didn't want to bother her even more than I already did by telling the producers about Harrison. It felt like a punch in the gut when I realized she wasn't going to respond, but it's my own fault. I deserve to feel like shit over her not wanting me anymore. At least I got to pretend to be in a relationship with her for what little time I had, and I even got to enjoy loving her…for a day.

Since then, I've gotten to love her in misery. From an ocean away.

Thoughts of Harrison send me to my phone to make sure there's no emergency before they take my electronics away again. The first day back at work after the show was surprisingly… okay. Harrison didn't yell, didn't fire me, didn't even look threateningly at me. And I was ready to stand up for myself or for her. But it wasn't necessary.

The first meeting was a little awkward, since Harrison wasn't even looking at me at all. But then he loosened up when we started to talk about some manufacturer issues that had come up. Now we've settled into a truce where we pretend that Naomi doesn't exist at work. I suspect that Mrs. Richmond might have a lot to do with that and I appreciate her for it.

Otherwise, watching myself fall in love with Naomi has been an…interesting experience. I'm happy because of how I felt when we were together, but then I feel a deep sadness when I realize it's over. And frustrated because I want more.

I've already bought the episodes, so I can see Naomi when she liked me, whenever I want, because that's all I'll get. Like the sad pervert I am.

Watching me, watching us, has actually led to me making a change, one that I'm afraid to tell Naomi about, because I don't know how she's going to react to it. I hope she'll be happy with it, but there's a chance she'll hate it.

"We'll need you out there in fifteen minutes. Are you ready? Do you need anything?" Aiko pops her head into the dressing room.

"A ride to the airport?" I ask hopefully. Only half joking. They're going to ask me questions I won't want to answer, that are going to be embarrassing and revealing and there's a live audience to deal with on top of everything.

And seeing Naomi again. Which is a terrifying prospect when she's already made her wishes regarding seeing me crystal clear.

"Cute." Aiko laughs at me.

"Actually, is Naomi already here?" Maybe her dad's lawyers did get her out of the contract. Good for her, but thanks for leaving me here to suffer.

"Yes, she is. Don't worry, you'll see her in a little bit. And we'll be there for all of it."

"Great." I smile, practicing my neutral smile before I leave the room. I've already given this show a lot of open, emotional responses. They don't need more.

Aiko, for her part, knows what she's doing because the fifteen-minute warning makes me even more nervous than I was when I walked in here, and I didn't think that was possible. I haven't been this nervous negotiating million-dollar deals. They're child's play in comparison to navigating this minefield of personal relationships and manipulative producers.

She finally knocks on my door and I jump up with all the alacrity of a puppy. "You ready? Oh, I guess so." She answers her own question when she comes in and sees me standing up.

"The sooner it starts, the sooner it'll be over, right?"

Aiko purses her lips. "After doing a lot of reunions during my time in reality TV, I can say it'll feel never-ending regardless of when we start."

"Great." I try the neutral smile. But the fear might leak through, because Aiko starts laughing as she turns and leads me to the shooting area.

The guys are already getting settled, one on each of the four couches set up in the same ballroom we started this show in. Two couches are set up on either side of a leather high-back chair, all framed by the elaborate decorations of the historic room, including moldings, murals and a gold chandelier.

I take a seat on the last empty velvet couch, crowding into one corner so Naomi can be as far away from me as she wants. But still, a part of me hopes she isn't mad at me anymore. I know I shouldn't have given the producers the ammo about her relationship with her father. They would have found out it was strained, but not as much as when I told them I was sent to get her back to New York. That told them the relationship was bad and that her father was rich enough to tell an employee to go to London for her.

Once we get last-minute makeup and sound checks, the women start coming in. They're all blurs that my eyes quickly pass over until Aiko ends my torture and brings Naomi out. Last, of course. She looks beautiful. I haven't seen her in modern clothes in a while, and my brain takes a minute to adjust to the fact that she's wearing a devastating short black dress that sparkles and fits her like a glove. Not the thousand layers of Regency wear she was in during the show.

She doesn't look angry. So either the time we've been apart have let her bury the anger down deep and hide it from me, or she's not angry at me anymore. I know which one I wish it is.

I stand when she gets close to me, the Regency gentleman still in here somewhere, even if I only lived that life for a week.

"Hi." That's a safe opening salvo. I pair it with a tentative smile and an unsure, slow arm movement that can transform into a hug or a handshake, or even an awkward wave, at the recipient's choice.

She moves in for a stilted one-armed hug, and the side of me that gets to touch her is ecstatic while and the side that's out in the cold erupts in angry jealousy. "Hi."

"How have you been?" Aside from what I can see on the socials. I'm clearly up to date on everything there, stalker that I am.

"Mostly good. This has helped my brand-new business as much as I thought it would, so I can't complain about the less than flattering bits that are out in the world. How about you?"

"Good. There has been some teasing, especially once we went viral. And the occasional outright disrespect. But at the end of the day, I work at a powerful company, so it hasn't been anything I can't handle."

We don't get any deeper into our reunion, interrupted by the actual reunion we're here for. Lewis comes into the ballroom from a door on the opposite side of where we entered from.

"Beautiful contestants!"

That voice. After all we've been through, it makes my body immediately flood with adrenaline, stressed for what's going to come.

"And beautiful audience at home! I've watched you all watching our little show and I love the love we're getting on social media and in the votes! The virtual voting booths have just closed, so while we count them all, we'll ask some of our favorite couples your burning questions. And we're start with the couple to my right: Hannah and Amir."

From there, the reunion focuses on one couple at a time, asking the couple questions and asking the rest of us questions about the couple. It makes me even more anxious, being next to Naomi but not touching her, or talking to her. A change from the last time we were together.

And we're last, of course. Before Lewis turns to us, we find out that Hannah and Amir have moved in together and Jessica is going to be on *The Only Way Is Essex*. George has a protein powder endorsement deal, which Naomi brokered, and Will is starting his own supplement store.

Finally. *Finally.* He gets to us.

"And now our last couple: Naomi and Nate."

CHAPTER 42

NAOMI

I clear my throat and take a deep breath before I dive in. The big movement on the exhale makes my side brush against Nate's, which tingles at the touch after two months of no Nate.

This entire day has been an exercise in slow torture, wondering when I would get to talk to Nate, waiting for it with equal parts anticipation and dread. Because I have some things to say and some things to do, but I have no idea how they're going to be received. I've already put it off longer than I should have, but I was afraid to contact him after initially ignoring him.

It's terrifying. But I need to do this as soon as possible, and if that means on camera, so be it.

"You two have found a strong following across social media." Lewis starts to read some of those supportive posts off his card. Which I've already seen since my job involves being very online. "'I would die for one of Nate's smiles. I canna handle this chemistry,' from one Scottish viewer. 'I need a relationship like that one.' 'They seem fun.' 'I can't believe Nate tattled to her father.' 'Get over yourself Naomi, it's not Nate's fault your dad is a wanker.' 'But are they together now?'" He taps the cards on his knee. "A lot to cover. Where should we begin?"

I raise my hand, not quite sure what the procedure here is. "Actually, before we get into that, I would like to say something."

"Of course. That's what we're here for." Lewis waves me on.

"Right." I turn to my partner. "Nate. I'm sorry for how I reacted at the end. I had a really good time with you and you know I have some issues with my dad. So I *might* have overreacted when he showed up and said some things that might not have been totally true, upon further reflection. I know you didn't know they would call Dad, and ultimately, it was his choice to come on the show."

"I would never do anything to hurt you. But it was my fault. I told them about your dad in the beginning. I'm so sorry for that."

"You have nothing to apologize for. Dad's actions are his own, and we have no responsibility over them. At the end of the day, he chose to come on the show and even signed an agreement to be shown on it. We've discussed it, and he's promised to try harder to respect my space. He's been doing it so far. Mostly."

Nate nods cautiously.

"I want to get over my hang-ups. And this is the part I wanted to wait for the reunion to tell you, because I wanted it to be in person: I want to date you. Long distance. You working for my dad. Whatever I can get, former fake fiancé, I would like to see where this could go with you, because I think it would be worth it. I've watched myself fall in love in these episodes, and I want that couple back. I don't know what's going to happen with us, and I can't guarantee anything, but I want to try. Because I love you."

I'm greeted by silence.

"And if Dad makes your life uncomfortable, I'm sure you'll have a good lawsuit on your hands." I know a promise alone might be hard for Nate to believe and it would be a leap of faith to start this relationship. But lawsuits are a language he does understand.

Nate doesn't say anything, but it doesn't look like he's disgusted by the offer. Maybe shocked? He could always be disgusted under the shock, I suppose, so I shouldn't go around assuming things. It makes an ass out of me, after all. I chew on my lip as the silence goes on.

"No need to answer now," I say when it becomes clear a response isn't going to be forthcoming whether I want it to or not. "I know it's a lot to dump on you, and you don't owe me anything. I…It's a lot to ask."

The silence is grating, so I keep needing to fill it so the world (or the UK audience of this show) doesn't see how awkward this is, getting rejected on television. But the lack of response is getting to me and I start to tear up, because this is not how I hoped this would go. "Okay, maybe I need a little break." I get up and start to walk across the stage and back to my dressing room. I'll be back out to finish this, I really will, I just need a second.

And I doubt any of the producers will stop me, because this is probably reality TV gold for them. And I naively gave them exactly what they wanted.

"Wait," Nate says. I stop mid-step, wondering if he would stop me to reject me now, or if this is good news. After that never-ending silence, I am scared to hope.

"Yes. I want that too. I want to be with you because I love you, too. Even if Harrison does end up deciding to fire me, it'll be worth it. You're always worth it. You're worth everything."

He moves forward and sweeps me up in his arm. He kisses me, my happy tears mingling with the unique taste of Nate on my lips. And accompanied by a giant wave of relief that I'm back in his arms. A wave that makes me feel so warm it's like I'm wrapped up in the thickest, softest blanket, sitting in front of a crackling fire while it snows outside Somehow Nate provides the warmth, comfort and coziness of my favorite season in portable form.

"Social media is going to love this." Lewis breaks into my happy moment, reminding me it isn't quite as private as I thought it was. It's frighteningly easy to forget those cameras are there.

"And I'd like to clear something up," Nate says.

"More twists? Always! Nate, tell us more," Lewis says, ecstatic that this reunion is giving him drama without him having to do much.

"The reason I was so quiet when you said you loved me was because I couldn't believe my luck. Because I came here to ask you to give us a try. Because I couldn't live with myself if I didn't try once more. I did a little more than that, actually."

"What? Tell me." Nate's gotten way too good at drawing out the drama since his stint on reality television.

"Well, we're an international company, and it's wearing on all of us to be up all hours, responding to the needs of our international clients. I told Harrison it would make sense to open an office in Europe…like in London. And he agreed. So we don't have to do long-distance."

"You're moving here?" I don't know if this is real or I'm imagining it because I want it so much, but if I am, I want to stay here in my fantasy.

"Yes. And I know that could come across as creepy if you wanted nothing to do with me, so I want to point out that there was nowhere for me to grow in New York, so this is kind of a promotion, and if you didn't want me, London is a big enough city to never see me. But when you said you wanted to try, I was shocked, and happy, because that's exactly what I want."

"And Dad knew this and didn't tell me?" He was awkward on our last phone conversation, but I assumed that was because the reunion was coming up and he didn't want to be reminded of it or the show.

"He's doing his very best to keep out of your life now. He said he would let me tell you the news."

Wow, he has changed. "You're going to be in London?"

"Indefinitely."

"And we're going to date?"

"Hopefully for a long time."

I kiss him again, so glad that not only am I dating Nate, we're doing it in the same time zone.

"Now, now. None of this will get you out of answering our questions, although you've already answered our first question: how do you feel about each other now." Lewis throws a card over his shoulder, then reads the next one. "Now, Naomi, what did you think when…"

EPILOGUE

NAOMI

he Next Fourth of July
We battle through the crowd that gets bigger every year at Bubba's. The British have apparently decided they aren't going to hold a grudge against the Fourth and instead they're going to embrace the extra day in the year to have festive alcohol and an excessive amount of fried food.

The great unifiers.

"Excuse me, Americans coming through. It's *our* day," I say as I squeeze through the crowds of drunk Brits.

"Sorry, we're only this entitled one day a year. It's the potent combination of her loving a theme and margaritas that really get her," Nate apologizes from behind me.

"If not now, when, Nate? I queue even when not asked. I bought an electric kettle and I say sorry even when I don't mean it. I have *adapted*. But today is my day!"

"Lots of margaritas," Nate tells the strangers.

"Ex-Pats, assemble!" I say as I find our table.

A chorus of "heys" greets us.

"Hollywood leprechaun, your show has been over for almost a

year. It's a bit much to still be getting places fashionably late," Zara says.

"I know, I know, giantess. There was an emergency with an extramarital affair that has been occupying my day." I steal a corn dog from the basket in the middle of the table.

The past ten months have been better than I could have imagined. Work is still slow to pick up, but it's getting there. Especially after the inevitable scandals my castmates (George) got into after tasting that first bit of fame. And after people saw me handle that, the referrals have been increasing at a very respectable pace for a new business. I've even hired people to help me. Okay, person. But it's a start.

Nate's been flourishing in London. Dad's company name is so strong that the European markets were ecstatic when they found out Nate was opening an office in London. He hit the ground running when he moved after that reunion, and he hasn't stopped since. We live together, so even though he's busy, I at least get to see him at night. I have to work most weekends at the events I organize, but he's happy to be dragged to them so we can spend some time together.

"Should I get the enchiladas?" Nate asks, looking at the menu.

"No!" five voices shout at him in horror.

"I'm not saying you can't find good Mexican food in London, but not at Bubba's. I would stick with something you could get at a state fair," Jaya says. "But if you did still want to order it, be prepared for not enchiladas. Maybe it's closer to a quesadilla."

Nate fits into this group perfectly, my friends loving him as much as I do. Well, maybe not quite the same way I do. He puts one arm absently on the back of my chair, rubbing my back while he contemplates his dinner choice.

He's fit in perfectly at home too. We went back to New York and Berkeley for the holidays to see the families and his were lovely. Dad is making an effort and he wasn't awkward at all. He did try to steal my date during White Elephant to talk business, but Mom put her foot down and we continued stealing presents from each other. And Mom is over the moon that I'm dating anyone, especially since it's someone she already knows and likes.

None of the worries we had going into this have manifested and I've been happier than ever, personally and professionally.

"I have news," Zara says.

"I'm not doing another reality show," I say, remembering the last time she announced something at a Fourth of July dinner.

"It's not that. Because of this streak of successes I'm on, which you definitely started, I've been offered a new job, this time as a supervising producer! I'll be in charge of everything…I'm getting my dream job!"

"Yes! I knew the world would see what we see in you!!" I bounce up and down in my seat, happy for my friend and former flatmate.

"Where is it?" Jaya asks.

"It's a British show but it films in Spain, so while you lot have rain, I'll be soaking up the sun."

"Enjoy it. You deserve it," Dev says.

I drop a surprise kiss on Nate's jaw, happy that we're all doing well, but pull away before he can respond. Because James, our favorite server, is back to our table.

"Six Red, White and Blue Margaritas, please. And a round of chili dogs for the table! We've got things to celebrate," I say, cuddling into Nate as I enjoy the night with some of the best people on the planet.

With my absolute favorite person on the planet. And all it took to get me to see what was right in front of me was an entire reality show, and joining the thousands of couples who took the road to Gretna.

And who knows, maybe someday we'll be back to Gretna, to

get married for real. Someday soon, if the ring I accidentally found in Nate's jacket pocket is anything to go by.

And this time, nothing will stop me from getting my perfect *I do.*

ACKNOWLEDGMENTS

Publishing is often a world of nos. But in this space, I want to highlight some of the yeses that brought me here today, to my first self-published book.

Farah Heron, you are my forever first yes (publishing edition). You picked my manuscript for Pitch Wars and polished it until it shone. You gave me confidence that someone besides me and my dog wanted to hear my words. Thank you.

Jana Hanson, you were my second yes. You made me feel like publishing had a place for me, and together, we set out to bring my words to the world. Even though we're not working together anymore, I'll never forget the feeling of signing that first contract. Thank you.

Deb Nemeth and Stephanie Doig, you picked my two stubborn enemies and introduced them to the public, making me feel that author was an attainable career. That was another contract I'll never forget signing. Thank you.

Venika Bibra, you have consistently created the best illustrations, bringing the characters in my head and on my page into the visual realm. Thank you, and I apologize that you have to see my initial sketches.

Mackenzie Walton, you took my manuscript and made it so much better, so much stronger, while having so much care and respect for my voice. Sorry for all the repeated words. But please let me have a last few for emphasis: thank you, thank you so much.

Readers, there are so many books you could have chosen and

I know those TBR piles can get out of cont-ol (including mine), so thank you for saying yes to this one.

Book reviewers, us publishing people might send books out into the world, but you bring our words to an audience, and I can't thank you enough for any like, share, and review you've done.

My husband, well, you've said yes to me a time or two. But here specifically, I mean the yes you gave without hesitation when I said I was going to be an author, a career with a famously bad return on investment. Thank you.

Oliver the Bulldog, you never bloody say yes to me. But I love your contrary face anyway. Thanks for being my writing assistant, even if you didn't make me one cup of tea and are in the process of giving me hip pain by sleeping on me.

My parents, you have a mixed bag of saying yes and no to me. But you've always supported and loved me and your yeses and nos have made me who I am today. Thank you.

ABOUT THE AUTHOR

Suleena Bibra has read romance in one form or another since she could pick her own books. She occasionally branches out to other genres, but really, what's the point if there's no kissing? She also loves to laugh, which probably has to do with her dad putting Monty Python on whenever her mom wasn't looking.

Suleena studied art history in college and loves to travel every opportunity she gets. A bit indecisive, she has worked as a museum intern, lawyer, workers' compensation adjuster, and private investigator. Author is best, though, so she can continue living out a bunch of other careers without changing out of her pajamas.

Suleena writes RomComs heavy on banter, shenanigans, and aggressive whimsy. She spends the rest of her time annoying her stubborn, but adorable, bulldog (who also doubles as her particularly lazy writing assistant) with her love.

www.ingramcontent.com/pod-product-compliance
Lightning Source LLC
Chambersburg PA
CBHW031208310726
48969CB00001B/263